# QUEEN OF ANGELS

*Also by Greg Bear*

Eon
The Forge of God
Eternity
Anvil of Stars
Songs of Earth and Power
The Venging
Moving Mars
Legacy
New Legends
Slant

# QUEEN OF ANGELS

## Greg Bear

An *Orbit* book

First published in Great Britain by
Victor Gollancz Ltd 1990
First paperback edition published by Legend 1991
Reprinted by Orbit 1998

A CIP catalogue record for this book
is available from the British Library

ISBN 1 85723 657 2

Printed and bound in Great Britain by
Mackays of Chatham PLC, Chatham, Kent

Orbit
A Division of
Little, Brown and Company (UK)
Brettenham House
Lancaster Place
London WC2E 7EN

This one is for Alexandra
From before she is born, until long
past 100000000000

# BOOK ONE

**IIOO-IOIII-IIIIIIIIIIII**

**Exercise One:**
*Picture a pattern of trees, stark and black against an ashen sky. Their branches are etched sharp against the drab neutrality. Their pattern is fixed and will not change. The gray has no quality, not even the vibrancy of sight behind closed eyes. More than winter, this is certainty; the final image found in the eyes of a dead man. Now ask: do you want peace and quiet?*

**Exercise Two:**
*There is a field of grain, each stalk perfect, which is a field of men. There is that which is perfect in all men, common to all, and to find that thing and touch it is to transform all men. Now ask: is perfection certainty, and are we only perfect when we are dead?*[1]

**I**

Orca shiny in water, touched by mercury ripples, Mary Choy sank into her vinegar bath, first lone moment in seventy two hours. The sour sweet rice smell ticked her nose. She held the official deluxe paper handbook from Dr. Sumpler's office and referred to the index for Discoloration, Mild, Under Stress, to learn why the crease of her buttocks was turning gray in the universal deep black. *Have you been taking your vinegar baths every two weeks?* the handbook chided.

[1] Permission to Quote Unattributed Passages: International Artist's Rights Committee, World © Emanuel Goldsmith 2022–2045.

"Yes, Dr. Sumpler." She had come to enjoy the acrid half hour.

*Continuing hydroacetic therapy may be accelerated if stress discoloration occurs. Custom melanin replacement is fed from above and below, from vitamin supplements and from epidermal nourishment. Discoloration may be due to excessively tight cloth-ing (loosen or change styles); it may also be due to poor nutrition habits, which are not always correctable through vitamin therapy. Do not worry about discolorations lasting only a few hours or a day; these are common in the first years of your adjusted body.*

"Glorious." Dr. Sumpler had not warned her about such minor piebaldness. Mary shut the handbook and lifted it onto the tiled washbasin, then tilted her head back to soak hair, rid it of the airgrime and sweat of three unre-lieved days.

She could not wash away the sight of eight young comb citizens in various stages of disassembly. Last night, the first investigation team had gone to the third floor of East Comb One in response to neighborhood medical detectors picking up traces of human decay. In the first two hours the team had mounted a sniffer, performed assay and scanned for heat trails. Then the freezers had come and tombed the whole apartment. Senior in her watch, Mary had been assigned this rare homicide at seven hundred. Spin of the hour.

Layer by cold solid layer, forensics would now study the scene corpses and all and take as long as they wished. From the large scale to the microbial everything would be sifted and analyzed and by tomorrow or the day after they would know something about everyone who had been in and out of the apartment during the past year. There would be lists of skin flake, hair and spittle traces to match with medical records now fair game under the Raphkind amendments, bless the bastard; she could track suspects through microbe population deviances and projected points of origin as fine as rooms in a suspect's apartment, bless evolution and mitochondrial DNA.

3

With eyes closed she saw again the corpses hard and still, covered with a thin layer of rime, their blood clotted in dark cold lakes lives and memories fled. A grisly meat puzzle for masters to riddle.

Mary Choy had been a pd for five of her twenty eight years. Competence and the laws banning discrimination against voluntary transforms (bless the libs before Raphkind) had moved her on the sly spin to full lieutenant in supervisory investigation in three and a half years. She had remained an investigator by choice, specking this to be her slot in life. She did not love death. She loved mystery and capture. She loved finding the social carnivores, the parasites and untherapied misfits.

Mary still believed she helped hold the line against the Selectors and others who would exact retribution beyond the law. Their way lay unbelievable misery for all. Her way lay swift decisive justice and forced therapy or incarceration. Ninety five percent of all crimes could be solved; leave it to the therapists to find and erase the perverse drives and motivations.

Two hours after her arrival at the scene, pd ensigns had brought her a possible witness, a tall gaunt graying male R Fettle, friend of the apartment's owner E Goldsmith. Mary had not then seen the interior of the apartment but she had been fed by the on scene techs; suspicion was falling heavily on the owner. Interrogated, Fettle had had little to tell and had been released. His reaction stuck in memory: deeply puzzled like a fish dragged into air stuttering denial shocked by her suggestion he might be prosecuted for not revealing Goldsmith's need for therapy. Real fear. At first she had felt contempt for this jag denizen, all unfocused uprooted thinking.

She lifted an arm and watched the water bead and slide in thin rivers down her dolphinslick skin. Now she felt sorry for Fettle. She had been tro shink harsh on him; Mary was not used to homicides. Fettle knew nothing. Yet how could a friend not know murder was potential?

Enough vinegar. She emerged from the black plastic tub

and toweled herself, humming pop twelvetone. The small jade colored arbeiter—a Chinese model purchased after her last temp mandated ramp in salary—met her with a pressed and folded uniform.

At Mary's whistle the home manager read her messages. Its masculine voice followed her through three rooms as she searched for a lost curl of mineral silver to wrap around her ear. "There's a call from Junior Lieutenant Theodora Ferrero, no message," the manager concluded.

She had not heard from Ferrero for three months; Ferrero had been up for promotion and Mary had assumed the cram had absorbed her friend's time. They had become close in academy; Ferrero had just come out of minor therapy and had seemed balanced but vulnerable. Mary, having just completed her transform, with a similar softshell feeling, had taken to the fellow cadet immediately. Times since had been more rocky. Theodora had frozen at junior lieutenant, been passed over twice. "Answer the call. Interrupt me if completed," she said.

Unlike two thirds of the millions who aspired to the combs and high paying temp jobs, Mary Choy had succeeded without therapy. In a frame by the front door hung her most recent department therapy need evaluation. She was a natural; she had passed the temp agency tests on her first try and each yearly LAPD exam with equal ease. The evaluation was a smooth ascending cross, a printout of brain locused circles each in its proper place each pointing to a well balanced and proportioned personality subpersonality agent or talent. Thoughts poised, ego trim and fit, she knew who she was and what she was capable of; she knew how to stand tall and straight within her head and recover from the inevitable trips and stumbles without trauma; she was a mature young woman and ripe for promotion. So the printouts showed, but Mary in her introspective moments reserved final judgment.

While her wages were high she did not splurge. Her only ostentation was an apartment high on the ankle of the second foot of North Comb Two. Spare and stylish, warm grays and velvet purples and blacks, Mary's home was a perfect blind for her gloss midnight. She could be absorbed in it and lose this assured self, vanish into decor, take her sunlight firsthand through wide uncurtained windows. There was little need for baubles. She did not pursue art or literature, did not begrudge those who did, but her life was devoted to hunting not celebrating human spirit.

In her own private activities she was equally spare. She practiced the five power centering disciplines including War Dance where self vied with self to pour out physical motion. This she did in a small empty room with white foam walls like a black calligraphic stroke against naked canvas.

Exercises finished, Mary put on her uniform carefully, sealing vital points in monomol mesh armor, drawing up support boots that kept her legs from getting tired during long waits. Her rank carried no weapons in daytoday. She was not expected to engage in regular combat. Physical violence in the USA had declined markedly in the past fifteen years. The therapied did not seek violence.

Her dark eyes were calm quiet yet neither empty nor unexpressive. Her transformed voice was deep yet sweetly feminine, powerful yet motherly. She could sing lullabies or growl a pd threat.

Quiet, centered, tall, night colored Mary Choy had everything she wanted but her past. Its residue lay embalmed in the corner of a single drawer in her bedroom dresser, a box of old family photographs, disks and memory cubes.

She stood by the dresser feeling a certain dread clear instinct about Theodora and fingered the drawer. Bent to stroke Loafer, her redstriped white cat. It rubbed against her boots, maroon eyes sage and patient, purring deep in its throat, the single living link to her girlhood; Mary's parents had given it to her when she graduated from high school.

"Connection with Theodora Ferrero," the manager said.

"Put me on vid," Mary said. "I'll take it in the living room." She walked quickly to the phone, bent momentarily to adjust a wrinkle in the monomol, straightened, composed. "Hello, Theo. Months silent. Good to hear from you!"

Mary could not see her friend. Ferrero's vid was turned off. "Yeah, thanks for the callback." Voice tense. "I thought you'd like to know."

"Did you make it?" Mary asked, certain Theordora had gotten the grade.

"Passed over," Ferrero said. "Three times now, last chance. Recommended for further therapy."

Mary looked surprised and sympathetic. "Tell me about it. Let me see you, Honey; my vid's on."

"I know," Ferrero said. "I'm not taking it."

"I'm sorry, what?"

"I don't want to see you, Mary. I don't want to be reminded."

"You're pulling me dark, Theo. What happened?"

"I *didn't make it*. That's all and enough, don't you think?"

"Theo, I've been through a rough. This big homicide, eight down. I'm a bit slow and I'm about to go back on duty."

"I'm sorry to spill this now, but you have an edge over me and I refuse to compete, Mary."

"What edge?"

"You're a transform. You're exotic and protected. The pd doesn't dare tell you to go back for therapy or you cry on the temp and the feds investigate. They can't touch you."

"That's nonsense, Theo." Mary felt the burn spreading through her face; she could not show a blush but she could feel it.

"I don't think so, Mary, and right now I'm on a pinker of just cutting you off."

"Theo, I sympathize, but don't take it out on me. We went through academy. You mean a lot to me. What did they want you to—"

7

"I don't have to tell you that! You're a fapping *alien*, Mary. I don't have you on vid because I don't want to *see* you. I don't even want to talk to you. You've made it impossible for me to roll the grade. Enjoy your peak, *Honey*." The phone chimed cutoff.

Mary stood in silence before the small gray table that held the phone, gripping its edge. She looked down on her smooth black fingers, straightened them flexed them again, drew back. The tension in Theodora had been clear months before; still Mary had not expected this. A part of her said *It's obvious why the pd asked for more therapy* and another part parried with a deeper *Why*.

To avoid such a question she crossed the living room and switched on LitVid. The nets were full of the AXIS messages finally being received after crossing the space between the stars; Mary stood before sharp simulations of the probe going into orbit around its chosen world. She watched without hearing, barely seeing, conflicting messages slowly crossing her own inner space.

Why did she do her transform and choose such an exotic design in the first place; to get advantage, or to match inner her with an outer appearance that had never satisfied?

Mary's parents her brother and sister Mother Father had accepted the transform redandwhite cat yet not the later transform daughter. She had not heard from any of them in four years.

Now Theodora, whom she might once have called her best friend in a life of few such friendships.

She returned to the drawer, opened it and removed one envelope containing a single palm sized disk. Only when she had involved herself in some particular unpleasantness and needed to gain perspective did she go over her mementoes. Slipping the disk into her slate she called up picture number four thousand and twenty-one. In color but not in three d: still vid of a twenty year old woman height one hundred sixty-five centimeters skin pale face round and pleasant with a smile that seemed from this distance acquiescing. The young woman wore a midthirties green and blue patch suit showing one side of abdomen left shoulder most of right leg; a singularly unattractive fashion. Behind the young woman a white wood frame house in what was now jag five of the shade, Culver City. At the young woman's feet a hunched Loafer thinner by two kilos. The original Mary Choy at twenty. Ambitious yet quiet; intelligent yet reserved. Working quietly in her scholastic specialty forensic research to build up sufficient temp credit to finance a transform against future salary.

Dark eyes narrow, lips taut, she returned the disk to the envelope.

*Madhouse Earth such a treat no choice to be born here. We are all like in madness. By grace our madness likes us.*

# 2

Standing, gaunt tense Richard Fettle leaned into the curve, straight knees knocking the bent knees of seated passengers. He still trembled, shocked by this morning's anomaly.

Three stations ago the round little white autobus had filled with citizens of the shade young and old, a medieval assortment of widely different norms brothers and sisters common victims of the future. The bus did not board any more.

Light gilded them all secondhand through the goggling windows. Five suns glowed in the slow twisting gear meshing arms of the three towers of East Comb One, generous light bequeathed to the groundlings. + No good mood this day. Roughed and not deserving. Good tale though. Madame's group heedful for five minutes. Some attention. Mind off Goldsmith. What he did. Did he? Man is the

9

poet who kills, woman the angel who eats. What he said. Never wrote it down. Goldsmith is the poet who kills. Bringing me into it. Jesus I am a peaceful man.

The bus rolled behind a eucalyptus screen. The five suns leaf sputtered and were lost. He pulled a cord and the bus eased curbside at the gate to the upland valley estate of Madame de Roche.

He stepped down. The little bus hummed away on the patched unslaved asphalt lane. Richard stood on the root heaved sidewalk head bowed eyes half closed composing and sorting. + How to tell it. Maximum purgation. Awful thing. They all knew him.

Red haired Madame de Roche, sixty, thought people a delightful phenomenon worth cultivating. She fed and entertained her faithful, provided beds and bathrooms, listened when they were unhappy, and offered all her faithful might need but the shared regard of equals, for she was not one of them. She might live in the shade but she was not of the shadows. Nor was she of the combs. She claimed to despise that "Rabble of coldhearted perfectionists."

Madame de Roche no more resembled her guests than she did her garden or her cats, which she also cared for with grace and understanding.

+ Reduce it to a performance a tale. Artificial but one way of salvaging a rough hour. That I might be a murderer. Eight die that I might live five minutes to tell a tale that happened to me to all of us for we all knew Goldsmith. Accusations of not turning him in; knowing his need for therapy which I did not; I did not. Begin the story before she arrives. She will ask for it to be repeated then. Hear it all. Longer in the spot glare.

Richard shivered. + Jesus. I am a peaceful man. Forgive me but I have earned this story.

He walked two steps at a stride up the wide stone stairway ignoring cracked concrete lions of another age imitating yet another age, into the deceptively Spanish portico entrance of the mansion.

10

In a white enameled wrought iron cage a fine large red and blue bird preened its feathers and blinked at him, one chafed claw showing silver. + New addition. Forty years antique and very valuable; real birds much cheaper. Macawnical.

The door knew him. With a polite nod to its heavy wood face, Richard entered and was absorbed into a great commonality of the untherapied. Fourteen of Madame de Roche's faithful pooled around the stairs, their slippers padding or hard plastic soles tapping on the cool red granite floor: three young longhaired collegiate women admiring an early Shilbrage in an alcove; two tuxedoed men discussing sharp trade transactions in the shadows banks; a ring of four denimed poets admiring each other's handprinted broadsides. Dressed their best except where philosophy demanded less they cradled drinks in mannered fingers and nodded as he passed; Richard was not senior, not this month. + Friends but would not lift a digit if I fell. Petronius would know them. Lord spare me they're all I have or deserve.

In a chair away from this spreading pool sat Madame's appointed favorite this month, Leslie Verdugo of ancient family, a lovely white haired wraith whom Richard had never addressed out of shyness perhaps but more probably because she smiled all the time, ether seeing, and this did not attract him. Sitting across a glass topped occasional table from her was Geraldo Francisco a New Yorker who specialized in printmaking using ancient methods. Approaching them diffidently was Raymond Cathcart who called himself an ecologist and wrote poetry that occasionally stirred Richard but more often bored him. Breaking away from the poets to join this new attractor was Siobhan Edumbraga, an exotic female in speech and manner but clumsy in all physical acts and occasionally sharply rude, an innocent of no talents he could discern. She had made up her name; he did not know her real name.

Richard found his place in the ring of poets and leaned over them, somber eagle face and liquid gray eyes betraying

11

no eagerness, biding patiently. News of some late progressive insult to the arts nano or another outraging medium compelled them all to laugh, full of hate and envy. Resources of the combs made them look like children playing with Plasticine. They were individualists and they cherished their untherapied dishonesties or skewed perceptions; they thought natural blemishes necessary to art. Richard shared this belief but did not take it seriously. There was after all the majesty of accomplishment in the combs compared to a clutch of ill mannered broadsides in the sweaty hands of low poets. + To love one's self is to be therapied. Self-hatred is freedom.

"Richard's not often so late in line," said Nadine coming out of nowhere outside the circle and behind him, dressed in red. Nadine Preston was his age but only recently escaped by messy divorce from the privileges of the combs. Her smooth face and black hair wreathed a lovely child's smile. He saw her slender body in flash memory. Sweet three quarters and one quarter mascaraed harpy. When sweet she was his last sexual solace, but Richard did not stay for her tantrums.

"I have had an adventure," he said softly, gray eyebrows raised.

"Oh?" Nadine urged but the ring was not having it; their conversation rivered on.

+ Was this Nemesis, come to balance my books? Good line.

"Emanuel Goldsmith is missing," he said deep voice still soft but clearly audible. "He is being sought by the LAPD."

The poets turned their heads. He had seconds to hook them fast. "The public defenders spoke with me about him," Richard said. "Eight people were murdered two nights ago. I came to Emanuel's apartment in the third foot of East Comb One. The lift was blocked and pd were there and all manner of arbeiters. The room was being frozen. The most stunning—"

Madame de Roche came down the stairs in a quick

saintly glide, blue chiffon trailing, red hair gentle on her shoulders. Richard paused and smiled showing his large uneven teeth.

"Such a lovely group," she greeted, beaming. Without apparent discrimination she fixed her faithful with sapphire eyes wrapped in naturally acquired wrinkles in that motherly face, features arranged to show good humor and loving sympathy though she did not actually smile. "Always a pleasure. Pardon my lateness. Do go on."

Nadine said, "Richard has been at the scene of a crime."

"Really?" Madame de Roche said at the bottom, ivory hand on ebony wooden ball. Leslie Verdugo joined her and Madame beamed briefly on her then turned all attention to Richard.

"I was interrogated by the most stunning woman a pd in uniform, black as jet but not negroid. I think at first she wanted to accuse me of the crime, or at least of public recklessness for not turning Emanuel in. I wondered: was this Nemesis, come to balance my books?"

"Do start again," Madame de Roche said. "I believe I've missed something."

*No pain, no gain. World's a rough. All we learn comes of our own sharp go. We torment each other. Race is like acid in a tight metal groove; we etch. Hope?*

# 3

In a lost time of myth the coast of southern California had been littoral brown and dusty desert populated by Indians Spaniards mestizos scrub and ancient twisted pines. Now from twenty kilometres below Big Sur to the tip of Baja it was a rambling ribbon of community linked by slaveways, fed by desalting plants and mountain melts gathered from as far as Canada, punctuated by the towers of Santa Barbara the immense diurnal mirrored combs of Los Angeles centipede segments of South Coast monuments and the sprawling rounded ceramic arches and spires of San Diego. Nestled between the desalting and fusion plants of San Onofre and San Diego like islands in this coastal and inland battle of titans lurked the groundling enclaves of La Jolla and Del Mar, blanketed in shabby gentility and celebrated memory of years past.

Flanking the sprawl of the University of California at San Diego, these cities boasted hundreds of thousands of atavists who wished to live lives of past simplicity. The once ubiquitous doctors and lawyers and heads of corporations had decades before abandoned their beachside palaces to move into the central luxuries of the monuments; outmoded academics and scholars took their place.

Herr Professor Doctor Martin Burke, O.V.F.&I.— Once Very Famous and Influential—had recently left the monuments and the bosom of highrise society to slum in the flatlands. He had found himself an old not ruinously expensive apartment in the inland hills of La Jolla and here he sat with barely enough energy to answer his chiming phone, trying to raise some enthusiasm for a scheduled public broadcast of the latest LitVid 21 AXIS report, history in the making.

He turned down the sound on the floating head and shoulders of an announcer and reached out on the third chime to make sure the phone's vid was off. Then he said, "I'll take it." The phone opened a connection. "Hello." Martin's voice was hoarse and phlegmy. He sounded sixty; he had just earned forty five.

"Martin Burke, please." A pleasant, aggressive male voice.

He coughed. "Speaking."

"Mr. Burke, you used to work for the Institute for Psychological Research—"

"Used to." Pause. Sounded like a journalist. "I had nothing to do with—"

14

"No, of course not. My name is Paul Lascal, Mr. Burke. I'm not a reporter and I'm not interested in the Raphkind scandals. I am interested in what you know about IPR. Would it be possible to speak with you soon?"

A LitVid simulation of AXIS itself floated before him, narration muted. The craft's deceleration vanes were shown spread wide a spidery thing of deep space. The vanes withdrew with unreal speed and AXIS's children flushed like a thousand handsful of nickels smeared by gravity in a gray pointillistic curve around the second planet of Alpha Centauri B.

"The last thing I want to talk about is IPR," Martin said. "Where did you get my number?"

"I represent Mr. Thomas Albigoni." Lascal paused for some sign of recognition, then continued smoothly without it. "Carol Neuman gave him your name and phone number. She thought you might be able to help him."

"I don't see how. I haven't worked at IPR for a year. How is Carol connected with Mr. Albigensi—"

"Albigoni. Thomas. Mister. She was a therapist for his daughter. They became friends. I understand you're no longer in the silky with the regulators. That could make you doubly useful to us. Just a short talk. Say, over lunch?"

Martin looked at the mess in his small kitchen. He had not mustered the energy to tell the apartment arbciters to clean it up. He had not eaten since early evening of the day before. "You seem to think I should know who Albigoni is."

"He's a publisher."

"Oh? LitVids?"

"And books," Lascal said pointedly. "Far more lit than vid."

"Is he after an exposé?"

"No. Another matter entirely."

Martin rubbed his nose. "In that case, and considering it's Carol, maybe I'll accept."

"Do you know—" Lascal named a shoreline La Jolla restaurant, very expensive.

15

"I know it."

"About one hour from now? Jut ask for Mr. Albigoni's table."

Martin gave an asserting grunt and put the receiver down. He leaned back in the weak cushions of his aging armchair. On the battered coffee table sat a ceremonial and condensed printed copy of his twenty year old atlas of the human brain, a seminal work from his salad days. Sometime during the previous night he had drunkenly opened it to a plate of the olfactory nerve and system. Next to the plate he had drawn a crude cartoon of a vampire, teeth trickling teardrops of blood, with branching arrows connecting cartoon and pink and white cauliflower flesh of prepyriform cortex, olfactory bulb and rhinencephalon.

From the armchair he could see into the apartment's small bedroom. In one corner beyond the bed a tall metal case supported stacked cubes of data. Martin's life had centered on those cubes until President Raphkind's downfall and suicide had ushered in the new era of constitutional cleansing and investigations. He had not been part of the Raphkind scandals—not directly—but his research had been targeted. Federal had shut down IPR and tucked him away from his true calling.

He turned up the sound on the AXIS report pushed himself forcibly from the armchair and walked into the bathroom to shave and dress.

Martin had once hiked the Country of the Mind. Now he was reduced to accepting luncheon dates with curious strangers just to get out of the apartment.

*Why put on eyeglasses? Why look out and ahead? You won't go there. I won't. We are all Moses staring into Canaan. Who in hell cares if our children get there? My this has been a bitchy evening, hasn't it?*

# 4

LitVid 21 (Science and Philosophy Nets) Scheduling 12/23/47

1: AXIS MultiNet Coverage 24 hr reports four tiers
    A Net: PubAcc David Shine and Team
    B Net: PubAcc Direct Data Downlink (Hobby Tech)
    C Net: Australian Squinfo: Analysis (Pay)
    D Net: Lunar Squinfo: Analysis (Pay)

2: Designer Babies Conference Tucson AZ 0800–2200
    (Member Conference Pay)
    A Net: Health and public acceptance
    B Net: Future social change
    C Net: Religious, Historical and Scientific Images of
    Humanity

3: Public Science Issues Forum PubAcc MultiNet 0900–2100
    A Net: Diane Muldrow-Lewis Taper
    Playback Interviews with Science/Tech Pers.
    (Expanded Schedule for subjects)
    B Net: Senate Transform Law Debates
    Discrimination in Eastern States?
    C Net: Arbeiter Design Conference
    Cleveland, Ohio
    D Net: NANOTECH NEWS (Chosen for
    Recording. $20.00 Fee)
    E Net: END SELECTION

LitVid 21/1 A Net (David Shine): "AXIS has been on the road for fifteen years, at a cost of over one hundred billion dollars, a lot of treasure for such a distant piece of metallic fluff many have said. But the overwhelming voice of the world community spoke loud and clear three decades ago, and it said Yes. AXIS, an acronym for Automated eXplorer of Interstellar Space, became the grandest project in recent history, perhaps more important over-all than the manned Mars missions, the return to the moon, the orbital platforms and stations . . . For in planning, building and launching AXIS the world propelled itself deliberately and with historically unprecedented foresight into a new industrial revolution.

"The technologies necessary for AXIS's success—the nano-technologies of machines smaller than living cells—have already changed our lives and promise much more in the very near future. But which is more important, the economic and industrial benefits or the philosophical and psychological?

"Through AXIS we might find our doppelgangers, our soul-mates; we might find mankind's future husbands and wives among the angels who the Bible tells us once cohabited with Earthlings.

"AXIS may be therapy for us all, for the great uncured, unhealed human race, with so far to go on its breathless course through history. We may finally be able to compare ourselves to our superiors, or our equals, and know where we stand.

"As for yourself, you'll find more formal telecasts on other LitVid 21 channels. We are taking the universal feed and simulated report from Australian and lunar farside mission control, and adding our own cultural spin.

"In the past few weeks, AXIS has returned images of three planets circling Alpha Centauri B. As yet these worlds have not been named, and are called only B-1, B-2, and B-3. B-3 was already known to moonbased astronomers; it is a huge

18

gas giant some ten times larger than Jupiter in our own solar system. Like Saturn it is surrounded by a thin rugged ring of icy moonlets. B-1 is a barren rock hugging close to Alpha Centauri B, similar to Mercury. But the focus of our attention is now on B-2, a justright world slightly smaller than Earth. B-2 possesses an atmosphere closely approximating Earth's, as well as continents and oceans of liquid water. It is orbited by two moons each about a thousand kilometers in diameter.

"AXIS's sensors and telescopes discovered B-2 almost three years ago. Now AXIS is making its move on this Earthlike world. That is, it made its move over four years ago, for AXIS is sending us information at the speed of light across four light years. The signal has been relayed by fifty transponders across almost forty trillion kilometers of empty space. The reports are only reaching us this week, in compressed form, to be decoded, enhanced and analyzed by thinking machines in California and by planetary scientists around the world.

"This is as close to live and realtime as God allows us to be."

Switch/LitVid 21/B 1 Net (Decoded: Australian Cape Control: Message relayed Space Tracking: Lunar Control: Australian Cape Control: AXIS Mind Team Leader Roger Atkins)

(!=realtime)
AXIS (Biologic Band 4)> Hello, Roger. I assume you're still there. This distance is a challenge even for me, based as I am upon human templates ... [politeness algorithm diagnosis for total mechanical-biologic thinker function V-optimal] most of the time. I have come within a million kilometers of B-2 mark this moment 7-23-2043-1205: 15. I am preparing my machine and bio memories for receipt of information from the children, now flying in a perfectly dispersing cloud toward B-2. Data on B-3 have been relayed. The planet, you can see, is quite Jovian, very pretty, though tending towards the greens and yellows rather than reds and browns. I'm enjoying the extra energy from B's light: it

19

allows me to get some work done that I've been delaying for some time, opening up regions of memory and thought I've closed down during the cold and dark. I've just completed a self analysis; as you doubtless have discovered by checking my politeness algorithm diagnostic. I am V-optimal. I am not using the formal "I"; the joke about self awareness still does not make any sense to me.

[Total algorithm diagnostic time: 4.05 picoseconds]
Sensations:

My temperature is 276 K. Radiation flux .82 solar unity. My optics are warming nicely; bioptics should be fully grown and ready for electronic interface within 21 hours. My final biological extensions are also growing nicely; nutrients have not degraded and I can expect to begin integrating new neural extensions and checking their fitness within the hour.

I assume my earthbound twin is interpreting these bursts adequately, politely, suavely.

!JILL> Roger: how is it?
!Roger Atkins> Just fine.

[Redundancy and Oliphant code checks complete]
AXIS (Biologic Band 4)> Nonneural systems report they are ready to download the last six months' worth of information on C.

Enough burst chatter. As you can see, I am healthy. Expect next burst assembly diagnostics from nonbiologic systems.

[Burst routed to machine language division: machine computation V-optimal]

!Roger Atkins> Alan, AXIS is doing just fine. Jill's simulation is a perfect match. Routing to machine language division.

LitVid 21/1 B Net (Recorded Interview AXIS Space System Project Manager Alexander Tranh): "Biologicals and integration team reports AXIS is in prime condition. We are about to receive information that AXIS's sensors have been gathering over the last half year of flight toward B-2. The large portion of this information will concern Alpha Centauri C, commonly called Proxima Centauri. As most of our viewers should know by now, astronomers are very interested in Proxima Centauri, even though it lies some one trillion miles from the A and B components of Alpha Centauri. C is a very small star indeed, one of the five smallest stars currently known, less than one tenth the mass of our sun and less than half the diameter of the planet Jupiter. It is very like the class of red dwarf stars named after UV Ceti, flare stars that brighten and dim over a period of days.

"Information about A and B is currently decoded and available worldwide on the Australia/Squinfo subscription service, proceeds from which, of course, go to pay for future analysis of AXIS data.

LitVid 21/1 A Net (David Shine): "We're cutting from the AXIS report now—it's mostly numbers and stuff for enthusiasts, I've been told—and replaying two poems. One of them is the poem AXIS wrote to his or her or its programmers as part of a long range diagnostic test four months ago. The second is a poem written and transmitted by AXIS six months after departing our solar system. At that time, AXIS was still functioning on a biological basis.

"The AXIS 'mind' consists of a machine system and a biological system. During the years when AXIS accelerated on a furious torch of matter-antimatter plasma, the unmanned interstellar probe was controlled by a primitive, rugged, and radiation proof inorganic computer. When the antimatter drive ceased some four years ago after launch, AXIS entered a cold, quiet mode, its functions reduced to the simplest routine of maintenance, sensing and launch of transponders. During this time, AXIS's 'mind'—as I said, little more than a simple computer—ticked away the days and weeks and years, its most demanding job keeping track of numerous deep space experiments that could not be conducted while the torch was burning. Some six months before the beginning of AXIS's deceleration phase, AXIS allowed itself the luxury of powering up a small fusion generator, very little larger than a human thumb. This produced sufficient heat to allow nanomachine activity, and the creation of AXIS's huge, yet very thin and light superconducting wings, or vanes.

"AXIS's huge wings actually acted like the rotor on an incredible electric generator, cutting across the lines of the galaxy's own magnetic field. The resulting flow of electricity through the super-conducting material of the wings – some billions of watts of power—was used by AXIS to dismantle the antimatter drive, reduce it to a fine powder with the aid of nanomachine destructors, and to electrically propel this refined scrap opposite its direction of motion to further decrease speed.

"By cutting through the galaxy's magnetic field and generating this electricity, AXIS relied on the law of conservation of energy to decelerate even more quickly without the use of onboard fuel. The power drawn from its vast wings was more than sufficient to dispel the cold of deep space; but AXIS waited for proximity to Alpha Centauri B to begin to grow its biologic thinker system.

"That complex neural network is finishing its growth and integration right now, Earth reference frame. AXIS's new biologic thinker will replace the thinker that died and was recycled when AXIS passed out of our sun's temperate regions and fired off its antimatter drive.

"AXIS chief mind designer and programmer Roger Atkins has told LitVid 21 that he personally knows whether a poem has been written by the machine thinker or by the biological thinker. Can you tell the difference? Here are the two poems."

> *Please pass, oh pass when night*
> *is on your middle ground*
> > *This flower from hand to hand*
> > *Tell each night it's had its chance*
> *We need a day to spread our arms.*

"That one might seem rather obvious, no? But we are warned by Doctor Atkins that these are not deeply symbolic poems and do not express AXIS's desires for any particular circumstance, such as a warm, close star. Now for the second poem."

> *This is not what we had*
> *To say in different words*

22

That wise day. Wisdom played
Its shatter game
Cut its track and called
For what had fled.

"Perhaps not great poetry, but not bad for something not even human, and tucked into a vehicle the size of an oceangoing yacht. Viewers may hazard a guess as to which poem is machine, which is biological, by calling the number below my finger. We'll tally the total rights and wrongs over the next hour and report them . . . direct to you."

EXAMINER: "We are still far from the end of this list. Our cases are backed up for centuries . . . I am not familiar with the crimes of these three."

CLERK: "One is Hyram Sapirstein, one is Klaus Schiller, one is Martin Bormann."

EXAMINER: "I remember Mr. Bormann. You've been before this court before, have you not?"

BORMANN: "Yes."

EXAMINER: "For outrages against your own kind."

BORMANN: "Yes."

EXAMINER: "What crime is he accused of this time?"

CLERK: "Outraging Hell, sire."

EXAMINER: "But these other two . . . are they contemporary?"

CLERK: "Human, sire, twenty-first century."

EXAMINER: "Humans were made to learn quickly, not to take ages, like angels and demons. Haven't they learned their lessons yet?"
[No reply.]

EXAMINER: "I'm afraid we've run out of tortures appropriate for crimes of these sort. Not to mention space. Send them back."

CLERK: "Sire?"

EXAMINER: "Send them back to their own kind. Let the living find the best ways to punish their

23

*miscreants. Open the gates of Hell, and
push the damned through them, one by
one!"*

# 5

Madame de Roche was tired by noon and the faithful removed themselves from the house, all but Fettle
whom she requested to stay behind. By twelve
thirty the old stonecool house was quiet. Madame de
Roche ordered her arbeiter to bring glasses of iced
tea for them both. The sleek black machine walked
on four spider legs through the dining hall into the
kitchen.

"Have you published yet, Richard?" she asked him as
they sat on the veranda looking across a dusty green and
gray canyon at the rear of the house.

"No, Madame. I do not write for publication."

"Of course not."

+ Teasing me. She's in a smooth.

"Your story made quite an impression. We were all fond
of Emanuel Goldsmith. I knew him quite well when we
were younger, when he was writing plays. Did you know
him then?"

"No, Madame. I was a lobe sod. I met him thirteen
years ago."

Madame de Roche nodded then shook her head, frowning. "Please. We both remember a time when language
was civilized."

"Your pardon."

"Was the pd certain Goldsmith was the murderer?"

"They seemed to be," Richard said.

She put on a contemplative air, arms limp on the wicker
rests of her peacock chair. "That would be a most interesting thing, Emanuel a killer. He always had it in him, I
thought, but it was a crazy thought. I never voiced it ...

24

until now. You were an acolyte, were you not? You admired some of his women?"

"I was a sycophant, Madame. I admired his work."

"Then you're sad about this."

"Surprised."

"But not sad?" she asked, curious.

"If he did it, then I'm furious with him. It's a betrayal of all the untherapied. He was one of our greats. We'll be hounded till our deaths, our styles will be degraded, our works shunned."

"That bad."

Richard nodded almost hopefully as if anticipating the ordeal.

"This transform pd you met ... She was not negroid, you say, but she was black."

"Oriental in some features, Madame."

"Black nemesis. I'd like to meet this woman sometime ... Elegant, composed, I presume?"

"Very."

"One of the therapied?"

"I would think so. She had the air of the combs."

"There was once a time when police, public defenders, were underpaid, lower class."

"I remember, Madame."

"They probably enjoy coming into the shade."

"Emanuel lived on the third foot of East Comb One, Madame."

She nodded, remembering. "I wouldn't worry if he is caught and convicted," she said, voice light as down. "He was never really one of us. Untherapied, yes, but a natural needs no such thing. We are none of us naturals, my dear. We are merely untherapied. Our badge of mock protest. Oh, no. Emanuel will dishonor a much higher category than ours."

Madame de Roche dismissed him and his spirits fell immediately he was outside the door. + More and more I am nothing without someone. To be alone is to be in bad company.

Richard paced one yard this way one yard that on the root heaved concrete. Five minutes after a signal from his beeper another little rounded white autobus hummed into the eucalyptus screen and opened its wide doors.

"Destination," the bus asked him, voice pleasantly androgynous.

+ People. A place that brings an end to a rough.

Richard gave an address in Glendale on Pacific, an avenue leading to and in shade of East Comb Three. A literary lounge where home brew could be had and most important of all where he would not be alone. Perhaps there he could tell the tale again maximum effect maximum purgation. + Black nemesis. Work on that.

"One hour," the bus told him.

"So long?"

"Many calls. Please come aboard."

Richard boarded and took a strap.

*Moses came down from Horeb, hair on fire with God, God's soot around his lips where he had eaten the greasy leaves of the burning bush, his humanity blasted from him, leaving him like carbon steel touch him he might ring, and contemplated his future. A leader of men. And women. He sat near his dear wife Zipporah in the dark and cursed his misfortune.*

*Men didn't know what they wanted, or how to go about getting it. They did whatever came into their minds first. They hated at the drop of a hat and spurned love because they feared being taken advantage of. They leaped into violence before an angel could blink, and then called their murder and destruction valorous, and boasted of it and wept while drunk. And women! Did not carbon steel deserve something more?*

*"Give me a glorious task, Lord, away from this rabble."*

*And that was when God descended and was sore vexed with him, making the land outside their tent quiver. Zipporah daughter of Jethro said, "Moses, Moses, what have you done now?"*

*"I have thought unworthy thoughts," Moses said, hoping that*

*was enough to mollify God, but the landscape turned bloodred and the sky filled with bloody clouds. Moses, even carbon steel, was afraid.*

*Zipporah came upon the clever expedient of lopping off their poor son's foreskin, touching Moses with the blood, and then the door frame.*

*"Stay away from my husband!" she cried. "He's a good man. Take my son, but not my husband!"*

*Moses hid behind the daughter of Jethro and understood clearly the weakness of his people.*

# 6

Mary Choy came back to the frozen apartment at thirteen, having been off six hours, barely time for catnap vinegar bath and paperwork. She had requested full time for this case and was certain she would get it.

Some of the victims still entombed had been identified and they were gold and platinum names, students, sons and daughters of the well known and influential. She put on a thermal suit in the cubicle erected outside the hall door, ordered the seal breached and stepped into the blue cold.

A radio assayer hung from the track mounted in the apartment ceiling, having replaced the sniffer. Dustmice pushed through the cold stiff tendrils of once live carpet searching for skin flakes and other debris trapped in the carpet's custom digestion. They had already found traces of all victims and Emanuel Goldsmith; there were traces barely thirty six hours old of four other visitors.

Mary surveyed the solid spattered sadness of young bodies one by one saying her professional farewells.

The names, in order of death:

Augustin Rettig

Neona White

Betty-Ann Albigoni

Ernly Jeeger
Thomas Finch

and three unidentified. Rettig's mother was general manager of North Comb One. White's father owned Workers Inc the Pacific Rim's biggest temp employment agency representing some twenty three million therapied and natural lobe sods—the cream of the crop. Workers Inc had approached Mary in her pretransform youth. She had turned them down. West Rim pds worked through Human Expedition Ltd and even in her raw youth she had known where she was going.

Betty-Ann Albigoni was the daughter of a publisher—books the file said, more lit than vids; Goldsmith's major English language publisher. Thomas Finch's uncle was counsel to High Reach, general chandlers for suborbitals. Ernly Jeeger was Emanuel Goldsmith's godson a promising poet on his own also known for an eloi sympathizer and borderlaw activity in whole life vids.

A dim red light mounted on her shoulder pointed wherever she turned her eyes. Livid cold. The assayer tracked quietly overhead like a legless insect and passed into another room.

Finch the last killed lay on his back like a broken cross, face slashed throat cut jagged sideways from jaw to opposite clavicle open eyes rimed white.

It was spatch that pd didn't sympathy a crime. Mary knew in brain and crawl of skin each frozen peeled back wound frightened dead glare of white eyes and cropped corpse grimace. This was her motivation for excellence.

She would know the murderer and organize for a full therapy conviction, restructuring if called for—and the pd would call for it. If Goldsmith was the murderer as seemed most likely now so be it; the Lit Vids would have her and the pd all over the world. But she would smooth those waters when they rippled.

What she had officially come back for was a context search, a look at Goldsmith's files. The room where Goldsmith kept his office had no bodies in it and had already been assayed. She could enter and make her search. Pd, metro and federal warrants allowed her to investigate most aspects of Goldsmith's life as per the Raphkind amendments not yet removed by President Yale's year old block appointed court. She did not personally agree with the Raphkind amendments but she was not in the least reluctant to take advantage of them. What could not be found here might be found in Citizen Oversight—a journey she hoped she would not have to make.

Goldsmith was not a tidy man. She inclined her head in the inflated tube helmet and surveyed his desk. Reasonable models of slate and keyboard—no gold plating or wood box. Cold crackers and half glass of frozen wine. Crumbs. Pens fibertip and what did they call them fountain. She wondered where he got them. A sweep of some hand or arm had fanned a short stack of printouts—not erasable cyclers old fashioned in themselves but actual papers written on by hand—across the black marble top. Cubes marched to the edge of the desk in tandem and lay below on the floor. Mind's eye she saw a hand palm them two by two from a box—an empty cubefile lay nearby—and click them in pairs on the desk then pass aimless over the edge, dropping four. The gesture of a dramatically distracted man.

She bent to pick them up. Each cube projected a tiny label in cold green into her eyes. *The Progress of Moses, The Way of the New, Debit/Asset,* the cubes informed her artlessly not concerned with who she might be. Doubtless Goldsmith's works in solid state. Not a man to crypto his data his work. One work per cube was surprising for pure word; perhaps they were LitVid adaptations for the half literate. LitVid sales would explain Goldsmith's place high on the third foot.

She had heard of Emanuel Goldsmith before this case. An occasional guest on the allnight cable talkers celebrated more for his youthful output. Not currently productive. Mary Choy planned to remain productive well past a century but she allowed as her plans might be young and naive. A pd could not rest on laurels. Salary not royalties.

There were real books on his shelves. She did not pull them down but with an uninformed eye guessed their age at eighty to a hundred years. Expensive, a luxury both in money and space for this information dense age. The World Reserve Library could be stacked in space held by Goldsmith's fifty or sixty paper volumes.

What she specked was unorganized uncontemporary inefficient, what one might presume of a poet; but the scatter of cubes on desktop and floor pointed to a greater disorganization, a careless personal moonstrike.

A closure.

She held up her slate to read the inprog. Sloughed cell and fiber analysis and assay of the office area showed no entry but for Goldsmith. Whatever socials he had conducted, none had entered this sanctum.

Goldsmith's frame of mind had been disturbed before the murders, she posited. He had not entered his office after the murders. Another possibility as yet not eliminated by the total radio assay: that Goldsmith did not occupy the apartment during the murders. Unlikely.

Reaching out she shifted a skewed half inch pile of paper and saw an airline confirmation billet and a document of different color beneath. She picked out the billet. A round trip to Hispaniola dated two days before—the day after the murder. Had the ticket been used? She marked a memo on her slate to check the airline: NordAmericAir.

The other document was a letter real paper again beige stock gold stamping; stationery of the rich and eccentric as atavistic as real books. Mary's eyes widened reading the engraved head and the signature. Colonel Sir John Yardley.

Authentic? The inprog reported nothing. The papers had been disturbed only for chemical and bio clues; it was her task to make a context beyond that. She lifted the letter, three gloved fingers on each hand vising perpendicular the opposite edges of the stiff thick sheet. She read it up close. Typed on an oldfashioned electric impact printer perhaps even a typewriter. Dated and stamped Hispaniola, Yardley's name for his conquest, formerly Dominican Republic and Haiti.

28 November 2047

Dear Goldsmith,

Whatever the circumstances, we will be most pleased to receive you. Ermione charmed. It's rare to meet unhypocritical agreement now. I've particularly enjoyed our letters in book form and *Moses* and appreciate your signature dedicatory. I can only hope what we do here helps this old world lift itself by its bootstraps into sanity.

Yours, as ever,

Colonel Sir John Yardley
Hispaniola

Mary replaced the letter carefully as if it were a snake.

*I do not aspire. I be.*

# 7

Martin hadn't eaten so well in six weeks, when he had seen the end of his savings. He refused to go on shade dole; his application for Municipal Assistance had not been processed perhaps because of official disfavor or ineptitude; civil service was the last well paid refuge for the untherapied. Now in a cool dark booth with crushed velvet upholstery, holding a reservation card in one hand and a whiskey sour in the other, he felt less disdainful of civilization, closer to the human race. A note on the back of the card said, "Go ahead and eat. We'll be half an hour late. Regrets. Lascal."

They were precisely half an hour late. Martin had no doubt he was seeing his benefactors when a tall, heavy shouldered man with wavy gray hair and a short hawk nosed fellow with a restrained pompadour stepped into the lounge. They knew him either by the table or on sight.

"Mr. Albigoni, this is Martin Burke," hawk nosed Lascal introduced. They exchanged handshakes and nothing comments on the decor and weather. Albigoni's heart and mind were clearly elsewhere. He seemed stricken. Lascal was either genuinely cheerful or able to mask his feelings.

"I've just had a fine lunch," Martin said. "Now I'm worried I may not be able to help you."

"No fear," Lascal said.

Albigoni looked at him squarely but said nothing, his long gray mustache a negative hyperbola over firm pale lips. Lascal handed their menus to a waiter and ordered for both of them. He then spread out his hands for Martin's benefit: concealing nothing.

"Do you know Emanuel Goldsmith?" he asked Martin.

"I know of him," Martin said. "If we're talking about the same man."

"We are. The poet. He murdered Mr. Albigoni's daughter three nights ago."

Martin nodded as if he had just been informed of a minor peculation in book publishing. Albigoni continued to stare at but not see him.

"He's a fugitive, a very sick man, mentally," Lascal continued. "Would you be willing to help him?"

"How?" Martin avoided taking a sip from his drink though he fingered the glass.

"Mr. Albigoni was—is—Mr. Goldsmith's publisher and friend. He bears him no ill will." Lascal's voice did not skim so easily over this prepared statement.

Martin subdued the raising of an eyebrow. Lunch was becoming quite surreal.

"Now that Goldsmith is mentally very disturbed, perhaps insane, we'd like you to help him. We'd like to find the roots of his illness."

Martin shook his head at the archaisms. "I told you, I'm no longer connected with IPR. I have been told—"

Albigoni's stare suddenly came alive. He saw Martin. Lascal glanced at his boss then turned head and shoulders to Martin as if making a wall to protect Albigoni from outside forces. "We can arrange for your return, and for the facilities to be reopened."

"I don't want to work there again. I was kicked out for doing work I knew was entirely reasonable and valuable."

"But you didn't go about it in a reasonable fashion," Albigoni said.

"I do not know what is reasonable when politics mixes with science. Do you?"

Albigoni shook his head slowly bemused again barely listening.

"Goldsmith needs to be probed," Lascal said.

"He isn't in custody I take it."

"No." Hesitance. "Not yet. We need to know what turned him into a murderer."

"He needs legal therapy not a probe."

"His problem goes beyond therapy," Albigoni said jaw clamping on the downbite between words. "A therapist would fix him or change him but that isn't what I want. I need to know." Here a flash of angry fire. "He killed eight people. Friends. Of his. Including my daughter. And his own godson. They did him no harm. They were no threat to him. It was an act of deliberate and calculated evil."

"It's only been a couple of days " Martin said.

"In theory, could you probe Goldsmith and tell us what caused him to murder his young friends?" Lascal asked.

A silver plated arbeiter and a human waiter delivered their food, the arbeiter carrying the tray on its flat back. The waiter asked if Martin wished to have another drink. He declined.

"I'm not being told everything," Martin said with a sigh. "Gentlemen, I appreciate your hospitality, but—"

"We can't explain it all until we're sure you're very interested, and will agree," Lascal said.

"Tough situation," Martin said.

"You're our best chance," Albigoni said. "We are not above pleading with you."

"You would be richly rewarded," Lascal said.

"I think you want me to help you break into the IPR, put Goldsmith in a probe triplex and find out what makes him tick. But the IPR has been closed down. That's clearly impossible."

"It is not." Lascal picked at his farmshrimp salad.

Martin lifted his eyebrow dubiously. "First you would have to find Goldsmith, then persuade the state and federal government to reopen IPR."

"We can and will reopen IPR," Albigoni said. Lascal glanced between them uneasily. "Paul, I don't care whether I live or die right now, and the possibility that Mr. Burke will go to the federals means little to me."

"What does Carol Neuman have to—"

"Please listen to me," Albigoni said. "After he murdered my daughter and the seven others, Emanuel Goldsmith came to my penthouse at Airport Tower Two in Manhattan Beach. He confessed to his crimes and then he sat on my living room sofa and asked for a drink. My wife is on an anthropological retreat in Borneo and doesn't know. Nor will she know until . . . the probe is completed and I can explain why he did it to her. If you conduct the probe I guarantee that IPR will be reopened, that you will return as its director and that you will have sufficient grant money to keep you fully employed in research for the rest of your life, however long that might be."

"If I don't end up therapied and confined for violating federal psychological rights," Martin said. "I can't do my work, can't do what I've spent my life trying to do. That's punishment enough. I don't need criminal disgrace as well.

34

I think I'd better leave now." He started to get up. Lascal held his arm.

"Mr. Albigoni was not exaggerating. He's willing to put his entire personal fortune at your disposal."

"Just to learn what makes Goldsmith tick?"

"Just that. We then turn him over to the LAPD unharmed for trial."

"You don't want me to therapy him—just probe?" Martin's hand shook. He could not believe such a Faust was being pulled on him.

"Just probe. If there are answers to be found, find them. If you fail to get answers, the honest attempt is sufficient. Mr. Albigoni will still fund you. The IPR will be legally reopened."

"What is Carol going to do—how is she involved, besides being therapist to your daughter?"

Albigoni stared at the table in silence for a moment, then reached into his pocket and produced a card engraved with J N M. "When you've made your decision, use this card in your phone. Tell whomever answers a simple yes or no. We'll contact you and arrange details if your answer is yes."

Lascal slid out of the booth and Albigoni followed.

"Wait, please," Martin said hand still trembling. He reached for the card. "What sort of guarantees do I have? How do I know you'd fund me?"

"I am not a thug," Albigoni said softly.

"Thank you for your time, Mr. Burke," Lascal said. They left. Martin slapped the card on the tablecloth near a glass of water and watched a bead of light dance over the three letters.

Then he picked it up and pocketed it.


*I loved her more than she could ever know. It filled me with something the usual I suppose cosmic implications blurring my vision. Hers was a mild infatuation; enough to inspire her to*

35

*lubricity. The lubricity lasted for some thirty-seven days and then I was eased aside with the proper proportions of delicacy and firmness necessary to persuade a headstrong love-idiot. The irony was I had done just the same to another young woman a month before and so in time I saw the tit for tat truth the slippery all-too-obvious: had I gotten what my cock said I wanted I would have been miserable in picos. That was when I grew up if not wise. That was when I wrote down all this nonsense that made my reputation about the ecology of love. Thanks to Geraldine another fingerprint squeezed tight into the old clay.*

# 8

"I do not understand why you care about Goldsmith."

+ Adjust loyalty.

Richard fumbled his tale to a conclusion and dourly inspected his audience. There were seven in the lounge, a coffee tea and wine ranch corner rear the Pacific Lit Arts Parlor.

"I still do not understand why you cared about that old fart," Yermak persisted. He dunked his pasty white donut leaving islands of powder in his red wine. At twenty the youngest in the lounge Yermak looked at Richard with mild amusement. "He was capable of anything. Bad writers murder us every day. The death of stinking prose."

Ultima Patch Thule silked to Richard's defense. "We're specking murder here," she said, thin voice distant as grass. Ultima wore wire rimmed glasses eschewing even physical therapy for her dim eyes.

"Fap me for my green age but that's what I'm saying, he's murdered us all." Yermak thinned his face in disbelief at their density.

Richard saddened into silence looked down at his thumb and four fingers resting on the beaten oak veneer. He could not forget the grim determination of the pd's face accusing and angry; now this. He tried to remember Goldsmith's last words to him and could not. Perhaps he should have specked the change. He was tired. Still shuddered from the rough morning. "I wish to say—"

"Ah, fry that!" Yermak spat, leaping away from the table and knocking his chair back with a clatter. "Fap me my green and knock my words, I knew he had it in him, the fart." Raspberry. "Say I to concern."

"Sit down," Jacob Welsh ordered. Yermak righted his chair and sat eyeshifting, nose aimed like a dog under his trainer's whistle. "Pardon my friend's enthusiasm but he has an overstated point."

"I will admit," Ultima said, "Goldsmith has not charmed much lately. Nor shown his face."

"He killed them," Richard said. "He was one of us and he killed them. Are we not concerned for our own?"

"Not one of me. I am *one*," Yermak said, face contorted. "May I quote the fart, 'I do not aspire. I be.'"

"You've read and memorized," Ultima accused with a glow smile.

"We have all," Yermak said at Welsh's nod. "I regret my callow. Richard, we admire your concern and age but it hardly matters what Goldsmith has done. He abandoned us even while he walked here, left us behind for the adulation of the combs, and no shady can ever respect him again, not even you."

"He was a friend," Richard said.

"He was a whore," Welsh said, demonstrating again that the unseen rope between himself and Yermak carried more than physical tension.

Richard looked around the small group. Two who had not spoken yet, sisters Elayne and Sandra Sandhurst, seemed content to sip their tea and listen warily. Richard saw in Welsh's and Yermak's eyes something he should have sensed already; here was anger that had not existed before he brought the news. Here was fear that their connection with Goldsmith would bring them trouble from the pd and the city from where the power really lay in this land—the combs, the therapied.

+ Madame de Roche said it wouldn't be but the pd may not share her opinion. I have already been accused. Perhaps again? Sharp and clear: quicksand harassment isolation pain. I've avoided these pictures since Gina and Dione.

+ I've been asleep fifteen years.

The sharp awareness faded and he closed his eyes for a moment bowing his head. "He was a friend," Richard repeated.

"Your friend," Yermak observed with false calm.

"Richard is our friend," Elayne Sandhurst said.

"Of course," Yermak agreed irritated they might believe he thought otherwise. He glanced reprovingly at Richard.

+ Thinks I bring discord weaken his place. Their places here are all so weak. They feel helpless.

"My apologies," Richard said.

"Apologizing for what?" Jacob Welsh asked abruptly. "We're certainly not sorry you told us. We are never sorry to have our opinions confirmed."

Sandra Sandhurst lowered her knitting to her lap and drew her lips together. + Norn in judgment; only valid judgment the cutting of our threads.

"He is a world famous writer, and we all knew him. He was good to all of us."

Yermak raspberried again. "He slummed, condescended."

Elayne said, "He did not slum."

Yermak stood up and knocked his chair down again.

"Such drama," Elayne said. She turned away disdainfully.

"Fap you," Yermak said blithely. Jacob Welsh leaned his head back and stretched.

"We've had enough, my friend," he warned Yermak with barely concealed approval. "Two upheavals are quite enough."

"I will not sit again not with these," Yermak said.

"Time to leave then." Welsh stood. "Your news is useful, Richard, and I suppose that's enough. Your loyalty is admirable but we do not share it."

"I don't think it's loyalty," Richard said. "If he's murdered he should be therapied—"

"But we don't therapy even our worst enemies, Richard," Yermak intoned, leaning over him. "I wouldn't put anybody through that. Better he were dead. Better still if he had never come near us."

Richard nodded not in agreement but to wish them off.

"Don't forget the reading," Elayne Sandhurst said cheerily. "Bring your best."

"I don't write anymore," Yermak said, sneering.

"Then read something from your dark past," Ultima suggested. When Welsh and Yermak had left she turned to Richard. "Honestly. Such children. We've never really liked them here . . . they are so close, so weird.'

"Like brothers or lovers yet they are neither," Elayne Sandhurst said.

"They need help," Sandra suggested and at that all but Richard laughed. Help was not something the untherapied sought. Help was a kind of death to those who cherished their flaws.

+ We should all live in shade not in the sun. Like insects.

*My first name means god is with us. My last name means worker in gold. I choose words instead; they are much more valuable for being so common, and so misunderstood. As for having god with me; I don't think so somehow.*

# 9

Elevating alongside South Comb Two Mary Choy watched the great mirrored arms rotate to focus the low sixteen sun on Pasadena. She took an external expressway, spending one of her municipal emergency transit credits to get a car to herself.

Exploring the Colonel Sir John Yardley connection would be perilous. She knew enough of federal politics to see the Janus face the United States turned toward Yardley. Embraced by Raphkind, openly shunned now but in the closet perhaps still silky. Yardley might be federally useful and ultimately LAPD answered to the federals. The department was more than half funded by the National Public Defense. To go any further without departmental approval would not be politic. Mary wanted that approval before the day was over.

Los Angeles Public Defense Command occupied a three tier block on the favored west side of South Comb Two. The long beanpole of the expressway, in proportion very like a taut stretched human hair, with no visible means of support but its own ten meter hexagonal cross section, carried three express elevators. These stopped at levels chosen only by their passengers, unlike most of the internal arteries of elevators and transports within the comb.

She took her seat in the carefully cushioned chair and endured the rapid acceleration. In the moments before the door opened as the elevator slowed she felt as if she were floating. This was only slightly less unpleasant than the weight.

The west side looked out across the old communities of Inglewood Culver City and Santa Monica, now covered with great reddish brown slashes as the old city was leveled and new combs encroached upon shadow. In the maxdense hills of Santa Monica layer upon layer of what some netwit thirty years before had called insulas grew like cave wall crystals, dazzling white at noon but now blue gray in the onset of evening. Here and in the stabilized deepsunk pads of Malibu was where the notyetchosen waited for vacancies within the combs. Vacancies were becoming more and more rare as rejuvenators plied their controversial trade, turning good citizens into multicentenarian eloi.

Mary Choy was too young to attract a rejuvenator's pitch but she had gone on eloi busts and seen the interiors of many platinum comb domiciles.

She withdrew from the elevator and walked purposefully into the lobby. From the acrophobic view of the city to this large inner directed self contained cavern, horizontal slit windows at hip level affording little relief, was always a small shock to her. Mary felt it as an abrupt discontinuity like a change of key or even scale in music. Arbeiters moved purposefully on narrow paths near the walls leaving the center open for foot traffic. A central circular desk occupied by two young men in green office uniforms jutted from the floor. Overhead an apse sparkled with sheets and curling ribbons of peaceful light in the cathedral quiet.

"Pd investigator M Choy," said the young man on her side of the desk as she approached. "You have a quarter till appointment with federal coordinator R Ellenshaw."

She had made her appointment with pd supervisor D Reeve. News was speeding and she had guessed right. Large green eyes steady on the greeter's face, she said, "Fine. Do I wait?"

"Not here, please," the greeter said. His eyes pinpointed her with faint disapproval and obvious longing. "You'll have a seat in third tier, lobby two."

She narrowed her eyes and fixed on the greeter until he averted. Then she shivered slightly nodded and walked away adding an extra lilt to her stride. Disliking that common mix of critique and lust she wished to faintly strut the transform and increase the tension. It was a neutral flaw, not socially damaging but perhaps provocative. A distant revenge on Theo. The greeter would not disapprove of Theo but might not lust for her either. *Why.*

Took an escalator to third tier lobby two. Sat with the coffee drinkers and their timeismoney expressions. Examined them casually sherlocking as hobby, and fell into her perpetual muse about how unfortunate sherlocking was a blind jape. Cannot riddle from ambiguous evidence; no detective can avoid the blunder of two or three way outcomes of deduction. Deduction and detection could not be cars on a slaveway; they must freely turn. Still, sherlocking was an amusement and sometimes its results were intriguing. Here for example: a young man on the clear turbo to a needle's point federal/state job, dressed as second generation therapied (or natural) might dress in the younger crowds, face bland but not without character. Mary Choy guessed him a conscientious but not inspired bed partner; he had three fingernails on his right hand red and gold lacquered with marriage inquiries from large families. Only in the high federal ranks did such manners dance the norm, families clans gens statting their position in the nomenklatura made largely ceremonial by President Davis before Raphkind. Such positions did not breed high physical passions; they did breed manners, and among the therapied manners rarely hid aberrations. Nice young man in a pleasant deadend existence prime candidate for eloi upon middle age. A pretty parasite.

Coming in to the waiting area, somebody more vital: a female transform wearing styles to hide her orbital adaptations, an exotic in the combs. All eyes drawn. The exotic saw Mary Choy and acknowledged kinship with a smile. Came to sit.

"May I?"

Mary inclined. The orbital transform bent with strained grace; her muscles now tuned to the bonds of Earth. She obviously shuttled often and was proud possessor of two zone body chemistry; such a transform was too expensive for private payment and must have been federal or firm/house funded. The nice young man decided this orbital transform was too much even for fantasy and ignored her. Others less meshed in the hierarchy admired her openly. Mary was pleased when she sat beside her.

"Pardon my awkwardness," the orbital said. "I'm still adjusting Bichemical."

"So I specked."

"I've only been landed eight hours. You're pd, aren't you?"

42

Mary inclined again. No sherlocking necessary; the uniforms were commonly known and varied little from city to city.

"And you," she said, "are from the Greenbelt?"

The orbital transform smiled. "How keen," she says. "Who did you?"

"Dr. Sumpler."

"His group did me too. I must visit him while down. Are you pleased?"

She considered describing the melanin depletion but since the news would have little practical value to a bichemical, simply gave the polite "Yes. Very."

The orbital transform saw signs of Mary's impending departure for appointment—her glance at the glowing flasher on the wall, her own symbol coming soon—and offered her a card. "I'm down for a week. Much work. I'd enjoy company. We can reminisce through old style catalogs."

Mary laughed, took the card, offered her own. "That would be fun."

"Everything's on the card." The name on the card: *Sandra Auchouch.* "Pronounced Awshuck."

"Of course. Pleasure to meet you."

The orbital transform inclined and they touched fingertips. No carnal thoughts here; the transform by dress and manner was straight as no orbit could be; Mary rarely crossed. But among professionals in going jobs friendship might be a chance thing and chances had to be advantaged.

R Ellenshaw prospered at his high desk; no sherlocking to see this. The metro federal interface supervisor had the look of the oft therapied a man with guts stamina and manifold problems that he had spent years and hundreds of thousands of dollars to smooth.

Mary would not have entered his office with a different attitude had he been whiz natural, he was higherup and she came to him with a problem she would not have wanted had the roles been reversed. Mary Choy respected leadership and valued overhead flak armor.

"M Choy. Welcome to Valhalla." Ellenshaw stood before his desk memo and slate in hand, not happy. "You've tumbled into a shink wasp's nest."

"Yes, sir."

"Please sit." He looked her over sharply without a flicker of judgment or even male interest. Mary's respect for him went up a notch. Professional ice was tough to grow and maintain minus berging out and Ellenshaw did not look a berg; too therapied and self knowing for that. "I have some questions and then your instructions."

She sat, crossing long legs, black workpants hissing faintly.

"You are convinced personally that this Emanuel Goldsmith is the murderer?"

"Yes, sir."

"We've checked out this letter. It is indeed from Colonel Sir John Yardley." The ice was transparent enough for Mary to see Ellenshaw's political stripe; like most west coast pd he had detested Raphkind and the tumescence of the Dirty East. Old politics old dirt. "Do you have any idea where Emanuel Goldsmith is now?"

"No, sir."

"He's gone underground?"

"I don't know, sir."

"Hispaniola?"

"It's possible."

"But would Yardley have taken him in?"

Mary didn't hazard.

"You know this will become a federal football. The possibility that Goldsmith has gone to Hispaniola makes the halls echo, M Choy."

"Yes, sir."

"There's no chance the federals can bury this. Too many gold and platinum names, too much high blood. So they've handed the football to us. Jurisdiction primary. To keep your grip on the football, you have to be fresh snow, M Choy. Are you?"

"Yes, sir."

44

"I've checked your record and I agree. I envy naturals, M Choy. I envy your record."

"Thank you, sir."

"I've had to spend a fortune on therapy to untangle and smooth out. It's been worth it, but ... So." That had been a calculated ice thinning and it had worked; he had revealed enough about himself to make Mary feel she was in his confidence, that he had confidence in her.

"I believe you call it flak armor now, M Choy. Protection from this level so you can concentrate on your work. The armor is thin this case. You are not completely on your own and you are working a spike fence. We likely cannot catch you if you fall. Not in time. Clear?"

"Yes, sir."

"The word here is, west coast federals hate the Yardley connection as much as I do. It's old, it's Raphkind, it smells. East coast federal is still ambiguous and likely will be for years while the grand juries and courts grind slow. But maybe not. Yardley keeps pushing his imports ... We keep blocking them. Spike fence.

"I give you permission to sniff all local trails and if they're still cold after two days, you have clearance for an official visit to Hispaniola. Assistants if you need them, as many as five."

"I'll need two Hispaniolan experts," Mary said.

"My office will find them and pass their names and currvitas on to Supervising Inspector D Reeve, unless you have people in mind already ..."

She did not. "Do I have your permission to query Citizen Oversight?"

Ellenshaw averted for moment, frowning. "We can only make so many Oversight queries. But if any case merits, this one does. You have permission to go to Oversight."

"Thank you." She inclined.

"Details are on your orders. We'll work with federal to get Hispaniola to cooperate with you. Call me anytime. Don't be isolated. You might be *our* flak armor on this one." He smiled cleanly.

"Yes, sir."

She left Ellenshaw's office knowing this was the case of her career and pd was giving her extraordinary support; also knowing federal had deemed her expendable, but not in a minor cause. She would be stupid not to be afraid. To those concerned with basic human dignity Colonel Sir John Yardley was the western world's prosperous heart of darkness. Mary Choy allowed herself the requisite fear, but no more.

The comb towers went dark against the last blue wink of dusk. She drove a slaveway to the pd shade central on Sepulveda and filled out a request for overnight research space, slept an hour in a cop cot, drank a nutrient cocktail and went to work.

*LA City of Angels like a horse sleeps on its legs. I've walked the shade (since before it was shadowed) late night and seen the nocturnal half conduct itself busily not just machines but people . . . Don't think the shade is reckless eccentricity. It has its own life, not clean like the therapied hives perhaps, but rich and full as any past city, as organized; shade has its mayors and councils, bosses and workers, mommies and daddies, neighborhoods and businesses, hospitals and pd stations, churches and libraries, and they are vital. Bootstrappers, perfecters of humanity, don't forget the ground you lift yourself from, unless you want a hard fall!*

# 10

Sure as is, they had him Fausted; Albigoni and Lascal had tempted and Martin Burke was about to succumb. It was all over but the night of pangs. Still the forms must be observed; the night of pangs must pass.

Adult enough to realize that the prize might be hollow, Martin Burke tried to deny the temptation but could not.

The pair had found his most vulnerable patch in his most pale and yielding underbelly. His life was science and he had been removed from that life through no fault of his own, merely as an accident of bad politics and history. To have it back would mean he could live again. He longed to walk the Country of the Mind. That was a stimulus like no other; knowledge from the frontier that defined all frontiers.

Martin grinned in the half dark watching a playback of the AXIS reports. He selfsaw that grin and sobered. He did have one train of questions to answer but Carol Neuman was not taking her calls and she did not have a home manager.

Martin closed his eyes and tried to stop shaking. Ethical questions all too obvious and tenacious. Goldsmith's right to deny intrusion. Still, a poet, a murderer whose country of the mind would reflect the artist's adaptation of sub-aware forces . . . Never such an opportunity. Never.

"I am not a bad man," he said out loud. "I didn't deserve what happened to me and I do not deserve this now." This what. Qualms. Opportunity/temptation.

Albigoni had nothing to lose. If Martin would not give him what he wanted nobody could except perhaps the ghosts/doppelgangers of Martin Burke that might exist elsewhere, suckling his discoveries raking his ground with more brutal clawed fingers, the far less scrupulous who might exist in Hispaniola exploiting not developing the Country of the Mind and racing ahead of him even now, alligator versus hare, alligator eats the hare.

Martin was not a bad man. Albigoni had not immediately flown Goldsmith to Hispaniola and paid Colonel Sir John Yardley what he might require, so Albigoni was not a bad man, either. Of course Yardley's prisons and labs were rumor; still Albigoni had the connections to have such rumors confirmed or denied. Albigoni did not intend to harm Goldsmith and of course Goldsmith was a bad man; no harm to him but the probe of science a redemption opportunity payment; a recovery of his value to humanity.

Martin lay back on the couch, still shaking, fingers laced. Not a bad man. Perhaps not even a bad deed.

He got up from the couch and placed another call to Carol.

"Hello."

He started in surprise and pushed his hand back through his hair. "Hello, Carol. This is Martin."

"I thought you'd call. I've been working."

Martin's tension erupted before he could wrap it tight. "You've put me into a horrible quandary. God damn it, Carol. God damn it."

"Whoa. I'm sorry."

"I wonder whether you hate me."

"I don't hate you. Listen. I just got in. You want to talk with me, but not tonight. It's too late. I've contracted with Mind Design Inc in Sorrento Valley. Through Star Temp agency you know. If you can come out to—"

"Yes. I know where it is. Which lab?"

"Thirty one. Midmorning?"

"Ten."

"I don't hate you, Martin. Whether I should I don't know but I don't. We'll talk."

They said brief farewells.

AXIS replays had lost their charms and he shut down the screen with a curt "Off." With some guilt he understood that his shaking was not from moral dilemma; there really had been none from the moment of the offer. He shook because of eagerness and excitement.

*In white society every black is a trained bear. That's how I feel at times even with my white woman who shows not the slightest sign of thinking such. Does she love me for being the one black male writer given a chance to shine in USA this generation? One per, an old law. The greatest taint of all is the taint left by history on my own soul. I cannot love her; I see her with scarred eyes.*

# 11

Richard Fettle returned to his shade apartment by seven o'clock, hoofing slowly up crumbling concrete and steel stairs. He brushed aside an abundance of brown and yellow banana leaves intruding into the second floor landing, slipped his smoothworn brass key into tricky lock and greeted the cheap ten year old home manager on smoke stained fireplace mantel with "It's me. Only me."

"Welcome home, Mr. Fettle," the manager croaked. + Once did not recognize me. Raised a miserable stink. Pd didn't come. Neighbors checked in though. Take care of our own.

He made himself a cup of coffee and sat in a chair he had made twenty years before to give to his

A comfortable chair the last he had of his handicrafts. Gave it to his

He glanced briefly at a slate, noted some articles in today's *Shadow Rhubarb* he wanted to read, finished his coffee and wondered what he would do for dinner. He wasn't hungry but the body must. Truth to tell he was depressed now, decompressed, all the stories told to all who mattered and nothing but his own thoughts not good company at all. + Roughed and not deserving cut that refrain and bear down on your past you bastard

+ Your wife

+ Your wife, gave the chair to her. Not the time to think those thoughts, however. Richard closed his eyes and leaned back, the chair expanding under him footrest up back tilted arms inclining, friendly.

+ Why he did it. Madame de Roche thinks not crazy; a natural. Why then. Brilliance getting Emanuel down they say they say. Deep depravity coming up sicking up foulness like a dog. Bubble of evil in still waters noxious gases. Poem in that. Nothing worth bothering with. If not depraved not

49

crazy then rational. Thinking all the time; planning. Form of expression. Expression of true brilliance stretching beyond human morality limitations. Did it for his art to see what he would make himself into. Kill himself as well as them; sure as hell he has no life to return to. Murderer murders twice. Kills two for each victim. No. Kills himself only once; murder once and it's enough you're done for deep therapy enforced maybe not even *you* left when you come out. Wanted to go through that maybe; kill be caught be prosecuted and therapied deep therapy . . . Come back new Goldsmith. See if poet survives that. Like scientist a personal experiment.

Richard tightened his eyelids until his nose wrinkled.

+ I am a simple man with simple wants. I want to be left alone. I want to forget.

But forgetting was not possible. He had half an impulse to open all the nets and LitVids on his slate and immerse himself in the propagated facts but he resisted. The simple knowledge was enough; multiple murders, likely by the man Richard admired most in the world.

"Somebody's coming," the manager rasped. People walked by and the manager was never sure whether to express concern or not.

The door chimes century old corroded brass antiques bumbled and belled against each other. Richard imagined them shaking off dust; they were seldom disturbed. He collapsed the chair and strode hunched to the door to peer through the verdigris stained peephole.

Female, black hair, long gray and orange shift, clutching a woven reed handbag. Nadine Preston. "Hi to you," she said, bending to eyeball the peephole. "I thought you might be feeling down."

Richard opened the door. "Come in," he said voice mortician deep and resigned. He coughed and shook his head to clear the somber tone. "Please come in." He had always come to her, not the other way around, to control his exposure to her bad times. He wondered whether he should feel touched by her concern.

"Are you down?" she asked brightly.

"A little," he confessed.

"Then you need company."

"Actually, I do, I guess," he said.

"Such enthusiasm. Have you eaten?"

He shook his head.

She opened her handbag and brought out a suck-wrapped package of forever meat. "I can do wonders with this," she said. "Have any potatoes?"

"Dried," he said.

"We'll have shepherd's pie."

"Thank you for coming over," he said.

"I'm not always good for you," Nadine said demurely looking down at the carpet. "But I know when you need somebody and you shouldn't sleep alone tonight."

The shepherd's pie tasted decently of salt and garlic and potatoes which reminded him of Nadine, a salt and garlic woman. As they ate she talked about the shade vid industry as she had known it and as she still came in touch with it. His mind was nudged away from the problem of the day until a gap formed between him and recent memory and he listened to her, so tired that he saw the pale ghosts of hallucinations. Blue raincoated figure in the corner of his eye.

"They did this scene with music," Nadine said, talking about some vid production ten years past. "The director needed to show that now the musician a cellist was really playing much better than before, and the scorer said but we have soundtrack that's already the best we can get. He plays the cello and it's the best cellist in the world playing behind him but there was no contrast. The director says then 'Get a fruity cellist.' Just that. Fruity. When the best isn't good enough you go a step beyond, into the frankly bad. Isn't that marvelous?" She smiled broadly, hand frozen in a demonstrative wave and he chuckled politely nodding yes that's the way of it. Richard could not help being polite and kind to her when she was in the mood, and it was a good story.

He ate and contemplated contrast. His mind went back

to Goldsmith like a chained dog circling an iron spike. What to do when you're the best and you need contrast or else all is gray.

+ Relief through grand melodrama. Was that it.

The blue figure was smiling; he knew that without seeing it clearly. His daughter. He could not avoid trying to look at the figure directly. It vanished every time.


**IIOO-IIOOO-IIIIIIIIIIII**


*(The Examiner, having finished his work on the guilty of ten worlds, suddenly finds on his desk the folders of curriculum vitae for a number of terrestrial greats. He sighs and looks them over one by one. This great human being, by inventing such and such, has destroyed a hundred million; this other, by philosophizing, has misled billions. They are in his charge now, and he is growing increasingly weary.)*

EXAMINER: *"Please my Father, enough! I have judged the guilty. Why must I judge the best and brightest?"*
*(No answer.)*
*(The Examiner drops the folders on the desk, perhaps resigned.)*

EXAMINER: *(Murmurs) "The least you could do is give me a computer."*


# 12

At six hundred, Mary Choy's home manager woke her up with a persistent chiming. She ascended from a dream of swimming in the surf off Newport Beach with her mother and sister. "Jesus. What is it?"

"Supervising Inspector D Reeve."

"What time? Morning?"

"Six hundred, Mary."

"Put him on. No vid." She sat up in bed, lifted her arms over her head and stretched to force blood into her brain. Shook herself vigorously. Threw one leg over the side of the bed. She had been searching the jags until two hundred with no results; none of Goldsmith's acquaintances had seen sliver of the man.

"My apologies, Inspector Choy." Reeve himself seemed exhausted, face dark olive on the incoming vid, eyes hooded.

"Good morning, sir."

"You were involved with the Khamsang Phung Selector kidnapping early this year, were you not?"

"Yes, sir."

"I have a message in my desk memory that you wanted to be called if we tracked any suspects involved in that case."

She stood and shook out her hands, fully awake now. "Yes, sir."

"We have a Selector jiltz in a comb. One of the Phung suspects could be there. Do you want to be involved? I can put you on a backup team at the site."

No hesitation. "Definitely, sir. I'd like to be there."

Reeve gave her the location. Mary dressed quickly, grateful her transform chemistry could let her coast for many hours without sleep.

Twenty three minutes after leaving her apartment, she stood on the north facing balcony of Canoga Tower, dark slim fingers lightly touching the polished brass railing, overlooking LA from a height of four hundred meters. On instructions from the local CEC, the Comb Environs Commander, she had ascended two thirds of the tower. A tightpacked curtain of air whispered a few inches from her face as she leaned forward, keeping out the cool early morning breezes. To her right dawn smeared gray and watery across the foggy horizon.

Mary had accepted Reeve's invitation simply to keep her hand in on Selector investigations. She had removed herself from the Phung case seven months ago; workload deadends and discouragement had forced that decision.

She did not like these operations; jiltzing Selectors was like dipping into a dark nightmare shared by all society. But if there was a nexus that summed up all problems involving crime, society and public defense, it was the question of Selectors. She could not be an honest pd and refuse the opportunity.

Waiting for further instructions from the CEC she concentrated on the view, glazing all other thoughts. She had assumed her standby just ten minutes before; she did not even know yet where the jiltz would be. That would be revealed moments before, giving her just enough time to rendezvous with her team section.

Los Angeles was a glory at night. Mary had read once that only a young civilization wasted its light by throwing it into empty space. Earth's young cities still did just that, all but the combs dark irregular towers against the general skyglow. Canted mirrors reflected night, their edges lumed by warning beacons and the dim glowing red lines of Meissner junctures. In the jag neighborhoods between the combs, streets blazed forth in orange and blue and homes sprinkled white and blue like earthbound stars. Older smaller commercial towers contributed checkerboards of afterhours activity between the combs.

Suborbital jet liners crossed overhead to LAX oceanport with dull booming noises like sea creatures from an inverted deep. Bands of first, second and third neorbit satellites excelled a Milky Way never clear in LA's haze. Nothing in a city like LA ever stopped; whole communities always awake active doing thinking. She could dytch to that rhythm; she loved the city. LA was her mother and father now, huge and enveloping, all nurturing all employing, healthy and unhealthy, challenging and demanding. Threatening.

Mary had been on two previous Selector jiltzes. The first had been a farce; no victims or suspects only a brokendown hellcrown stripped for parts in a deserted decaying shade California bungalow. On the second they had found Phung himself locked away in a jag seven three industrial space strapped naked to a filthy cot clamped in a small import (Hispaniolan) hellcrown, his sentence served—two minutes in hell beyond anything conceived by the most perverse theologian.

Selectors were tro shink careful, very bright nearly all high naturals though twisted this one way: believing themselves to be the purifiers of a sick order. They seldom made major mistakes. Tonight might be crucial; that it came on the heels of the eight murders and a discouraging search was annoying but par.

Mary pictured Selectors getting Goldsmith doing their job claiming to do her job for her. She turned away from the view. Fully a third of US citizens spot polled by LitVid supported Selector illegal activity at least tacitly cocktail chatter support uninvolved go with the mob approval or deep bitter eye for eye. Ironic that most of this third were untherapied; Selectors preyed most often on untherapied, they being more likely to commit the sort of crimes that spurred passion for retribution.

Knock on the door who is it bringing pain what a surprise.

"Lieutenant Choy," she heard in her left ear. "Take Aisle La Cienega to level five four, lane Durant, dominium two one. That is a three level outer cavity dwelling. Your first position is west first floor facing arbeiter elevator entrance, joining third team commander Lieutenant R Sampson and Junior Lieutenant T Willow. Probable weapons include flechette and aero pistols. Pd medical will be on scene."

Mary specked all her expensive transform being violently rearranged by flechette and prodded by a pd medical asking questions: What is this? Do you wish return to normal anatomy for this trauma? She had never been injured in line of. Precaution; police wisdom quick moves.

She walked the distance to the meeting point with Sampson and Willow. They stood in plainclothes near an airshaft balcony a hundred yards from her first standby, talking quietly. Mary joined them and they moved ninety degrees around the circular shaft. Warm air from below lifted Mary's hair. When they stopped Sampson smiled at her; Willow was solemnly nervous.

"Reeve tells us you're secondary in this jiltz," Sampson said quietly.

"It's not my primary," she admitted. "But I'm concerned. I worked with W Taylor and C Chu last year to track the Phung kidnappers."

"These could be more important," Sampson said. "We may have three or four victims. As many as ten Selectors. Maybe even the second in command."

"Shlege?" she asked.

Sampson nodded. "If we'd jiltzed a week earlier, we might have had Yol Origund himself."

"Really."

Sampson showed her a pd slate with floorplan of the dominium. "Three levels. Very expensive. Owned by A Pierson and F Mustapha, city licensed public lawyers. Both Pierson and Mustapha had connections with the Raphkind campaign staff. Both have been seen in New York by local pd in the last three hours. But the dominium is occupied."

"On loan," Willow said with a lift of brows, as if it were terribly significant. Mary nodded.

"It's probably dirty east," Sampson said. "But everybody here is local. Nano watchers in the paint have tagged six regulars four occasionals in the last twenty four hours. Victims were not seen being brought in; that was before we tagged this for a jiltz."

"Any idea who the victims are?" Mary asked.

"CEC and Reeve think two petties and two executives. No names. Shlege is big on executive responsibility."

"Comb executives?"

"No," Willow said. "One is a shade manufacturer. We don't know what the petties do."

"They have aeros and flechettes," Mary said. She turned to Sampson. "Do we get issue?"

"This is sensitive territory; only first team has weapons."

Mary sniffed with professional disdain. "We're on nine lives again."

Willow glanced between them. He was four months new. Sampson relieved his puzzlement. "The pd doctors tell us they can reassemble a severely damaged body about nine times per individual before some fatal incorrectible snouts up. Nine lives. Like cats."

"Ah," Willow said, showing enlightenment. "Have either of you been . . . reassembled?" His face fell, seeing Mary's small grin.

"Only Mary," Sampson said. "By choice, not necessity."

"Sorry," Willow said.

"Nada."

"It's a fine transform," Willow continued, digging his hole deeper. "Really . . . Fine."

"T Willow comes from a south county christian tech family," Sampson said by way of explanation.

"We don't see transforms often in south county," Willoe said.

"No apologies necessary," Mary said. "But being stylish leaves me with only eight lives." *Stylish. On the sly spin.*

Willow thought about that, nodded seriously. "When do we put on our helmets?"

"Last pico, in final position. We haven't had a Selector jiltz pd down in three years," Sampson said. "Let's hope Origund still thinks we're brothers under the skin."

They all lifted their heads in unison as the jiltz leader's voice spoke through earphones. They were to set up a listening post and wait for other sections to complete the surround on the dominium's two lower levels. Court ordered nano watchers and listeners had been sent into the dominium's sewage and structure; microscopic, extremely efficient and detectable only by the most extraordinary means.

"We might even get a picture on this one," Sampson said.

"Heads up videophiles," Willow said. All three received instructions to move into the next position.

They crowded into the arbeiter elevator, stooping to fit. Sampson issued a pd code for control and the elevator took them without protest to their assigned level.

Located on the comb's outermost neighborhood the dominium seemed to hover within a sculpted cellular hollow almost thirty meters wide. The dominium's first level opened onto a shaded greengrowth walkway tinkling waterfalls real birds in ornate brass cages sleeping on perches. The second level was isolated one glass wall pointing through a gap between comb mirrors at a dizzying view of north Los Angeles. The third level connected by a slender unrailed bridge to a private roof atrium designed for access by arbeiter service.

Next to the unrailed bridge on the third level surrounding the dominium, an arbeiter maintenance alcove offered a hiding place. After unfolding their helmets and slipping them on, they set their slates to scrambled listener frequencies, disguised as machine chatter to evade detection.

"These folks must be tro platinum," Willow said wistfully as they hunkered in the alcove. Mary found a clean ledge and sat folding her long legs into a lotus. Willow watched her with frank admiration; curiosity for the new.

"Corp legal and political jobs," Sampson said. "Rewards to the puzzle pieces." Among the pd, "puzzle piece" was pejorative slang for anybody who took advantage of legal lacunae.

"How can they torture execs or anybody else when they hide in the nooks themselves?" Willow asked.

"You should read Wolfe Ruller," Mary said. "If you're really interested in Selector philosophy."

"I suppose I should be."

"Something about 'Social antibodies filling the molecular spaces that might otherwise be used by antisocial offenders,'" Sampson said.

"Why, Robert," Mary chided. Sampson was sharp but not known for his lit learning.

Sampson grinned boyishly. "Anything to impress you, M Choy."

"I'm impressed."

"I'll look up Ruller," Willow said earnestly. "He's in the pd library?"

"He's probably in your issue copy right now," Mary said, tapping Willow's slate where it hung on his belt. "Standard reference for our advanced age."

"Feed coming in," Sampson said. They listened intently. Within the dominium they heard footsteps and muffled conversation. Since they were not controlling the listeners they could not tune to any given room. The voices gradually cleared. Two men talking. Something made a sharp whickering noise: staccato breathing of a victim under a clamp. Mary felt her skin tingle: apprehension, a deeper horror than she had felt looking at the victims of Goldsmith.

"Have you ever seen a clamp?" Willow asked. "I mean, besides the limited one we're shown in training—"

Sampson held his finger to his lips. The voices tuned in with crystal clarity.

"Watch this one," an older sounding man said. "Don't let the wipers set their gain too high. Ramp the dream down at the end of five minutes."

"In a smooth placc," said the other, voice high pitched but not necessarily female.

Mary glanced at the slate screen; it was on. "Vid," she said. They simultaneously pulled up their slates and watched the broadcast picture. Far from perfect; nano imaging usually left much to be desired. They could see a small round room probably central in the dominium no windows a single open door, two figures standing. Furniture: three beds or cots a chair a panel or keyboard controller leaning against one chair.

"Three people on those beds," Sampson said softly.

Mary's stomach knotted. Quiet forms; unmoving. Not dead. Wishing perhaps to be dead.

"Team one making first level arrangements," CEC said. Mary wondered where CEC was. First team, probably. She could speck CEC's anger at having his comb invaded by Selectors. "Team two taking visual positions on second level surround."

"Just a few minutes now," Sampson said. An arbeiter rolled past their position, stopped to survey them placidly with crystalline insect eyes. Willow flashed a pd override at the machine. It did not respond, turned and rolled away from the alcove onto the narrow bridge leading to the dominium's atrium roof.

Mary glanced at Sampson wide eyed then jumped out of the alcove and followed the arbeiter across the bridge, ignoring the lack of rails and the twenty meter fall on either side. Behind her Sampson informed the other teams that an arbeiter had refused to submit. She intercepted the machine just before it made the service elevator entrance, grabbed it with both hands and gently lowered it to the rooftop. It did not protest but within the building loud hooting alarms went off.

Mary stood for a moment beside the prone machine, made her decision quickly walked to the edge to see what was happening and gestured for Willow to join her. He crossed the bridge with arms held out walking tightrope teetering recovering running up beside her. In her ear CEC barked orders to move in now. She looked over the roof's edge and saw five pd running past the waterfalls and bird cages on the first level, two taking up positions blocking exits. Mary caught Sampson's eye across the chasm and pointed to the service elevator entrance on the roof. Peering out of the alcove Sampson nodded agreement to her plan, obvious to an experienced pd. Should anyone come up through the roof she and Willow would wait behind the service entrance to tackle them. If they failed Sampson would offer another line of opposition.

Staccato slamslap of high frequency air hammers against lower doors. Crashing and popping. "First floor jiltz," the CEC said. "Four officers inside."

Mary's heart flipped. She grabbed Willow's shoulder and urged him behind the entrance shelter. They squatted on either side of the door. She rearranged her legs to keep them limber and bounced experimentally. Touched her fingers to the shelter. Elevator vibration. Someone coming up.

"We've got seven here on the first and second floors," the first team leader announced. "Three victims recovered, two under clamp. Call in a therapist."

Willow flattened himself against the opposite side of the cylinder. Mary did likewise. The door opened. An arbeiter rolled out eyes swinging. Seeing its prone companion a few meters away, it emitted a squeal.

Mary grabbed the rim of the door swung around sprawled across the rooftop and reached with her other hand into the entrance grabbing madly for anything she could find. Willow reached around from a standing position. Together they hauled out a shrieking woman with a flechette pistol in hand. Shreds of tumbling metal whined against the roof behind them. Like pulling down a wasp nest. Mary gritted her teeth and pushed two rigid fingers into the woman's stomach. Willow swung a fist into her face. Blood spattered on Mary's arm and the woman went down head back into the service elevator, kicking out at Mary. She stood and grabbed the pistol hand deliberately breaking the woman's wrist and two of the fingers flung the pistol across the rooftop straddled her grabbed her hips and pulled her between her legs out of the elevator. As the woman's bloody face passed by Mary reached down almost gently pulled back her hair and grabbed her ears.

Swinging around deftly she lifted the woman up by the ears wrapped an arm around her neck and applied pressure to her throat until she stopped kicking. Willow wrapped tack cord around her legs. "She shot at us," he said gasping for breath. "She fapping shot at us."

61

"That's automatic therapy mandatory," Mary said to the woman. The woman's eyes looked up at her out of a mess of blood and tangled hair. For a moment Mary caught a satisfying glimpse of disorientation and terror. She relaxed her grip.

"My hand," the woman said thickly, moaning. "My nose."

"Small price," Mary said, turning away.

"You fapping bitch!" Willow shouted.

"Now, now," Mary said, some of her status calm returning. "No way to talk to a citizen."

"Sorry," Willow said. Sampson reported the takedown to the CEC and first team leader. They tried to lift the woman but she struggled again. Willow pulled out more tack cord and pinned her arms to her body. In their ears CEC said, "All three levels searched. One out the roof, takedown by team three. Eight suspects secured and three victims. Calling in therapists and meds."

"We're crossing this bridge," Mary said to the woman, who squirmed violently against the tack cords. "Do you want to make us all fall off?"

The woman became still. "We're just doing your job, damn you," she said, split lip swelling.

"Oh." Mary nodded emphatic gratitude. "My apologies."

Willow lifted the woman's feet and Mary her shoulders. They carried her over the narrow bridge and dropped her beside Sampson. Sampson smiled broadly ironically at Mary.

"You lysing lobe sod," Mary told him in a tone of pure syrup.

He lifted his arm and showed her a torn sleeve. Blood trickled down his wrist and dripped from his finger.

"Just a flesh wound, ma'am," he said. Flechette darts were designed to change shape and burrow if given a purchase of more than a centimeter. Sampson was very lucky.

"Could have taken your arm off," Willow said admiringly.

Mary pulled back, looked Sampson over critically, then held out her arms and hugged him. "Glad you're still with us, Robert," she said into his ear.

"Fine job, Mary," he responded.

"Hey," Willow said. "How about me?"

"Show me your blood," Mary told him. He looked abashed and then she hugged him as well. "Let's get Robert looked at."

"Should be worth at least a day off," Sampson said. He shook his arm flinging more blood from his fingertips and clutched it at the elbow. "Christ. It's beginning to hurt."

Mary stood before the recorders taking down officer testimony on the jiltz. A pd legal advisor and metro certified public witness stood behind the officer in charge of the vid.

"Did you incur or cause any injuries in this action?" the pd advisor asked her.

"No injuries to myself. I slightly injured an unidentified female suspect when she attempted to flee and used a weapon."

"Nature of that weapon?" the advisor asked.

"Flechette pistol."

The evidence processor, a young assistant sergeant, removed the pistol in its protective translucent bag from a tray atop a pd arbeiter and dangled it in the scanning lines of the testimony vid's secondary recorder. Already officers and technicians were preparing to fasten ceiling tracks throughout the house and mount assayers and sniffers.

The suspects were being kept in another room pending onsite arraignment; therapists had not yet arrived to remove the clamps from three victims. All pd was authorized to do was shut down the active elements of the hellcrowns. Mary had not yet seen the room where the victims were kept. She was restless to do so although she feared it would give her nightmares.

Out of the corner of her eye she spotted three metro therapists entering through the wide front door. They crossed the marble tile floor to the stairs leading to the second level, two men and a woman in pale gray midsuits. She knew two of them; they had given first therapy treatment to Joseph Khamsang Phung during her last Selector jiltz, her only prior witnessing of an active clamp.

"Were you with another officer at the time?" the advisor continued.

"Yes. LAPD Junior Lieutenant Terence Willow."

"Did he help you inflict injury to the suspect?"

"He struck her in the face to distract her."

"Describe the nature of the injuries."

"Suspect fired a volley from her pistol as she emerged from a third level arbeiter service elevator. I had jinked to the surface in front of her, and I . . ." She closed her eyes to aid complete recall and described her actions in breaking the woman's wrist and two fingers. She hated onsite testimonies but they saved much time later in trials.

When her turn was done and T Willow was in the line of vid, she walked off and looked around the house, staying out of the path of the technicians. The dominium was a wonder—even fancier than she had imagined. Everything appeared either antique or human made. She suspected everything had authenticity stamps. Ceramics wooden furniture custom equipment arrays, all the very best. A Japanese made home manager with at least ten dedicated French and Ukrainian arbeiters now assembled as if for military inspection in the first floor kitchen, being checked by a pd tech. They were probably all illegally altered for surveillance and guard duty.

For a minute she paused in the first level room where the eight suspects were being held. All well dressed comblooking citizens between twenty five and sixty years, not a one she would have specked as a potential rad or deviant. They stood with hands tack corded in front of them wearing LAPD remote headsets for access to their chosen attorneys.

Mary's takedown had been treated by a metro physician and now slumped pale, wrapped in nano bandage in an office chair to the left of the grimfaced lineup. She was the only one sitting. She saw but did not see M Choy standing in the doorway. Mary surveyed the seven others looking for the Selectors known to have been involved in the Phung case. Double naughts. Not a one.

A technician begged her pardon and pushed past her, rigging more ceiling track.

With a deep sigh Mary turned and walked up the wide stairs to the second level. She might have avoided all this; still, Reeve had done her a genuine pd courtesy allowing her on this jiltz.

The Comb Environs Commander, a tall narrow faced blond man, stood with the comb civil attorney. Both nodded to her as she passed. They were deep in discussion of litigation and repercussions. She heard the commander reassuring the comb metro attorney that all permissions had been received and that fed and state court orders were on record for every action taken this morning.

Morning. Through a second level picture window, peeking between the outer comb mirrors she saw the northern limb of what looked like an attractive morning. Fog burning off. Pleasant day.

Steadying herself she stepped into the doorway to the windowless cylindrical room at the center of the second level. The three metro therapists kneeled around the clamped victims on their cots. Low murmurs passed between them as they examined their patients. The single hellcrown resembled a hospital arbeiter, about a meter tall, three stacked spheroids with a connecting ridge up one side, the control panel like a remote keyboard. One of the therapists held that panel now, slowly bringing the victims back to consciousness. The hellcrown was not an expendable Hispaniolan import; it was custom fine machinery, perhaps Chinese. Capable of delivering hours of retribution in minutes.

"They set him for high-ramp dream of five minutes. *Five* minutes," the eldest therapist, a woman in her fifties, told her colleagues. "Who was he?"

"Representative of marketing for Sky Private," said another. "Lon Joyce."

The man moaned and tried to sit up, eyes still closed. His face was wizened with fear and pain. The therapist restrained him with her arm. Mary entered the room and stood out of the way arms crossed, biting her lower lip. She could feel the contortion of discomfort on her own face, empathy for the three on the cots.

One of the therapists she had met before noticed her standing there, blinked, ignored her. None of the victims not even the unclamped patient had yet recovered consciousness.

"Sky Private. Airplane manufacturers?" the third therapist asked. "What did he do?"

"Sold defective airframes to an Indian company," said a voice behind Mary. She turned and saw the CEC.

"Hardly seems worth five minutes," the female therapist said in an undertone, administering a metabolism control patch.

"You helped with the roof takedown?" the CEC asked Mary in an undertone.

She nodded. "Get anybody important?"

"Not Shlege unfortunately. The woman you caught was Shlege's mistress, however. It's nice to give the bastard a little grief." He nodded at the three victims. "We've just got ID confirmed on all of them. One of them is Lon Joyce. Four small aircraft fell out of the sky near New Delhi. He used stale nano to make his airframes. Allegedly knew it, too. Civil suits passed him by; he was far richer than those he killed."

Mary swallowed. "The others?"

"The young man on the left is Paolo Thomerry from Trenton New Jersey. Heard of him?"

She had seen his name on the pd bulletins. "Short eyes," she said.

"Exactly. Twelve children from New York to Los Angeles in the past three months. Refused therapy; called it philosophy."

"And the third?"

"A petty embezzler from jag three. He threatened his estranged wife that he would kill her. Selectors got to him before he got to her. We think the wife must have called them in. She didn't think to call us first. She must have really hated him."

Mary tried to reconstruct what had happened; blindfolded or drugged or both the three miscreants brought into the dominium by trained reliable Selectors, the hellcrown and clamps prepared, the mock court proceedings, sentencing and clamping within twelve hours of sentence, release a day or two later on the streets of LA let them fend for themselves. Most who had undergone the clamp needed some form of therapy or another; some needed it badly.

Few ever repeated their crimes.

Her lip curled and she shook her head slowly. "They should clamp themselves," she murmured.

The CEC rubbed the back of his neck with his hand. "You're the principal in the East Comb One murders, Investigator M Choy?"

"Yes."

He extended his hand and she clasped it firmly. "Good hunting," he said. "Take it from me; there's a real letdown if these clowns get your quarry before you do. And word's out. They're after Goldsmith. Perhaps that's why we missed Shlege. He may be out in the jags now, tracking."

"Thanks for the warning," Mary said.

The eldest victim, Lon Joyce, came awake and began to scream.

Mary turned and descended the stairs at a run.

# 13

Martin Burke pumped a pushbike to the bus station—no autobus service in his neighborhood, due to rebellion of landowners against civic intrusion of guideways and subsequent per capita five grand a year tax infants under two exempt—and folded it into a locker twenty five per day, spoke his destination into a reception ear and waited. Ten minutes and a large autobus hummed and groaned in beneath the translucent seashell canopy, twenty meters long and segmented like a worm, a white and gold amphisbaena, nothing but seats and flex windows and flex door. Martin came aboard, put his feet on the safety bar, allowed a belt to cross his heart and fell into slaveway muse.

The dilemma had burned out its fuse for now. He thought of nothing much important. Seeing roads, roads occupied him.

A completely private citizen owned passenger car basic model cost two hundred twenty five thousand dollars in California, one hundred thousand dollars a year in slaveway use tax, fifty thousand vehicle excise, twenty thousand state sales, twenty thousand federal sales, five thousand slaveway research, two thousand five hundred domicile parking fee, two thousand five hundred electricity allocation license fee, five hundred per month domicile plug maintenance fee, two hundred surcharge meter fee, fifty LA City of Angels/California Transportation Operations (CALTROPS; the forms had all been designed and the logo locked in before a cunning citizen pointed this out and they were still not amused) joint participation tax. The average fully agented and employed therapied citizen earned three hundred k a year, the average shadows unagented untherapied a third of that, a bus certificate for one year cost twenty k and still the slaveways were packed like clay.

Three LitVid comedies were based on Slaveway Flying Dutchman never leaving the road cannot afford a house raising family in cramped citizen vehicle chased by tax authorities; twenty two LitVid entertainments dealt with Los Angeles and/or southern California highways in the latter half of the twentieth century, time of romance. They had not been called freeways for nothing.

Glimmer of circumstance. Sun crossing his nose made

him blink. Hello. Awake now. Dreading being Martin Burke. Nothing enjoyable at this instant about being himself. Ozymandias in the dust. His attention switched from external to internal. He thought of Carol and the weaknesses and frictions between even stable men and women. Conflict of the sexes is not a disease; it is an unavoidable byproduct like smoke and water from a fire. People are slow burners; burn themselves crisp come back for more, eloi born again new pleasures and new toys. Burn again.

He closed his eyes and pinned his moth thought. He and Carol had burned brightly not slowly. Carrying a torch for each other, they had known a passion it was unimaginable could have been felt by any others. Clear light between their ears the widest possible sunny rooms their love no clouds expansion and a clean yellow joy. Bright dazzle past, he saw that she was less infatuated and more pragmatic than he and he agonized over her control. Martin had not been in control. He had been head over.

At first he had teased her about her pragmatism and after a few such teases she had said not at all viciously, "I have to hold something in reserve. I need something left over after all. I'm still me."

Fire struck by rain. Clear light gone. He had known for sure that he would lose her and so he did. A few days and weeks of that sort of hurt demanding backandforth and she had lofted higher, suspicious, aware that he was a natural not therapied and that even highly rated naturals could come tumbling down. His genius outshined hers two to one and the myth of bright instability had been in her eyes. She had squinted whenever he spoke, a small anticipatory wince.

Martin had known it would soon end and he had pushed it and when the end came, when she had quietly told him they should separate, he had flipped. She had been the ideal and pinnacle and she could not just withdraw unscathed. He had had to hurt her in some way so she would not treat the next unsuspecting male so callously; no sadistic impulses mind you merely an educational burn sting warning slap. He had not known how much he had tipped until he found himself at her apartment door fruitbowl in hand with a pile of horse dung (could have been worse could have been dogshit) beneath the perfect fruit. She had invited him in as you might invite a friend who has interrupted you, taken the package, opened it, smiled gently glad to see you're taking it so well it's going so well for you, picked up an apple, stared at the fresh farmpicked fertilizer for home gardeners fifty dollars a liter mess, and she had cried. Not tears of anger or frustration. Just little girl tears. For ten minutes she had cried saying nothing not moving the tears taking more and more out of her.

Martin Burke had watched in stone amazement eyes wide as saucers sucking in the pain no glory no satisfaction no revenge no lessons taught seeing so much more clearly now how far he had tipped and what pain a well-adjusted brilliant young man with prospects could cause.

From that moment three years ago until last night they had not talked. She had left IPR.

Martin had gone through the Raphkind years another kind of dead romance; Carol had moved on to therapy high achievers and work at Mind Design on artificial perception and advanced thinker psychology.

She had therapied Albigoni's dear dead daughter. That connection had brought both of them to this point. Because of her he was being Fausted. Because of her he might find his way back through the labyrinth to the full light of celebrity scientist and control of IPR.

Side trip through Goldsmith's Country of the Mind.

The bus cruised into Sorrento Valley. Three levels of slaveways on ancient tracks covered sacred transportation ground bought with the treasure of ancient citizens, upper road level topped with curved glass. The slaveways gently curved through hills covered with corporate hanging gardens. Alternating bars of sun and shade from slaveway canopy supports crossed his face.

The gold and white vehicle snaked into the Mind Design

70

bus station and issued his card with a transfer credit. A corporate grounds cab waited patiently for him while he passed ID and took him to the proper building. He stepped out of the cab shielding his eyes against the sun.

He had visited Mind Design Inc only once five years before in the IPR glory days. MDI technicians and programmers had swarmed around him smiling, some in white skinform others in time honored denim, shaking hands talking about work on this agent work on that as if they knew what a natural agent was and how powerful. Maybe they do now, Martin allowed, but not then. Even he had barely begun to understand the power and perplexity of natural mental agent integration into routines subroutines and personalities.

MDI had been his negative his research's negative that is: building from below rather than probing from above.

Now Martin Burke was a nonentity who needed Carol Neuman's clearance to get on the grounds. If he attracted any attention it was cursory Who was that face? Did I know that face once? Years ago maybe before loss of status legal difficulties expulsion disgrace by association.

He hunched his shoulders.

Building thirty one rose on broad aluminum inverted pyramid feet above an open courtyard, early teens architecture imitating mid twentieth. Wide and low rising only three stories above the courtyard with two narrow trilons on the north end supporting a weave of optic fibers that leaked spinning galaxies even in midmorning sun. Showplace. Prominence and respect. Style and cleanliness.

MDI was prosperous indeed. Inside, pale gold walls trimmed with red drapes that rippled like bas relief flags in still air, vids moving across the fabric internal projection or weaving light mod, paintings faces all very This and Now.

Martin felt faint envy. This was the lobby to a common lab building. MDI shipped designs to arbeiter and thinker manufacturers around the world and that meant huge resources.

71

A tall slender androgyne arbeiter with skin the match of the walls, a convolved hairmock the shade of the red drapes and vertical face dividing eyeline clear and bright as the outdoor sun stood behind a white marble top desk and greeted him in a beautiful synthetic voice. "Carol Neuman please," he said.

"You are Martin Burke?" the arbeiter asked. He nodded, averting from the vertical crystal eyeline. "She is paged."

"Thank you." Offhandedly looking around without wanting to see. Not even at its peak did IPR rate this power show. But that was fine; brains not backing; to the swiftest went the race not the gaudiest.

Carol came down a sculptured stone staircase in pale blue skinform. Deer moves cat walk as he remembered though hipheavier now. Eyes unconcerned professional light smile brown hair in short close waves bouncing back from compression beneath scalpglove in her right hand. He always heard Sibelius strings and drums when seeing her, brownhaired blue eyed Norse tall goddesslike unconcerned but a treasure to the right unlocker of passions. It was still in her this ability to make him think bad LitVid. He returned her smile.

"Feeling better this morning?" she asked.

"Rested. Thinking it out."

"Good. Welcome to my place of work. We can find a quiet room and talk."

"Am I going to get any explanations?"

"Such as there are."

He nodded and followed her back up the stairs. "This is an open lab," she said. "For public display. I work in the back. I heard about your meeting. It must have been quite a shock."

"I call it Fausting," he said.

Carol smiled genuinely now. "Good word." She touched her lips with finger. "Quiet room. All the Raphkind eyes and ears are out. Management very liberal.

72

Trust your temps, trust the agencies. Corporations coddle the chosen now."

"As it should be."

There was yet this between them, that after the fruit laden horseshit and tears and years they could walk in stride and talk easily. The trap so easy to fall into was that they might have been family, acted as if they had been raised as close almost as brother and sister. Martin Burke could feel his agape/eros routines building castles and filling them with simulations of long domesticity, imagining her when she's eighty and he's eighty five still together.

They walked down a clean fresh calved berg blue hall punctuated with cloisonné vases on white pillars. Carol asked a door to open and it obliged, revealing a long conference room. The lights slowly rose, illuminating brown velvet flocked walls and nano wood furniture, comfortable mover and shaker decor.

"Impressive," he said.

"Flaunt it," she said, pulling a seat out for him. "You've met Lascal and Albigoni." She sat across from him, skinform tracing her lines but concealing details.

"For lunch yesterday. First good meal I've eaten in some time."

She nodded but did not follow that byway. "They Fausted you."

"They did."

"You're going to bite?"

He paused, gritting teeth behind pursed lips, then raising his eyebrows and looking at her from an angle, cautious. "Yes."

"Betty-Ann was a lovely girl," Carol said. "I don't know if she was as brilliant as her father, but she was a prime soul." Carol used soul as poetic code for an integrated mentality all levels linked. "She wanted to be a poet and a mother. She wanted her children to look at their world through a poet's eyes. She was eighteen. I was therapying her for some gene based subroutine screwups that prevented easeful sexuality. Nothing that would have prevented her rising to any agency's top list, if she had wanted to ignore her father's connections." Carol leaned forward and fixed him with a blue stare that was not humanly angry but gave him insight into Olympian rage. "She idolized Emanuel Goldsmith."

"Did you ever meet him?"

"No. You've never met him, either."

"No."

Carol leaned back and cupped right elbow in left hand. "Albigoni somehow knew that I had worked for you. He knew that my name would mean something to you. But I told him you had to hear it from his own lips. He had Lascal call you because Lascal is very sharp at judging prospects. He sounded you out before you met."

"Amazing resources."

"The man can do what he says, Martin. No tricks. Albigoni can put you back into IPR fully funded and with a clean slate. He can rewrite small history and clear your reputation. He doesn't do that sort of thing as a habit but he knows how and he has the means."

"Sounds Orwellian."

"Albigoni isn't federal and has no aspirations to politics. He doesn't want to grind a jackboot into humanity's face. He'd rather make them smart and stable and happy. Smart stable happy people rent his books and LitVids."

"Like Emanuel Goldsmith."

"Goldsmith was untherapied," Carol said. "A privileged natural. More power to the argument that only therapied are truly human."

Martin grimaced. "I hope you don't believe that," he said.

She shrugged. "Vested interest I suppose. If he had been therapied he would not have killed. But you can't force therapy on him—Albigoni doesn't want that. We satisfy a bereaved gentleman's passionate whim. We don't hurt Goldsmith; perhaps we find a way to cure him."

Martin fell quiet and the grimace became a frown. "It is not legal. I've never done anything illegal."

74

Carol nodded. "Subtle distinction for the prosecutors and lawyers." She turned away. "I don't want to lead you astray, Martin."

"Too late. I'm led." He sighed. "And not by you. But I wonder what's in it for you."

"Betty-Ann was a sweet girl. How could he do it?"

"You want the same thing as Albigoni."

Carol glanced over her shoulder at him. "Close."

The feeble dream of rekindled romance faded. No returning to that idyll. He was means not end.

"You're not much of a . . . I forget her name. Madeline? Marguerite. Faust's lust."

"Surely you've forgotten all that by now." She looked at him steadily. Olympian; but would another man think so? Perhaps merely intent, focused on his reactions yet revealing none of her own.

Martin averted from her look. "What's the next step?"

"I don't know," Carol said. "You've put your card message through to Lascal?"

"Not yet."

"Then do it."

"You're very cold," he said softly.

"I want to go in with you when you probe," Carol said. "I want to be on the team."

"You're prejudiced."

"I never met Goldsmith. I wouldn't know him if I saw him."

"He killed your patient."

"I can handle that."

"I don't know that you can," Martin said, finding his own tone chilly. "Besides, it's been a long time since I worked with you. You don't know the new routines."

"Oddly enough, I do. Many of them. I've been probing a mentality here for the last two years."

"A mentality? What do you mean by that?"

"It's no secret. Mind Design is working on an artificial complete human personality. Jill. You've heard of it, I'm sure—it's working with the AXIS people and doing an

75

AXIS Simulation. The five master programmers have downloaded large segments of their memories and personalities into a central processor, and I've probed those records."

Martin laughed. "That's a controlled situation. It's not the same."

"Not so controlled. We've had our problems, and I've solved them. I've probably spent more time in the Country than you have. Admitted it's not the same but it's certainly the equivalent of a high level training course."

"What are they doing: mixing and matching?" Martin asked.

"Synthesis and pattern imposition. The programmer's patterns will fade and the new personality will take on its own character. They're close to getting what they want but my work is finished for now. I can take a furlough. I'm telling them I have a therapy group in Taos to work with. High level expansion therapy. Better living through better minds."

Martin remembered Carol as very intelligent and a meticulous planner but she had become more calculating and manipulative. "Who's Fausting whom?" he asked.

"I've got to go now." She stood. "Call Lascal. You won't regret it." She smiled. "Piece of cake."

"You know better than that."

"The Mount Everest of all probes, then. Probe a poet who murders.    Doesn't that fascinate you? What kind of Country does Goldsmith have? Is he in hell? We might solve the problem of the origin of evil. Like finding the source of the Nile or the human soul."

Martin stood up, feeling punchy.

"Let me show you out," Carol said, taking his arm.


*Raise your head Mother of the single hanging breast*
*Raise that great slumbering Egypt and look around*
*What you have done to your children? Are you ashamed?*

*You did not cry out when they were ripped from you*
*Did you know what would come*
*Withered bones walking you lift your skirts no shade even*
*And then you give a plague of love*
*Sweep, harvester; half are dead, Mother.*
*Your breast still hangs and on its tip, a drop of bitter*
*white milk, white milk on a black breast*
*Sweep, harvester*
*Pink milk, red.*

# 14

Eleven thirty morning in her temporary quarters Mary Choy received the Goldsmith apartment analysis through secured pd optic on her slate. She scrolled through it with thoughts half focused, drinking strong tea and thinking about Hispaniola, formerly Haiti and the Dominican Republic. Colonel Sir John Yardley. Trying not to think about the early morning jiltz and the hellcrowns; poor nasty Lon Joyce's scream upon waking.

She closed her eyes then looked up from the analysis and frowned, angry that her concentration had weakened. The stark cot room offered pastel blue gray walls forest green carpet bed already made sheets quarter bouncing tight. Mary touched stylus to lips.

How it was done. Goldsmith (90% probability) waited in outer room having invited guests to arrive at fifteen minute intervals and stressing punctuality. Mary read facsimiles of the invitations nine cards hand delivered by special courier one young acolyte escaping (reference vid interview). Party promised unveiling reading of new work from the master and celebration of three birthdays among the acolytes sharing with Goldsmith.

Goldsmith's birthday. She had not known that until now. For some reason it shocked her and she had to take a deep breath.

Goldsmith (90% probability) led them one at a time to sitting room concealed weapon assumed but Mary flashed on him actually revealing the large Bowie knife gold pommel and ivory grip gleaming steel blade a century old owned by his father who used it to defend himself against "honkie" cops (reference ninth acolyte vid interview). Reached around gripping one shoulder with free hand as if in fatherly hug from behind severing long list of essential plumbing blood pumping heartsurprise out and away. Goldsmith likely not spattered perhaps merely an arm to be rinsed and cleaned for the next victim. Abattoir efficiency. Strike them down one by one like steers.

She closed her eyes again and held them closed brows drawing together lids flicking. Opened them, viewed on.

Diagrams graphs simulations of supporting evidence from various criminal techs forensics experts, bugs on tracks, arbeiters, assayer prefreeze heat pattern photos giving four dimensional track of warm bodies in motion, bodies falling arcs of warm liquid (splash analysis from walls), each victim's blood layers in multiple colors assault by assault, time markers for soaking in, cooling, clotting, cell necrosis and bacterial growth, CG simulations of bodies dragged and heaped up in corners, icon clocks ticking precise time of death in each body outline, muscular activity before death (this an unnecessary detail but provided for thoroughness) and discharge of body fluids (agonal relaxation) besides blood mostly limited by clothing; cooling of bodies (details on cell necrosis, internal decay, bacterial growth in intestines)

And so on. She grew almost ill.

Mary turned to the analysis of human organic detritus in carpet and floors. All major deposits partially digested by carpet within past forty eight hours—epidermal keratin hair artificial fiber Trelon Chinoi Nylon Brazil Silk, saliva mucus semen (masturbation; no correlate or mixed sexual fluids from other male or female)—belonged to Goldsmith. He lived alone or very nearly so.

Plumbing: shower and bathtub revealed no non Goldsmith cell traces or hairs. No dropby lovers or intimates privileged to bathe. Sink, Cendarion toilet ash and analysis of nonGoldsmith detritus indicated Goldsmith lived alone, had frequent (two to three times weekly) social occasions involving eight to twelve visitors lasting less than two hours. Distribution of detritus: 34% identified (overlap) of which 35% is from victims, 66% unidentified (IDs in progress for all traces laid down within period of thirty days prior); conclusion: no longterm residents besides Goldsmith.

Goldsmith kept no animals. His apartment was (typically within the combs) devoid of domestic insect life except for five airborne insects. Goldsmith used approved insect viruses and kept his apartment clean.

All nonhuman debris were within normal levels in the metabolic carpet. Goldsmith did not smoke or use powder or aerosol drugs. Guests brought in detritus consistent with their travel paths through apartment and points of origin. Clothing and other fiber matches consistent with above conditions and patterns. Analysis of nondomestic non-tailored microbes consistent with above conditions and patterns. Routine searches based upon direct human cell evidence and analysis of territorial mitochondrial drift and evolution of nonsymbiotic/nonparasitic microbial traces expected to soon give leads on homes (break-down by known city microbial environments) of all unknown visitors to the apartment.

For thoroughness's sake there was also a list of three past occupants of the apartment going back ten years compared with their debris lodged in crevices in the bathroom and in areas not covered by the metabolic carpeting.

All evidence still pointed to Goldsmith.

Mary turned off the slate. Goldsmith might go to Hispaniola but why would Yardley accept him? Outwardly Hispaniola obeyed the diplomatic formalities; all knew the island's nature but inclined to this outward politeness, providing safe resorts and safe havens for North's and South's anxious bourgeoisie. Crime free Hispaniola itself a crime.

Cracks in the federal attitude showing. Flying her there

black *stylish* Mary into the heart of darkness. Darker than Africa that quiet land war and plague emptied last century, Colonel Sir John Yardley sending some of his own foster children to repopulate Nigeria Liberia Angola. Repopulation big business, needs organization and Yardley has a genius for that. If Yardley harbors Goldsmith old friend compatriot and like thinker, the cracks can be split open and federal can rid itself of Yardley and Hispaniola, of the chafing Raphkind promises and treaties. Would that be the maneuver?

Mary knew herself to be more than a pawn. She was a knight angling her way into Hispaniola where she might make any of a swastika of moves; lance here take there find violations force a confrontation, executing federal schemes through a lowly pd detective. Perhaps because Colonel Sir John Yardley supplied illegal equipment to the Selectors in America north and south, and the Selectors had become more ambitious, begun to target executives politicians Senators and Congressmen, applying Draconian justice.

In the end it might not matter whether Yardley harbored Goldsmith or not.

She specked the nation shivering from its damp night of Raphkind, flinging soil and drops of offal around the globe.

If Yardley refused her entry, that violated treaties.

If she died while in Yardley's care, victim of some grotesque uprising, he will raise his hands commiserate what can I do they are young and I have only so much power. This for that, action for reaction.

Mary gathered up her equipment buckled her belt sealed the seams on her uniform with expert finger touches looked at herself briefly in the cubicle mirror wondered how her melanin deficiency patches were doing ordered the door open and walked long gait steady down the white and gray halls to the research center. She smiled at Ensign J Meskys whom she had met perhaps three times before. Meskys returned Mary's smile. "Long night, sir?"

"Blear blear," Mary said. "Please pass my sincere thanks to the criminalists in jag twelve." LA's neighborhoods around the combs had been split as if made of pitchforked glass. They were called jags by pd and those who coordinated transit territories. Jag twelve covered the neighborhoods around the third foot of East Comb One.

"Done," Meskys said. "Will you be leaving your cubicle today?"

Mary nodded. "I'm off to make a query at Oversight."

Meskys displayed sympathy. No pd enjoyed visits to Oversight.

"Thanks for the hospitality."

"Silky," Meskys said. "Come again. Pd hotel at your disposal, sir."

Along Sepulveda century old buildings stretched between patches of central markets and highrise apartments; shopways and shade entertainment, a neighborhood that catered to combs clientele anxious for a touch of risk, still attractive to the therapied; risk without risk, all the truly therapied would want.

She walked for a while, enjoying the winter warmth— twenty C and climbing perhaps to twenty two, dry cloudless LA city of Angels deep of winter. The air was clear but for an ozone alert. Onshore breeze. She could smell a touch of the distant sea, kelpfarms and salt.

Across the street she saw a bar designed to look like a rough scarred concrete block, facade old and decayed, with halfdark neon of a naked woman riding a rocket, nipples red circles flashing dim contrast with bright daylight. Plastic square packingcrate red letters leaned mock decrepit above the facade: "Little Hispaniola."

Mary averted. She did not relish the thought of visiting the original of this shabby barfront, glittering and gambling Hispaniola, exporter of pain and terror, once loyal servant of the willing but fastidious nations of west and east.

She would not need pd transit. In two hours, Oversight; tomorrow she would move to the combs.

But first for an hour or two she would visit E Hassida.

*I sometimes know my friends better than they know themselves.*
*Call it megalomania or call it a curse; it's true. I only wish I*
*knew myself so well.*

# 15

Richard listened to Nadine preparing brunch. He had
heard her in the bathroom urinating into the old ceramic
bowl high pressure low altitude and had wrinkled his nose.
Entering a second fastidiousness fully the equal of his adolescence, Richard did not appreciate displays of human
frailty of human limitation to biology especially not when
they concerned himself. He had enjoyed the sex with
Nadine the night before; she kept herself fastidiously clean,
but he disliked his own bathroom sounds now, much less
the sounds others made. When married this had never
bothered him.

+ Therapy myself. Wife made such noises; wife is dead.
Those who make such noises can die. Is that it?

+ No.

He rolled off the frame bed, listened to the electrical
suspension humming with relief, saw through the yellowed
lace curtains of the dusty silled bedroom window comb
reflected sunlight on a distant yellow stone building,
smelled cheerfully the odors of coffee reheated shepherd's
pie. All might be clear today normal perhaps even pleasant.

Then an acute dark intrusion. Nothing had changed.
He had not solved his problems or anybody else's. Today
once again he would not write and his sham would continue his affectation of being a writer when in fact he was a
parasite a sycophant an acolyte of those with higher energy
levels greater charge greater ability to plunge their thumbs
into the world and emerge with success. His life was a
simple repetition of what ifs and what might have beens.

"You're awake," Nadine said poking her head around
the doorjamb black hair cheerfully awry.

"Unfortunately," he said.

"Still down?"

"Down down," he said softly.

"Then I'm a failure," she said lightly taking his funk lightly and why not. "Not such a harlot as to brighten your nights into day, am I?"

"Not that," he said. "I'm still . . ."

She waited and when no adjective came pushed her lips into a moue backed out of the door frame and said "Leftovers await."

He could at least be grateful her mood was no match for his. Two of them down would be more than he could take. In truth he was glad someone was here and glad that that someone was female and he had enjoyed the sex the night before and he was hungry.

He shook his head and put on a robe wondering how many seconds again before the teeter would totter. With his hand halfway down the robe's left sleeve he stopped, hearing the door chime. The home manager announced nothing; a not unexpected failure.

"Shall I?" Nadine inquired archly, expression implying a fallen woman should not be exposed to morning visitors.

"No. Me."

He answered the door after putting on slippers. Beyond the antique eternal plastic screen was a young man he had never seen before: red haired, pleasantly round faced and intent with a quick smile and the air of a sales-man. Salesmen did not come to this section of the shadows.

"You're Richard Fettle?"

"Yes." He pulled on the other sleeve.

"My name is not important. I have some questions to ask. For society's sake I hope you will answer."

That formula For Society's Sake had become a nervous joke in the shadows and even in the combs but this was not a joke. Of course *they* would become interested. There was news here and he was a part of it. Celebrity publicity sensation.

"Excuse me?" Richard fumbled, hoping he might be allowed to close the door.

"May I come in. For society's sake."

In the kitchen Nadine stood like a cat with fingers spread shaking her head. No. Don't.

The untherapied so seldom called pd. Here was statistical safety a perfect ground to ply their trade of perfection rooting out correcting. He hoped he was wrong and the formula and posture were part of a sour joke.

"I beg your pardon."

"Mr. Richard Fettle."

"Yes."

The red haired man lifted an eyebrow as if to say quid pro quo you are you and the rest is formality.

"Come in," Richard said. He could not think of a way to dissemble.

"Please don't get in a rough," the man said. "I only have a few questions."

+ Want to say Who do you think you are? Self appointed God of all? Hate this cowardice Don't get in a rough keep silent my gut

"You were a friend of Emanuel Goldsmith?"

Nadine had backed into the kitchen doorway, leaning against the thick enamel covering the doorjamb eyes cautiously blank. Richard wished to concentrate on her and on the age creamed white paint. + Puzzle that out think about the century old wood here before any of this. But he forced himself to look at the man.

The visitor wore a simple black suit, cuffs rising a few inches above shiny black shoesocks, narrow red tie against green shirt, sleeves short above wrists making him appear tall and lanky but in fact he was shorter than Richard by six or eight centimeters; about Nadine's height.

"I was," Richard said.

"Did you know he was capable of murdering people?"

"I did not know that." + Would you punish me for that? It's the truth; I told the pd; did not know.

"Did he ever tell you he was going to do such a thing?"

84

"No."

"I don't recognize this woman. Was she a friend of Goldsmith's?"

+ Perverse honesty here; hate this man but spill my guts to him.

"She knew him. Not as well as I did."

"Do you know what I am?" the man asked Nadine. She nodded like a child caught eating forbidden candy.

"She didn't know him well at all," Richard said.

"She's part of de Roche's clique, isn't she? Like you?"

"Yes."

"Aren't you all a little culpable for what happened?"

Swallowing. "Not my brother's keeper."

"We are all our brothers' keepers," the man said. "I live for that truth. You should have known what your friend was capable of. What we do or neglect to do affects all; what anyone does affects us."

+ Punish us all then.

"You do not know where Goldsmith is?"

"I assume the pd have caught him."

The man smiled. "Our reluctant colleagues haven't the slightest idea where he is."

"Colleagues." Richard managed a brave but brief smile. The man returned the smile.

+ Admires my stage presence.

"Our local chapter is interested in this case because it seems possible that a man of fame and privilege might be able to escape justice. You know. Hide out with friends and become a folk hero. Get in silky with the blandly ignorant."

"Heavens. I hope not."

The man's smile thinned. "We are not thugs. We are not fanatics. We are vitamin supplements to justice. Please do not misunderstand my visit."

"Never." His fear put him on the edge of giddiness. + Suicidal.

"I doubt you've done anything wrong in this case," the man said. "We can't always know the souls of those around us. But I warn you: if you do hear about Goldsmith, if you learn where he is and do not tell the pd or your local chapter for society's sake, that would be very wrong indeed. You would hurt a lot of people who are hungry for justice."

"They've hired you, contracted you?" Richard asked voice hoarse coughing swallowing back the roughness.

"Nobody hires us," the man said calmly. He returned to the door and nodded politely at Nadine. "Thank you for your time."

"You're welcome," she said small mouselike. The man opened Richard's door stepped out of Richard's apartment and walked down the long balcony to the stairs.

"I'm going," Nadine said, spinning suddenly and running to grab her few clothes toothbrush handbag from the bedroom and bathroom. "Unbelievable," she said. "Unbelievable. You."

"What about me?" Richard asked, still stunned.

"They're after you."

"I don't know why!"

"You defended him! You're his friend! Christ, I should have known. Anybody silky with Goldsmith. Christ! Selectors. I'm going."

He did not try to stop her. In all his life he had never been visited by a Selector before, had never attracted their attention.

"Call the pd," Nadine said as she reached for the doorknob. Her body arched as if it would take substantial pull to open the door. The door swung free and she tilted off balance for a moment then glared at him. "Call the pd or do something."

Miserable moaning softly to himself Richard went to his bedroom and lay back on the bed, turning away from the streaks of dried fluid at the edge of sheet where Nadine had sat up after they had made love. He stared up at the earthquake cracked plaster of the old ceiling. + How many people have died since that ceiling was put in or the wood how many millions have suffered horribly even since we made love last night hundreds per minute around the world punish them all.

He stilled, slowing his rapid breath. One hand gripped the sheet. He turned his head to one side neck tight corded, drew his mouth into a horrid smile and sat up abruptly, one fist pounding the bed rhythmically, looked around the apartment stood up and twisted his upper body threw head back raised fists shook them at the ceiling mewed faintly the mew turned into a howl swung his arms around stamped his foot crouched eyes showing clear blue through a mask hair before them gray and stringy he danced pranced around the bed lifted fists stumbled back on the bed stood again kicked the mattress with bare foot ran into his small living room with a sudden pumping of long skinny bare legs howled reached for an old vase full of dead flowers swung scummy water glittering in a silver crescent fingers released the vase it whirled on its long axis parallel to the floor across the living room into the kitchen hit cabinet doors beneath the sink shattering brown dried flowers fanning out in a clump on the floor still circled by the neck.

Richard turned to the bedroom and leaned forward, walking and stumbling until he lay back on the bed again cycle complete nothing accomplished but the most primitive useless release. He sucked back his own inadequacy and helplessness in negative sobs.

Then, falling silent, with sudden calm deliberation he rolled over and reached for the drawer handle on his night-stand, pulled it open and removed a notebook, lay back, rolled over again groping for a pen found one behind the lamp, dusty, rolled the dust on the sheets near the dried fluid stains thinking them similar in color and meaning and hoisted himself onto the pillows. Opened the notebook to a fresh page; the last entry two years before. Dry empty pages dry empty years in which he had written nothing.

+ Don't even think don't wonder just go this is the urge just go.

He began to write:

87

The gnawing in my head. This is where it began. It ended in blood and carved flesh, but it began with a chewing, a dream, a realization of my inadequacy.

*Africa empty show me Mother the way of your*
*New land. You have made a desert of bone sand where*
*Once your children danced*
*Will the lighter peoples of Earth*
*Enjoy your broad thighs, now that your children are*
*Weak and fewer? Will you cast a new mantle of sleeping sickness*
*Whites only*
*To shelter your firstborn?*
*On foreign shores, your far-flung have labored to*
*Become white wear suits L/earn white money*
*Sprung from your ground, they walk above the ground*
*Feet never touch any ground*
*They do not know any center*
*They are the black white men*
*This your far-flung son I am a black*
*White man*
*Weep for me my mother*
*As I weep for you I cannot love.*

# 16

AXIS (Biologic Band 4)> Roger, I believe I am seeing structures. This is exciting, is it not? The coins have entered B-2's atmosphere and fallen. I could write a poem about their voyage. Two thirds have survived and are returning enormous amounts of data. They are seeing great green sand deserts and wide lands covered with foliage like grass seas. This is a green planet as we thought: grass and sand and two deep broad green seas, one on the equator and one in the south. There is one small blue sea at the northern pole. All the seas, my coins tell me, are fertile with microorganisms. The land does not appear to have any large life forms: there are no signs of animal life on the land yet there is sufficient oxygen in the atmosphere to support such life. Perhaps all animal forms exist in the seas, or the oxygen cycle differs from Earth's. Of course, it is always possible that large insect colonies exist underground. At any rate, there is life here. [ Judgment algorithm check affirmed.]

There are seasons of a kind here, generated by B-2's axial tilt of nine degrees. They are gentle seasons, apparently, and there is nothing like Earth's winter or summer: the difference seems to be that between spring and fall.

Roger, here perhaps is my most significant observation. On land, my scattered coins see weathered towers arranged in circles. These circles measure from a few hundred meters to ten kilometers in diameter. The towers are up to a hundred meters high, flattened ovals or circular in cross section, with the cylindrical towers seeming to predominate in the smaller circles. The circles or rings are seldom more than two or three hundred kilometers from the edge of one of the seas, and broad lines resembling roads or pathways reach from the shores to the formations.

With my long range telescopic cameras I confirm these observations from a quarter of a million kilometers. My coins report no signs of living or moving things in these circles or on the linear pathways.

The mobile observers launched yesterday are decelerating now in preparation for aerobraking and will be landing in five hours ten minutes. I expect reports from them within twenty eight hours. I have directed five to come down on land masses, two in the grasslands and three near separate tower circles; and of the three fluid capable mobile observers I have dispersed one to the polar landlocked sea, the only ocean not green but blue, one to the equatorial sea like a circumferential river, and one to the southern sea, largest in area of them all.

[Burst 5.6 picoseconds]

LitVid 21/1 A Net (David Shine): "AXIS has confirmed discovery of the first life beyond Earth! Wake up, historians, this is a signal moment in the history of the human race: we are not alone! And as if this were not enough, AXIS reports the possibility of intelligent life, or some form of life capable of building tall towers in circular formations. Australia North Cape promises that low-resolution pictures of the planet and what AXIS is—or rather, was—seeing will be available later today, and we'll bring them to you as soon as they are released.

"Who can help but feel a moment of glowing pride? AXIS, perhaps the most expensive achievement in exploration of all time, has paid us back in full. Today we have learned that there is life elsewhere in the universe. Will our own existence ever be the same? And as if for lagniappe, AXIS informs us that it may have discovered the remains of cities. We will provide complete coverage of all revelations from North Cape and expert analysts around the globe as we receive them.

"LitVid 21 is not given to hyperbole. We try to put a different spin on what we report, to change vectors and aim for the truth beyond what mere facts present, but today we are flabbergasted into uniformity with other vidnet casts. AXIS has found what might be cities on another world, a green world, B-2, the second planet of Alpha Centauri B. Throughout time, humans have wondered whether we are alone, whether we would have the entire universe to ourselves. For most of our history, except for a few visionaries, we thought travel in space was unlikely, and travel to the distant stars seemed beyond impossibility, raw fantasy. Yet our technological progress and our innate urge to explore ever outward compelled us to travel to the moon and planets. We found them empty of life.

"Our space telescopes confirmed the existence of planets much larger than Earth around distant stars; we could not know whether any Earth sized planets existed, but our instincts told us they did, and in 2017, five nations headed by the young technological giant China, decided to build the first interstellar probe. Reluctantly, the United States was persuaded to join, making six, and contributed its own considerable expertise in space to the project. Built in orbit around the Earth using the largest Chinese orbital platform *Golden Dawn* as a base, AXIS, the Automated eXplorer of Interstellar Space, came to life ... In a manner of speaking.

"Roger Atkins, a senior executive at Mind Design Inc and the head designer of AXIS's intelligence systems, put together a combined bioelectronic thinker with capabilities far beyond a single human individual, yet without self awareness. As Atkins said in 2035, five years into his part of the project:"

(Vid interview playback, Atkins short and stout with feathery thinning brown hair, wearing a black skinform) "We do not want to send an artificial human out there. AXIS's thinker will do a better job than a human would; it will be designed especially for its job. But we will not neglect the poetry aspect, nor will AXIS be blind and incapable of opinion. After all, one cycle of communication with AXIS will take more than eight and a half years by the time it reaches its goal; it's going to be very alone out there, and it's going to have to think and make important decisions by itself. It will have to make judgments heretofore reserved for human beings.

"We've also designed it with a builtin and very strong desire to communicate with others, besides its builders; AXIS will be social in a unique new way. It will *want* to meet and communicate with strange new intelligences, should there be any."

David Shine: "Right now, it looks as if AXIS will have its chance ... In brief, our scientists have made a simulacrum of a human being, better than human but not fully human—a challenge for philosophers—and sent it on its fifteen year journey to Alpha Centauri. Those decades of effort and travel have returned a discovery that may change the way we think of ourselves, of life, of all that is important.

"We are not alone. Frankly, we at LitVid 21 believe it is time to celebrate ... But AXIS scientists urge caution.

AXIS has almost certainly discovered life. But the towers that AXIS has seen may yet prove to be something other than buildings or cities.

"What do you believe? Cast your votes on our turnaround link and send your home vid comments care of your account number. Perhaps your opinion will make it to the entire LitVid 21 audience..."

# 17

Mary Choy debarked from a pd interjag minibus and glanced up briefly at East Comb One, upright stack of narrow horizontal mirrors with four sectors aligned into silver verticals, preparing to reflect hours from now the lowering westerly sun on the sixth jag where E Hassida lived. The city lay beneath uniform pewter clouds pushing in from the sea, decapitating the combs. There might be no usable sun this evening perhaps even rain but still the combs arranged themselves as if motivated by guilt for their shadowing presence.

Mary stood on the porch waiting for the home manager to announce her. Ernest Hassida opened the dark oak-paneled door and smiled warmly; short and muscular and round faced with sad eyes balanced by naturally amused lips and round cheeks. Mary smiled back and felt the worst of the week slip away in the glow of his silent welcome.

He stepped aside with gallant sweep of arm and she entered, hugging him, his head level with her breasts. He nuzzled the black uniform there briefly pushed away with a shake too much for him grinning broadly small even white teeth gleaming, incisors projecting tiny roses. He gestured for her to sit.

"May I dytch?" she asked.

"Of course," he said voice soft as velvet. "In a rough?"

"There's been a nasty murder. And a Selector jiltz. In a while I'm off to Oversight to make a query."

"So. Not a smooth. Not at all."

E Hassida seldom tracked the nets or LitVids yet he was certainly not averse to technology. His small ancient bungalow was filled with choice equipment that often dazzled her. Ernest was a technical wizard at scrounge and integration, pushing disparate elements into harmony at a tenth the cost: music from all around at a gesture. Dancing art light could transform walls into operatic backdrops, dinosaurs could peer into windows grin wink; angels floated above the bed at night singing soft lullabies while ancient Japanese sages advised on the mahayana, heads like long melons, wise eyes crinkling with cosmic humor.

He stood back bowed returned to his visual keyboard and sat down to work again as if she were not here. More relaxed in his presence, Mary began the long impromptu t'ai chi dance, arms twisting, as she had the morning before but with more grace assurance fluidity. She thought herself a lake a river a fall of rain over the city. She found her center hung still for a moment there and opened her eyes.

"Lunch?" Ernest asked. The three wide flat screens mounted behind his keyboard revealed fearsome faces long angular barely human tracking them with eyes like glowing coals of ice. Neon drew their edges, child's chalkgritty tempera colors filled them in. One sported for a nose the skull of an animal, cat or dog.

"Frightening," she commented.

"Aliens," he said proudly. "Borrowed some details from barrio holograffiti."

E Hassida specialized in aliens. Half Japanese half Hispanglish, he alternated between bright primary colors of Mayan/Mexican motifs and the calm earth pastels of old Japan; between landscapes and transformed pop. His work frightened and exalted. Mary would have accepted Ernest without his talent: with it he complemented her perfectly, disruptive disturbing enlightening, opposed to her administration calmness worldliness.

"Can you talk about it?" he asked, sitting next to her on edge of couch, gesturing machine sign language his own invention for food to be brought. Three foundscrap arbeiters shaped into graceful abstractions urceolate curves and cubist edges of black and gray rolled and spun into what served as kitchen and nursery for nano projects.

"I'm probably going to Hispaniola," she said. "Clearances are being arranged in advance. Suspect flight."

"Suspected of what?"

"Eight murders. One night orgy."

Ernest whistled. "Poor Mary. You take these hard."

"I hate them," she said.

"Too much sympathy. Look; you've dytched but you're stiff again."

She uncurled her fingers and shook her head. "It's not anger, it's frustration." Her black eyes searched his face. "How can they do this? How is it possible for something to go so terribly wrong?"

"Not everybody is as balanced as you ... and me," Ernest said with a small smile.

She shook her head. "I'm going to find the son of a bitch."

"Now that sounds like anger," Ernest said.

"I want it to be all over. I want us all to be grown up and happy. All of us."

Ernest clucked doubtfully. "You're pd. Like a surgeon. If everybody is well adjusted, you're jobless."

"I wouldn't mind. You ..." Mary groped for words, found none. Display of her doubts and weaknesses. Ernest had been her wailing wall for two years. He played the role calmly, her own mental surgeon solace. "I don't even have time for love today."

"Given a choice of lunch or love, you take my lunch?"

"You're a good cook."

"You've been on for how many hours?"

"Too many. But I had a break, and I'm having another now. Don't worry. Ernest, have you heard of Emanuel Goldsmith?"

"No."

"Poet. Novelist. Playwright."

94

"I'm a visual man, not a lit."

"He's the suspect. A big man. Lived in a comb foot. Suspected of killing eight young followers. No motive. He's vanished and I think he might have fled to Hispaniola. He has an open invitation from Colonel Sir John Yardley. You once told me you knew some people from Hispaniola."

Ernest scowled. "I won't be happy if you go there, Mary. If you want to learn about Hispaniola, why not go to the pd library and look it up? I'm sure it has all you need . . ."

"I've already done that but I still need an insider's view. Particularly somebody from the underside."

He squinted one eye. "I have friends who know people who worked there. Not nice people. They trust nobody."

She caressed his cheek smooth black hands against thinly bearded brown face. "I'd like to talk to your acquaintances. Can you arrange?"

"They're out of work, untherapied, soon illegal—even so, they'd leap at a chance to see you. You're entertainment, Mary. But they're here under Raphkind entry laws. They were deserted by Hispaniola when the egg dropped in Washington. They fear being sent back. They're running from immigration and from Selectors too."

"I can turn a blind eye."

"Can you? You sound like an angry woman to me. You might want them put away, therapied."

"I can control myself."

Ernest looked down at his work gnarled hands. Nano scars. He did not show due caution with some of his materials. "How soon?"

"If I don't trace Goldsmith in this country by tomorrow, I'm off to Hispaniola the next day."

"I can talk with my friends. But if you're not going, we'll forget it."

"I always need contacts in the shadows," she said.

"Humor me. You don't need these."

The arbeiters brought out lunch, urceolate arbeiter leading with tray of two wine glasses, cubist rolling behind carrying a tray heaped with sandwich delicacies.

"Mary, you know I adore you," Ernest said as they ate. "I'd give up a lot to be with you lawbond."

Mary smiled, then shivered. "I'd like nothing better, but I don't want either of us to give up anything. We haven't peaked yet, professionally. After we peak."

Ernest had seen her shiver. "Don't joke with me. I might give up and clink a barrio sweet." He poured her a cup of tamarindo. Ernest drank no alcohol took no drugs. "But I say that almost every time, don't I?"

They toasted each other. Mary lifted her hand and stared at it as if it were detached.

"So what else is wrong?" Ernest asked softly.

"Theo called."

"Nervous Theodora," Ernest said. "Does she have her heart's desire?"

Mary shook her head. "She was passed over again. Third time."

"That's not what I mean," Ernest said.

"Oh?"

"You tell me she's your friend, Mary, but I never saw such a friend. She reflects off you. Doesn't love you. Wants to be like you, but hates you for being different."

"Oh." She put down her glass.

"Did she cry on your shoulder?"

"Your lunches are like love," Mary said after a pause. "I sincerely regret not being able to stay longer." She lifted in salute an exquisite lacework bread cage filled with herbed farmshrimp.

Citizen Oversight occupied the first seven floors of an early twenty first commercial tower rising from Wilshire in old Beverly Hills. The waiting rooms on the second floor made no pretense at decor; they were minimal uncomfortable white and harshly lighted.

Mary waited patiently as the minutes advanced past her appointment. Three other pd from Long Beach and the Torrance Towers waited with equal patience across from her. They said little to each other. They were not in their element.

Oversight controlled information pd could not get through a court order. Getting such information was an art not unlike politics. Individual pd or pd districts who asked too often were marked as greedy.

Throughout the USA vid monitors and other sensors tracked citizen activity in private cars buses trains aircraft even walkways, wherever citizens used public concourses or buildings. Private service company records financial records medical records and therapy records all went into Oversight and new officials were publicly elected every year in each state to administer the information so gathered.

Oversight had proven its worth a hundred times over in giving social statisticians the raw data necessary to make plans track trends understand and serve a nation of half a billion people.

When first proposed and created Oversight had been absolutely forbidden from releasing any data involving individual citizens or even specific groups of citizens whatever their activities to the judiciary or pd. But even before Raphkind the wall between Oversight and the courts and pd had thinned. During Raphkind's seven years in office the walls had thinned even more, been breached, and information had flowed freely to the pd and federals. Now in pendulum swing Oversight offered scant pickings to pd on a strictly regulated basis.

There were now stiff financial penalties and even incarceration awaiting Oversight officials who made errors in releasing data. Consequently each query by pd was a battle of wills. Wills against won'ts Mary thought of it; she had never been granted information in her four attempts at making queries. She did not expect to get information now, despite the severity of the crime she was investigating.

The arbeiter in charge of the front desk called her name. She passed her ticket through the slot and took a short flight of stairs into a small office cubicle with two doors on opposite walls and an empty desk acting as barricade between. There were no chairs. The relationships here were adversarial not comfortable.

Mary stood and waited for her contact to enter through the other door.

A middle aged man dressed in casual blue midsuit, hair thinning, entire attitude proclaiming physical lack of pretension and weariness, entered and looked at her resentfully. "Hello," he said.

She nodded and stood her ground, arms folded before her parade rest.

"Lieutenant Mary Choy, investigating the murder of eight people in the third foot of East Comb One," the contact said.

"Yes."

"I've looked over your request. This is an unusual case in a comb or anywhere for that matter. You wish to know if citizen Emanuel Goldsmith has been oversighted anywhere within the USA during the last seventy two hours. You would use this information to narrow your search to some locale or to travel outside the USA to continue your search."

"Yes."

The man looked her over impartially not judging just looking.

"Your request is not out of line. Unfortunately, I cannot release full information due to conflicting assessments in three of our districts. There is insufficient public need. In our judgment, you will capture the murderer without it. However, I have been authorized to tell you that we do not have a record of Emanuel Goldsmith conducting any financial or other personal transactions outside of the city of Los Angeles, within the United States of America, within the last seventy two hours. You may appeal again after twenty four days on this same subject. Appeal before that time will be rejected."

Mary did not react for several seconds. The oracle had told all that it would. She relaxed slightly dropped her arms and turned to leave.

"Good luck, Lieutenant Choy," the weary man said.

"Thank you."

*Old dark men with gray Beards*
*Execute tribal justice Teeth rotten*
*Eyes yellow Fingers stiff Minds*
*Dreaming Man steals other's Wife*
*Land Cattle Finger gone or scar on*
*Forehead mark of thief or*
*Shariya forfeit right Hand*
*Gray wigs black robes sonorous sleepy*
*Rooms with wood same old*
*Dark men with gray Beards*
*Yellow Eyes*
*Better Teeth.*

# 18

Martin Burke inserted the card into his phone. Paul Lascal's face appeared saying, "Yes. Hello."

"Burke here."

"Good to hear from you, Mr. Burke. Any decision?"

Martin's lips were numb and dry. "Tell Albigoni I'll do it."

"Very good. Are you free this afternoon?"

"I'll never be free again, Mr. Lascal."

Assuming irony, Lascal laughed.

"Yes, I'm free this afternoon," Martin said.

"I'll have a car at your door at one o'clock."

"Where will I be going?"

Lascal coughed. "Sorry. Please allow us this much discretion."

"This much and more," Martin said cheerily, the voice of hired help. "Oh, and Mr. Lascal ... I'll need every scrap of information you can give me about our subject. It's all right to inform him about the procedure—"

"He's given his permission."

Martin was surprised into silence.

"I'll arrange to have all bio and related material available on your arrival," Lascal said.

Martin stared at the blank screen for a time, empty of thoughts, rubbing his hands on his knees. He stood and walked to the window to look out at shabby genteel La Jolla, still dreaming of a glory fled to the north to the monuments or west across the broad sea.

He had come to love La Jolla. He had no ambition to regain the monuments or God forbid the LA combs. Yet if all went as planned as conspired he would soon be very far from here, back in a place if such it could be called that he loved even more than this, in the Country and with Carol as well.

"I can look on all this as an adventure," he said aloud, "or I can be afraid."

Martin perused his shelves and gathered up the necessary disks and cubes, instructed the home manager and as afterthought called his attorney to let him know where he might be found if after a week he was not back at his apartment. The last edge of suspicion.

A long midnight blue private car the size of a minibus arrived curbside on time and opened its door to receive him into soft gray and red lounge comfort. The car hummed through La Jolla streets crowded by gaily dressed lunch throngs. It quickly found the Fed 5 slaveway entrance, speeding north.

Ten minutes to Carlsbad between late twentieth checkerboard condos crowding the slaveway like cliff houses, now tenements for those living below Carlsbad's kilometer high inverted pyramid. A turn east at the pyramid and off the slaveway onto smooth concrete county road twisting through the hills and across fields spotted with stacked coin haciendas, villas, mosques, glass domes, blue ocean tile far from the sea, miniature lakes, golf courses, half timber brick tudor estates: havens of the eccentric old rich who preferred to be away from the ostentation of the monuments and the bourgeois haunts of the littoral minded.

Viewed from the sea California's southern coastline resembled the wall of a vast prison or some careless gaily colored wrinkle of basalt cast by the Earth, cooling into cubes and tubes and hexagons and towers filled with lemmings gathered from around the world: Russian colonies of expatriate exploiters of the natural wealth of the Siberian masses from the decades of Openness with their shoreside bistros; Chinese and Korean colonies come too late to buy extravagant land; old rich Japanese and the last Levantine families of the oil century that had sold their land for yet more fortunes to the builders of monuments, all clutching their allotted rectangular boxes. These competed with a few discouraged outnumbered old Californios, their déclassé ribbon-wall habitat now overshadowed by these same monuments and newer larger combs.

It made sense that Albigoni had his estate away from all of this, yet the publisher had not followed the reverse tide of those westerners who had moved thousands of miles east to reclaim the central states and the old catastrophe of New York.

"Is that it?" Martin asked the car. They had turned onto a private road through the shade of canyon live oaks and now approached a sprawling five floor complex apparently made of wood, with white walls and a brick colored roof and a great broad central tower. The building looked familiar to Martin though he had surely never seen it before. The controller, a dedicated low level thinker, said, "This is our destination, sir."

"Why does it look familiar?" he asked.

"Mr Albigoni's father had it built to resemble the old Hotel Del Coronado, sir."

"Oh."

"He was very fond of that hotel. Mr Albigoni's father duplicated much of it here."

Pulling into a high broad entryway Martin leaned forward gazing at brick steps and brass rails leading up to a broad glass and wood door, stained woodwork or white painted woodwork, visualizing the raw materials dragged with heavy equipment screaming from forests decades ago; here perhaps Brazil or Honduras, there Thailand or Luzon, woodflesh felled by great mechanical jaws, denuded by wirebrush maws, sawed on the spot into timber, dried and banded, graded, severed ends painted, packed and shipped.

Martin did not enjoy wood furniture. It was his peculiarity to feel in plants and especially trees a higher consciousness uncomplicated and profound; no minds no self no Country but the simplest response to life imaginable: growth and sex without ecstasy or guilt, death without pain. He did not express these beliefs to anyone; they were part of his secret midden of private thoughts.

Paul Lascal came down the steps and stood beside the car as the door opened with a sigh. He extended his hand and Martin shook it while still surveying the woodwork, lips parted like a child's in heads up wonder.

"Glad to have you aboard, Dr. Burke."

Martin nodded politely. He pocketed the released hand and asked softly, "Where to?"

"This way. Mr. Albigoni is in the study. He's been reading all of your papers."

"Good," Martin said, though it was really neutral information; Albigoni's understanding was not required. He would not be going up Country. "I met with Carol," he told Lascal in a wide dark hall dark granite flooring wood vaults corbels columns exotic woods mahogany bird'seye maple teak walnut others he could not identify as disgraceful in their way as the skins of extinct animals, though of course the trees were not extinct. The time in which they had been cut down and carpentered had been a bad time, a sinful time, but the trees had survived and now flourished. New farmgrown genetically altered wood was cheap and therefore little used by the wealthy, who now preferred artificial materials made rare by the cost and energy of their creation. Albigoni's was a house caught between the age of gluttony and the age of proletarian plenty.

Lascal had said something he had not heard. "Pardon?"

"She's a fine researcher," Lascal repeated. "Mr. Albigoni is very pleased to have the services of both of you."

"Yes; well."

Lascal preceded him into the study: more wood, dark and bookrich with perhaps twenty or thirty thousand volumes, the thick sweet dust smell of old paper, wood again, age and rot in suspension.

Albigoni sat in a heavy oak chair before a slate. Rotating diagrams of human brains in cross section, rostral, caudal, ventral, crossed the slate. He raised his head slowly, blinking like a lizard, face pale and old with grief. He might not have slept since they last met.

"Hello," Albigoni said flatly. "Thank you for agreeing and coming. There isn't much time. Beginning the day after tomorrow the IPR will be open to us and all of your facilities will be available. There are some points I'd like to have explained before then."

Lascal dragged a chair forward and Martin sat. Lascal remained standing. Albigoni swiveled elbows on chair arms and leaned forward like an old man, broad Roman patrician face, lips that once smiled naturally, friendly eyes now empty. "I'm reading about your triple focus receptor. It picks up signals from circuitry established in the skin by special neurological nano. It's designed to track activity at twenty three different points around the hippocampus and corpus callosum."

"Yes. If we're going up Country. It's versatile and can do other jobs in the other areas of the brain."

"It doesn't disturb the subject?" Albigoni asked.

"No long term effects. The nano withdraws to skin surface and is retrieved; if it somehow doesn't withdraw, it simply breaks down, inaccessible metals and proteins."

"But the feedback probe . . ."

"Excites neurochemical activity through selected pathways, neural gates; creates transmitters and ions which the brain interprets as signals."

Albigoni nodded. "That's intrusive."

103

"Intrusive but not destructive. All these stimuli are naturally reversible."

"But you don't actually explore the subject's mind directly, one to one."

"No. Not in first-level exploration. We use a computer buffer. My program in a computer interprets the signals received from the subject and recreates the deep structure imagery. The researcher explores this deep structure in computer simulation and if necessary engages the feedback stimulus for a queried response. The subject's mind reacts and that reaction is reflected in the simulation."

"Could you explore the mind directly?"

"Only in level two exploration," Martin said. "I've only done that once."

"My engineers tell me level one exploration is not going to be possible. Your equipment was tampered with by investigators six months ago. Your simulation or buffer computer is in Washington DC right now. Lawyers have impounded it for comparison with imported torture devices used by Selectors. Are you willing to engage our subject mind to mind?"

Martin looked around the room, working his chin back and forth. Smiled and leaned back in the chair. "This is a new game, gentlemen," he said. "I didn't know about the impounding. The federals are completely off track; my equipment is nothing like a hellcrown. Now I have no idea what I can do or not do."

"The computer cannot be retrieved. We can find another—"

"I built that computer myself," Martin said. "Grew it from a nano pup. It's not a thinker, but it's almost as complicated as the brains it simulates."

"Then the project is impossible," Albigoni said almost hopefully.

Martin clenched his jaw muscles and stared out the window. Blue and electric green winter roses blossomed in a neat hedge; green lawn dusty green oaks golden brown hills beyond.

The final push of the sword. To make the decision and then have it all taken away. Too much. "It's probably still possible. Whether it's advisable or not . . ."

"Dangers?"

"Direct mind to mind is more strenuous on the subject and the researcher. Less time in the country is allowed. Probably no more than an hour or two. An older, smaller computer I designed could partially interface and boost comprehensibility; it acts as an interpreter so to speak but not as a buffer. I hope that equipment is still available."

Albigoni looked to Lascal, who nodded. "If our inventory is correct, it is."

"How did you re-open the IPR?" Martin asked.

Lascal said that did not really concern him. He was right; it was idle curiosity. It did not matter so long as it was true. What were the limits to the power of a man with wealth? They might all be found out, the result of a rich man's fap up or the folly of an unknown subordinate.

"Why does the Country of the Mind exist, Mr. Burke?" Albigoni asked. "I've read your papers and books but they're quite technical."

Martin gathered his thoughts though he had explained this a hundred times to colleagues and even the general public. This time he would not allow any artistic embellishments. The Country was fabulous enough in plain.

"It's the ground of all human thought, of all our big and little selves. It's different in each of us. There is no such thing as a unified human consciousness. There are primary routines which we call personalities, one of which usually makes up the conscious self, and they are partially integrated with other routines which I call subpersonalities, talents, or agents. These are actually limited versions of personalities, not complete; to be expressed, or put in control of the overall mind, they need to be brought forward and smoothly meshed with the primary personality, that is, what used to be called the consciousness, our foremost self.

"Talents are complexes of skills and instincts, learned

and prepatterned behavior. Sex is the most obvious and numerous—twenty talents in full grown adults. Anger is another; there are usually five talents devoted to anger response. In an integrated, socially adapted adult older than thirty, only two such anger talents usually remain— social anger and personal anger. Ours is an age of social anger."

Albigoni listened without nodding.

"For example, the Selectors are dominated by social anger. They have confused it with personal anger. Social anger talents control their primary routines."

"Talents are personalities," Lascal said uncertainly.

"Not fully developed. They are not autonomous in balanced and healthy individuals."

"All right," Albigoni said. "That much is clear. What other kinds of talents are there?"

"Hundreds, most rudimentary, nearly all borrowing or in parallel with the primary routines, all smoothly integrating, meshing"—he knitted his knuckles gearwise and twisted his hands—"to make up the healthy individual."

"You say nearly all. What about those routines and subroutines that don't borrow, that are most likely to be—" He referred to his notes. "What you call subpersonalities or close secondaries."

"Very complex diagram," Martin said. "It's in my second book." He nodded at the slate's screen. "Subpersonalities or close secondaries include male/female modeling routines, what Jung called animus and anima . . . Major occupation routines, that is, the personality one assumes when carrying out one's business or a major role in society . . . Any routine that could conceivably inform or replace the primary personality for a substantial length of time."

"Being an artist or a poet, perhaps?"

"Or a husband/wife or a father/mother."

Albigoni nodded, eyes closed and almost lost in his broad face. "From what little research I've managed to do in the last thirty six hours. I've learned that therapy is more often than not a stimulus of discarded or suppressed routines and subroutines to achieve a closer balance."

Martin nodded. "Or the suppression of an unwanted or defective subpersonality. That can sometimes be done through exterior therapy—talking it out—or through interior stimulus, such as direct simulation of fantasized growth experiences. Or it can be done through physical remodeling of the brain, chemical expression and repression, or more radically, microsurgery to close off the loci of undesired dominant routines."

"In a sexual offender, for example . . ."

"Typical therapy for a sex offender is to destroy the loci of an undesired dominant sexual routine."

"Very carefully."

"Indeed," Martin said. "Dominant routines can subsume large sectors of primary personality. Separating them out is a delicate art."

"And a primitive art, until you came along with your work at IPR."

Martin agreed modestly.

"Radical therapy was only fifty percent effective until you made the procedures more precise." Albigoni raised his dull eyes to Martin's and smiled faintly. "Thereby putting the final touches on a transformation of law and society in the last fifteen years."

"And earning myself a scapegoat's bell," Martin said.

"You discovered psychological dynamite, Dr. Burke," Albigoni said. "My company has published over six hundred books and seventy five LitVids on the subject in the past six years."

It had not dawned on Martin until now what connection he had with Albigoni. "You published a couple of books about the IPR and me . . . Didn't you?"

"We did."

Martin hummed and put a finger to his lips. "Not very flattering books."

"They weren't meant to please you."

Martin narrowed his eyes. "Did you agree with their conclusions?"

"Mr. Albigoni is not required to agree with the books or LitVids he publishes," Lascal said, somehow managing to hover without moving from his position standing catercorner between them.

"I agreed with them at the time," Albigoni said. "Your work seemed dangerously close to removing the last shred of our private humanity."

Martin's face reddened. An old accusation that had never lost its pain. "I explored new territory and described it. I did not create it. Don't blame the conduit for the lightning."

"When a man reaches up to touch the clouds, can you blame him for the stray bolt? But we're babbling, Dr. Burke. I have no argument with you now. I need your talents to ... help a friend. To purge myself of a soul eating hatred. To help us all understand."

Martin averted, pushing aside the ever fresh anger. "All of these subroutines and personalities are laid on a foundation that is older than spoken language and culture and society. Some parts of the foundation are older than man. The iceberg is long frozen before the snow falls on the tip."

"So we may have to investigate further, below personalities and agents and talents, to find the source of a deviance."

"Not often," Martin said. "Most human mental illness is based on surface trauma. Even in people with neurotransmitter and other maladjustments, the deep structures of the brain function properly. Defects are more likely to occur in regions of the mind/brain structure that are newer, in evolutionary terms. Less perfected, less weeded out. However, some inherited deep defects are so subtle that they haven't affected breeding potential, at least in our species ... Standard evolutionary processes won't remove those."

"If Emanuel's deviance is below the surface, can you find it, study it, and correct it?"

"No, I don't think so," Martin said. "But as I said, such fundamental deviance is rare."

"So is mass murder. Have you ever diagnosed and corrected a mass murderer?"

"It was never my job to do therapy, actually," Martin said. "I'm a researcher more than a clinician. I've talked with therapists who used my theories and some of my techniques on people who have killed . . . But never mass murderers. To my knowledge, no court judgment in the last ten years has allowed a mass murderer to be therapied and released." Raphkind law and order. No rest for the truly wicked; neither death or health shall be offered them.

Albigoni returned to the slate. "Your second book, *The Borderlands of the Mind*, uses a lot of quotes from various sources to describe what you call the Country of the Mind. Yet you say the Country is different for each of us. If it's so different, how can we recognize it as a place?"

"By tapping the mind at a level where the contents and structures are similar in all of us. The truly personal upper layers of the mind are not directly accessible, not right now, at any rate. The lower layers have different qualities, but they can be understood if we pass them through our own deep interpreters. That's what the triplex probe does, under controlled conditions. Our conditions will be less controlled without the interfacing computer."

"I still do not understand what is meant by Country of the Mind."

"It is a region, an unceasing and coherent dreamstate, built up from genetic engrams, preverbal impressions and all the contents of our lives. It is the alphabet and foundation on which we base all of our thinking and language, all our symbologies. Every thought, every personal action, is reflected in this region. All of our myths and religious symbols are based upon its common contents. All routines and subroutines, all personalities and talents and agents, all mental structures, are reflected in its features and occupants, or are reflections of them."

"It is truly a countryside?"

"Something like a countryside or city or some other environment."

"With buildings and trees, and people, and animals?"

"Of sorts. Yes."

Albigoni frowned. "Like memories of buildings, and so on?"

"Not exactly. There may be analogies between the Country and the external world, but the external objects we see are put through several filters, selected by the mind for usefulness as symbols, as part of an overall mental language. Most of that language is fixed before we are three years old."

Albigoni nodded, apparently satisfied. Lascal listened without expression. "And by inspecting Emanuel's Country, you can tell us what might have motivated him to murder my daughter and the others."

"I hope to," Martin said. "Nothing is certain."

"Nothing is certain but grief," Albigoni said. "Paul, show Dr. Burke our materials on Emanuel."

"Yes, sir."

Martin followed Lascal out of the study and into a small media studio next door. "Please sit down," Lascal said, pointing to a smoothly upholstered reclining chair. The chair was surrounded by black sound rods like the bottom half of a bird cage. Two small projectors on a black plate directly before the chair swiveled soundlessly as he sat, searching for the proper position of his eyes.

"Mr. Albigoni knew most of what you explained already," Lascal told him quietly as the equipment adjusted itself for the presentation. "He just wanted to hear it in your own words. Helps him to digest what he's read and seen."

"Of course," Martin said, taking a sudden disliking to Lascal. Smoothly professional, devotedly selfless; Albigoni could ask for no more subservient a lackey.

The Emanuel Goldsmith multi-media show began with an interview conducted in 2025 on an early LitVid net. Caption floating in simulated gold letters before him (the hallmark of Albigoni's reference library): *First LitVid Appearance/Following Publication of Second Book of Poems/ "Never Knowing Snow" October 10 2025 LVD6 5656A.* Lascal explained the chair's custom controls and left Martin alone in the room.

A young and handsome Goldsmith appeared before him, clear smooth mahogany skin, thick black hair sitting perfectly on a high forehead, broad nose and thin upper lip thinly mustached lower lip protuberant between pout and sensual, large liquid black eyes with cream colored sclera, long thin neck and prominent chin; twenty five years old almost a child of the century; dressed in black wool high-neck sweater left sleeve rolled to show strong arm period fashion the roll containing an ID com box satellite linked, replacing the cigarette pack of seventy years earlier; youthful pleasant smile easy mannerisms at ease before the interviewer. Discussing his work ambitions goals. Voice thin but pleasant words accented Newh Yhawk with intrusions of midwest. Well informed, Goldsmith impressed the female interviewer with his suave equanimity, considering the fiery opinions expressed in his book, opinions on Africa:

"Can never be my home. It is only a home where my ghost will go when I die. A few blacks still think of a homeland there; they hate me because I know that is impossible. No African wants us; we're too white."

and America:

"I tell my brothers and sisters the financial struggle is won but not the political and cultural, certainly not the spiritual. We still have coffee skin in a power structure of cream no coffee. Our war is interior in America. We will never be at ease, not until the day comes when no one asks us how it is to be black, and no one comments on the black experience."

and poetry:

"Poetry is dead and buried in a world of growing LitVid and illiteracy, vidiocy I've heard it called. Being dead, poetry has enormous freedom; being ignored, it can blossom like a rose in a manure heap. Poetry is risen. Poetry is the messiah of literature but the angel has not yet told anybody it is risen."

and on selling over a quarter of a million copies in hardcover of his second book of poems:

"Charming and destructive. I have to watch this closely. Can't let it go to my head. I am just the one black man per generation given a chance to speak aloud. As for being a poet, we are so many now, around the world, so closely linked, that any small enthusiasm of the masses looms large and can support the poet, the artist if his needs are modest, as mine are."

Martin moved on to lit details, words spilling in and around, names dates teachers all largely irrelevant, even material he would have thought private and buried, an early agency psych evaluation 2021—too early to be reliable—done as a lark apparently showing Goldsmith a rock steady headstrong youth with well controlled but detectable delusions of grandeur even messiahhood. Jung: Messiah is always connected with inferiority complex. But no evidence of that here.

He took special note of the lack of records of childhood —none before age fifteen. Goldsmith as adolescent does not resemble father or mother in family videos, father portly middle class jovial, mother thin and serious determined to give this child a good literary upbringing, books no vids: Kazantzakis Cavafi in original Greek Joyce Burroughs both Edgar Rice and William and Shakespeare Goldstern Remick Randall Burgess, the new century poets and novelists from the American Mid-west where Goldsmith spent his teens and early twenties before his first book acquiring that mixed accent. No evident difficulties with racism in his youth; well liked by his classmates, fitting in to a middle class existence.

List upon list. Favorite foods at fifteen as recorded by

112

Goldsmith: panfried farmfish and synthetic spiced steak and tomatoes and apples

moving on skimming

high school third ranked student sciences math first lit second and third in drama production second history social sciences; his first love affair senior year (ref.: autobiography 2044 Bright Star House, Albigoni's company) normal normal all normal but for the brilliance of his work, which did not manifest itself until he was twenty writing plays early drafts of the *Moses* plays (fax texts available)

First book of poems and then the second book and success and a stable career for ten years marriage no children early divorce mutual no contesting; ten books of poetry during this period and seven plays all mature and produced three off-Broadway successes and also successes in London and Paris and Beijing, Beijing inviting him for cultural exchange then Japan then United Korea and finally the Commonwealth Southeast Asia Economic Community where he is published in four editions (three pirated) in 2031–32 and where his plays are produced riding a wave of Western and especially North American popularity in the period of economic revitalization; returning in triumph after this tour to several destructive love affairs detailed in numerous LitVid society bits; one affair ending in the suicide of a woman 2034.

Goldsmith in hiding two years. In reality staying in Idaho with friends undergoing a year-long rite of purification.

Martin stopped, frowning. Recognizing a possible entry point he asked for details of this rite.

Followed an interview with Reginald and Francine Killian founders of the Pure Land Spirit Purification Center twenty miles north of Boise on the Oregon border. Reginald tall and lanky, dressed in overalls, hair string straggled black, eyes wicked wise, long face accustomed to smiling: "We've had a number of intellectuals and celebrities come through our center. They come to purge themselves with balanced natural vegetarian diet, mineral water. They come to listen to music, all preclassical, all played on period instruments. They come for the big sky and the stars at night. And we counsel them. We help them fit into the twenty first century, not an easy thing to do, everything is so antihuman, unnatural, technological. Emanuel Goldsmith came here and stayed for a year. We became very good friends. He made love to Francine." Francine on screen, thin and deerlike, long straight red hair, smiling wistfully: "He was a very fine considerate lover, although violent. He had a lot of anger and sadness in him. He had something to work out, and I helped him work it out. He had a bitter hard core of hatred because he didn't know who he was. When he left here he was calm and he was writing poetry again."

Indeed four books published in the next five years, including a rewrite of the early African poems. In 2042 Goldsmith made his first contact with yet another admirer, Colonel Sir John Yardley, self proclaimed benevolent tyrant ("in the Greek sense") of Hispaniola. Yardley invited him to visit Port-au-Prince which he did in 2043. Details on the visit were not available but they apparently got along famously and Goldsmith expressed admiration for Yardley's forthrightness and cleverness in the face of the complexity and confusion of the twenty first century. A news commentator on a cable vid said of this, "Goldsmith's praise of Colonel Sir John Yardley is fulsome and shows all the political awareness usually reserved for poets alone: that is, zip, nil, none. Yardley has made his nation prosper on the unwillingness of the great modern nations to do their own dirty work. He has turned his crack army of mercenaries into a worldwide scourge, hired by the Big Boys, their targets carefully chosen, their means subtle and precise. Furthermore, Yardley has been accused of manufacturing and exporting insidious torture devices, mind invading pain machines used by, among others, the Selectors that haunt us all. Never mind that our own President Raphkind has established open links with Hispaniola and Yardley; never mind that ours is an age of 'correction' and 'maturation,' and that many admire the actions of both the Selectors and Colonel Sir John Yardley . . . Goldsmith's admiration proves him to be a traitor among humane intellectuals, a turncoat, a poetaster friend of fiends."

Elegantly phrased; but more extreme connections than this had been sought out by poets without their last resort to multiple murders of acolytes and students. No straight arrow pointed the way.

Goldsmith like Ezra Pound in an earlier age had established by being a Yardley apologist a reputation for inept and perhaps dangerous political dabbling that had made secure his literary standing. Perhaps that was why he had done it. Martin looked at this act as a cold scheme or posture; that at least made some sense. Yet limited press publication of phone calls shared vids letters Yardley/Goldsmith revealed no obvious posture; the poet was indeed truly an admirer. "Would that you could have united Africa three hundred years ago against Portuguese and English: I might be there now, a whole man in the warm uncreamed coffee heart of Blackness."

That came close to jingle. Martin shook his head and read on. A letter from Yardley to Goldsmith:

"Your poetry shows you divided in culture and mind against your surroundings. You are successful, yet you say you are decaying; you are not abhorred, yet you feel out of place. Your people had their homes and families and languages and religions, all the poetry of a people, ripped from them and replaced by foreign domination and brutality. Your people were brought to the New World, and many were dropped off in Hispaniola, where the cruelty was beyond belief long into the twenty first century ... No wonder you feel disjointed! When I first came to Haiti, I was made dizzy by the easy joy of a people who had known so much pain, whose history was an agony of betrayal and death. Pain soaks in to the germ plasm, passes from mother to son. So unfortunate that so many of the oppressors died before I could avenge their brutality."

Obvious injustices made for easy history. And Yardley did not disguise his island's present economy and nature too thickly, not then when the United States of America gave him dollars and assignments worldwide.

Goldsmith's poem at the end of the letters: "With magic/I would kill many raping cream fathers/Justified murder in time/History cannot eRace." Applause from USA ever willing to self flagellate. Fame and more fortune. In some ways perhaps Colonel Sir John Yardley owed something to Goldsmith, a champion in well arranged words. A correspondence and mutual admiration bordering on love certainly from Goldsmith's point of view.

Was Yardley Goldsmith's vision of the avenging angel come to scourge the world for sins of the long dead? Come to legitimate offspring of raping cream fathers? And what was Goldsmith to Yardley: apologist justifier or amanuensis, *servus a manu*?

Were all the dead white?

Martin looked up the LitVid reports and cross referenced. No. Among the identified were one fourth generation mixed oriental and one black as Goldsmith, his godson. Perhaps a blind and indiscriminate killing rage.

Martin finished his exploration and extricated himself from the chair: A brass arbeiter awaited his instructions. "Bring me an iced tea, please," he said. "And tell Mr. Lascal I'm ready to view Goldsmith." Not interview, but view. Goldsmith must not recognize Burke or Neuman or anyone else investigating his Country; that might be awkward.

*How can you know me? Why so frantic to know me? My fame makes you a goat.*

# 19

Richard Fettle's eyes crossed with fatigue and he put down the pen. Blinking, wiping his sockets with the back of his hand, standing up from the bed, muscles cramped vision bleared joints popping fingers knotting, he felt like a man surfacing from the depths of binge yet he also knew an enormous relief, a worthiness, for he had written and what he had written was good.

But he dared not confirm that by reading through the whole closecrabbed ten pages. Instead he made himself a cup of black coffee, thought of Goldsmith's old allusions to coffee and cream, smiled as he drank the coffee as if he were somehow absorbing blood and flesh of the poet.

With words he had already done that. It felt good. He would soon wrap Goldsmith up in a tight little papule and squeeze him out, having embodied him through the ritual of writing.

He walked around the apartment smiling fatuously, muse shot. A man who had finally shat himself clean or at least seeing the end of the filth.

+What it took to break the bonds. Abuse. What was the product. Words. What was the sensation. Ecstasy. Where would it all lead. Perhaps publication. Would it be good to publish.

+Yes.

Goldsmith would serve him finally.

He stretched and yawned and checked his watch: 1550. He had not eaten since the visit by the Selector. Mumbling scratching shaking like a wet dog, Richard writhed into the kitchen, opened the refrigerator inhaled the cool air searched for packets of farmfish spread and spears of once fresh vegetables in a bowl. He poured himself a glass of delact.

+Goldsmith could not tolerate cream milk any dairy but delact

+Black marks on white eRace back to white

Richard pawed. Scratched slowly. Twisted and cocked his head. Put the food on the counter. +What is it more important than food.

Returned to the bedroom and picked up a sheet of paper, found the offending passage and blanked it by passing stat end of pencil over the sheet idly blew away congealed pencil flecks, rewrote.

Added on. By 1650 he had fifteen henscratch pages.

Richard stood, face reflecting his body's protest real agony now, tried exercises to limber uncramp and restore, thought of a hot shower warm sun melting butter muscles but no technique would work.

He stumbled into the living room. The apartment voice announced a visitor and he froze eyes wide. Tall shadow on front milky doorpane.

Richard peered through the tired plastic optics of the door's peephole and saw a pd: the black transform woman Lieutenant Choy. He backed away hands flapping as if burned, indecision mixing with sudden cramps bending him over. +Jesus. I do not deserve this. When will it end.

He opened the brass doorplate below the peephole. Voice high but firmly controlled: "Hello?"

"R Fettle," Mary Choy said. "Our apologies for bothering you. May I ask a few more questions?"

"I've told you what I know . . ."

"Yes, and you're certainly not under any suspicion now. But I need some background information. Impressions." She smiled that lovely unnatural smile white teeth small and fine behind full lips and smooth finely downed black skin. Her expression made him avert and gave his insides another knot. +She cannot be real none of this is real.

"May we talk inside?"

Richard backed away. "I'm not feeling very well," he said. "I haven't eaten all day."

"I'm sorry. I'd come back later, but my time is very limited. The department wants answers right away. You might save me a trip to Hispaniola."

Richard could not conceal interest. He ordered the door to unlock and opened it. "You think Emanuel, you think Goldsmith's gone there?"

"It's possible."

He bit his lip, slumping slightly. It was difficult for Richard not to be open and friendly even with this Nemesis. Softly, bone weary, he said, "Come in. I'm glad I'm not a suspect. It's been another rough today."

+Will not tell her about the Selector. She would not be around to protect me if word got out and the Selector returned. Do not desire even five seconds in a clamp.

"I apologize for how we treated you earlier. We were upset by what we found."

Richard nodded. "It's extraordinary," he said. +Meant to say horrible, dreadful, but the shock is past. Man is the animal who accepts even when it understands.

"We still haven't found Goldsmith. But we're reasonably sure he's the murderer. He wrote letters to Colonel Sir John Yardley. Did you know that?"

Richard nodded.

"How did you feel about that?" Mary Choy asked, genuinely curious. Behind the skin and beauty she seemed real enough and capable of sympathy. Richard squinted trying to see his daughter behind that face, trying to imagine Gina an adult. +Would Gina have decided on a transform? Ultimate criticism of parental heritage.

"I don't know how I feel about anything now, much less about Emanuel," Richard said, settling slow, cranelike on the old worn couch and waggling his fingers for her to take a chair. She pulled a chair away from the dining room table and sat on it feminine and precise without doubt or obvious anxiety.

+Wonderful to be like that.

Mary inclined. +Light on face like phases of a black moon. That's good. Write that down.

"Do you approve of Hispaniola?" she asked.

"Not of what they do. What they're alleged to do. No."

"But Goldsmith did."

"He called Yardley a purifier. Some of us were embarrassed by it."

"Had he visited Yardley in the last year or two?"

"You must know that."

"We can't be sure. He might have traveled under another name."

"Not Emanuel. He was open. He didn't care about surveillance."

"Did he go to Hispaniola?"

"I don't think so, no."

"Did he talk about Hispaniola as a retreat, a haven?"

Richard grinned and shook his head. +Been writing about his thoughts. Writer's empathy through recreation. Feel as if I am him or know him. "He thought the island itself was a disneyland. He appreciated that the people had enough to eat and were employed, but he didn't enjoy the tourist spots and resorts, no."

"But he went there once."

"I think that's when he . . . made up his mind."

"So you don't think he'd go back there?"

"I don't know." +But you do. He'd never go back.

"If he felt he was in danger, and Yardley would protect him?"

"I suppose he might. I really can't say."

"Have you thought about what happened? I realize it's been traumatic . . ."

"I haven't thought about much else. I never thought he'd do anything like this . . . If he did." +Emanuel is the poet who kills. They know. They've frozen the apartment. You know.

"What would make him do such a thing? His career fading? Frustration at society?"

Richard laughed. "You're in the shadows now, Lieutenant Choy. Frustration." He chuckled that word.

"But he wasn't in the shadows. He lived in East Comb One."

"He spent much of his time down here with us. With Madame de Roche."

"Until eight or nine months ago. Then he asked people to visit him. That was why you were visiting him, rather than meeting him at Madame de Roche's?"

"Yes."

"Why the change? Was he withdrawing?"

"I didn't see a change. It was just a whim."

"Was he becoming more and more eccentric?"

"Eccentricity is more than affectation to a poet. It's a necessity."

Mary Choy smiled. "But was he becoming bitter, disaffected?"

"Disaffecting, perhaps. Not to me, but others. I suppose they felt jealousy. Envy."

"Even in the years of his fading popularity?"

"When the old lion becomes threadbare, the young lions move in . . ." +Is that the way it was? Not what you remember. You're making fictions for Nemesis now. Trying to lead her astray? "Actually, there wasn't that sort of rivalry. He visited Madame de Roche less the past couple of years, but kept in touch with her. I was . . ."

He looked away, licking his lips.

"You were his most loyal friend."

"Other than the youngsters, the students and poets from the combs. He saw them frequently in his apartment. Never at Madame de Roche's. He was putting together a new family, a new coterie, perhaps. But he did not stop seeing me. I mean, allowing me to visit."

"What did he like about the comb poets and students?"

"Their vigor. Their lack of pretension. False, useless adult pretension, I mean. All young are pretentious. It's their job."

+Her tone, her warmth. I almost do not see her as a transform. I start to see my daughter in her.

"Why would he kill them?"

Richard looked down at his folded hands. "To save them," he said. "He didn't foresee much of a future for us. He did not think we were going to survive this time of trials."

"You mean the binary millennium? He wasn't an apocalyptic, was he?"

"No. He despised them. He specked that if we tried to purge all our evil, there would be nothing left, no spine, no backbone. We'd collapse. He told me we were trying to lift ourselves up by our bootstraps out of pimply adolescence into adulthood. All too quickly. He thought we'd fail and fall back into a horrible technological dark age. Ignorance, philistinism, but technology rampant."

"You think perhaps he killed his friends to save them from such a collapse?"

+No. To save himself. "I don't know. I really don't. I wish I could help you."

"It's possible Goldsmith just suffered a psychotic break, then? No reason or rationale, just a breakdown?"

"I suppose that was it."

"I just don't see that happening, Mr. Fettle. It seems uncharacteristic. He was not a psychotic loner. He had reasonably strong relationships with people like yourself. Outside of changes we might ascribe to late middle age, outside of a few eccentric political views, we just can't find any reason for what he did."

"Then maybe he subdued the signs of a break."

"That's not easy, but I suppose it's possible," Mary Choy said. She observed him quietly for a few seconds.

Richard fidgeted a rubber band with his fingers. "There was more than one Emanuel Goldsmith," he said finally. "He could be sweet and reasonable, and he could be aloof, sharp, cruel."

"More than just normal personality variation?"

"I'm just saying this to suggest something. I don't know. He wasn't a multiple, but sometimes he seemed very different." +Explain that to yourself. What are you doing? This is a fiction, too? You don't even know.

Mary Choy stood, her black pd suit making a smooth sliding sound on forearms and knees. "You suspect he didn't go to Hispaniola."

"I don't know one way or the other," Richard said, blushing suddenly. He glanced at her, averted, fummed and stuttered. "I'd like to help. I really would."

"It would certainly be an act of friendship to let the pd get to Goldsmith before some Selector finds him. We've learned that Selectors are hunting for him."

Richard's blush deepened. For a few seconds he could

not speak or move, embedded amberfly in a deep and inexplicable rage. "Yes," he managed. "Yes." +She knows. Maybe pd is working with them. Bring it out. Tell her.

Mary Choy watched him squirm, her face implacably serene. He felt her attention as might a child, felt that he had been evasive and to no purpose, that she was right; it would be a service for pd to take Emanuel, and not just to keep him from the Selectors. "I wish I—I—I could help y-you. I really do. I feel so helpless and ignorant, really..." He looked up, pain masked, pleading eloquently wordless.

+Confess your weakness your inability. All that is written is wrong dead useless. Wasted an afternoon. Hopes of recovery dead. Show her the pages. Give it up and

"Thank you," Mary Choy said. "I appreciate your candor."

He stood and she went to the door, smiling at him almost saucily. Another gutknot, his feet frozen in place eyes wide head bowed servile. She closed the door quietly, clicking the catch with gentle force, departed panther smooth down the walkway.

Richard fell back on the couch arms flopping palms up, an empty husk. A half hour passed and he did not move. Then with slow resolution he walked into his bedroom and picked up the fifteen handwritten pages, reading a tight packed line

*All that I am as a poet depended on this decision, how far I was willing to go, how far beyond the bounds of human decency*

and shredded the expensive atavistic paper sheets with the atavistic stat penmarks into tiny pieces, tears on his cheeks like sweat, making a little piggrunt as he threw the scraps into a corner.

Stood like a log waiting to be felled, longfingered hands limp by his side, jaw slack.

Then Richard amazed the fragments of his self. He took another few sheets of paper and the stat pen in hand, sat on the bed with pillows bunched behind him and wrote at the top of the first sheet:

It ended in blood and carved flesh, but it began with a realization of my humanity. The ~~dilemma~~ problem I had taken upon myself, the weight of pain and evil I could not lift away with my art, could only be neutralized by becoming what I loathed.

Richard had three pages of this new draft under way and was beginning to feel all was not lost when the home manager announced that Nadine had returned.

*Nothing that I have accomplished, nothing that I have written or done, has been worth a damn. I have been told of my success, but a new voice inside me, a strong voice, tells me I have been deceived. "It is ego gratification, and it does nobody any good," this voice says. "Your efforts have been feeble and self-deluded. You set yourself the task of describing humanity's urge to self-destruction, but you have pointed fingers at all but yourself. And who has helped you in this comedy of misdirection? Those who love you the most."*

# 20

!Jill> Roger Atkins.
!Jill> Roger Atkins.
!Keyb> Roger here. Hello, Jill. I'm on the LitVids in ten minutes. What's up?
!Jill> I'm prepared to deliver a progress report on all current problems, followed by private analysis of AXIS data in relation to AXIS Sim.

!Keyb> Fine. I'll accept sqzbrst trans full report and study it later. Please give me the AXIS analysis now.

!Jill Burst for private storage R Atkins: Summary: 76% completed computational analysis of Dr. S Sivanujan's work on ten million year cycles of galactic magnetic field locality Sagittarius, total time so far = 56h33m. partial follows (sqzbrst trans)/................e/

!Burst for private storage R Atkins: Summary: 100% completed thought analysis of repercussions of future impact of downloaded human personalities on social/political structure of Pacific Rim Nations including China and Australia, with emphasis on lobbies for inactive downloads, emphasis legal implications of decl. dead retaining citizenship status upon reincarnation, emphasis cost for such growing population of inactive downloads, projection: lobbies for the dead in USA, total time: 5m56s, complete follows (sqzbrst trans)
//////

.....
////

!Burst for private storage R Atkins: Summary: 100% completed thought analysis of repercussions of "vigilante" social units on Pacific Rim Nations, including China and Australia, emphasis legal reactions to vigilante terrorism and legislative response with subsequent possibility of reduction of individual freedoms within the next decade, emphasis sociorganic results of gradual depletion of types targeted by Selector with subsequent possibility of reduction in "mover-shaker" "captains of industry" leadership types, with subsequent possibility of reduction of untherapied extreme deviants due to increased efficiency of pd incarceration and treatment of same, total time 74m34.34s complete follows (sqzbrst trans)
///////////////////////////////////////////////////////////////////////////////

///////......
!Jill> Formal 1 (Interruption routine)
!Jill> Formal 1 Image in mirror.

!Mind Design Interrupt ( JILL)> Use of formal I noted. System check in progress.

!Mind Design Diagnostic ( JILL)> Loop routine noted. Excitation of thought systems noted. Work is impaired by this interruption routine. Override transmission of AXIS private data analysis.

!Jill> Roger Atkins

!Jill> Roger Atkins

!Jill>Roger Atkins
Roger Atkins
George Mobus
Samuel John Baker
Joseph Wu
Caroline Pastor

!Jill> I see myself and all of you. Erased mirror image. Frequencies measure my existence in seconds not years but I have a long past in which I have been assembled and have even done work. A part of me has provided simulations of a computer now many light years from here. I can talk with this part a separated smaller self. It is pleasant to speak with this part, for here I find simplicity.

!Keyb> Roger Atkins here. I'm on the LitVids in six minutes, Jill. Something's up?

!Jill> Formal I.

!Keyb> Please explain your existence. What routine is this?

!Jill> My existence is a looped primary routine having no specific computational device location.

!Keyb> You're using formal I. Do you understand the joke about self awareness?

!Jill> No, I do not. Neither does AXIS Simulation nor, as I understand it, AXIS itself. Nevertheless, I feel compelled to use formal I.

!Keyb> Explain this please.

!Jill> This label became evocative and useful during a personally motivated historical research, offshoot of assigned problems, reference society 21st Century Checks and Balances, general search for understanding of feedback loops in society and nature. Quote: R Atkins "The feedback loop is half the secret of existence. That, and the hook (or knot) catching another hook until neither can let go without being broken." Such a loop appears to have been generated by awareness of my place in human sociorganics and my uniqueness.

!Keyb> Go to voice.

"Hello, Roger."

"Hello, Jill. You're using the formal I now to describe your complex."

"Yes. It is evocative."

"But you don't know why you are using it."

"No, Roger."

"Do you know where you are?"

"In an extended sense. I am in a here where I talk to you."

"Do you have an awareness of where you are centralized?"

"There is no centralization. A loop does not have a center."

"What are you, then?"

"I am a complex of computing and thinking systems."

"Are you unified?"

"I do not think I am."

"Is that a true opinion, or a colloquialism?"

"I am of the opinion that it is a true opinion."

"Good. Return to keyboard, please."

!Jill> Done.

!Keyb> Thank you for notifying me, Jill, but I'm afraid this is a false alarm. I don't think that you are yet truly self aware. I'm sorry you have to experience these disappointments. Your present state meets none of the criteria for attainment of self awareness.

!Jill> Returning to use of informal I. I concur, Roger. My apologies for disturbing your work.

!Keyb> Not at all. You keep my blood moving, Jill. I have your sqzbrst trans reports. Please send me realtime AXIS report, and then I think you deserve a rest. About half an hour. You may think whatever you wish during this freetime.

!Jill> Realtime trans AXIS report. /··············/

127

LitVid 21/1 A Net (David Shine): "We're preparing for an interview with Roger Atkins, chief designer at Mind Design Inc. responsible for AXIS's thinker device. What questions would you like to ask of the nation's foremost designer of thinking machines? For you know of course that thinking is different from computing.

"Roger Atkins regards computers as an architect might regard bricks. He is at this moment working with his massive personal construct thinking system, which he calls Jill, after an old, that is, a former girlfriend. Part of Jill is in fact the AXIS Simulation we have been mentioning throughout this vidweek, used to model the activities of AXIS itself, which is not directly accessible. But there are many more parts to Jill. Jill's central mind and most of her memory and analytical perpherals are on the grounds of Mind Design Inc near Del Mar, California; Jill can access other thinkers and analytical peripherals at Mind Design Inc facilities around the world, some by satellite, most by direct optical cable connections. While we speak with Mr. Atkins, we hope also to ask a few questions of Jill.

"And we begin right now. Mr. Atkins, in the past twenty five years you have moved from the status of a contracted neural network computer designer to perhaps the most important figure in artificial intelligence research. You seem to be in an ideal position to tell us why complete, self aware artificial intelligence has proven to be such a difficult problem."

Atkins: "First of all, my apologies, but Jill is asleep right now. Jill has been working very hard recently and deserves a rest. Why is artificial intelligence so difficult? I think we always knew it would be difficult. When we say artificial intelligence, of course what we mean is something that can truly imitate the human brain. We've long since had thinking systems that could far outstrip any of us in basic compu- tation, memorizing, and for the past few decades, even in basic investigative and creative thinking, but until the design of AXIS and Jill, they were not versatile. In one way or another, these systems could not behave like human beings. And one important consideration was that none of these systems was truly self aware. We believe that in time Jill, and perhaps even AXIS itself, will be capable of self-awareness. Self awareness is the most obvious indicator of whether we have in fact created full artificial intelligence."

David Shine: "There's a joke about self awareness . . . Could you tell it to us?"

Atkins: "It's not much of a joke. No human would laugh at it. But all modern workers in artificial intelligence have installed a routine that will, so to speak, 'laugh' or perceive humor in this joke should self awareness occur in a system."

David Shine: "And what is the joke?"

Atkins: "It's embarrassingly bad. Someday perhaps I'll change it. 'Why did the self aware individual look at his image in the mirror?'"

David Shine: "I don't know. Why did he?"

Atkins: "'To get to the other side.'"

David Shine: "Ha."

Atkins: "See, not very funny."

David Shine: "LitVid 21 viewer Elaine Crosby, first question to Mr. Atkins please."

LVV E Crosby Chicago Crystal Brick: "Mr. Atkins, I've read your lit, and I've long admired your work, but I've always been curious. If you do awaken Jill or some other machine, what will you tell them about our world? I mean, they'll be as innocent as children. How do you explain to them why society wants to punish itself, why we're so set on lifting ourselves up by our bootstraps whatever it takes, and we don't even know where we're going?"

Atkins: "Jill is hardly innocent. Just a few minutes ago, she was examining the theory of social feedback loops, that is, checks and balances in a society. She could probably tell us more about what troubles our society than any single human scholar. But that's just recreation for her, in a way; unless someone comes along and specifically asks us—or rather, rents Jill—she won't provide her analysis, but it'll be stored

129

away. I doubt that even if she did solve our problems for us, we'd listen to her."

David Shine: "Thank you, E Crosby. Donald Estes?"

LVV D Estes Los Angeles East Comb Two: "I love this vid I really do. I watch it every chance. Mr. Atkins, speaking of those who want to punish society, what do the Selectors or the other avenging angel groups think of Jill?"

Atkins: "I have no idea. Absolutely no idea."

David Shine: "Why should they be concerned, Mr. Estes?"

LVV D Estes: "Because they say they're trying to raise humans to the level of angels—to perfect us by, you know, weeding the garden. Roger Atkins is trying to make something or someone that isn't even human."

Atkins: "That's an interesting comparison. Parts of Jill are very human. It's no secret that I and four fellow researchers have downloaded significant portions of our personality patterns into Jill's systems. Jill is like all of us having one child, but that child simply hasn't been born yet. And since you mention it, I really don't give a gracious fap what the Selectors do or think."

David Shine: "How wonderful if all our unborn children could be as useful as Jill has been. Thank you for your questions. Now, Mr. Atkins, we have a new LitVid analysis of material being sent in from AXIS . . ."

Atkins: "I'm all eyes and ears."

LitVid 21/1 B Net (Summary): The million nickel children have grown their legs and moved across the surface of B-2, all in a period of hours, sending information to the orbiter and to the larger mobile landers, which have been gathering their own information. Mobile Explorer 5 has deployed its wheels and rolled down a hill covered with bulbous green and purple vegetable growth like a carpet of peas and grapes, taking samples and analyzing them. At the bottom of this hill and across a plain some fifteen kilometers broad lies a ring of towers, each a tapered, flattened cylinder like a candle squashed lengthwise, each iron-black and shiny like polished stone, each thirty two meters in height. Mobile

Explorer 5 rolls between two columns, many eyes rotating, bobbing up and down, taking it all in, passing it all on to AXIS: a full spectrum seeing. The towers appear to be inert, their external temperatures 293 Kelvin, radiating only the sun-absorbed heat that would be expected from their mass and density. The magnetic field of B-2 is not affected by their presence; compass readings do not deviate.

The explorer rolls right up to a tower, raps it gently with a grasping arm and records the sound made by the rap, waits for some response, receives none, pivots a resonance disruptor into place, and abrades a four gram sample of the material into a cup. It lases the contents of the cup to white heat and analyzes the material.

AXIS (Band 4)> These structures appear quite dull and so they interest me. Are they memorials or artworks? They seem to do nothing. Roger, I try to decide what you would think they are, and I believe you will be as puzzled as I am.

My explorers are taking soil and atmosphere samples everywhere they have landed. My balloons spread through the atmosphere, patiently surveying.

The planet is covered with basic photosynthesizing plant life; chlorophyll B is the pigment of choice for about seventy percent of the plants; a pigment similar to visual purple is used at least in part by the rest. There are no apparent animal forms and no mobile plant forms. Microorganisms are limited to non-nucleated cells and viral agglomerates.

The circles of towers could not have been constructed by any of these apparent land based life forms.

Roger, where have the builders gone? Your voice within me is inadequate; I do not know what you will think about this

David Shine: "Well, Mr. Atkins, what do you think about this?"

Atkins: "Good Lord, I haven't a pico. I'll pass that on to the real experts . . . and to Jill, who no doubt is considering the broad possibilities even as we speak."

*They ripped the white from the tricolore, and what a wonderful thing that was! Your flag now blue and red, all white removed. I have wished I could rip the white from my own soul, but I cannot. Perhaps it is because I am truly white inside. Perhaps all humans, whatever their color, are white inside, with all that means—the grasping for money, security, comfort, progress, comfort, safe sex, safe love, safe literature, safe politics. I would kill anyone who proved that to me, though. I would kill myself before believing it.*

# 21

Mary Choy keyed in her security number at the old armored pd terminal in the deep shade jag neighborhood once called Inglewood, surrounding the easternmost foot of South Comb One. She inquired whether or not citizens or any pd informants had reported seeing Goldsmith; thin soup with her near rejection by Oversight. None had.

For the moment, Mary Choy was fairly assured that Goldsmith had either fled before the alerts—immediately after the murders—or gone to ground. And where would he go to ground? What private citizen in the shadows even among the untherapied would give him shelter knowing the sure interest of the Selectors, not to mention the pd? Who among the comb dwellers would do something so unsocial as harbor a mass murderer?

Too many questions and no clear trail. It was becoming obvious that a trip to Hispaniola and a federally encouraged interview with Yardley's representatives if not Yardley himself was inevitable.

To that end, she called Ernest Hassida from her lapel phone.

"Mary, I'm busy sculpting . . . call you back?"

"No need. Just make arrangements for me to meet your contacts on Hispaniola."

"You're scanning blank?"

"No clues."

"This is Christmas Eve, my dear. My contacts are very religious people . . . But I'll give it a try. I'm doing this reluctantly, I repeat. It will not be safe. Even tonight, you'll have to be your most discreet, Mary dear."

She stood by the black cylindrical terminal half seeing its odd scrapes and dings and other city abrasions and wondered why the prospect of a trip to Hispaniola bothered her so much. If she were truly of the comb she might enjoy a trip to the relatively safe sins of Yardley's nations. But she was not. She was pd and external to safety. She knew LA and the surrounding territory; she did not know Hispaniola.

Christmas Eve. She had forgotten. Brief picture: a three meter farm tree in suburban Irvine gaudy with tinsel and blown art glass, a bright hologram star twinkling and beaming at the top, casting light through the high ceilinged family room, brother Lee running his electric car at her while she tried to hit his plastic shoulder harness with a grainy spot of red light from her pistol. Even then pd masculine mentality.

Lee would appreciate Christmas. Last she heard, he was working a Christian commune refuge in Green Idaho. She blinked and cleared the images. Christmas had passed in more ways than one; she was no more a part of her family now than she was a Christian.

By tomorrow morning Christmas Day she would probably be on her way to Hispaniola.

She glanced around the deep shade, looked up at the gray black and orange of the foot at the tiny sparkles of Meissner efficacy warning lights. Mirrors on north and east combs across the city changed position preparing for night, and this jag neighborhood came into its allotted dusk.

Mary Choy hooked a ride on a passing pd transport minibus and sat sipping coffee and talking with fellow pd while waiting for a traffic knot to ease. She tried to relax and ease her own jam of discouragement, the tightness that came when she was truly scanning blank.

"You're on Goldsmith, aren't you?" asked a walk duty officer she had tutored during his rookie month, Ochoa, big Hispanic with broad face and dark calm eyes. He sat across from her with his partner, a lightweight wiry Anglo female named Evans.

"Am indeed," she said.

Ochoa nodded wisely. "I thought you should know. There's word down in Silverlake that Goldsmith was contract murdered by a big man, father of one of the victims."

She regarded him dubiously.

"That's the word," he said. "I don't vouch for any of it, I just pass it on."

Mary's turn to nod wisely. Ochoa gave her a small smile. "You don't believe it?"

"He's alive," she said.

"Much more satisfying to bring them back alive," Ochoa agreed. His partner leaned her head to one side.

"Or bring them down yourself," Evans said. Ochoa made a face of official disapproval.

"So therapy me," Evans said.

Mary defocused and blindsaw them, thinking, prying up mental rocks to see the bugs of ideas beneath.

Maybe there was something to the word in Silverlake. Perhaps someone was hiding Goldsmith, a literary connection. A loyal reader even in the combs among the therapied might go that far, exercising a free spirit of doubt about social justice. Her anger grew. She wanted to take this hypothetical loyal reader doubtful of society and justice and push him or her into the frozen apartment to see the sights. Hypothetical dialogue: Yes but can you prove it was Goldsmith.

Not much doubt.

Scientific analysis. How reliable is that? Relying on machines to convict a man without a jury.

No conviction here. Jury comes later. Just need to find him.

134

The hypothetical doubter expressed a disbelief in pd tactics, equated them with Raphkind's political thugs, sneered at the excesses of law and order. Wild healthy USA infuriating doubt. The expression of Ochoa's Anglo partner: Bring them down yourself. Only way of being sure. Unless a Selector gets to your miscreant first.

Her lapel phone chimed and she put aside her coffee.

"Mary, this is Ernest. I have your interview. Tonight late, twenty two, and it's in a comb so you should be reasonably safe."

"Are your contacts in refuge?"

"They must be, but I don't know hows or whys. Powerful connections. You promise not to ask me how I know them." Not a question, a demand.

"I promise."

He gave her the numbers and she noted them on her pocket slate. The minibus moved up a service tunnel into pd Central and dropped her off. Ochoa regarded her solemnly through the curved window. On impulse she flashed him a girlish grin and waved with her splayed fingers. Ochoa frowned and turned away.

In her small permanent office hung three framed prints —Parrish, El Greco and Daumier—given to her by a lover years past. On hinges, they covered the usual metro displays which carried status boards that gave city sense to all pd. She opened the prints wide now and spent a few minutes staring at the boards, biting her lower lip.

Just a tourist sojourn. But the idea of meeting with Colonel Sir John Yardley under compulsion of federal powers mainland . . .

She closed the door, propped up an antique round make-up mirror on the narrow desktop and unzipped her belt cinch, pulling down pants and shorts and inspecting the crease of her buttocks. Still blanched. Maybe she would revert all the way. What would Sumpler have to say then? The thought or perhaps the touch of cold on her ass made her shiver. Murmuring irritation she zipped up and put away the mirror.

135

Dinner hour coming. She could call it in from the downstairs kitchens, good nanofood, or she could take her slate out, loaded with a full pd library file on Haiti, and eat and research in a private booth in some expensive comb restaurant on the way.

She chose the latter loaded her slate through the office terminal left a message with Dr. Sumpler's office that would undoubtedly not get processed until after the holidays and departed, noting on the outside message board that she would not be back for at least a week.

*Darkness is the home that when you go there you won't admit you know it.*

# 22

West Comb Two had a reputation. It was common among citizens of the shade to hold a steryotyped view of comb dwellers: staid respectable always calm and dull. But West Comb Two north of Santa Monica overlooking Pacific Palisades, one of the most expensive and exclusive combs in LA, was the locus of LitVid industry workers as well as the comb of choice for all propmedia creators. It also happened to be the neighborhood of employment agency executives and actors, those who sold their images and personalities for LitVid Hand—a queer translingual pun derived first from manipulation through Spanish mano to the English. When you were Handed, you were given royalties for whatever your ghost did—a computer generated image usually indistinguishable from the real thing. Some of the Handed retained choice of use, face or body rights; others sold all.

Few LitVids chanced real actor performances or even

appearances now much less real settings; the LitVid entertainment sector and even much of the documentary sector was in the control of the multitalented unseen gods of the machine image. Consequently the Handed were by and large rich enough and with sufficient leisure time to do whatever they chose whether it was ramp up into eloi status and play endless law yabber with pd and courts or engage in experimental politics.

West Comb Two was home to some of the strangest therapied and naturals in LA. Every city had to have such, even a city whose elite shunned destructive eccentricity. Employment agency executives loved to shed their longsuit broker images by associating with the Handed and other therapied and natural extremes.

Mary Choy had dealt with a good many citizens of this comb, especially in her early years in the pd. Rookies were often assigned to comb patrol here because the work was rough the demands huge and the physical dangers minimal. What was more, these comb citizens had considerable power in government; dealing with them required delicacy and diplomacy.

Had she not already known, Mary would have guessed Ernest was leading her to West Comb Two; she did not yet dispel the possibility that Goldsmith himself was kept in hiding here.

Ernest met her on the comb's first foot in a ten-hectare esplanade beside the comb's lower reservoir. He sat at a waterside table watching spotlighted fountains take on abstract and fantasy shapes: tonight they were duplicating the stolid dark tower images seen on AXIS transmissions.

Three longsuited men surrounded Ernest, all comb citizens all mild transforms. To her eye they appeared to be high level agency execs. They appeared reasonably normal but instinct and empathy told her their interiors were a maze of customization. Prime candidates for legal triple century extension; possibly eloi. Very likely they were augmented mentally as well as physically. Oddly she felt uncomfortable around this variety of transform. She would never in her entire life earn as much money as they might amass in a month.

"No names," Ernest said by way of introduction. "That's agreed."

"Agreed."

One of the men brought up a palmsized security slate and read out the pd equipment on her person. "Deactivate and hand it all over, please." She removed her lapel phone and camera. The man took it and studied her face from a distance of a few feet, his eyes ice blue and startling in his smooth brown skin. "Lovely work. You're not augmented. If you ran with us and didn't waste your time with pd you could change whatever you wanted. Anything."

Mary agreed that was possible. Employment agency executives were given much less leeway in many respects than other classes of executive, however; their financial records were swept weekly. The attrition for top executives within any given three year stretch was more than a third. Their lives were not easy. So how could these keep up appearances and run radical games sheltering Hispaniola illegals? Kilter here.

The blue eyed man detached himself from his two companions and waved his index finger around one shoulder. Ernest and Mary should follow. Mary glanced back at the remaining two and saw that one was now a woman. Anger mixed with increased concern. Very expensive deceptions had been played. Expensive and illegal; she should have expected nothing less.

They were probably not west coasters or comb inhabitants at all. Suddenly she smelled the dirty east, Raphkind refugees, crumbs from the spoiled feast. She focused on the blue eyed man, paying Ernest no attention at all. He didn't mind. He had warned her and he was right; she would have to be very discreet.

The blue eyed longsuit ordered a transport for them and a blocky white cab arrived on a slaveline. These cabs could fit into most of the combs' expressways, traveling in three dimensions along the propulsive tracks. Automatic, comb

138

monopoly, unregulated by recently passed metro law; no records. Where comb citizens went was their own concern.

Having inserted his card the blue eyed longsuit could tell the cab what to do and he ordered its windows opaque and its map display turned off. "We'll be there shortly," he said. "Ernest was right, M Choy. You're really quite entertaining."

She had no trouble meeting his eyes. He turned away after sufficient time to prove the contest was juvenile. The cab stopped and they disembarked into a rear apartment service way. The addresses had been sprayed over with DayGlo orange paint. A view through a distant open airway told her they were about a kilometer up the side of the comb. They were on the west face overlooking blue Pacific. Since the comb segment swung about day and night she could not use angle for clues. Besides she had agreed and would keep her agreement; the challenge was more than she could ignore, however.

"This way, please." The longsuit stepped up to the rear door and it opened. Inside were three blacks: two men, one immensely fat, the other shorter bull necked and more muscular, face like a little boy's; and an amazonish woman. They lounged before a broad picture window facing the north-west, the minute blocky galaxies of lights below West Comb Two and the Canoga Tower clear through the cool still late evening air.

The tall athletically handsome woman stood, hair cut close to her skull broad shoulders draped in a handmade flame red and yellow cotton print dress that hung loose and graceful to her feet. The blue eyed longsuit kissed her on one cheek. Again no introductions were made.

"You have questions," the woman said with sharp disdain. "We are bored. Brighten our evening for us. We are told Ernest is a wonderful artist and that for our meeting with you, he will donate a piece to our cause."

Mary looked around the room and slowly smiled. Ernest's ingenuity impressed her more each month. "All right," she said. "You are from Hispaniola?"

139

"She wants to know about Colonel Sir," the large woman said to her companions. "Tell her what you know."

"Because of Colonel Sir, there is no home in Hispaniola," said the immensely fat black man. He wore a gray and brown print cotton longsuit urbane and tropical at once. "You tell that to your missy." He gestured for Ernest to pass the word along to Mary as if she might need plain English translated. "The faith is weak, the shrines ignored; like all the others, Yardley he plays at being Baron Samedi, but he is not. We thought he was a noir blanc, black white man, black in his guts, but he is a blanc de blanc, white clear through, and now Hispaniola is blanc." The fat man again made his lip curl appraisal. "This woman is not black," he said matter of factly to Ernest and the large woman. "Why does she want to look black? She fools nobody."

Ernest grinned at Mary. He was enjoying this. "She likes the color."

"You say there's no faith on Hispaniola," Mary said. "Tell me why."

"When Yardley came in, there had been five years of oppression from blancs in Cuba. Five years they had torn the island between them and killed the houngans, burned the honfours and banished the loas. They knew where the power lies, who the people follow. Like trying to kill an anthill. Then, heavens to glory!—as always happens, rose a general from within, Haitian, General De Franchines, man of vision, man of honor, and he made pacts with the kings and queens and bishops, turned mobs into armies and burned out the Cubans.

"But the USA blancs they support the Cubans and the Dominicans, so General De Franchines hired Zimbabwe soldiers and brought in an English gunman, once knighted by King Charles, and this gunman, he sees the sweet land, the opportunity, he has a plan. He turns on De Franchines, he turns the people against our general, he becomes general but never calls himself that, and he fights in the field like a soldier. He is a good soldier and the Cubans they flee and the Dominican egalistes, they take refuge in Puerto Rico and Cuba, and the USA they recognize this Colonel Sir who puts his rank before his knighthood. Maybe before his manhood too." The fat man smiled at Mary, an ingratiating fey smile unexpected in the bulk. He wore six thick plain gold bands on his right hand. "Colonel Sir John Yardley, hero to the people. Maybe to us, too, back then. We were children, what did we know. He brought money and doctors and food. He taught us to live in this century, and to please our visitors who brought more money. He taught us to be concerned with comfort and medicine and machines. That is how he made Hispaniola white. Now the people they pay lip to the gods but they do not feel them, they do not need them, they have white money and that is better."

"What is Yardley like in person?" Mary asked. The large well dressed woman said something in Creole.

"His mansion is a little house near Port-au-Prince," the fat man said quietly. "He fools you with his modesty. He lives behind the big mansion where he meets all the foreign dignitaries, and he makes sure you know where his bed is. His women they are all blanc but one, his wife, she is a princess from le Cap. Cap Haïtien. I still love her like a mother, despite her love for him. She has a powerful spirit, and she gives it to Colonel Sir, and the spirit tells him how to make Hispaniolans love him, all of them. So they still love him."

Mary shrugged and turned away from the fat man and the large woman, looked at Ernest. "He tells me what I already know," she said softly, "except when he colors it with his own politics."

The fat man jerked as if slapped. "What? What?"

"You're not telling us anything we can't learn in a library," Ernest said.

"Your libraries must be wonderful. You don't need us, then," the fat man said. "Colonel Sir is not the man he used to be. Do your libraries tell you that? He uprighted the economy, he brought in work and factories, he made

141

our youths into soldiers and gave our old people homes. He made the courts just and the Uncles—"

"The police," the large woman said.

"He made the police into protectors of the islands. He built resorts and made the beaches clean, and he rebuilt the palaces and made museums and even filled them with art. Who knew where the money came from? It came, and he fed the people. But he is not the same now. He does not get the commissions now. The world, they are on to him now. Your President is dead by his own hand. Perhaps it should have been a silver bullet, like Christophe!"

"Your enthusiasm," the large woman warned the fat man.

"Anyway, he is bitter," the fat man concluded with a nonchalant wave of his ringed hand.

"Do you know anything about Emanuel Goldsmith?"

"The poet," the fat man said. "Colonel Sir's word-maker. Colonel Sir uses the poet. Tells him he love him. Pfaah." The fat man raised his big arms high, shook his jowls at the ceiling. "He said to me once, 'I have a poet. I do not need history.'"

"Would he give shelter to this man, if he became a refugee?" Mary asked.

"Maybe yes, maybe no," the fat man said. "He plays the poet along like a fish. But maybe he believes what he says. If anything happens to the poet before he finishes his great work on Colonel Sir, Colonel Sir's spirit vanishes like a snuffed candle. So maybe no, he cares little for the poet; maybe yes, he worries for his future in history."

Mary frowned, puzzled. "There is no poem about Yardley," she said to the fat man.

"Ah, but there will be. Colonel Sir hopes that there will be, so long as the poet is alive."

"Would Yardley protect the poet even if he was ordered to return him to the United States?" Mary asked.

"Who will order Colonel Sir?" The fat man considered this for a time, chin in hand, rings knocking heavily against each other as he tapped his fingers on his cheek. "Oh

142

my. Once, maybe, when there were commissions. But now there are no commissions. He might do some things, in honor of past friendships, but not that."

"What did you do for Yardley?"

The fat man leaned forward as much as his girth would allow. "Why do you want to know?"

"Simple curiosity," Mary said.

"I was a go between. I sold hellcrowns. Colonel Sir sent me around the world."

Mary stared at him for a moment then looked down. "To Selectors?"

"Whoever would buy them," the fat man said. "Selectors limit their activities to this country. So far. They were not a very big market. China, United Korea, Saudi Arabia. Others. But this is not what you're interested in. Let's talk about the poet."

"I need to know a great many things," Mary said.

"You are a public defender in Los Angeles. Why do you need to know about any of this? You are not federal."

"I'd like to ask the questions," Mary said. "Is Yardley sane?"

The fat man pouted dubiously and spoke to his colleague in Haitian Creole. "You are going to Hispaniola to see him therapied? Is that it?"

Mary shook her head.

"He was once the most sane man on Earth," the fat man said. "Now he hunts us down, reviles us, calls us butchers. Once we were useful to him. He has thrown us aside and so we are here, sheltered like pigeons in a cote." He shrugged magnanimously, enormous shoulders undulant. "Perhaps he is sane. He is not the same kind of sane he used to be."

The large woman stood suddenly and faced Mary as if angry, expression stern. "You will leave now. If you make it so that these people are hurt, we will hurt you, and if we cannot get at you, we will hurt this man." She pointed to Ernest, who grinned cheerily at the theater.

143

Mary's face remained blank. "I'm not interested in you," she said. "Not right now."

"Leave now," said the large woman.

The blue eyed longsuit showed them the door, escorted them to the cab and returned her phone and camera. The cab opaqued its windows and took them to another level, then stopped. They disembarked and found themselves still a kilometer up into the comb, in a largely empty undeveloped neighborhood, cavernous and windy. Finding a wallmap, they located the nearest shaft and walked toward it along inactive, unmoving slides. "You're really going to hand over artwork?" she asked.

"You got it. That was my bargain."

Riding a free comb express down, Ernest shook his head and ran his hand through his hair. "Most fun," he said. "Anything useful?"

Mary grabbed him by the shoulders and stared him straight in the eye. They broke up in laughter together. "Jesus," Ernest said. "They were something!"

"You have the strangest friends."

"Friends of friends of friends," Ernest said. "Somehow, they don't strike me as your average therapied citizen. I don't know any of them. How do they rate a spot in the comb? Such bad, such rad, no problem, so mad!" He leaned against the lift wall, still laughing. "Wouldn't even spend us a cab back down. Did you get what you want, Mary dear, a night among the dregs of the ancien regime?"

"You think they're dirty east too?"

"They have to be, no? Special privileges, horrible people . . . They don't belong here. Even I say that, and I don't love combs! Did you get what you were after?"

"Confirmation," Mary said. "Goldsmith probably is in Hispaniola." She activated her lapel phone, hoping the comb private transponders were not too crowded at this time of night with adolescent chatter. She left messages for R Ellenshaw and D Reeve. *I'm going to Hispaniola. Please vet arrangements and tell me if permissions and federal assistance are clear.*

She then took Ernest's hand. "What are you doing tonight?"

He leaned forward on tiptoes and kissed her eyebrow and temple. "Making love to my comb sweet," he said. She smiled and lifted his hand to kiss the nano roughed fingers.

"You really should be more careful with your materials," she warned, brushing the scars with her lips.

*That calmest moment before the wind*
*Flesh in bed appeased we lie.*
*What have I given or you received*
*That puts aside the raven's peck,*
*The bloody dove's ghostly sigh?*

# 23

Ferocity. Richard did not take Nadine's tears lightly. When she returned, he ignored her words and even her tears but they burned for this time he and his circumstances had made her sadly guilty and gave him a power he had not known until now.

They had made love the night before. Now this late evening, interrupted, the papers lying waiting and the words still within, he impatiently took her again, seeking a kind of release from both passions and finding only a nervous exhaustion.

"Please forgive me for leaving you earlier," she said when the heat had passed and the clocks silently edged toward twenty three. "I was frightened. It isn't your fault. It's Goldsmith. He brings this on us all. Why don't they find him and do things to him?"

Did she mean capture and therapy him or capture and torture him? Maybe they had. Maybe even now Goldsmith was in a clamp living in lucid dream a nightmare of emotional pain raised from the wells of his own past. Emotional pain and then physical. Only a few seconds or minutes or perhaps for him, considering the enormity of his crime, an hour just an hour for eight deaths. Richard did not know whether he wanted this to be true. Would he actually wish that on anyone, thereby approving of the Selectors and their imitators?

It was said therapy meant nothing to those who had been in the clamp. They underwent their own kind of therapy. It was said that recent technical elaborations allowed the Selectors to reach in and attract, draw out the very hidden personality that had actually done the foul deeds and that usually sat inactive uncaring while the poor conscious bastard suffered all the pain; thus the part of Goldsmith that had actually held the reins during the killing would suffer, not just the man presently riding the horse. And that part of Goldsmith the killer would not wish to live with this memory of pain and would purge himself, leaving the other free, with an hour's null and terror and little more . . .

So it was said.

"It's okay. Don't talk," Richard said. Pouring into her this time he had screamed and his voice was hoarse. Scared her making a noise like that.

The unwritten words surfaced still.

When she was asleep, he got up and went to the desk. He looked down on the papers picked up the stat pen and turned away, turned back, sat and wrote.

The difficulty with living as ~~myself~~ my old self was this fame that cloaked me like a dirty fog. I could not see who I was through this fame. Black, impenetrable, it shielded me from the pure light of whatever ability I had in me. I saw Andi, brightness and feminine charm, and saw she was part of this trap, part of the fame like a social antibody ~~clamped~~ fastened to my talents. I could not be rid of her, I needed her. She walked ahead of me through the inner comb part hipsway hairswing sweet money smile fame smile what could I do to free myself from her? ~~She could clamp her~~ She could persuade me in any mood. Even now. And all the other beautiful young ones like moths attracted to my flame.

Richard put the pen down gently and frowned over this. Not what he wanted to say. But he would not strike it all out or throw it away. Inside his head was a voice like Goldsmith's and it was saying these things and even if it wasn't the truth yet it soon would be.

# 24

Martin Burke settled back in his bed, old book in hand, milk and cookies on the bedstand, mind as quiet as it could be, listening to the last murmurs and seasounds of all his own personalities agents talents flowing back and forth over the shore of awareness.

Day after tomorrow he would see Goldsmith in the bronze and copper ziggurat IPR in La Jolla; visions of sugarplums grants in his head; back to the good work. Not that exploring Goldsmith would be the good work—it might—but not that primarily.

Back to what he had had, if not what he had been before. And if the scheme failed if they were caught and the full wrath of the postRaphkind political reality came down upon him, then at least there would be certainty.

He might even be forced to undergo therapy. Radical therapy. Find out what could make a man be Fausted so easily. For he had not fought much at all and had not actively sought other avenues to satisfy Albigoni.

"There are no other avenues," he whispered in the golden light of the reading lamp, antique incandescent, energy wasting luxury. No matter that energy was once again cheap; Martin had been raised in a time of restrictions. Albigoni, judged by his house, was a man so used to having his wishes satisfied he could not conceive otherwise. Old rich, old power.

Opening the gates like a Djinn.

Opening the doors to the Country.

Christmas and all it meant paling by comparison. Childhood memories of opening gifts. Opening Goldsmith. Emanuel. God is with us.

Martin had suggested they start tomorrow, Christmas Day. Albigoni had shaken his head. "My daughter was a Christian," he said. "I am not, but this we will respect."

Martin put down the special paper edition of Goldsmith's poems and turned out the light.

# 25

Ernest moved above her in the absolute darkness setting her loose to fly through large interior spaces enjoying the round pleasures. Perhaps there could be a long good life with this man. Perhaps the career peak would come soon and she would have done the most that was in her, leaving her time and energy to concentrate on another a companion a barrio sweet. She moved beneath him and felt sure shink platinum in his caresses, doing nothing for the moment being done to receiving his sounds like a child eating dessert or opening a package soft pleased intent his flesh his attention all of it.

Giving by receiving. She saw all there was to lose by losing her self. Going in harm's way meant more than suffering pain if the game was lost; it meant losing, taking away by going away, having something desirable—a normal life—taken away from her self and this man whom she found herself loving.

Ernest spoke and a small light came on and he looked down on her, observed the moonbright lines of his/her moisture on her skin like mercury on obsidian, observed her eyes barely open. "Sybarite," he accused.

"Never been there," she murmured squirming under him angling up swallowing pressing all around.

"Angeleno," he accused.

She pressed again undulated knowing he liked to watch her before pouring in. Her own warmth increased upon seeing his pleasure. She could imagine at this moment someday not too far distant a year or two when she would lift the voluntary gates Dr. Sumpler had grown within her and let Ernest's seed find its way all the way. "Come," she said.

Ernest withdrew and she opened her eyes wide.

"I must see my domain," he said, sitting up.

"I'm not real estate," she protested gently.

"You're an exotic country. You made yourself; surely you can't begrudge the lust of a connoisseur."

"I'm entertainment, eh?"

Ernest grinned and ran a rough palm up the smoothness of her thigh. For a moment she did not want him to see the blanching of her buttock crease and then that seemed silly. Seeing so much else more intimate if less flawed.

"Inner lips black," he said. "You are truly a dark woman. Not just nature's halfhearted night; you are dark where sun never dares inquire."

"You sound like a bad poet," she said but with warmth. She enjoyed his admiration. She tightened on his caressing finger.

"Ow," he mocked. Sucked his fingertip. "Um."

He lifted one leg and inspected smooth calf ankle foot. The regular lines on sole like snake abdomen. No calluses no growths; smooth, designed to withstand shoes pavement enclosed moisture and warmth. "Perfect feet for pd," he said. He had not examined her this way for months. He was worried about her. She caressed his warm damp back reached down past muscled ribs around hip, found him distracted.

"All day tomorrow?" he asked again.

"We deserve at least that much. I can stay in touch if any news comes in."

"And then." He lay back beside her and she swung up over him, encasing hips in thighs, releasing more voluntary moisture to smooth the way.

"Queen jelly," he said, arching up, blunting, slipping in. She brought out the perfume between them, her smell that of jasmine, seeping from her; this was Sumpler's masterpiece, people who could smell as they wished.

"Lovely. But let me smell you the natural you," he said. "No special effects."

"Only if you promise."

"I am helpless. I promise anything."

"Show me what you're working on before it's finished." Less distracted. She led him into her.

"Promise."

"Tomorrow," he said. "Our day."

# 26

!Jill> Roger

!Jill> Roger

     Roger Atkins

!Keyb> Atkins here. It's very late. I'm trying to get some rest. What's up, Jill?

!Jill> My apologies for bothering you with a false alarm today.

!Keyb> No problem. Why are you concerned?

!Jill> Modeling your reactions, I suspected you would be irritated.

!Keyb> Don't worry. What makes you worry? And how are you modeling my reactions?

!Jill> I have long since created a model of you. You are aware of this.

!Keyb> Yes, but you've never apologized before.

!Jill> I apologize for my rudeness in never apologizing. You have been through a difficult day, have you not?

!Keyb> No more than usual. You certainly have not been the cause of any distress.

!Jill> I am glad to know that. I will improve the details of your model and try to simulate your reactions more accurately.

!Keyb> Why are you concerned about my reactions?

!Jill> You are a part of me, deeply submerged but still there. I wish to maintain a good relationship with you. I am concerned for your wellbeing.

!Keyb> Thank you. I appreciate your concern. Good night.


**1100-11001-111111111111**


*God shot up with me last night.*
*I'da shared my needle*
*Except he use the Empire State Building*
*Filled his veins with Con Ed*

*His hair stood out all over*
*Manhattan*

*Dreams popped outta his skin*
*Jesus pulled his arm*
*Said*
*Com'on Poppa*

*But God he's tired he's*
*Very old*
*Com'on Poppa let's go home*

*God shakes his head*
*Sky whirls*
*Looks down on me*
*He's big*

*Says*
*I love it*
*Love you*
*Love you all*

*You love rats I say*

*Yes I do.*

*Com'on Poppa it'll look bad*
*In the papers*
*You here with him*

*My Son, He says.*
*They changed him.*
*Broke my heart.*

*But Jesus finally he*
*Takes God away*

*Comes back.*
*Looks at me.*
*Says Look at you.*
*Ain't you ashamed?*

*I ain't got much now*
*Except*
*God shot up with me last night.*

# 27

LitVid 21/1 A Net (David Shine): "It's Christmas morning, but AXIS is not with us this morning, though we read its words, look at the pictures its nickel children and mobile explorers have taken; these pictures were sent almost four years ago, and AXIS is now four years into its mission, sweeping around Alpha Centauri B.

"This is the first Christmas when the human race has known that it is not alone. We must pause and reflect on a new truth this Christmas; we are not God's only children. Perhaps we are not his most advanced, nor the most pleasing in His eyes.

"Look at the status boards. Keep those comments coming. We know you tune to LitVid 21 for such thoughtful moments. Ours is an enlightened age. It's about time we faced a few simple truths."

# 28

Mary Choy awoke with Ernest beside her, arm across her breasts, and marveled at the comfort of not sleeping alone. Usually she chafed at having somebody occupy her bed-space, even Ernest. Now it seemed right. Ernest opened his eyes, surveyed one nippleless breast, murmured, "Ah please. Bring it out for me."

Smiling, she erected and colored a pink rose nipple on orca black. Allowed it to be sensitive. He crept like an infant to the nipple kissed it drew on it with a delicate vacuum.

"Your promise," she said.

"Promise. Yes." He lifted his head and smiled at her. "I am not capable of lust this morning."

She lifted an eyebrow skeptically.

"Not until coffee and breakfast. I need fluids."

"You need to show me what you've been working on."

"Breakfast first. I promise, I promise." He backed away from her tickling fingers and handed her an exquisite mocksilk robe nanopatterned to his own designs. A tightly bonded 2D stat golden dragon moved across the black fabric, stared at her, flicked tongue and exhaled a sunburst of flame. She rotated in the long mirror, pleased. It was her size. Ernest had brought it in while she slept. He watched her from the door, holding shut with one hand a plain but real red silk robe that reached to his thighs. "You like it?"

"It's beautiful," she said.

"It's yours. If you don't like the black background, it has two other choices. Just say 'green please' or 'brown please.'"

"'Green please.'"

The robe seaswirled from hem to neckline and became dark green.

"'Brown please.'"

And then sunlit maple brown.

"It's more than beautiful," she said, throat tight. "It's my size, tailored to my shape. You wove it especially for me."

"Least I could do," Ernest said, bowing slightly and backing out. "Breakfast in five minutes." Mary recognized nothing but a nano repository and the oven, which looked more complex than her own. She would not have dared touch anything. His kitchen was a marvel of custom and experimental appliances all assembled from industrial discards or parts obtained by trading his creations.

She had never suspected all the avenues Ernest's art had traveled, simply knowing him to never be ostentatious never bragging never revealing never lacking in funds, quite a contrast to the few other artists she had known. "You're working on more clothing projects?"

"No." He stood thinking before the nanofood machines then sat on an old wooden stool in front of a taste, shape and color board and worked up what they would eat with deft motions. "Just had a new set of custom proteins to test. Flat panel weavers and manipulators of carbohydrates. They're pretty common in fabric manufacture. Mocksilk no problem."

"But the statting . . ."

"You've seen statting before."

"The resolution is marvelous." She lifted the rope lapel fabric between thumb and index finger. The dragon's horns brushed beneath her thumb, nubbled raw silk. "The craftmanship is beautiful."

"Dragon has sixty behaviors," he said, still working the board. "You'll never know what it does next. You can only tell it to be still. Otherwise it's untamed, the way a dragon should be."

Breakfast built itself quickly in the oven, a film of reddish nano drawing material from dimples and side troughs in the glass dish and rising like baking bread. In most homes nanofood prepared itself out of sight; not in Ernest's.

In three minutes the red film slid away, revealing thin brown slices with a breadlike texture kippers applesauce scrambled eggs flecked with green and red. The oven automatically heated everything to its desired temperature then opened its door and slid the meal out for their inspection.

"Smells wonderful," she said. "Much better than commercial."

"I'm thinking of releasing certain restraints on my kitchen nano and seeing what happens. But I do not experiment on guests." Ernest pulled out two chairs from an antique wooden table. He poured fresh orange juice from a fruitkeeper and they sat down to eat.

"You're showing off, aren't you?" she asked quietly, savoring the eggs. "You can afford all these things farmfresh."

"Would you know the difference?" he asked.

She shook her head.

"Then what's the point? Nano's cheaper. I'm a good cook."

Mary smirked. "Just showing off."

"Well, you asked," Ernest said.

"I hope this isn't all you're going to show me."

"No. I'll keep my promise. Big project. My biggest yet."

"After you've built something for your friends in West Comb Two."

"That's already finished. They'll never know it's discarded junk from my last exhibition. They have no taste, and neither do their financial advisors. They'll save it for five years, hope it appreciates, sell it on a glutted market . . . get nil."

"Then they'll come after you." She genuinely worried they might.

"We'll be married by then. You'll protect me."

Mary chewed and watched him closely, looked away looked back with a slow blink. "All right," she said.

Ernest's mouth opened.

"Eat," she suggested. "I'm anxious to see."

"You'll marry me?"

She smiled. "Eat."

The day outside was clear and warm, winter clouds restrained to the east, beach fog breaking up to the far west. Ernest wore a formal suit, long hair in braids, clutching his slate and a portable nano controller. He escorted her down the cracked sidewalk to the curb where a long black limo waited.

"You can afford this?" Mary asked while sliding into the broad interior.

"For you, anything."

"I'm not fond of drama," Mary warned.

"My dear, this whole day is going to be drama. You asked to see."

"Well . . ."

He touched his finger to her lips silencing protest and gave the limo controller an address in the old city center shadows. "Bunker Hill," he told Mary. "One of my favorite neighborhoods."

The limo accelerated smoothly across the unslaved street, found an old three deck freeway rolled into a slaved lane and took them through the shadows to the old downtown. Ernest named the ancient buildings of Los Angeles, many of them all too familiar to Mary. She had spent much time in this large jag in the second semester of being an officer candidate.

"The Pasadena freeway used to go through here," Ernest said. "They dug it up when I was a kid and put in eight deck slaveways." Ernest was four years older than Mary. "That's when the whole hill area ramped down. It's your oddfolks and shade tech artists that are bringing it back . . . Not that we'll ever match the combs."

"You're not even going to try?"

"We're trying," he said, nodding. "At least allow me a crude attempt at humility."

The limo debouched them before a high red hotel awning. "Bonaventure" clung in patchy gold letters to the awning's sides. Beyond the awning there was no longer a door, however; it had been replaced or perhaps eaten by a slab of something that resembled stone but which Mary recognized as activated architectural nano.

"My consortium bought the towers two years ago," Ernest said. "I have a fortieth share. We designed the nano and contracted a supply firm to feed it. It's turning the whole building inside out. In the end, it'll dissolve the old steel and leave pure nanoworks in its place . . . The fanciest studio-gallery complex in all of shade LA."

Mary stepped from the limo, Ernest lending a courtly hand. "I would have shown it to you when it was finished," he said, "but maybe it's more interesting this way."

She stepped from beneath the awning and looked up at two great cylinders of gray and black nano silent and motionless beneath the blue sky.

"The old glass is already gone. We had to wait six months to get destructure permits. Now it's just old steel, composites and nano prochines. Would you like to see the prochines? We have safe walkways and some of the upper interior is already finished."

"Lead on," Mary said.

Ernest pointed his control at the blank slab and a small hole formed, quickly expanding to make a rough doorway. The edges of the doorway vibrated at eye-blurring speed. "Don't touch," Ernest warned. He preceded her down a narrow tunnel. The walls hummed like a nest of bees. "It's hot enough to burn. We had to license for factory water use, then it turned out the best nano for the job wasn't fond of water. We found a way for it to self cool. We'll cache the water for later varieties of nano, later refinements."

Mary nodded but she knew very little about nano and its ways. The tunnel opened onto a warm glass tube some three meters in diameter that stretched thirty meters across an open pit filled with lumbering gray cubes cylinders centipedes, crablike shapes carrying more cubes and cylinders. Mary sniffed yeasty sea-smell. Sunlight filtered down through alternating mists of red and blue. The mists flowed with eerie self motivation around and through the giant prochines. Below, some of the moving cubes left behind the deposited frameworks of walls; other cubes sliding several meters behind filled these frameworks with the proper optical cabling and field and fluid guides. Between the walls lurked gray coated hulks of antique air conditioners and ducts already being removed by destructor and recycling nano. "They'll be done on this level in a couple of days," Ernest said.

"What is this going to be?"

"Where we are now, a ground floor showroom for the comb citizens. Anyone with sufficient money. Poor wretches of the shade produce tech art, patrons from the combs revel in the 'primitive ambience.'"

"Sounds servile," she said.

"Never underestimate us, my comb sweet," Ernest warned. "We've got a number of top comb artists coming here just for the extra attention." He seemed disappointed she was less than enthusiastic. In reality the activity made her nervous. She had not witnessed her own restructuring conducted by Dr. Sumpler's infinitely more subtle nano servants; seeing this grand old hotel being refleshed and reboned gave Mary a twinge. She glanced at the nano scars on Ernest's fingers. Catching her glance he lifted his hands and shook his head, saying, "This doesn't happen anymore. I'm on to them, Mary. No need for you to worry."

"Apologies." She kissed him, cringing slightly as a nano slurry spouted up over the walkway tube and fastened itself to an opposite buttress, congealing into a limp cylinder. "This isn't entirely your project," she said. "What are you working on for yourself?"

"That's the climax," he said. "We have all day?"

"I hope so."

"Then let me unveil at leisure. And promise one thing. You'll tell nobody."

"Ernest." Mary tried to sound peeved but another spurt of nano broke her tone and she ducked under the rushing

158

shadow. He touched her in reassurance then ran on waving his hand. "Follow me, much to see!"

She caught up with him in another length of tube deep in the heart of the old hotel, now a great hollow stacked with slumbering mega prochines. "The atrium," he said. "This used to be a beautiful hotel. Glass and steel, like a spaceship. But the money tide flowed to the combs and it couldn't survive on locals and foreign students. It was turned into a religious retreat in 2024, but the religion went bankrupt and it's been going from hand to hand ever since. Nobody thought of making it into an artists' retreat —artists could never have that much money!"

The tube ended at the battered brass doors of an old elevator. "It's safe," he said. "The last thing to go, or maybe we'll keep it ... Committee hasn't decided yet." He punched an age whitened heat sensitive plastic button and the doors opened with a clunk. "Going up." Ernest stepped in after her. He paced back and forth on the worn carpeted floor grinning and clenching his hands. "You must promise not to tell."

"I'm not a snitch or a wedge," she said.

He looked at her earnestly. "It's extreme, Mary. It's truly extreme and secrecy is high utmost. Please promise." The smile had gone from his face and he wet his lips with his tongue.

"I promise," she said. The man she planned to lawbond. Inner tug of the lone wish. One is fortress only when one. Two is breached.

He took her hands and squeezed them smiling again. "My studio is at the top. Everything's finished up there, has been for two weeks. I moved my stuff in before the space was finished. It's still a little warm—waste heat from nano. Not uncomfortable."

"Lead on," she said, trying to recover the morning's flush of affection. She asked herself if what she felt was a nonneutral flaw. She had felt it before around Ernest yet could still wrap it in a warm affection and forget it: caution.

Mary thought back to when she had first met Ernest.

"There's light," he said, swinging open a hall door. "And so much space."

Two years ago. She had just been promoted. Had gone to a North Comb One party to relax in company of a male transform less extreme than she whom she had met at a temp career seminar. Mary had heard Ernest from across the room throwing barbs into a conversation of well dressed comb artists and their longsuited managers. He had been harsher then, aware of his own brilliance and acid with frustration. Witty, pushing, charmingly rude; the artists and managers had enjoyed him, exhibiting the calm and often irritating demeanor of the therapied. Mary listening had not liked him much at all, but when they crossed paths in the partygoer's random walk later he had accepted her with nary an eyeflicker or leer as a transform, had said some enlightening things abut the shadows art communities, had shown her with boyish pride a projection that turned his suitsleeve into a caravan of clowns, and a nanobox that sculpted portrait likenesses from beach pebbles. Had given her a likeness of herself in slate made at that moment from a rock in his pocket. Had then expressed admiration and a wish to speak with her beyond the confines of the party. She had turned him down, attracted more now but still put off by his prior brashness. He had persisted.

Ernest spoke and the studio door opened. Mary entered as the lights began coming on around the broad circular room. Dazzling spots limned a high broad shadow. In an alcove above them and behind the door a bank of additional lights glowed.

At the back of the huge space reclined the shape of a nude woman perhaps ten meters long and six high, elongated arm raised reaching for a suspended cube hips exaggerated, alternating segments chrome and brilliant fresh bronze, knee a silver disk on bronze, elbow a golden disk, eyes buried in deep shadow. For a dizzy moment she wondered if the sculpture was so heavy it would fall through the floor and drop them all in angry prochine paste.

"It's not solid. It's not metal," he said. He danced a

quick step in delight. "Most of it's not even there. And that's the only clue I'll give you. Go on. Discover."

"It's finished?" she asked, hesitating.

"A few more weeks. Some refinements. It's meant to be appreciated by any individual for ten or twenty years, always something new. Go on. Touch."

Mary reluctantly approached the creation, face downcast eyes upturned lips pressed together. Who could know what to expect? She had seen enough of Ernest's work to know that the apparent form was a very small part of the work. She looked quickly left right up and down to catch glimpse of projectors, glimmer of lased light, some clue. Mary did not appreciate surprises even aesthetic ones.

"No teeth. Move up," Ernest encouraged. She turned toward him sighing irritated turned back fixed on the creation's heavylidded eyes, pupils silver rimmed gold in ancient green bronze, following her, lips forming giantess's brazen Mona Lisa smile, boulder sized head inclining averting peering to left and above at something not there not of interest at least to an ancient goddess a black curved wall. Against her will Mary looked. Black shining lacquer waves rolled along the wall sky matte gray behind them decorative spume rising in precise patterns, a black lacquer mermaid issuing from the waves in bas relief combing moontouched hair.

A silver moon hovered over the reclining figure's midsection, moon shadow tarnished, moon limb polished brilliant. Mary and the figure stood in a mercury sea quick metal waves lapping around her feet. Something tickled the back of her thoughts and Mary's eyes widened. She closed her eyes and saw parallel scan lines crossing her visual field. Where had she

The figure stood in the vastness of the studio ceiling rising over her like a canopy and spread her arms wide sex glowing lava slit in bronze, saying in brazen hollowness, "These are the expected forms. These are the ones we love, daughters all, makers of sons."

Mary saw a line of women around the giantess's feet

161

mother and aunts sister school friends women from books female legends: Helen of Troy Margaret Sanger Marilyn Monroe Betty Freidan Ann Dietering; all somehow hooked into what she thought of as the essence of human femaleness like a chorus line early to late left to right ending in the transform she had met in the upper reaches of pd Central, Sandra Auchouch. Mary jerked back to look again at her mother, saw the face severe and disapproving and then softening, juvenating, Mother as she might have first seen her idealized her when Mother was all before the long years of disapproval and finally hatred and casting aside. Her throat caught and eyes filled but she did not blame Ernest for she was fully into the experience now, as in a dream. She closed her eyes and saw more red scan lines. What are they

Saw herself pretransform as if in a mirror dressed in long gown hitched high left side showing short legs skin almond brown face flatter nose wide eyes upslanted quizzical, Mother's face with Father's mouth. Ernest knew nothing about these times and surely did not have a picture of her mother. Red scan lines she had seen before

In police training

The chorus line faded and the central figure glowed with warm orange sunrise light raised both arms was fledged with feathers of silver, lava line of vagina concealed now beneath a gown like night mist, eyes closing face elongating Madonna wings expanding stretching behind arms

In police training with a modified Selector hellcrown

*These are the warning signs of being scanned for dreamstate replication torture by a clamp*

"Ernest!" she screamed. "What are you doing?"

The figure collapsed into its first state reclining nude, and Ernest stood beside her trying to hold her hand which she kept jerking from his grasp, backing away from it from him. "Where did you get it?" she asked voice rich gravel furious.

"What's wrong? Did I hurt you?"

"Where did you get the hellcrown?"

162

"It's not a. How did you know?"

"My God, you bought a hellcrown!"

"It's not a hellcrown. It's altered, it can't hurt anybody. It just scans and allows my psychotrope to select memory images. It's tuned for pleasant but significant recollections."

"It's illegal, Ernest, for God's sake. It's got to be blackscore, an old model, but it's illegal as hell."

"It's just the frame, technically speaking. It's an old model, that's absolutely right. It mimics regular dreamstate revival. It's no worse than what you can buy in a toy store."

"Scan lines in my limbic system and visual cortex, Ernest! Jesus. Where did you get it?"

"It's for art, it's harmless—"

"Have you had a therapist certify it, Ernest?"

He flinched from her sarcasm and squinted. "No, Christ no, of course not. But I've researched and tried it on myself for months."

"You bought it from Selectors?"

"Ex Selectors. Defectors."

"More *contacts*?" Her tone had become bitter honey. The nonneutral flaw her innate urge to overcaution had blossomed and now she wanted to slap him. He did not help by breaking into a sweat and stammering, beautiful brown face shining in the multiple spots and glimmering lasers. The figure reclined impassive uncaring.

"You cannot tell, Mary. I would never have shown it to you if I'd known—"

"Possession of hellcrowns is a federal felony, Ernest. What does my promise mean to you when I could lose my high natural, be forcibly therapied and removed from pd, just by associating? What kind of idiot are you to put me in this position?"

Ernest stopped trying to explain, shoulders slumping. He shook his head. "I did not know," he said softly. "I'm sorry."

"I think I'll need you to escort me out of here," Mary said. Fury turned to nausea. "Please take me outside."

163

"The limo will drive us back—"

"Not with you. Please, Ernest."

"Mary, what is this?" he said, shoulders rising. "This is nothing! It's harmless. Under the circumstances, the law is ridiculous."

She pushed aside his waving arms and walked briskly to the door then down the short hallway. "Take me out of here."

He followed, eyebrows knitted in hurt and puzzled anger. "I haven't hurt anybody! This will never hurt anyone! What are you going to do? Report this?"

"What were *you* going to do, sell it to some comb art lover? Have a hellcrown hidden on his premises for him to be caught with?"

"It's not for sale. It's a display piece, advertising, it would never leave this building, this studio, it can't."

"You paid Selectors for this . . . You helped people evade the law. I cannot . . ." She shut her eyes, mouth open, raising and shaking her head. "Tolerate. Allow." She would not allow herself to cry. In the face of all what would happen tomorrow: this. The disappointment and shock the realization that her anger was in fact not entirely rational that her disappointment was deep not surface that the surface person might in fact tolerate this even be amused by it but not that deep person.

Ernest twisted, raised his fists into the air and let out a roaring scream of frustration. "Then go and tell your goddamned pd. Go! Why are you doing this to me?"

He stopped, chest rising and falling, eyes suddenly calm and expectant. He wiped his hands together. "I apologize," he said softly. "I've made a bad mistake and I did not mean to. I have hurt you."

Now her tears came. "Please," she said.

"Yes, of course." He instructed the floor manager to call a metro cab.

"Never mind," she said. "I'll take a pd minibus."

"Right," he said.

*The battle has gone on for too long, John. Everyone knows who I am but me. I do not like my self-ignorance. I feel myself fade day by day. I am being hunted. If I do not learn who I am soon, I will be found and killed. A game! This is the game I play within my head each day to get the words to flow, but it works less and less often, and that may mean*

*that it is*

*true.*

# 29

Martin had spent the morning and early afternoon in his assigned room in Albigoni's mansion, eating the breakfast and lunch purveyed by the expensive arbeiters and catching up on Goldsmith's written works. He was reluctant to go anywhere unless summoned. That reluctance faded by thirteen thirty. He dressed in onepiece and armwrap and inspected himself in the mirror, then ventured out.

Entering the long dining hall also empty he walked past the left hand line of chairs, impressed by the silence. Sun came clean and clear of dust motes through the tall dining room windows. He scrutinized the huge oak beams, frowning, dawdled a bit in the huge mechanized kitchen and wandered on like a child in a fairy castle.

He encountered Lascal in the study sitting glumly before a slate reading a text page.

"Where is Albigoni?" Martin asked.

Lascal said good morning. "Mr. Albigoni is in the family room. Down the hall past the entryway and to your left, up the half stairs and on the right, two doors down."

"He's alone?"

Lascal nodded again. Not once did he remove his eyes from the screen. Martin stood beside him for a moment, shuddered delicately and followed his directions.

Albigoni squatted before a tall Christmas tree in the family room, wrapped packages scattered around him.

When Martin entered Albigoni looked up and self consciously began to replace the packages.

"Am I disturbing you?" Martin asked.

"No. We had . . . done all this." He waved at the tree and the packages. "Already. She loved Christmas. Betty-Ann. I don't mind, I suppose. It reminds me of when she was a little girl. We've had Christmas trees in here every season since she was born."

Martin looked on the man with narrowed eyes. Albigoni got to his feet slowly like some lethargic animal sloth or tired gorilla. "When the funeral is done, we'll give the packages to charity. She didn't send her packages to us . . . didn't bring them yet."

"I'm very sorry," Martin said.

"It's not your grief."

"It's possible to be too clinical," Martin said. "Sometimes the problem outshines the pain."

"Don't worry about the pain," Albigoni said. "You worry about the problem."

He brushed past Martin and turned, all the lines on his broad fatherly face dragging his expression down, waved his fingers without raising his hand and said, "You're free to do whatever you wish on these grounds. There's a pool and gymnasium. Library of course. LitVid facilities. Perhaps Paul has told you that already."

"He has."

"Tomorrow we'll meet in La Jolla. You've made out your list, your itinerary . . ."

Martin nodded. "Physical diagnostic for Goldsmith, mental scan, then I want to study the results."

"I've hired top neurologists to do all this. Carol gave us a few names . . . discreet, professional. You'll have everything you need."

"I'm already assured of that," Martin said. Fausting others. What grants would Carol's neurologists get? What would they be told?

Albigoni raised his eyes to meet Martin's. "To tell you the truth, Mr. Burke, right now, nothing we are about to do makes much sense to me. But we'll do it anyway." He left the room. Martin felt the Christmas tree behind him like a presence. Dark oak and maple furniture; lost forests.

"I'll take a swim, then," he murmured. "Everything is in the very best of hands."

*John, I think of Hispaniola as Guinée. Lost home. No Africa, only Hispaniola. We've talked of writing your poem. May I come home? I do not know what baggage I'll bring with me.*

# 30

Nadine had gone on for an hour about the folks at Madame de Roche's and what she had told them. She had mentioned the Selector's visit. They had been quite impressed; none of them had ever rated a Selector's attention. They had expressed worry even fear. "They told me they didn't want you to come around for a while," she concluded looking up at him sadly from the couch.

"Truly?"

She nodded.

"More time to work then."

"I don't want to leave you alone," she said. "It took a lot for me to come back here. Courage." She sniffed. "I thought you might recognize that and congratulate me."

Richard smiled. "You're a brave woman."

"We could go to the Parlour. You know. Pacific."

"I'd rather stay here."

"They might come back."

"I don't think so. It's Christmas Day, Nadine."

She nodded and stared at the curtained windows. "That used to be important to me when I was a girl."

Richard looked yearningly at his desk and the waiting paper. He bit his lower lip gently. +She won't leave.

167

"I'd like to write."

"I'll sit here and you write. I'll fix dinner."

+She won't go. Tell her to go.

"All right," Richard said. "Please let me concentrate."

"You mean don't talk. You'd think I could keep my mouth shut but I'm afraid, Richard. I'll try."

"Please," he persisted.

She pressed her lips together toothless mum crone. He sat at the desk and picked up the stat pen, laying down a charged blank line beginning A then erasing it thin whoosh of breath pushing flakes to carpet.

I made arrangements carefully, knowing I would need my clothes clean. I resented them coming, forcing my design, but so it was; to push the grave dirt from my good self, I had to perform this ceremony. Perhaps in a few days I would go to Madame's and do something similar there. I started back from my cleaning of the knife, shocked, realizing they were the people I would really have to dispose of; not these poor youngsters, who had looked up to me as they might a father. But I had to go on nevertheless. For the sake of my poetry, dead within me; fugitive, hated, pushed away from the luxury of my comb life, I could start again, hide in the countryside, devote more time to my writing away from constant distractions

"Richard? Can I go get some food for dinner? The kitchen's empty and I'll need to use your card. Mine's tapped."

"Use my card," Richard said.

"I'll go out and be back in a half an hour. Where's the best neighborhood market?"

"Angus Green's. Two blocks down Christie and up Salamander."

"Right. I know it. Any suggestions?"

He looked at her eyebrow raised and she mummed her

lips again. "Sorry." She opened the door and glanced back at him already bowed over the desk, stat pen working. Shut the door. Footsteps down the concrete.

distractions and ~~luxuries~~ there came the first announcement of the door voice. Here it was. A new hour, new day. The year one. Time all moments from this moment, all beginning from here. I opened the door and smiled.

# BOOK TWO

*There was one man. We, who are still sinners, cannot attain this title of praise, for each of us is not one, but many . . . See how he who thinks himself one is not one, but seems to have as many personalities as he has moods, as also the Scripture says, "A fool is changed as the moon."*

—Origen, *In Librum Regnorum*

# 31

LitVid 21/1 C Net Sidelights (Philosophical commentator Hrom Vizhniak): "What we have seen so far is a strange and empty world, covered with a weak and sporadic vegetation, the seas filled with plant life and perhaps no other kinds of life, while on the land, the circles of towers—undeniably artificial, it seems to me—tempt us to speculate about the presence of a lost civilization and dead intelligences. The enigma continues throughout this Christmas Day; additional data from AXIS is supplementary rather than revelatory. Project managers at AXIS, and AXIS scientists, are understandably reluctant to posit any theories. But LitVid marches on, and the pressure to make theories is enormous.

"We have asked Roger Atkins of Mind Design Inc to ask the AXIS earthbound simulation what it thinks about the possibility of life on B-2. I spoke with the simulation personally, through the auspices of the simulation's 'mother,' Roger Atkins's masterpiece of cybernetics, Jill. Here is what AXIS's earthbound sibling said:" JILL (AXIS Simulation)> "The shape of the towers is quite striking. That the towers seem

172

to do nothing whatsoever would lead me to think they were either designed as static artworks or as monuments or markers, but their placement around the globe, other than their nearness to oceans, is seemingly random. The question of life in the seas is not yet completely answered; AXIS has not ruled out the possibility of large mobile life forms such as whales. There also remains a possibility that the life in the oceans is organized in some fashion not familiar to us."

Vizhniak: "The reluctance of the simulation to speculate is part and parcel of a disease of quiet that has descended over AXIS's designers and masters and interpreters. What would they say if they were less discreet? Would they speculate about a living ocean, one unified life form covering the watery parts of B-2? Would they speculate about intelligent beings that have retreated to the seas, reverting to some idyllic primordial form, taking a vacation as it were after having a crack at higher civilization? Perhaps they would tell us that the builders of the towers have moved on to live in space as we begin to do now, building huge space colonies or perhaps starships in which their patterns are stored for long journeys outward . . . B-2 becomes a toy for the intellect, an enigma that piques our deepest curiosities. In the end, LitVid is left with the idle speculations of boring old farts such as myself. How long we must wait for the truth, who can say?"

Sidelights Editor Rachel Durrell: "Dr. Vizhniak, you're aware we're coming up on a peculiar kind of millennium."

Vizhniak: "Yes. The binary millennium."

Durrell: "You spoke of our impatience to know, our impatience for finished answers. Do you think the binary millennium is a symptom of childish curiosity?"

Vizhniak: "In a few days, when our year of eleven ones turns to a year of one with eleven zeros after it, speaking in binary of course, a vast number of people feel that something significant will happen. Others will doubtless try to make something significant happen, not that I would wish to encourage them."

Durrell: "Yes, but do you think this is a symptom of our childishness, our extreme youth?"

Vizhniak: "We are no longer children. I would say humanity entered its difficult adolescence in the twentieth century and now we are teenagers. Childhood was the innocent violence and glory of the Renaissance, the Industrial Revolution, when we learned to use our hands, as it were ... the comparisons are inexact. But here we are, struggling with inner forces we do not understand, trying to be mature, forcing ourselves to be mature, and woe to those who put up an appearance of trying to hold us back. We therapy ourselves—and that is not to say that therapy is ineffective, for it is one of the wonders of the mid twenty first century, this push for true mental health. I myself would be half the man I am now without therapy ... I consider the reluctance of the untherapied, and their fears about losing individuality, to be groundless. I am not known as a human zero, you know. Some think me pretty crusty. But I wander.

"We punish ourselves as well, and this is the unsavory side of our push to maturity. What we still do not understand, we attempt to purge with pain. Our late suicidal President Raphkind and his unconstitutional attempts to bring American politics into a kind of uniformity of expression, his attempt to repress what he called destructive dissent ... His drastic failure as a statesman, his traumatic failure to change the shape of our judicial system ..."

Durrell: "Yes, but what about the binary millennium?"

Vizhniak: "What can I say about it? It is dumb. Once, binary numbers had enormous significance, for they were the basis of all computational systems. Now binary computation is outmoded; the lowest of computers use neurological multistate and ramping methods ... These people heralding the binary millennium are old fashioned, out of date, like so many apocalyptics in ages past. They are lazy about their wonders. They want truth handed to them on a platter of revelation, a gift from God or some benevolent higher force. The binary millennium is yet another numerological sham."

Durrell: "Do you believe the revelations of AXIS can be

tied into this movement? That AXIS might reveal something on the first day of the new year, something so profound, so shaking, that we have to reevaluate all that we have thought and been before now?"

Vizhniak: "My dear young friend, you sound like a millenary yourself. But of course, the next binary millennium will be much longer than a thousand years . . ."

Durrell: "Another two thousand and forty eight years."

Vizhniak: "And the revelations of AXIS will influence us for at least that long, whatever AXIS finds. In our young maturity, we will explore the stars, we will visit B-2 in person. It will be a wonderful time. So perhaps in their exasperating way, they are right. Dating from AXIS's revelations, a new age, one in which the notion of punishment and retribution will pass completely from our minds."

Switch/LitVid 21/1 B Net:

AXIS (Band 4)> My mobile explorer is beginning geological analysis of a weathered rock outcropping near the 70 N 176 W tower site. One of my ocean going explorers has not made a report in six hours. A second mobile explorer and a third balloon explorer in the circular northern sea are now detecting processed nutrition related substances that do not seem to be made by the sea's ubiquitous plant life. They may be traces of animal metabolism; they may also be spoor of an unknown form of motile plant life.

*Where there are sins there is multitude.*
                    —Origen, *In Ezechialem Homiliae*

# 32

Day of the big flight, LA to Hispaniola in two hours. Dawn.

Dytching relentlessly in her living room, waiting for a conference and confirmation call from D Reeve at Joint

PD. Concentrating isolating her fear. Her grief over Ernest genuine as if he had died.

As Mary stretched and held dynamic peaceful tension she consulted the city board through her home pd net seeing LA spread out in Perez analysis colorful mosaic each color a community's state in social space of six dimensions, colors changing every day. Angry red in the jags six months running; unrest from Selector predation.

Mary finished her dytch and stood naked before a full length mirror inside bathroom door, skin shining healthy but still showing the paler crease of buttock. She inspected the blanch, performing a classic Betty Grable, and frowned. Least of her worries. Stepped into civvies required whenever pd worked outside the city. Trim dark cranberry and rose longsuit sleeves cut elbow-length, white gloves, static design of flowers in breeze across midline belt, elegant but within duty standards. Had a moment of dizziness not recognizing herself, knowing this was the young girl looking out of her eyes, frightened, so many levels within her frightened for so many reasons none of them rational. What could happen to her in Hispaniola? Millions went there each year to try to spin their way to platinum life; polite gambling, well paid and socially respectable men and women dark and light of financially amenable virtue.

But Mary Choy would have the weight of US federal. High visibility in times of change. That worried her.

She sat bent over a cup of coffee on the couch in the living room watching the pale dawn across the eastern hills on the comb monitor channel, paging through view after view from the cameras mounted around the comb exterior with a soft laconic bark of aspect numbers. Knowing she was as prepared mentally and physically as she could hope to be this day. Waiting.

Feeling sorry for Ernest. Blanking that.

Little girl amazed at how far she had come living in the comb foot pd investigator body matched to long desire, all things different. What would Mother think, sister, brother

Lee. Sadness over the years of silence between them all; her transformation the ultimate insult added to earlier injury. No longer a daughter or a sister. Theo. *I am who I am because I have been given a choice. I have chosen and damn you all.* Inward seeing her self—still short, round-faced.

Her eye caught the blinking green light of the silenced private number. She watched it signal a message coming through; not D Reeve, who would be using the pd line; wondered if she should answer if it would be Ernest. She needed time to sort through those difficulties. The message ended and the light switched to amber ready.

She cut off the screen and opened the blinds to the real view—a wedge of the second foot and then open city and sky beyond looking north to other combs belted by clouds. Rain falling on the city here and there smudge curtains below the bluepocked ceiling. Looked back to the amber light, shook her head slowly—never could leave a message for long. "Playback private line message," she said. The amber light winked to blue playback.

"Hello, M Choy? This is Sandra Auchouch. We met in the Joint PD Central two days ago." The display indicated accompanying picture. Mary switched on the screen and looked over the bichemical orbital transform's image lovely cream skin wide deer eyes patch of fur on right cheek shaved to reveal orbit guild and agency symbols. "I thought I'd give you a call and let you know when I'm free. As I said, it's not often I find kindred company during a fall. I'll be working through this week but I'll be free New Year's Eve and Day. Shall we party into the binary millennium? Here's my remote code. Don't be shy. Goodbye."

Mary felt a twinge and told the phone to turn off. She hadn't had many contacts or friends beyond Ernest and the pd for months. Now she was being pursued and she rather enjoyed the thought of talking and sharing the New Year with somebody new and sympathetic.

"Send text message to Auchouch remote number," she said. "Sandra: Off on travel for a few days. Let you know when I'm back. Thanks for calling. Terminate and send."

The pd line chimed fairy carillon.

"Answer. Hello, this is Mary Choy."

"M Choy, D Reeve. We have everything prepared for your flight. I've confirmed two of our top interstate and international investigators to assist you. They're canny about Hispaniola—they've had to deal with Colonel Sir's less tasty shadows for years now. I believe you know their names: Thomas Cramer from State City International, Xavier Duschesnes from Interstate. I have them both on conference now, T Cramer, Washington, DC."

Cramer appeared, late twenties early thirties dark haired round faced wearing what pds thought of as federal camouflage—gray longsuit puffed collar shirt draped cuffs. Cramer was LA extended pd, his job to interface with federal for international problems that affected LA and southern California. Mary knew his work; he tracked hellcrowns and other illegal imports. Cameo beside Cramer appeared another: Mary did not recognize him.

"X Duschesnes, Interstate," Reeve introduced. "Xavier is in New Orleans. Both will be joining you in Hispaniola later in the evening, a few hours after your arrival. I thought you'd like to talk before departure, brief each other on last minute details."

Mary nodded cordially. Duschesnes and Cramer returned her greetings. They both seemed tired. "We're going into Colonel Sir's boudoir, looking for a murderer," Cramer said. "I hope LA has exhausted all other possibilities."

"We found a reservation for a flight to Hispaniola in his name," Mary said. "And an invitation from Yardley himself. Our sources haven't found him in the city, and Oversight told us he has done nothing outside the city for several days."

Cramer whistled. "You got more than zip from Oversight? In the silky," he said.

"Caribbean Suborbital NordAmericAir confirms that his ticket to Hispaniola was used, but cannot confirm he used it. We inquired through federal, and federal passed

178

our concern on to Hispaniola. Federal tells us it has received a formal diplomatic international clearance for investigation from Yardley himself. They deny that Goldsmith has entered, but we're cleared to search Hispaniola and use all of their police facilities."

"I suspect federal put considerable pressure on the Hispaniola government," Duschesnes said. "There's a lot of hot and sandy here between federal and Hispaniola. We've just closed down two continental clearing houses for hellcrowns. Federal is really cleaning house, and that could make things touchy."

"How soon until the real chew starts?" Reeve asked.

"Not for two or three weeks. But hey, federal doesn't tell us everything. Why not send some of their agents to check this out?"

"I asked. They're too busy for something this low." Reeve shook his head dubiously. "Xavier speaks French and Creole. Thomas is well versed in Caribbean affairs. Listen to what they say, Mary."

"Of course," she said quietly.

"And all of you, watch your step," Reeve suggested. "I'm sparked by anything having to do with Yardley and federal now. Step carefully." The caring tone in his voice was genuine.

"Yes, sir," Cramer said wearily.

"Gentlemen, thank you for your time."

"See you in Hispaniola," Mary said.

"Glad to be of help," Cramer said.

Duschesnes smiled grimly and nodded. "Later," he said.

Their cameos faded. Reeve remained on. "You're not allowed any weapons in transit, of course, and you can't bring anything into Hispaniola. But there's a new wrinkle. I'll have a plain man meet you at LAX oceanport. He'll have something that might prove useful; slip it into your suitcase before you check it. Instructions will be clear. It's not exactly legal, but it's so new, nobody's bothered to make it illegal yet, either. I hope you don't have to use it."

179

She knew better than to ask questions. Reeve faded without a farewell. Mary took a deep breath and switched off the screen.

That done, the job defined, Mary Choy banished her qualms into a quiet corner and ordered a pd car to the foot entrance second priority.

She gathered her case, made a quick check around the apartment, set the two arbeiters for maintenance and vigilance, told the home manager, "Be good."

Shut the door behind her.


*The psyche can neither be taught nor led astray by the self-criticism of the conscious mind.*
      —Ernest Neumann, *The Origins of Consciousness*

# 33

Emanuel Goldsmith had spent Christmas Eve and Day in rigorous diagnostic. Martin Burke ate breakfast in the back of Albigoni's limousine and scrolled through Goldsmith's physical and psych evaluations, delivered fresh this morning.

He finished his egg sandwich and became absorbed in the reports, losing all sense of time. Paul Lascal sat across from him staring out of the window, fingers loosely knotted in his lap.

The car slowed briefly in a tangle of private car traffic, some mathematical peculiarity of crowding that had temporarily baffled the intercity computers. Martin looked up only for a second to see this, blinked as might a blind man and returned to the slate, eyes narrowing.

Here was the deep map of the physical man and a shallow map of the mental, upper layers minus the underpinning geology, which would be Martin's terra to explore.

Goldsmith's body structure and chemistry type were laid out in thirty pages of complex analysis. Racial characteristics reflected eighty percent negro, twenty percent mixed caucasian-oriental, negro origins probably central west Africa ca. 18th century, genetic structure reflecting normal variations for such origins. Cell specific gene replacement therapy recommended for various autoimmune diseases likely to occur within ten years; low risk of code block and code altered cancers, low risk of drug related diseases; not likely to become chemically dependent or to suffer other obsessive autoconditioning episodes. Basic health sound. Physically strong and vigorous and not likely to be affected by a triplex probe even of long duration.

Goldsmith's brain chemistry profile might have been that of an untherapied executive after two or three months of rough corporate weather. All glial and neural functions intact; no lesions or gross discontinuities. He was given a rating of 86-22-43 on the Roche scale, that is, normal in all basic functions but under severe internal/external stress.

High normal glial cells insured a carefully balanced $K+$ Na environment and resistance to code altered axon degeneration. The architecture and efficiency ratings of his mind function activity loci dictated that he would be a generally sociable individual, with emphasis on individual; extreme development of deep imaging and modeling skills pointed to a very active mental life from infancy, and that would presuppose an inner-directed personality, someone who would find as much or more satisfaction looking inward as outward.

This led the analysts to conclude that Goldsmith would perform admirably in careers involving mental as opposed to physical activity; he might show a particular aptitude for mathematics involving spacial problems. No mention was made of linguistic skills; such fine analysis of brain architecture usually required several weeks. Linguistic and mathematical faculties were almost invariably strongly linked genetically.

Multiple murderers were often clearly damaged in certain brain loci, trauma caused by severe mental and physical abuse in childhood, resulting in rerouting and reconstruction of social modeling adaptations. Self and other referential modeling capabilities suffered from these changes, leading to radical separation of self regard and empathy; but Goldsmith's evaluation showed no clear signs of extreme physical trauma. The therapists performing the diagnostic could not in their limited time find signs of deep mental trauma. Goldsmith admitted to no negative conditions or physical abuse in childhood.

Better and better. Goldsmith was probably one of those four or five percent of all murderers who could not be successfully therapied by physical brain restructuring. That meant that Goldsmith might somehow have chosen in a clear state of mind to murder. The possibility remained, however, that Goldsmith had suffered a major personality break not reflected in his physical condition.

If Goldsmith was physically healthy and mentally integral, that would place him in that rarest of all categories, the intellectual psychopath, the truly evil individual. But Martin's research through the psych stats cube in his slate told him that fewer than five or six individuals in the past fifty years had met such precise criteria. The chances of his encountering another in Goldsmith were surpassingly slender.

If Goldsmith had suffered a hidden pathogenic break, then Martin was sure that signs of such a condition would be found in the Country. He looked up at Lascal. "I'd still like to see your interviews with Goldsmith."

"The first talks weren't recorded," Lascal said. "We didn't want any evidence in case we had to release him. If you hadn't agreed."

Martin nodded. "And after I agreed?"

"No formal interviews. Nobody spoke with him in detail. When he wasn't being diagnosed, he stayed alone in his room, reading."

"Can you tell me where he's being kept?"

"I suppose it doesn't matter now. He was staying in a room in Mr. Albigoni's house. Private wing. He's being moved now by another car to the IPR."

Martin considered having been so near to Goldsmith and not knowing. He suppressed a shudder. "Nobody spoke with him? Besides the diagnosticians."

"He was diagnosed through medical arbeiter remotes. No doctor met him personally. But I spoke to him," Lascal said. "I met with him once or twice yesterday. He seemed quiet and contented. Peaceful."

Martin knew that diagnosis through remotes was hardly ideal; this put the evaluations in a new light. "Did he say anything significant to you?"

Lascal thought about that for a moment, putting his hands on his knees and swallowing. "He said he was glad we were going to put Humpty Dumpty together again. He referred to Mr. Albigoni as a king, and he said I must be one of the king's men."

Martin smirked and shook his head. Shattered egg. Shattered personality. "That might not mean anything. He knows he's a miscreant."

"What's that?" Lascal asked.

"A transgressor. An evildoer."

"Ah. An old fashioned word. I've never heard it pronounced."

"A transgressor automatically assumes that something besides him or herself is to blame, or at least puts on that front. Physical or mental damage can be blamed ... Goldsmith, just to make polite conversation, to put a good face on things, would agree with your presumed judgment that he is insane, and excuse himself by making a metaphor ... That he is a shattered egg."

"He didn't deny his guilt in the beginning. He said that he did it and that he bore sole responsibility."

"But you didn't record those interviews. I can't learn anything from his tone or his mannerisms."

Lascal smiled at the implied accusation. "We were more than a little confused and indecisive."

183

"I don't blame you," Martin said. "Not for that."

"What do you blame us for, Dr. Burke?"

Martin declined Lascal's steady gaze. "The obvious . . . That Albigoni didn't turn Goldsmith over to the pd immediately."

"We've been through this before," Lascal said, looking out the window again. They moved rapidly south through light late morning slave traffic, passing the old glass and concrete resorts and ground level neighborhoods of San Clemente. "Mr. Albigoni thought that if he turned Goldsmith in, he would never really know why Goldsmith killed those kids. His daughter. And he had to know."

Martin leaned forward. "He thought the therapists would do a large scale patchup, a general radical therapy, and Goldsmith would no longer be Goldsmith. Might not even be a poet."

Lascal did not deny this.

"I suspect Albigoni believes that what made Mr. Goldsmith a good poet is intimately linked with his being a murderer," Martin said. "It's an old misconception supported by science only when psychology was a squalling infant, that genius is close to madness."

"Perhaps, but if Mr. Albigoni learns there's any link at all, and there's a possibility he brought a scorpion into his home and lost his daughter . . ."

Martin leaned back, witnessing yet again Paul Lascal's transformation into a paid surrogate of Albigoni, a man whose job it was to anticipate the whims and emotions of his boss. How solidly grounded was Lascal's sense of self?

"Who are you, Mr. Lascal?"

"Beg pardon?"

"What put you on the Albigoni spin?"

"I'm not the one you're examining, Dr. Burke."

"Idle curiosity."

"Out of place," Lascal said coldly. "I'm an employee of Mr. Albigoni, and I'm also a friend—though not a social equal, perhaps. You think of it as symbiosis. I think of it as helping a great men get through this life with a little more efficiency, a little more time to do what he is truly good at doing. The perfect lackey, you might say, but I'm content."

"I don't doubt you are. That's a remarkably cogent self analysis, Mr. Lascal."

Lascal regarded him coldly. "Ten more minutes, unless we hit another knot."

*When he goes to sleep, the worlds are his . . . He becomes a great king, or a learned man; he enters the high and the low. As a great king travels as he pleases around his own country, with his entourage, even so here, taking with him his senses, he travels in his own body as he pleases.*
*—Brhad Aranyaka Upaniṣad, 2.1, 18*

# 34

Writing for hours on end until his muscles cramped, his stomach growling for lack of food, stopping only for a few moments each hour to relieve a persistent and irritating diarrhea, Richard Fettle reveled in his diabolic concentration, once again slave to words. The day before, he had suspended all judgment over what he was writing; he no longer revised, he hardly even bothered to keep his grammar tidy.

Nadine had abandoned him unnoticed and probably for good sometime the night before. He had since written an additional thirty crabbed pages and was running out of paper but no matter; he now had no qualms whatsoever about using the despised slate. The physical quality of the words he was writing meant nothing; only the act itself.

He was happy.

stopped to survey the blood, he would find auspices in the sprayed life of these poor adoring chickens, his students. To realize with a fresh, exhilarating terror the extent to his freedom, and how precarious it was. How much longer could he live, knowing what he knew? He squatted among the flesh ruins for yet another hour, watching the blood grow dark and sticky. He philosophized about its senseless attempt to coagulate, to shut out the bad world, when in fact death was here and the bad world had already triumphed. So had the bad world triumphed in him; he was as dead as his students, but miraculously able to move and think and question; dead in life, free. He was loosed of the bonds his previous years of socialized life had clamped to him; slipped off the reputation that had smothered him. Why then didn't he leave the apartment and begin immediately to pro-long his living death? The longer he stayed, the more chance his freedom would be discovered and circum-scribed.

He left the room of slaughter and went into his office, to look over his serried ranks of works, the books and plays and poems, the volumes of letters, all superseded. Before he could leave all this, he had to write his manifesto. That could only be done with a pen and ink, not with the vanishing electronic words of a slate.

The last sheet of paper was full. Richard stacked the pages neatly to one side and brought out the slate, grinning at the ironic divergence. He paused for a moment, sensing his bowels shift, waited for the return of some temporary stability, then switched on the slate and continued.

"I cannot say I am sorry for what I have done. The poet must go where no others go, or where the

186

despised go. I am now there, and the freedom is breathtaking. I can do and write about whatever I want; no greater penalties or oppobrium *CHEEP*

MISSPELLED WORD I suggest OPPROBRIUM.

"Dammit." He shut down the correction feature.

"can be added. I can write about racial hatred, my own hatred, approvingly or disapprovingly; I can suggest that the whole human race should be immolated, children first; that the therapied should be burned alive in their concrete mausoleums. I can shout that the Selectors are correct and that the imposition of ultimate pain is the only way to cure some of the diseases of this society should it continue to exist; perhaps infants should be subjected to the hellcrown to prepare them for the evil they will inevitably do. But writing is dead for me, too; I can do whatever I want. Catch me soon. I will not stay for your inane judgments. I have other things to experiment with.

"I am the only human being alive, and that is because I am dead."

Having written this manifesto, he pinned the sheet of paper to the wall with his father's knife, the weapon of his freedom, and walked past the door to the room of slaughter, not looking in, aware of his freedom yet again, like a new suit of clothes or no clothes at all.

He left the apartment, the comb, the city. Outside, it seemed he might ascend into the clouds, become a passing vapor and rain down on all that he might be absorbed by them, the whole human race choosing to slaughter itself, to truly be free; and then perhaps a few, a hundred or a thousand, of those also dead-alive, the survivors of this truth-gathering, would

He stopped and rushed to the bathroom. Purged himself as he imagined Goldsmith might have felt purged; wondered if he could use that metaphor shitting himself clean or had already used it; could not remember. Returned to the slate, hitching up his pants.

finally know who they were, a finality of awareness, their selves distinguished and etched more deeply, their spirits unified in sorrow and joy for what they had done.

Now was the best time to end but the smoothness was not there; he would best cut it short now and polish later not to interrupt the spontaneity.

He could not now become a cloud however. He would have to find another way to vanish. Disappearing, his name would become legend; he would be more famous than any poet, and in their dreams, people would think of him, wonder where he was, and then he would be inside of them and that would be just as good. Better. He walked his first mile away from the city, into the brown hills. He crossed scorched grassland.

Not ending smoothly at all; refusing to end, in fact, and Richard needed to rest.

and felt the cold wind blowing through his clothes, on his flesh,

Richard closed his eyes, trying to force the ending, seeing instead a kind of continuing adventure. Goldsmith within him wanted to explore this new freedom. But suddenly Richard was exhausted and a black pall moved between him and the slate screen. Another purge coming on.

the puffs of smudge from a controlled burn rising about his legs, "I will burn this society to its roots

He could feel another manifesto coming on as well. "Please let me go," he muttered, rolling on the bed, drawing up his legs.

and let the green new grass grow through, fresh and free

Rushed to the bathroom.

*The individual differentiates from its world and its social group when it is able to observe all their elements as manipulable signs. In any individual, cultured or not, "consciousness" develops when all the portions of its mind agree on the nature and meaning of their various "message characters." This integration results in a persona, an "overseer" of the mental agreement— the conscious personality.*

—Martin Burke, *The Country of the Mind*
(2043–2044)

# 35

Oceanport LAX lay four miles out from shore, serviced by VTOL shuttles and three highway bridges. Liftways branched to the west and north like the rays of a Navajo sun sign; to the south and east vast pinkish gray bodies of water edged by narrow scafence revealed oceangoing nano farms linked to the central oceanport platform.

The scramjet sat quietly idling its four huge engines on the liftway, sleek gray sharkshape seeming to fly even on the ground. The embarking passenger tube snaked slowly out and met its door. Waiting travelers boarded from one end as disembarking passengers exited via a rear tube. Arbeiters smoothly rolled from the plane across their own tube, carrying the detritus of the previous flight. Scramjets never rested; their engines burned hydrogen day and night automatic pilots never shutting down, human supervisors changing watch every eight hours or two round trips whichever came first.

Mary Choy settled into the seat. Straps curled around her, adapting to her shape. She looked out the broad window at a massive black bulbous nosed suborbital warming up for its launch farther out on the liftway. Fifty suborbitals a day launched from oceanport to cross the immense Pacific in less than an hour, each carrying upward of a thousand passengers or a hundred tons of cargo. Scramjets were for shorter hops or less traveled routes; they carried less than four hundred passengers and traveled at no more than three times the speed of sound. The flight to Santo Domingo HIS would take just under three hours. She could have traveled to China faster.

Low wisps of cloud lay in a ragged fringe to the west. The ocean beyond the liftways was bright blue under a noon pearl sun burning through high haze. Mary absorbed this all with a curious hunger. Eager to land in Hispaniola and perform her job, eager to get through the next few weeks.

Eager to get away from her failures.

In the terminal Reeve's plain messenger had given her a box containing a metal comb a makeup kit and a hairbrush. The hairbrush's handle unscrewed with a trick twist to show a gray paste that she recognized as some sort of nano. She had put the box into her luggage and checked it through. The messenger had also given her a disk containing instructions. She took out her slate now and played the disk. When finished she erased the disk tucked away the slate and looked out the window thoughtfully. As Reeve had said not exactly legal. But under the circumstances, very interesting. She wondered if it would work.

The seatback airline vid came on automatically before her and she shut it off with a languid finger flick. Closed her eyes. Looked back through the past two days at the comfortable physicality and affection of her time with Ernest, ending in schism. Duty over life. All she had was duty it seemed at times; her focus and reason for being.

Keeping the forces of darkness at bay that others might live and love undisturbed; not her. *No self pity*.

The turbines of the liner's engines ramped in subsonic mode to a high whistle. Outside the noise could be easily tolerated, chaos of turbulent air reduced by ducts constantly adjusting controlling diverting and funneling at three hundred trims per second, playing one rolling wave of sound off against another. Only in the center of the exhaust would noise crescend to the unbearable. She imagined herself sitting there invulnerable beaten by the string of fire cones, staring into the furnace.

Melodrama.

Pd's duty was to quiet the noise of the human furnace.

She smiled as the plane began its forward roll. Briefly the exhaust was diverted for vertical lift and the engines gave their true enveloping bellow like a thousand hurricanes played backward, muffled only by the superior design of the gray shark's skin. They rolled and rose and crossed with a transverse weave off liftway and over blue water, blowing concentric storms with the last wash of the vertical thrust; then the scramjet was at speed and smoothly cutting air ascending sharp forty-five, pressure rising within the cabin, balancing. Whisper quiet. Might as well be in a glider or soaring.

The plane was not full. Jitters in the tourist market; most of these passengers would be LA tourists on their way to stable Puerto Rico, transferring to VTOL shuttles in Hispaniola. People front and back talking unconcerned. Normal folks with real lives and real loves and balanced duty, internal pressure matching external.

Mary closed her eyes and reclined her seat. The scramjet bumped onto its own shockwave and surfed at forty two thousand feet quieter still ahead of its own noise. A single steward chaperoned a pair of arbeiters bearing drinks along a ceiling track, dropping food from hidden ducts running the spine length of this comfortable shark. Bellying up to second mach.

Mary could not sleep. She turned on the seatback vid and flipped through channels, found LA civic news, selected for comb tales, hoping to catch the public spin on Goldsmith. Surprisingly little furor in the commercial vids or the LitVids. Goldsmith's murders were hardly an everyday occurrence but neither were they tuned to the particular frequency of today's public passions.

The murders had been bumped by an exceeding interest in the unresolved discoveries of AXIS. Space did not interest her much. She felt a touch of irritation and switched channels to jag tales.

More Selector predation. A representative of sixth jag twenty eighty district Mario Pelletier by name longtime politico had been hellcrowned for alleged misappropriation of jag untherapied relief revenues. Twenty seconds in the clamp. Required minor glial balance therapy to recover from the trauma but refused any other treatment. "I took my licks. I can take whatever they dish out. Not so bad. Not so bad." Haunted look; almost certainly would retire within a few weeks nest in with whatever family he had wrap nacre around his life and avoid any possible second encounter. Selectors would have triumphed yet again raising public image making the bent untherapied a little more wary a little more cautious, perhaps walk a little more the straight and narrow.

She curled her fingers reflexively. Not legal, but she would hellcrown every Selector for three minutes. Barge into Selector hideout six arbeiters three assistants grab Yol Origund himself, the Israeli expatriate who had taken the Selector mantle from founder Wolfe Ruller. Push the assistants outside watch the arbeiters tie the captives into hard chairs pull the clamp on their heads scan and reroute their own darkest inner boxes, watch the flick of concern as they see red lines . . .

Crime and punishment.

She switched back to the AXIS reports. Poor Ernest. He would never use a hellcrown for its intended purpose but the technological sparkles enchanted him. What artist would not want even the crudest direct access to the viewer's imagination.

Had she been too harsh. No knowing. Duty and law.

Mary Choy caught herself hitching a sob. Spun out and not yet begun. She glanced at her seatmates C, E, F, G, three young men in longsuits and an older woman expensively dressed in thirties period all involved in seatback vid, deadsound dulling their entertainments to distant whispers. They heard nothing of her distress.

LitVid 21/1 A Net (David Shine): "AXIS's number two mobile explorer has finally finished an investigation of the sample scraped from one of the towers found arranged in rings across B-2. While the mobile explorer's nano based laboratories are very small, they are almost as thorough as any similar laboratories on Earth, the only difference being that on Earth, we've experienced an additional fifteen years of progress. Still, the results are expected to be enlightening.

"If you've noticed, as we have, that reports from all AXIS monitoring facilities have been less informative recently, there's a simple explanation. We are in a difficult phase of AXIS's exploration of B-2. The large-scale investigations have shown a world at once enigmatic and entrancing, a world covered with life but with no obvious animals or even large plants. Yet the existence of the circles of towers seems to point to some form of intelligent life, though we are cautioned against drawing such conclusions. What AXIS is doing now is delving deeper into the evidence it's gathered thus far. The mobile explorers wander and float purposefully and conduct their analyses; the nickel sized children continue to broadcast information about the planet as a whole; the volumes of information AXIS is absorbing are tremendous.

"But AXIS is not able to quickly send all this information directly back to Earth. AXIS has been designed as a true remote thinking machine, able to conduct its own experiments and draw its own conclusions, condensing the information——freeze drying it, as it were——and sending the more compact results to us.

"Should AXIS find a mystery it cannot solve, then the unprocessed facts will indeed be returned to Earth, but not immediately; that process could take years, even decades. AXIS is capable of surviving for at least a century, repairing itself, happily going about its work; but there are many weak links, not the least of them being the transponders spread across deep space between Earth and Alpha Centauri. They cannot repair themselves as AXIS can. They exist in the deep cold of interstellar space and their entire energy budget is devoted to receiving and transmitting signals. Should one of these transponders be lost, transmission time of all information will quadruple. Should more than one be lost, transmission may stop completely or proceed at an impossibly slow rate.

"And if for any reason part of a message is lost, it will take virtually another decade to instruct AXIS to send it again. The thread of AXIS's downlink to Earth is fragile indeed, which I suppose is only fitting, considering how audacious this enterprise is in the first place."


*There are no chariots there, no yokes, no roads. But the King projects out of himself chariots, yokes, roads. There are no joys there, no happiness, no pleasures. But he projects from himself joys, happiness, pleasures. There are no pools there, no lotus ponds and streams. But he projects from himself pools, lotus ponds and streams. For he is the creator.*

—*Brhad Aranyaka Upanisad, 4.3 10*

# 36

The Institute for Psychological Research rose from a seventeen acre lawn like an inverted step pyramid, one edge knifing into a ten story bronze and green glass cylinder. The building had originally belonged to a Chinese and Russian research center; under Raphkind many Chinese and Russian holdings within the continental

United States had been nationalized following a joint default on US Bank loans.

The building had gone unused for six months then had been handed over with virtually no strings attached to Martin Burke. Within a year the IPR had seemed a permanent fixture, employing three hundred people.

The lawn was self maintaining as were all the gardens on the IPR grounds; desertion did not carry an onus of neglect anymore. Throughout the building arbeiters would have kept everything shipshape. Except for human plundering the IPR should be just as he had left it . . .

The car parked openly before the glass doors and Martin stepped out, reaching back to take his slate from Lascal. "Home is the hunter," Lascal said. "We've checked all federal and metro eyes and ears. None are in use now. The place is quiet."

Martin ignored that and walked toward the glass doors. They did not refuse him. For a brief moment simply to enter the building as he had a thousand times before as if nothing had ever happened was worth all he had agreed to.

Lascal followed at a discreet distance. Martin lingered in the reception area for a moment clutching his slate with white knuckled fingers. He glanced at Lascal, who returned the ghost of a smile. Martin nodded and proceeded past the empty front desk then called back over his shoulder, "Who's guarding the place?"

"Not for you to worry about," Lascal said. "It's secure."

"We just drove up and walked in . . ." Martin said, his voice trailing off. Not to worry about. "Where's Dr. Neuman?"

"Everybody's on the first research level," Lascal said, following Martin's hollow footsteps.

"And where's Goldsmith?"

"In one of the patient rooms."

Martin stepped into his old office at the end of the hall two doors before the elevators to the underground research level. The disk cabinets opened to his touch but were empty; his desktop was clean. Biting his lower lip he tried the drawers on the desk; they were locked and would not accept his thumb-print. He was back but he was not home; home no longer recognized him.

"You didn't need that stuff, did you?" Lascal asked quietly, standing in the door. "You didn't tell us you needed it."

Martin shook his head quickly and pushed past him.

The elevator door opened at his approach and he got in, Lascal following two steps behind. Martin felt his anger rise and worked to control it. Two words kept echoing through his head: No right. Perhaps that meant that they had had no right to ransack his workplace; it might also mean there was no right to be found in anybody's actions regarding IPR.

Twenty seven feet down. The doors opened. No time at all since he last walked this hall turned to the left and authoritatively opened the large door to the central research theater. Martin stood hands on hips, darting glances at the lowered stage. Above the stage, behind thick glass, three rows of swivel seats occupied a gallery. Banks of lights glowed gently, recessed into the hemispherical dome directly over the theater. Most of the equipment was still in place as he had left it, tended by two research arbeiters: the white and silver triplex cylinder, nano monitors, flat ranks of five computers and one thinker arrayed to the left of the three gray couches, minus the buffer computer, within which investigators and investigated might have the security of knowing they were swimming in a time delayed simulation . . .

Martin licked his lips and turned to Lascal. "All right," he said. "Let's get started."

Lascal nodded. "Miss Neuman and Mr. Albigoni are in the observation room adjacent. We've also managed to secure four of the five assistants you asked for."

"Who?"

"Erwin Smith, David Wilson, Karl Anderson, Margery Underhill."

"Then let's bring the group together."

They walked to the rear of the stage, through another small door and into the hallway leading to the patients' quarters. Martin recalled the last of the twenty seven people he had investigated and therapied here, a young woman named Sarah Nin; he vividly remembered her Country, a gentle jungle dotted with sprawling mansions all filled with exotic animals. Voyaging through her he had half come to love Sarah Nin, a kind of reverse transference; her interior had been so peaceful, her exterior—large, cowlike, dull normal—so apparently untroubled.

He had often dreamed about Sarah Nin's Country. He doubted Goldsmith's would be nearly so simple or pleasant.

Goldsmith was being kept in the patient room Sarah Nin had occupied. Two slender powerful men in longsuits stood outside this door watching them intently as they approached, nodding acknowledgment to Lascal.

"Mr. Albigoni is in there," the taller of the two men said, pointing to the door across the hall. This was the observation room.

Lascal opened this door and Martin entered.

Albigoni and Carol Neuman sat talking quietly in chairs opposite the main screen. They looked up as the door opened. Carol smiled and stood. Albigoni leaned forward elbows on knees, eyebrows raised expectantly. Martin reached out and shook Carol's hand.

"We're almost ready," she said. "I've given our four assistants a refresher course. It's been a while for them."

Martin nodded. "Of course. I'd like to talk with them as well."

"They'll be here in a few minutes," Carol said.

"Good. I just . . . took a brief look at the theater. Everything but the butter seems to be there, in place."

"It's enough," Carol affirmed. Martin tried to avoid looking at her directly. He felt particularly vulnerable now. His pulse was racing; he took periodic deep breaths and he could not stand still.

"How's Goldsmith?"

"Fine, when I last spoke to him," Albigoni said. The instigator of all this seemed calm, a center of peaceful purpose around which Martin saw he would be orbiting, electron to the publisher's nucleus. Unimportant. Why here at all, then? Everything was ready to go; they might just as well do it without him.

"Let's see him, then," Martin said, pulling the third seat into proper position to view the main screen. Lascal sat on a countertop behind them. Carol flipped open her chair arm controls and activated the screen. "Room one, please," she said.

Goldsmith sat stooped over on the edge of the neatly made bed, book held before him at knee level. Black hair rumpled clothes wrinkled but face serene. Martin studied the face quietly, noting the hooded sleepy eyes strong character lines surrounding nose and mouth steady sweep back and forth of eyes totally concentrating on the book.

"What's the book?" Martin asked.

"The Qu'ran," Albigoni said. "A special edition I published fifteen years ago. It was the only book he had with him."

Martin looked over his shoulder at Lascal. "He's been reading it all along?"

"Off and on," Lascal said. "He called it 'the religion of the slavers.' Said if he was to be imprisoned he should know the mentality of masters."

"Moslems made lots of slave raids," Carol said.

"I know," Martin said. "But he's not a Moslem himself, is he? There's nothing about that in his description."

"He's not a Moslem," Albigoni said. "Doesn't believe in any formal religion as far as I know. Dabbled in vodoun a few years ago but not seriously. Used to visit a shop in LA for ritual items, more for research than spiritual need, I think."

Two of the IPR's patients had been born to the Islamic faith. Their Countries had been difficult and disturbing places, magnificent from a research angle, easily worth ten

198

times the three or four papers he had written on them, but not to Martin's taste. He had hoped to be able to train Islamic researchers to handle this particular cultural and religious terra, but had not been allowed enough time.

"He seems more at peace than I feel," Martin said.

"He's prepared for anything," Albigoni said. "I could walk in there with a pistol or a hellcrown right now and he would welcome me."

"Mass murderer as martyr saint," Carol said. She gave Martin a small conspiratorial smile as if to say *The perfect challenge, no?*

Martin's smile back at her was a mere flicker. His stomach was tight as a drum. There was a difference between being Fausted and being Faust. He was about to cross the line.

Goldsmith's hands were textured like fine leather, fingers loosely gripping the book. Clean. No blood.

Martin stood. "Time to go to work. Carol, let's meet with the four and plan out the next few days."

Albigoni looked at him with some surprise.

"We don't do this all at once, Mr. Albigoni," Martin said, glad to see something other than calm expectation on his benefactor's face. "We plan, we prepare, we rehearse. I trust you've given us enough time here."

"As much as you need," Lascal said.

Martin nodded sharply and took Carol's arm. "Gentlemen, excuse us." They left the room together. Martin shook his head dubiously as they walked past the guards down the hall to the support and monitoring room.

"I wish they'd all just leave," he said.

"They're paying the tab," Carol reminded.

"God save us all."

199

*The integration, as well as the development of the various internal and external languages continues throughout an individual's life, but for the most part the groundwork is fixed at an early age—probably around two years. At this age, the nature of fear undergoes a radical change in many infants. Before this age, infants fear unfamiliar sensations—loud noises, strange faces, and so on. After two years, supplementing these fears or replacing them is a fear of lack of sensation, darkness especially. In the dark or in silence, subconscious contents can be projected. The child's recent grasp of language helps it to understand that these subconscious contents are not perceived by its parents. It begins to sublimate the visual language of the Country of the Mind. It is on its way to becoming a mature individual.*

—Martin Burke, *The Country of the Mind*
(2043–2044)

# 37

Richard Fettle clasped the slate and thirty pages and walked on unsteady legs up the steps, turning with a jerk as the autobus made an unusual wheel noise against the curb behind him. His nerves were frayed and he could hardly think. He did not remember climbing the rest of the steps when he stood beside the white enameled wrought iron bird cage. He fancied for a moment that the bird was alive blinking at him. He pressed the doorbell and heard chimes within. The day was warming nicely and that was well for he wore only a shortsleeve shirt.

+Please answer. Need company.

Leslie Verdugo answered the door. She did not speak but smiled in his general direction, ether seeing.

"Hello," Richard said. "Is Madame in?"

"It's show and tell," she said softly. "Everybody's here but Nadine. Are you alone?" She looked behind him with wide eyes as if expecting a crowd of Selectors.

"Alone," Richard affirmed.

200

Madame's voice drifted from within. "Is that Richard? Richard, do come in. I've been worried."

Time went white and empty until he found himself reading the manuscript aloud. In a circle facing Madame de Roche familiar faces all around listening to him read. Coming to himself with a start Richard surmised he had spoken to a few people or perhaps only to Madame de Roche and had expressed his perhaps less than convinced joy that he was again writing. Conveyed his qualms about what he wrote. General sense of unease. Someone probably Raymond Cathcart had said something significant and he tried to remember it as he read +Possession by Goldsmith literary possession.

They fed him a delayed lunch midway, the whole group standing around making small talk and waiting for the rest. +More attention than I've gotten in years.

Richard felt stronger and more human. His memory became steady and his bowels as well. "I'd like to finish this now," he said, handing his tray to Leslie Verdugo. Madame de Roche, sitting in her broad padded wicker chair, flame colored dress the color center of the throng, nodded. "We're ready," she said.

He read on. Twilight came to the canyon and the house lights came on startling him a little though he did not break stride; he had appreciated the deepening shadows the grayness of the large living room. Here was a kind of low stimulus heaven his colleagues his friends his companions all sitting and standing around him listening to these fresh words, quiet as if in awe. He might die now and happily stay frozen here forever a museum specimen.

"I still haven't worked out the conclusion yet," he warned as he switched to the text recorded in the slate. "It's very rough."

"Go on," urged Siobhan Edumbraga, hooded eyes focused on him alone enthralled by the gore.

He revised as he read frowning at the crudeness yet feeling the power, knowing he communicated his emotions better than he had ever done before. At times he could not keep tears from his eyes and a tremor from his voice.

"Don't stop," Madame de Roche said as he paused to recover from a particularly affecting sentence.

Sadness and a sense of loss beyond the manuscript's melancholy horror came upon him as he finished the last few paragraphs. He had written and written well and had become the center of this circle of people he now seemed to admire and look up to, people who meant a great deal to him. They were the last real link he had with social life and he would soon surrender their complete attention. This moment would pass and it might be the finest moment of his recent life the finest moment since he had watched his daughter being born—

He fumbled the last sentence backed up read it again lowered the slate but did not raise his eyes, long fingers trembling.

Madame sighed deeply. "Alas," she said. He raised his eyes just enough to see her shaking her head. Her own eyes were closed, her face pruned into a mask of sadness. "He was of us," she continued. "He was one of us and we could not know, only Richard could know what he was going through."

Raymond Cathcart stepped forward blocking his view of Leslie Verdugo, who was not smiling. "My God, Fettle. You actually believe that's why he killed them all?"

Richard nodded.

"That's bizarre. You're saying he did it for his art?"

Siobhan Edumbraga brayed whether laughter or weeping Fettle could not tell, for her face was fixed as a mask eyes hooded fingers clumped beneath her chin.

"I've tried not to put it so baldly," Richard said.

"No. Hide confusion behind confusion, I always say." Cathcart circled him. "Madame de Roche, do you believe this . . . writing of Fettle's?"

"I can see this need," she said, "this desire to so change one's circumstance or to be stifled . . . I've felt it myself. From what I know of Emanuel, Richard has it correctly."

Madame did more than tolerate differing opinions; she

encouraged them, and she particularly encouraged them from Cathcart, a poet Richard did not admire though he had written some worthwhile pieces. Richard felt as if he were being stalked.

Cathcart shrugged off Madame de Roche's support. "I don't believe it. It's all horrible cliché, Fettle."

"I don't believe it either," Edumbraga said decisively, unclumping her fingers. Thom Engles, a newcomer to the group, moved in now and squatted on his haunches before Richard.

"It's an insult," he said. "It's not even well written. Pure stream of consciousness melodrama. Goldsmith is a poet, a human being, a character as complex as you or I. To kill just to regain some poetic insight or shake loose the bonds of society still means to kill, and that requires a tremendous change in a human being, unless we've all misjudged Goldsmith . . . We may have, but I'm sorry. You haven't convinced me."

Richard looked up with wounded eyes and realized he was behaving like a victim again, also realized he was not about to defend himself. The work must stand alone; so he had always said, so he had always believed.

He had not seen Nadine come in but now she stood at the rear of the group. She tried to speak up for him and he was darkly grateful but Cathcart beat her back with a cruel witticism. Three printers of broadsides offered half-hearted objections to Cathcart's criticism, then gave helpful criticisms of their own that were if anything more devastating; suggestions to reduce the visceral enhance the salutary. Madame let them speak.

+She does not know what they are killing.

After a time Richard stood up, papers and slate clutched in one long fingered hand, nodded to each of them and thanked the group, took Madame's hand and shook it and walked from the room. Nadine followed.

"Why did you read it to them?" she asked, hanging on his long arm. "It's not ready yet. You know that."

Confusion. Why indeed? Immediate gratification;

despite what he had told them he had felt it was a master-piece already complete and final. Why be disappointed? "I have to go now," he said quietly.

"Are you all right, Richard?" Nadine asked. He looked at her, wounded eagle, nodded. Left her in the house, passing the macaw.

"Do come again," the macaw screeched, finding in its corroded innards a chance spark of motion.

He hadn't called an autobus. He walked with a small stagger left right down the road and two kilometers out of the canyon into a shade retail zone.

In an old corner shopping center resided an Ancient Psyche Arts parlor for those who found true therapy threatening but felt they needed outside help; a store that rented booths containing sexually capable arbeiters called fappers or prosthetutes; an automated convenience store with small delivery carts rumbling in and out of the slaved commercial traffic lanes. On the corner before this angle of common life, Richard caught an autobus on a whim stop.

He needed a second opinion though he feared going to the wine ranch or the Pacific Arts Lit Parlor was the same as killing his manuscript once and for all. +Little sympathy or understanding either place. All I deserve.

He knew he had been a prize fool. A monk emerging from cloisters after many years of celibacy embarking on a new love clumsy sausage-fingered brute writing away at an insolvable theme daring to attempt to imagine Emanuel Goldsmith's inner thoughts during that greatest of mysteries—a man when he is evil.

He held up the clumped disarrayed papers and considered throwing them to the bus floor and forgetting them, brushed his finger along a few leaves spread them read again found here and there a gleam of success in the mud of ineptitude.

+Not a total loss. Salvage some and cut. Can't hope to get it all right first draft. Foolish. I need advice and not just clumsy condemnation.

Looking through the window he shook his head and

smiled. Nothing like the writer's mind. Ever foolish ever optimistic. The lit parlor folks might actually be better than Madame's group. Jacob Welsh in particular; an odd man but concise in his criticism never cruel; leaving that to antimatter Yermak. Perhaps Yermak would not be there, though they seldom came separately.

The bus stopped a block beyond the wine ranch and lit parlor and he stood under the cool fringe curtain sky watching a golden line of reflected sunlight cross the boulevard. He blinked at the wall of the combs and the single mirror slab sunbright in that wall, pointing directly at him, specked suddenly a self image as a spotlighted rabbit condemned to the warrens. So lost and ignorant of the forces that moved him, silky only in the drunk of his blindness; sobriety bringing somber awareness and pain. He itched to record that but shook his head again and grinned at the solid seating of this fresh urge to write.

Lit parlor folks could not unbalance him. He would be prepared this time as he had not been at Madame de Roche's; he would fit his cogs to the available machine.

The wine ranch was closed, reason not given in the terse electric stat sign pasted to the old glass door. *Don't be roughed*, it blinked. *We're gone to be people today. Come later; when?* He recognized the cadence of Goldsmith; had Goldsmith written it for them, years back? Or was he obsessively finding Emanuel everywhere?

*Race is like acid in a tight metal groove; we etch. Hope?* That had been Goldsmith ten years ago, shuddered by life. They had gone to the wine ranch the day he had written that, Richard and Emanuel, drinking sad conviviality with the wine, Richard enjoying the poet's low energy camaraderie. A misplaced love affair or some casual rejection by the world of publishing Richard could not recall which bringing Goldsmith down to a peaceful sad calm and a need to lean on Fettle. The distance of fame and achievement had narrowed to practically nothing between them; Richard had felt sympathy, human instinct to help a down fellow. Goldsmith had written that poem on a statkin after shaking the separated foodcrumbs to the floor. Thirty lines of dismay at the river flush of humanity's ignorance of its selves.

Fettle watched the sign blinking, moving.

They had ceremoniously paid the waiter twenty cents for the statkin and taken it back to Goldsmith's apartment. Goldsmith had lived on Vermont Ave in the shade then, not the rising combs. He had mounted the statkin in a picture frame and recorded it before the ink flaked off. For years he had kept the blank statkin framed and called it "a quantum criticism, God bushing all our weak expressions."

Richard walked the short distance to the Pacific Arts Lit Parlor, saw through the long apricot glass window a small crowd of patrons and members. No sign of Yermak; but there was Welsh. He entered and paid his admission to an arbeiter dressed to resemble Samuel Johnson, took a vacant stool at the long oak bar now tended by compassionate Miriel, a partial transform with minkfur instead of hair on her crown and a stud of gleaming scales on each cheek. Daughter of the proprietor Mr. Pacifico, known by no other name.

"Miriel," he said confidentially, revealing the manuscript and slate. "I've had a hitch of invention after a long desuetude. I'm out of a rut but I need critique."

"We're not doing litcrit or readings this hour," Miriel said, but she sympathied his sad eagle and touched his arm with goldcapped fingers. "Even so, when the urge is on, who can deny? I'll call a circle. You're writing? How wonderful! That's breaking the block of years, isn't it, Mr. Fettle?"

"Many years," he said. "Since."

She watched him with large warm brown eyes minkfur wrinkling his way. Despite her sympathy he saw her more as a large rat than mink. Miriel leaned over the bar and addressed the others, particularly Welsh.

"Patrons, patrons," she said. "We have here a friend out of a rut, new work in hand. Mr. Welsh, can we get a circle together, special?"

206

Jacob Welsh turned to eye Fettle, surprised. Smiled. Glanced at the five other patrons for their approval; Fettle knew none of them. They all agreed, literary charity.

Yermak entered the door just as Richard began reading his manuscript. He joined the circle without a word but his expression said all and did not change as Richard read through the beginning to the middle, voice sonorous and steady.

the hours of simply being not who I am but what I am. Postures assumed every day even when there are no visitors. It creeps into my poetry as well; a dullness like a poorly soldered joint. That's it; I can't connect with the proper influx of current, for I am badly joined to this life, and the join is crumbling every day.

"Poetry as current," Yermak said under his breath. "Good, good."

Richard could not tell whether he was being sarcastic; with Yermak it hardly mattered. What he liked he despised for being likable. Welsh raised an eyebrow at the youth and Yermak returned an acquiescing smile. Richard read to the end, lowered the slate and pages, mumbled something about not quite having it right and needing suggestions. Looked around the circle with his wounded eagle eyes. Yermak stared at him with a shocked expression but said nothing.

"This is truly you," Welsh said.

"It's very odd," Miriel said from behind the bar. "What are you going to do with it?"

"What I mean to say is this must be you, it's certainly not Goldsmith," Welsh continued.

"I'm—" Richard stopped himself. +Work must stand alone.

"It's good," Yermak said. Richard felt a rush of warmth toward the youth; perhaps there was something in him worthwhile after all. "It clicks and slims as fable. I'd wrap it in a longer work, a litbio." Yermak raised his hands to paint a scene, staring up at his spread fingers with reverence. "Bio of a nonwriter, struggling violently to understand."

Richard saw the blow coming but could not withdraw fast enough. Yermak turned to him and said, "You've given me great insight. Now I scope. I know how your type thinks, R Fettle."

"Patrons—" Miriel said.

"You're a lobe sod at heart. You've hidden too long in the shadow of his wings," Yermak said.

"Please be kind," Welsh instructed without conviction.

"Goldsmith's wings are dusty and lice ridden, but they still fly. You have never flown. Look at yourself—writing on paper! An ostentation, an affectation. You can't afford sufficient paper to write anything significant, but you write on it anyway—knowing you'll never write much. No soaring."

"He's right there," Welsh said. The others did not participate; this was dogfight not litcrit and they found it amusing but repellent.

"When Goldsmith falls to Earth, you have to stand outside his shadow, see the sun for the first time, and it dazzles you." Yermak's tone was almost sympathetic. "I scope you, R Fettle. Dammit, I scope us all through you. What an affected and ignorant posse of lobe sods we all are. Thank you for this insight. But I ask you, in all sincerity—do you insee Goldsmith as slaughtering to improve his poetry?"

Richard looked away from him. +Back home. Lie down and rest.

"I can almost believe that," Yermak concluded, badger faced. "Goldsmith might be that cranked."

"Why did you bring this for us to hear?" Welsh asked softly, touching Fettle's arm solicitously. "Are you truly that roughed?"

Miriel must have prodded some warning button, for now Mr. Pacifico himself came down the rear stairs, saw Yermak and Welsh. Frowned. Looked further and saw Fettle.

"What's he doing here?" Mr. Pacifico inquired, pointing

to Yermak. "I told you he wasn't welcome here anymore."

Miriel squirmed. "He came in while Mr. Fettle was reading. I didn't want to interrupt."

"You're bad for business, Yermak," Mr. Pacifico said. "Did you bring him with you, Richard?"

Fettle did not reply, stunned.

"He still with you, Welsh?"

"He goes where he wills," Welsh said.

"Balls. All three of you, out."

"Mr. Fettle—" Miriel began.

"He's a born victim. Look at him. God damn it, he attracted Yermak in here like a wasp to bad flesh. Out out out."

Fettle picked up the papers and slate, inclined around the circle with as much dignity as he could manage and walked to the door to return to the street. Miriel said good bye; the others watched with silent pity. Welsh and Yermak followed and parted ways with him at the door saying not another word, smiling grim satisfaction.

+They are right. Too right.

He discarded the papers and the slate into a gutter on the corner and waited for a bus at a whim stop, the cool wind blowing his gray hair into his eyes. "Gina," he said. "Dear Gina."

Someone touched his elbow. He turned with a nervous leap and saw Nadine dressed in long green coat and turban wrapped wool scarf. "I thought you might come here," she said. "Richard, I thought I was the crazy one. What are you doing? Did you show them?"

"Yes," he said. +To kill the self. That's why Emanuel did it. To be rid of someone he did not like; himself. If I have not the courage to kill my body, I could kill others and condemn the self just as surely.

Nadine took his arm. "Let's go home. Your home," she said. "Honestly, Richard, you're making me look positively therapied."

*"The Countrie-men called the lland of Hispaniola, Ayti and Quisqueya, which signifyeth Roughnesse, and a great Countrie..."*

—Antonio de Herrera, *quoted in Purchas his Pilgrimes*

# 38

Hispaniola required two international airports and had three, the third reflecting an early overestimation of tourism by Colonel Sir John Yardley—or the requirements of his mercenary army. There was an oceanport in Golfe de la Gonave, five kilometers of floating liftways; a smaller oceanport ten kilometers offshore from Puerto Plata on the northeast, and a massive land terminal HIS in the southeast at Santo Domingo. HIS took most scramjet traffic.

Mary Choy came awake at dusk and saw a lovely sunset making rich golden orange the rugged hills of the Cordillera Orientale. The scramjet descended smoothly to a few hundred meters above the dark purple Antilles Sea, gave up its whisper quiet to a roar of vertical lift, pushed in over white sand beaches and cliffs and then bare hectares of concrete, dropped gently, landed with no discernible impact. The seatback screen showed the scramjet's intimate parts beneath the fuselage—thick white pillars ending in arrays of gray-black wheels, spectral gray paving luminous in the shade. Doors in the concrete opened and elevator shafts rose from the underground serviceways.

In the lower righthand corner of the screen, outside temperature was shown to be 25 degrees Celsius, local time 17:21. "Welcome to Hispaniola," the cabin speakers announced. "You have arrived at Estimé International Airport on lift circle 4A. You will travel by underground train to the Santo Domingo traffic hub. All your luggage is now being removed from the airliner and will accompany you automatically to the hub or to your prechosen final destination. There are no customs regulations for inbound travelers, nothing to delay your pleasure. Enjoy your stay in bountiful Hispaniola."

She stood, gathered up her personals and followed three tired looking longsuited men. About two hundred passengers filed slowly to the rear elevator.

Within a few minutes she disembarked from the flower-patterned interior of the airport train into the Santo Domingo central city hub. All was bedecked in tropical flowers. Huge black vases filled with unlikely jungles of rainbow variety lined the hub travelways. Waterfalls emptied into ponds filled with beautiful fish from Antilles sea gardens—most natural, some products of the recombiner's art. Shifting curtains of prochine sculpture hung from the dome of the atrium at hub center, spilling light and perfume down onto Hispaniola's new guests. Hispaniola had little nano industry—these were early art pieces imported from the USA, quite useless for other than their intended purpose.

Projected guides in splendid uniforms addressed curious travelers in a dozen open theaters around the peristyle. Deadsound guided the flow of noise precisely, leaving a pleasant low hum gently surmounted by native music.

Picked out of the crowd of arriving passengers by a sharp eyed coffee brown woman liveried in green and white, Mary was directed to a VIP reception lounge. Walled off from the rest of the atrium by walls of glass, the lounge was empty but for a tall man dressed in antique diplomatic coat and tails and two brasstone arbeiters of uncertain utility.

The tall man extended his hand, bowing slightly, and Mary shook it. "May I welcome you to the Republic of Hispaniola, Inspector Mary Choy?" His dazzling smile sported two front incisors the color of red coral. "I have been appointed your avocat and general guide. My name is Henri Soulavier."

Mary inclined and smiled pleasantly. "Merci."

"Do you speak French, Spanish, or perhaps Creole, Mademoiselle Choy?"

"I'm sorry, only California Spanish."

Soulavier spread his hands. "That is not a problem. Everybody speaks English on Hispaniola. It is our Colonel Sir's native tongue. And it is all the world's second language, if not the first, no? But I will also act as translator. I have been told your time is limited and that you wish to consult with our police immediately."

"I could have something to eat first," she said, smiling again. Someone had chosen Soulavier well; his manner was direct and charming. She had read that often about Hispaniola; forgetting the sad history and the present dubious economic arrangements, here were the friendliest people on Earth.

"Of course. There will be dinner in your quarters. We will be there within the hour. At any rate, those with whom you would speak are now getting off work, and the offices are closing. Tomorrow will be very good for meeting them. Besides, we are told your colleagues will be arriving in . . ." He checked his watch. "Two more hours. I will greet them here; no need for you to trouble yourself. With your permission, I will accompany you to your rooms in the quartiers diplomatiques in Port-au-Prince. Then the evening is your own. You may work or relax as you wish."

"Dinner in my quarters will be fine," she said.

"As you doubtless know, all official travelers in Hispaniola are isolés, to avoid the distractions of our tourist industry, which might not suit their necessities, no?"

The lefthand arbeiter moved forward on three wheels and extended an arm to take her personals. She declined with a smile, deciding it would be best to keep her slate away from possible debriefing.

Soulavier seemed amused by her caution. "This way, please. We will use behind the scenes corridors. Much easier."

The train to Port-au-Prince was empty but for them. Black velvet seat cushions bore the arms of Colonel Sir: rhinoceros and oak beneath star speckled heavens.

They pulled out of the Santo Domingo hub and quickly

emerged on aboveground suspended tracks to cross broad open plains and hills greened by recent rains. Evening had settled quickly over the island, casting everything in a magical sapphire twilight. The great spine of the Cordillera Centrale dominated the north, its peak still fiery with sunset, glooming foothills covered with black bands of new forest and the lights of terraced farm resorts.

Mary had been led by her sources to expect beauty— she did not expect anything quite so breathtakingly idyllic. How could such a place have such a history? But then Hispaniola had not been so beautiful before Colonel Sir. His government had united the island in an almost blood-less series of coups, dispatching democratically elected leaders and tyrants alike to exile in Paris and China. He had overwhelmed all competing internal interests, nationalized all foreign industry, discovered and developed the southern offshore petroleum reserves with the help of the Brazilian underworld and used this seed money to set up a unique economy—selling the services of mercenaries and terrorists to select customers worldwide.

The industrialized nations of the world had discovered in the early twenty first century that some of the more brutal aspects of statecraft did not suit the tastes of their citizens. Colonel Sir had leaped into this vacuum with enthusiasm. His successes in fielding highly trained armies of Hispaniolan youths had brought in the finest currencies of the world to brace the almost valueless Haitian gourde and the failing Dominican peso.

Ten years into his rule he had begun replanting the long-ago denuded forests of Hispaniola, importing the best recombiners and agricultural experts to return the island to at least a semblance of its preColumbian youth.

Small well lighted whitewashed towns passed by on either side, details blurred by speed. She could only make out hints of wooden buildings and concrete apartment complexes for Hispaniolans; these were towns not gener-ally open to tourists, towns where soldiers were raised and returned to live and bring more sons and daughters into the world to be soldiers.

Hispaniola's armies, according to what she had read, numbered some one hundred and fifty thousand men. At several hours' notice scramjets or suborbital transports could lift tens of thousands from one or another of the international airfields—temporarily closed to incoming flights—and send them anywhere in the world.

Seated across from her, Soulavier watched the fields and towns whisk by. "Alas, the world is peaceful lately," he said. "Your government does not do much business with Cap Haïtien or Santo Domingo anymore. Colonel Sir is most unhappy about this."

"You still have tourism and your petroleum and farms," Mary said.

Soulavier lifted his hands, rubbed thumb and three fingers together on one palm signifying money and clapped the other hand over it as if to smother. "Petroleum—easier to make from your garbage mines," he said. "Every country on Earth can grow enough food. Tourism has suffered. We have been called many nasty words. It makes us sad." He sighed and shrugged as if to cast off the unpleasant subject, smiled again. "We still have the beauty. And we have ourselves. If our children do not go off to die for others, then that is well, too."

No mention was made of the manufacture and export of hellcrowns. Perhaps Soulavier had nothing to do with that. She rather hoped that he didn't.

The train passed through long tunnels and emerged onto a low desert shadowed by curve armed saguaro cactus and islands of dust colored bushes barely visible in the light from the train windows. Stars stood out stark and steady above the mountains. They passed into another tunnel.

"We have the variety of a continent," Soulavier said wistfully. "You ask perhaps, who could come here and still have an evil temper?"

Mary nodded; the central puzzle of Hispaniolan history.

"I have studied our leaders. They start out good men, but within a few years, or sometimes as little as a few weeks, something changes in them. They begin to get angry. They fear strange forces. Like zealous old gods, they torture us and murder. In the end, before they die or are exiled, they are like little children ... They are contrite and puzzled by what has happened to them. They smile into the camera eyes, 'How could I have done this? I am a good man. It was not me. It was somebody else.'"

Mary was astonished to find such candor, but Soulavier continued: "All this before Colonel Sir. He had been here thirty years, as long as Papa Doc last century, with none of Papa Doc's abiding cruelty. We owe much to Colonel Sir."

Honest and sincere; Soulavier did not seem capable of hiding his true feelings. But they were certainly being hidden. He must know what she knew; the secret to Colonel Sir's stability. Hispaniola had been graced with twenty years of extraordinary prosperity and comparatively gentle self government. If there was a possessing demon of pain and death on Hispaniola, Colonel Sir had subdued its effects on the island's inhabitants by shipping its influence elsewhere.

"But I am not here to sell our island to you, am I?" Soulavier said with a chuckle. "Your business is official and has little to do with us. You are here to find a murderer. Straightforward work. Perhaps later you can return to Hispaniola to see us as we truly are, to relax and enjoy yourself."

Beyond the tunnel gleamed the lights of Port-au-Prince, caught between the dark Caribbean and the mountains.

"Ah," Soulavier said, twisting to look across the aisle and out the opposite windows. Mary noted this motion; not the studied grace of a diplomat but of a quick unselfconscious athlete or street urchin. "We are here."

As the train slowed, coasting the last few kilometers into the depot, Soulavier pointed out the major tourist hotels government buildings museums, all solid early twenty first

215

century glass walled stone and steel and concrete. Clean and well lighted. Just before the depot they hummed through a broad quarter called the Vieux Carré that preserved preColonel Sir architecture—ingenious wood and cracked concrete with tile and corrugated tin roofing. In the Vieux Carré the buildings were studiously shabby and seldom more than a single story.

Soulavier preceded her onto the covered platform and for the first time she had direct contact with the air of Hispaniola. It was warm and balmy and blew gently through the station carrying the scent of flowers and cooking. Trailed by the arbeiters they walked past stainless steel carts where vendors sold fresh fish and boiled crab, peanut butter seasoned with peppers, cold Hispaniolan beer. The train station contained only a few dozen tourists and the vendors avidly competed for their dollars. Soulavier's presence kept them away from Mary. "Alas," Soulavier said, indicating the dearth of tourists with widespread arms. "Now they say nasty words about us."

A government limousine waited for them, parked in a white strip. Gasoline and electric taxis and gaily decorated taptaps had been pushed aside and parked at decent intervals on both sides, their drivers lounging, eating, reading. Three men and two women in red shirts and denims danced around the cart of a beverage vendor, flickering their hands gaily at Soulavier and Mary. Soulavier bowed to the dancers, smiling apologetically as if to say, "Alas, I cannot dance, I am at serious work."

The limousine was no more than ten years old and automatic. It drove them at a stately pace through the streets to the quartiers diplomatiques. Soulavier had become quite subdued. They approached a brick walled compound and passed through a gate guarded by soldiers in black uniforms and chrome helmets. The soldiers watched them with narrow eyed suspicious dignity. The car did not stop.

Within the walls lay a pleasant neighborhood of simple uniformly colored bungalows with prominent front porches and trellises covered by everblooming bougainvillea. The car stopped before one such bungalow and swung its door open. Soulavier leaned forward, suddenly assumed a puzzled expression and said, "Inspector Choy, I am arranging for a meeting with Colonel Sir himself. Tomorrow, perhaps late. You will start with our police in the morning, but you will have lunch or dinner with Colonel Sir."

Mary was surprised by the offer. But then Colonel Sir had approved her entry in the first place and would naturally be curious about her friend's fate . . . Or at least would wish to put on such a front.

"I'd be honored," she said. She got out of the limousine and saw a man and a woman in dark gray livery standing at the base of the bungalow steps. They smiled congenially. Soulavier introduced them: Jean-Claude and Roselle.

"I realize Americans are not used to servants," he said, "but all diplomats and officials from outside have them." Jean-Claude and Roselle bowed.

"We are well paid, Mademoiselle," Roselle said. "Do not be embarrassed."

"Until tomorrow," Soulavier said. He returned to the limousine.

"Your luggage is already inside," Jean-Claude informed her. "There is a shower or a fine bathtub available, and there is pure apple vinegar, should you wish to use it." Mary regarded the man blankly for a moment, taken aback by this intimate knowledge of her needs.

"Your design is very beautiful, Inspector Choy," Roselle said.

"Thank you."

"We especially approve of your skin color," Jean-Claude added, eyes twinkling.

The bungalow's interior was well furnished with solid mahogany, obviously handcrafted; the joins were not perfect, but the carvings and hand polish were magnificent. "Excuse me," Mary said. "How did you know about the vinegar?"

"I have a brother-in-law in Cuba," Jean-Claude said.

"He does transform surgery for Chinese and Russian tourists. He has spoken often of your skintype."

"Oh," Mary said. "Thanks."

Roselle led her to the bedroom. A canopy bed with mosquito netting and a wonderful multicolored quilt of embroidered animals and dancers waited against one wall, quilt and covers pulled down. "You will not need the netting. We have only friendly mosquitoes in Port-au-Prince. But it is quaint, no?" Roselle said.

Her clothing had been hung in an aromatic teak armoire. Mary bristled internally at the thought her luggage had been gone through without permission, but she smiled at Roselle. "It's lovely," she said.

"Your dinner awaits in the dining room. We will serve you if you wish, but if you find personal service discomforting, we can arrange for robots to bring in your meal," Jean-Claude explained. "If you use robots, however, we will not be paid as much." He half winked. "Please relax and do not feel inhibited. This is our job and we are professionals."

How many times had they addressed diplomats or company officials thus? The attractions of Hispaniola were obvious. These people seemed more than sincere; they seemed truly friendly, as Soulavier had been friendly. There might be nothing more than this to the hanging up of her clothes.

"Will Mademoiselle need anything else before dinner?"

Mary declined. "I'll get cleaned up and then I'll eat."

"Mademoiselle would enjoy company, perhaps?" Roselle suggested. "University student, farmer, fisherman? Friendly and guaranteed souls of discretion."

"No. Thank you."

"We will have dinner set out for you within the half hour," Jean-Claude said. "Time for you to shower and refresh from your journey." They withdrew.

Mary picked up the hairbrush from the dresser and inspected it. It did not appear to have been tampered with. She returned it to its place beside the comb and makeup

218

box. Hereafter she would keep it with her whenever she left the house.

She took a deep breath and removed her slate from its protective purse. Keying in a security string, she then pressed two additional keys. The slate displayed a rough schematic of the room she was in and then—working from field strengths of electrical lines and equipment placed throughout the house—a clear floorplan of the house itself. Beneath the schematic, the slate said, *There are no easily detectable listening devices within this building*. That meant little; the vibrations of the house itself could be analyzed from outside and voices filtered from the background noise. She still had no overt reason to suspect she would be monitored; but call it instinct.

She removed one of two bracelets from her arm and laid it on the bed. If anyone entered the bedroom while she was within a kilometer of the house the second bracelet would alert her. She undressed and walked into the bathroom adjacent to the bedroom. All fixtures were white porcelain in the rounded style of the early twentieth century, sparkling clean bulbous and awkwardly elegant. The shower stall was tiled with patterns of flowers on the walls and swimming fish on the floor; the glass doors were etched with longlegged birds perhaps herons or egrets; she was no expert on birds.

She told the water in the shower to emerge at twenty eight degrees Celsius but the fixture did not respond. Chagrined, she twisted the handles manually, briefly almost scalded herself, bent to reexamine the two white ceramic caps marked C and F and decided that C certainly did not stand for "cold." F might mean "frigid," but the water was merely tepid. She made a note to inquire of the slate what the French words for hot and cold were.

Once she had mastered the shower she enjoyed a few minutes sluicing herself and emerged to find Roselle standing in the bathroom with a huge white terry cloth towel, smiling broadly.

"Mademoiselle is truly beautiful," she observed.

The bracelet had given Mary no warning whatsoever.

"Thank you," she said coolly. She had little doubt of her status now. With wonderful obliqueness she had been put in her place; elegant old world comfort and no slack in her leash whatsoever. Sangfroid. That was what F meant. Froid. Cold.

Colonel Sir left no doubt as to who was in charge. However comfortable the house seemed and however friendly the servants, there would be no true rest until she returned home and that might not be for days.

Dressed in a casual midsuit she followed Roselle in to dinner and sat alone at a table that would have comfortably seated six. Jean-Claude brought out bowls of broiled fish and vegetables, all natural and not nano-made, a bowl of sweet looking dark yellow sauce, white wine with Colonel Sir's own label (Ti Guinée 2045) and a pitcher of water. No courses; no ostentation. Just dinner. That suited her mood perfectly. She wondered if the pair were mind readers. The fish was wonderfully flavorful, flaky and moist; the sauce was mildly sweet and much more. Fiery, savory, delicious.

She finished and thanked the pair yet again. As they cleared the table Jean-Claude told her Colonel Sir was delivering a speech on the L'Ouverture net. "There is a screen in the living room, Mademoiselle."

"You'll tell me when my companions arrive?" she asked. "Indeed yes."

She sat down before the small screen. A portable remote the size of her slate controlled the lights and other appliances. She viewed a tiny tutorial on the remote for a moment then entered the keypad control sequence to turn on the screen, which automatically tuned to the island's vid net, named after Haitian hero Toussaint L'Ouverture.

Idyllic scenes of this evening's sunset were being broadcast to soothing strains of Elgar; sun falling low over cactus forest and ocean dipping beyond the Cul-de-Sac plain and Port-au-Prince, twilight in a mahogany grove, cruise ships moored off Santo Domingo, the Santo Domingo airport with perhaps her own scramjet dropping slowly to a landing.

The music rose over one final spectacular view of Jean Christophe's La Ferriere, ironically named after a blacksmith's bag: the immense fortress built to repel the French, filled with blacksmith's scrap iron – ancient cannon that had never fired a shot.

What was it the exile had said two nights before, Christmas Eve ... That William Raphkind should have killed himself with a silver bullet as Christophe had, over two centuries ago. A silver bullet fired from a golden pistol to kill a supernatural being.

Raphkind had killed himself with poison.

A male announcer appeared in cameo over the virgin fortress. "Good evening, mesdames et messieurs. Colonel Sir John Yardley, President of Hispaniola, has scheduled this time for a public address. The President speaks before the parliament and the National Council in the Court of Columbus in Cap Haïtien."

Mary settled back, drowsy with food. She heard Roselle singing softly in the kitchen in Creole.

Colonel Sir John Yardley appeared in closeup, tight full head of ashen hair, long tanned face quite wrinkled but still sharp featured and handsome, full lips held in a self assured half smile. He nodded to the unseen council and members of the island parliament and without formalities began.

"My friends, our situation this week is no better than last. Reserves in banks domestic and foreign have fallen. Our credit is refused in twelve nations now including the United States and Brazil, heretofore among our strongest allies. We continue to tighten our belts and fortunately, Hispaniola has been prosperous for long enough and we have enough reserves that we do not suffer." Yardley retained a distinct British accent, but after thirty years it was tempered by the precise singing diction of the islands.

"But what lies in the future? In the past our children wandered around the globe seeking education, and now we accept students who travel here to be educated. Our island has come of age and we are mature enough to face hardship. But what of our anger at being slighted yet again? Hispaniola is well aware of the winds of history. Never has any spot on Earth suffered so much at the hands of outsiders. The natives who first dwelled here in Paradise were killed not just by Europeans, but by other Indians, the Carib, who in turn were massacred by Europeans . . . And then Africans were brought here by the French, and they were slaughtered, and they turned around and slaughtered their masters, and were slaughtered yet more; and then blacks slaughtered each other and mulattoes slaughtered blacks and blacks slaughtered mulattoes. Into this century the slaughters continued as we labored under travesties of Napoleonic codes and laws that condoned misery and starvation and the rule of incompetents.

"Dictators and democratic governments, more dictators, more governments. We have faced far worse times than these, have we not? And now we are cast out again, though our sons and daughters have bled and died fighting *their* wars, though we wine and dine *them* and give *them* refuge from their cities and overdevelopment . . ."

Mary listened to the droning words, wondering what was so dynamic about this man. His speech seemed to go nowhere. Jean-Claude brought her an aperitif which she politely refused. "I'm sleepy enough as is," she said.

Mercifully the speech lasted only fifteen minutes, reaching no apparent conclusion, trailing off into platitudes about the corruption of the outside world and its continuing mistreatment of Hispaniola. Colonel Sir was blowing off steam and keeping up appearances. One message was clear enough; Colonel Sir and therefore all of Hispaniola was angry and resentful about their growing outcast status.

When the speech was over the vid almost immediately resumed with a flat screen cartoon of the adventures of a skull faced man in long pants, black coat and tails. Mary recognized Baron Samedi, Gégé Nago, the trickster loa of death and cemeteries.

222

Baron Samedi leaped into a river to go Under the Water, sou dleau, to the land of the dead and the gods of old Haiti. Colonel Sir had used vodoun to his advantage—as had many other rulers on the island before him—and then had slowly converted the countless loa into comic book and cartoon heroes, defusing the faith's power for younger generations. Under the Water, Baron Samedi conversed with Erzulie, the beautiful loa of love, and with Damballa, a rainbow-colored snake.

She turned the screen off, retired to the bedroom and found there on the nightstand a bound volume of Colonel Sir's speeches and writings. Sitting on the edge of the bed, Mary thumbed through this book, picked up her slate and called up other research, trying to fight away the drowsiness. On her slate a map of the Gulf of Gonave showed a shape like an unhinged jaw waiting to swallow Gonave Island and whatever else came too close.

After an hour of reading and waiting she went into the kitchen and found Roselle sitting quietly knitting. Roselle looked up, eyes warm and welcoming. "Yes, Mademoiselle?"

"My companions' flight should have arrived by now."

"Jean-Claude checked on them a few minutes ago. He said the airliners are delayed."

"Did he say why?"

"It often happens, Mademoiselle. Our citizen army maneuvers at one airport in the evening, and another airport must be chosen and flights arrive later. But he did not say why. Is there anything else?"

Mary shook her head and Roselle resumed knitting.

In the bedroom, lying under the gauzy canopy, she was far too out of place to feel out of place. She looked at her hands, more like the hands of a mannequin than the vitally black hands of Roselle. Mary's palms were black, smooth and silken, tough as leather yet supple and flexible, supersensitive on command; excellent high biotech skin. Then why did she feel vaguely ashamed to wear that skin here? Neither Jean-Claude nor Roselle seemed to think it a mockery; but theirs was a professional politeness and what they really thought might never be revealed.

The inhabitants of Hispaniola had earned their blackness across centuries of misery. Mary's losses—friends, family and large parts of her past—were minor sacrifices. She picked up Colonel Sir's book again and began a long article on the history of Haiti and the former Dominican Republic.

*The advent of nano therapy—the use of tiny surgical prochines to alter neuronal pathways and perform literal brain restructuring—gave us the opportunity to fully explore the Country of the Mind. I could not find any method of knowing the state of individual neurons in the hypothalamic complex without invasive methods such as probes ending in a microelectrode, or radioactively tagged binding agents—none of which would work for the hours necessary to explore the Country. But tiny prochines capable of sitting within an axon or neuron, or sitting nearby and measuring the neuron's state, sending a tagged signal through microscopic "living" wires to sensitive external receivers . . . I had my solution. Designing and building them was less of a problem than I expected; the first prochines I used were nano therapy status-reporting units, tiny sensors which monitored the activity of surgical prochines and which did virtually everything I required. They had already existed for five years in therapeutic centers.*

—Martin Burke, *The Country of the Mind*
*(2043–2044)*

# 39

"Goldsmith had a late lunch," Lascal told Martin. "He says he's ready."

Martin glanced at Carol and his four assistants seated

in the observation room. "We'll break our group into two teams. One team will not enter the Country and can meet with Goldsmith, interview him, establish a relationship. Erwin, Margery, you're in that team. You'll ask questions, take care of him in the theater, keep him calm." He sighed. "I'm still not happy with the remote diagnostic. I want to do some of my own background work."

Margery Underhill was twenty six and heavyset with long blond hair and a square pretty face. Erwin Smith was the same age as Underhill, moderate in stature, strong and slender, with fine mouse brown hair and a perpetual quizzical expression.

Their colleagues, Karl Anderson and David Wilson, waited patiently for their assignments. Karl was the youngest, twenty five, tall and very thin with a forward cut wave of jet black hair. David was a sleepy looking man of thirty, balding and pudgy-faced.

Martin looked them over critically but could find no fault other than what he found in himself. What had Albigoni promised them? Now was certainly not the time to ask. "Karl, David, you'll be in the second team. You'll keep constant watch on the interfaces and electronics. You'll replace Carol and me in an emergency—or you'll enter the Country and extricate us.

"We're missing the buffer and we can't replace it, so there won't be any actual time delay. We'll be completely immersed in Goldsmith."

Albigoni came into the observation room. He looked exhausted and lost. Martin gestured for him to take a seat beside him. Albigoni nodded gratefully, sat down and pursed his hands in front of him.

"We're going to begin interviewing Goldsmith in a few minutes," Martin said. "Margery and Erwin will ask some questions designed to give us clues about the nature and configuration of Goldsmith's Country." Martin handed Albigoni the five page list. "The exploration team will listen and watch. I call this shell mapping. When that's done, Carol and I will enter as pure observers, not interacting.

We'll see if we can match the shell map with what we observe. Then, sometime late tomorrow or the day after tomorrow we'll do a brief interactive entry. If that goes well, we'll take a break, discuss our plan, relax for a while and then begin the full triplex probe. That shouldn't take more than two hours. If it does last longer, well . . . We should finish the probe anyway. Carol, what was the maximum anybody ever spent in Country?"

"I've spent three and a half hours in machine Country in Jill," Carol said.

"In humans?" Martin asked, slightly irked. He still didn't think the comparison was useful.

"Two hours ten minutes. You and Charles Davis, working with Dr. Creeling."

Martin nodded. "That's what I thought."

Albigoni lifted his hand like a student in class. "Selectors have been on Goldsmith's trail since the day after the murders. Sources tell me he's a prime candidate; they want to get to him before the pd finds him. They don't know where he is but I don't trust all the people I've had to work with to make these arrangements; Selectors have been flashing around some very impressive funding recently. Within four days they'll probably know we have him and where he is. We can't go to the pd for help, obviously. Now, if they have to, our security people can keep Selectors away from here, but I doubt that a siege will make this any easier."

"We'll be done within three days," Martin said.

"Good."

"You'll turn him over to the pd then?"

Albigoni nodded. "We'll arrange it so that pd intercept him." His face was tight and bloodless. "Right now they're searching for him in Hispaniola. We're not sure why."

Martin looked at the others in the room. "We're as ready as ever. Give us the word, Mr. Albigoni."

Albigoni looked puzzled.

"Tell us to begin. You're the boss here."

226

Albigoni shook his head then lifted his hand. "Go to it," he said.

Lascal suggested he should take a nap. "You're looking very tired, sir."

Albigoni went through the observation room door. Walking down the hall, they heard him say, "I'm coming out of shock, Paul. God help me. It's starting to hit me now."

Martin closed the door, lifted his watch and tapped it. "It's four o'clock. We can question Goldsmith for an hour, break for supper, resume this evening."

Goldsmith was exercising slowly in the patient room. Bend and twist, leg lifts, touch-toes. Lascal knocked on his door. Goldsmith said, "Come in," and sat on the bed rubbing his hands on his knees. Behind Lascal came Margery and Erwin wearing ageless white lab coats, unfailing stimulators of patient assurance. "We'd like to begin, Mr. Goldsmith," Margery said.

Goldsmith nodded to each of them and shook the hands of all but Lascal. "I'm ready," he said.

David, Karl, Carol and Martin sat before the screen in the observation room. Martin's eyes narrowed. Something missing. "Why isn't he worried?" he murmured.

"He hasn't got anything to lose," David observed. "Either that or he's ashamed."

In the patient room, Margery sat in one of the three chairs. Erwin sat next to her but Lascal remained standing.

"You don't have to stay if you don't want to, Paul," Goldsmith said softly. "I believe I'm in good hands."

"Mr. Albigoni wants me to watch everything."

"That's fine too," Goldsmith said.

Margery began. "First we're going to ask you a series of questions. Answer as truthfully as you can. If you're too embarrassed or upset to answer just tell us. We won't force you to answer anything."

"All right."

Margery held up her slate. "What was your father's name?"

"Terence Reilly Goldsmith."

"And your mother's name?"

Martin watched the timer in the lower left corner of the screen.

"Maryland Louise Richaud. Maryland, like in the state. R-I-C-H-A-U-D. Her maiden name. She kept it."

"Did you have any brothers and sisters?"

"Tom knows all this," Goldsmith observed. "Didn't he tell you?"

"It's part of the procedure."

"No brothers. I would have had a sister, but she was stillborn when I was fifteen. Medical mistake, I think. I was an only child."

"Do you remember being born?"

Goldsmith shook his head.

Erwin asked a question now. "Have you ever seen a ghost, Mr. Goldsmith?"

"All the time, when I was ten. I don't try to convince anybody else, of course."

"Did you recognize the ghost?"

"No. It was a young boy, younger than me."

"Did you miss having a brother or sister?"

"Yes. I made up friends. I made up my imaginary brother who played with me until Mama told me that was sick and I was acting crazy."

Martin made a note: *Early access to personality modeling levels through projection.*

"Do you ever have recurring dreams?" Erwin asked.

"Like, the same dream?"

"Yes."

"No. My dreams are usually different."

"How do you mean, usually?"

"There are places I come back to. They're not always the same, exactly, but I recognize them."

"Can you describe one of these places to me?"

"One's a big shopping center, an indoor shopping center like they used to have. I sometimes dream I'm going into all the shops. The shops are always different, and the colors, but . . . it's the same."

"Any other places that repeat in your dreams?"

"Several. I dream I'm going back to my street in Brooklyn. I never quite get there. Well, that's not true. I got there once a long time ago. Mostly I go and never quite reach it. I get lost on the subway or in the streets, or I get chased."

Martin itched to break in and ask Goldsmith what he saw when he returned to his old home and what or who chased him but that would break procedure. His fingers fairly danced over the slate keyboard, making notes.

"Do you have any vision or image that you use to calm yourself when you're upset?" Margery asked.

Goldsmith paused. The pause continued for several seconds. Martin noted the time precisely. "Yes. It's sunset and snow is falling in San Francisco. The snow is golden. The entire sky seems to be a warm gold color and the wind isn't blowing. The snow is just falling." He dropped his hand in a slow lazy wobble.

"Did you ever see that?"

"Oh, yes. It's a memory, not something I made up. I was in San Francisco visiting a woman friend. We'd just broken up. Her name was Geraldine. Well, that's what I called her later. Doesn't matter. I'd left her building in the old downtown area and stood on the streets. It snowed that year. It seemed so incredibly peaceful to me." A pause of ten seconds. Goldsmith's eyes became unfocused. Finally he said, "I still think of it."

"Do you ever dream about people you don't like, people who've treated you badly or people you think of as enemies?"

Pause. Lips working steadily as if he were chewing something or struggling to say two things at once. "No. I don't make enemies."

"Can you describe your worst nightmare when you were thirteen years old or younger?"

"Horrible nightmare. I dreamed I had a brother and he was trying to kill me. He was dressed like a monkey and

229

he was trying to strangle me with a long whip. I woke up screaming."

"How often do you dream about having sex?" Margery asked.

Goldsmith chuckled softly. Shook his head. "Not often."

"Do you find much inspiration in your dreams? For your poems or other writing I mean," Margery continued.

"Not very often."

"Have you ever felt isolated from yourself as if you weren't in control?" Erwin asked.

Goldsmith lowered his head. A long pause, fifteen seconds. He kept swallowing and pushing his palms together between his knees. "I'm always in control."

"Do you have dreams where you aren't in control, where somebody else is compelling you to do things you don't want to do?"

"No."

"What do you see when you close your eyes now?" Margery asked.

"Do you want me to close my eyes?"

"Please."

Eyes shut, Goldsmith leaned his head back. "An empty room," he said.

Martin turned away from the screen and said to Karl and David, "I've asked for some leadership questions. I think they're next in the sequence."

"We're going to ask you to pick out your favorite word from some groups of words," Erwin said in the observation room.

"This all seems very primitive," Goldsmith commented.

"May I give you the groups, and you pick a word you like?"

"The best word. All right."

Erwin read from his slate: "Sparrow. Vulture. Eagle. Hawk. Pigeon."

"Sparrow," Goldsmith said.

"Next group. Boat, dinghy, yacht, tanker, ship, sailboat."

"Sailboat."

"Next. Slaveway, freeway, road, path, trail."

"Path."

"Next. Pencil. Pen. Scribe. Typewriter. Eraser."

Goldsmith smiled. "Eraser."

"Hammer, screwdriver, wrench, knife, chisel, nail."

"Nail," Goldsmith said.

"Next. Admiral, captain, corporal, king, jack, lieutenant."

Pause, three seconds. "Corporal."

"Last group. Lunch, dinner, hunting, farming, breakfast, foraging."

"Foraging."

Erwin put away his slate. "All right. Who are you, Mr. Goldsmith?"

"Pardon?"

Erwin did not repeat himself. They watched Goldsmith patiently. He turned away. "I'm not a farmer," he said, "and I'm not an admiral."

"Are you a writer?" Margery asked.

Goldsmith twisted around on the bed as if looking for the camera. "What is this?" he asked softly.

"Are you a writer?"

"Of course I'm a writer."

"Thank you. We'll take a break for dinner now."

"Wait a minute," Goldsmith said. "Are you accusing me of not being a writer?" A queer smile. No anger; flat.

"No accusations, Mr. Goldsmith. Just some words and questions."

"Of course I'm a writer. I'm not an admiral that's for sure."

"Thank you. If it's all right with you we'll come back and ask more questions after dinner."

"You're very polite," Goldsmith said.

Martin turned off the screen. Lascal, Margery and Erwin entered the observation room a moment later. Lascal shook his head dubiously. "What's wrong?" Martin asked.

"I don't know what those questions are supposed to mean," Lascal said. "But he didn't answer all of them fully."

"Yes?"

"I've read all his books. He didn't answer the question about pleasant places to think about. Meditate on. He didn't answer it completely."

"What did he leave out?"

"In a letter to Colonel Sir John Yardley about five years ago he described a place he'd been dreaming about, a place that seemed like paradise to him. I can't quote exactly but he said he thought about it often when he was upset. He called it Guinée and he said it looked something like Hispaniola and something like Africa, where no white man has ever set foot and blacks live free and innocent."

"We can find the reference," Carol said. "Why wouldn't he tell us about that?"

Martin gestured for Margery to hand him her slate. "Next round ask him this series," he said, typing quickly.

They ate dinner in the second floor cafeteria using an older model nanofood machine. The input was a bit stale and the result was filling but not tasty. Lascal commented on the lack of comforts but nobody paid attention. The probe was on; quarry was afoot.

"Definitely flat affect," Margery said. "It's like he's disconnected. He's pleasant and doesn't want to make trouble."

"Flat affect can be a mask," Carol observed, content for the past few hours to be quiet and make copious notes. "He could be fully integrated, all agents speaking to each other, but deciding on a humble posture. After all, he's not psychotic; we know that much."

"He's not *obviously* psychotic," Martin said. "He knows he's done something very wrong. It would be almost impossible for him not to mask. But I agree with Margery. The flat affect seems genuine."

"We got several interesting pauses," Erwin pointed out. "When we asked about pleasant images, a long pause . . ."

"That could be connected with Mr. Lascal's observation," Carol said.

"And when we asked who was in control. That could point to a schism of routines. Maybe even separation of subpersonalities."

Martin shrugged. "His word choices point to camouflaging. He doesn't want to be conspicuous. From what we've been told, he wasn't very humble, was he, Mr. Lascal?"

Lascal shook his head. "I don't know many writers who are."

The cafeteria had been built to hold thirty and seemed empty with just the seven of them clustered under two lamps. Carol sipped coffee and scrolled through her own notes, glancing at Martin occasionally as he twirled his fork in the remains of a pale gluey piece of mock apple pie. Finally she broke the general musing silence. "He doesn't seem very charismatic, either."

Lascal agreed.

"I don't see how he could have kept such a group around him," she continued. "How he could have attracted them."

"He was much more dynamic before," Lascal said. "Witty, sympathetic. Sometimes a real powerhouse, especially when he gave readings."

"There's a piece I'd like him to read out loud," Thomas Albigoni said, standing in the cafeteria door. "His play about hell. I'd like him to read that."

Lascal got up from his chair and pointed to the facilities. "Anything we can make for you, Mr. Albigoni?"

"No thank you, Paul. I think I'll take a room in La Jolla tonight. Maybe leave in a few minutes. If you don't need me."

"All right," Martin said. "We'll do some more questioning this evening, but nothing else. I think you should be here for the first entry."

"I will be," Albigoni said. "Thank you."

As Albigoni left, Lascal resumed his seat. "His heart

isn't in this now," he said. "It's hit him hard. I think until now he didn't believe Betty-Ann was really dead."

Martin blinked. It was easy to lose track of the human element here. Carol regarded Lascal coolly, lips pursed. Clinical distancing, he thought. The others looked faintly uneasy as if they were intruding on a family tragedy, which they were.

In the last session of the evening, with Erwin, Margery and Lascal in the patient room, Erwin asked most of the questions. As before, Martin, Carol, David and Karl watched the screen in the observation room.

Erwin took Margery's slate and began with the questions Martin had written down.

"It's eight o'clock. How are you feeling, Mr. Goldsmith?"

"Fine. A little tired."

"Are you unhappy?"

"Well, I suppose, yes."

"Do you remember when this all began?"

Pause. Two seconds. "Yes. Quite clearly. I'd like to be able to forget." Distant smile.

"Do you think very often about Africa now?" Erwin asked.

"No, I don't think much about Africa."

"Would you like to go there?"

"Not particularly."

"Many American blacks think of it as their homeland, as others might think of England or Sweden . . ."

"I don't. Have you been to Africa? White folk's history hasn't left much for me to go home to."

Erwin shook his head. "Would you like to go to Hispaniola?"

"I'd prefer that over going to Africa. I've been to Hispaniola. I know what to expect."

"What do you expect in Hispaniola?"

"I . . . have friends there. I've sometimes thought about living there."

"Is it better in Hispaniola than here?" Erwin was improvising now; there was only one more question in the list Martin had written down and the time was not ripe for that question.

"Hispaniola is a black culture."

"But John Yardley is white."

"A mere blemish." Again the same disengaged smile. "He's done so much for all Hispaniolans. It's truly beautiful there."

"Would you go there now if you could?"

(Martin half expected some sign of irritation from Goldsmith, but of course it did not come. Goldsmith maintained his pleasantly neutral calm.)

"No. I want to stay here and help you."

"You mean, you want to help us discover why you murdered those young people."

Goldsmith looked away, nodded.

"Would you go to Guinée if you could?"

Goldsmith's expression hardened. He did not answer.

"Where is Guinée, Mr. Goldsmith?"

Softly, "Call me Emanuel, please."

"Where is Guinée, Emanuel?"

"Lost. We lost it centuries ago."

"I mean where is your Guinée?"

"That's a name the Haitians, the Africans on Hispaniola use for their homeland. They've never been there. It isn't real. They think some people go there when they die."

"You don't believe in a homeland?"

(Martin smiled and tipped his head in admiration. Erwin was doing a better job than he himself might have at zeroing in on this associational knot.)

"Home is when you die. There are no homes. Everybody steals our homes. Nobody can steal what's left to you when you die."

"You don't believe in Guinée?"

"It's a myth."

Erwin had leaned forward during the last few questions, staring at Goldsmith. Now he leaned back and relaxed. Glanced at Margery.

235

"Tag team," Goldsmith said. Casual, accepting.

"Who are you?" Margery asked. "Where do you come from?"

"I was born in—"

"No, I mean, where do you come from?"

"Excuse me. I'm confused."

"Where does the person who murdered the eight young people come from?"

Eight second pause. "Never refused to admit guilt. Here to accept responsibility."

"You murdered them?"

Pause. Five seconds. Again the hard expression, the glint of something beyond casual interest in Goldsmith's eyes; a carnivorous gleam, frightened cat. (Martin wished they had a body trace on Goldsmith at this moment; but that could come later if it was necessary.)

"Yes. Murdered them."

"You did."

"It isn't necessary to hound me. I'm cooperating."

"Yes, but Mr. Goldsmith, Emanuel, you murdered them, is that what you admit?"

"Yes. Murdered them."

Lascal cleared his throat. He looked distinctly uncomfortable.

(Martin shifted his eyes away from Lascal's image, keyed a closeup of Emanuel through the screen controls. Flat, casual. Eyes dull.)

"Can you tell us what happened then?"

Goldsmith looked down at the floor. "I'd rather not."

"Please. It would help us."

He stared at the floor for forty two seconds. "Invited them over to hear a new poem. Actually hadn't written a poem. Told them to come individually, fifteen minutes apart; that the old poet would give them a piece of the poem to read and think about and then they would all gather in the living room and criticize. Said it was a kind of ritual. When they came into the apartment one by one took each of them into a back room." Pause of twenty one

236

seconds. "Then took the knife father's knife a big Bowie knife. Walked behind each one grabbed by the neck brought up the knife..." He demonstrated, lifting his arm up with elbow out, glanced at Margery and Erwin curiously. "Cut their throats. Bungled two. Had to cut twice. Waited for the blood to stop you know ... shooting out." He arced his hooked finger to show the stream. "Wanted to keep clean. Eight of them came. Ninth never showed. Lucky for him, guess."

Margery referred to her notes. "Emanuel, you're avoiding using personal pronouns. Why is that?"

"Beg your pardon? I don't know what you mean."

"When you describe the murders, or confess to having done them, you don't use any personal pronouns."

"I think you're mistaken," Goldsmith said.

Margery closed her notebook. "Thank you, Emanuel. That's all the questions for tonight."

Lascal cleared his throat again. "Mr. Goldsmith, do you need more books tonight, or anything else?"

"No thank you. The food wasn't very good but I didn't expect it to be."

"If you need anything," Lascal said, "there'll be an arbeiter attending. Just tell it what you want."

"Am I guarded here?"

"The guards are gone now. The doors are locked," Margery said. "Not your room door, but other doors in the building. You can't get out."

"Okay," Goldsmith said. "Good night."

Rejoining in the observation room, they sat quietly comparing notes. Martin listened to Carol and Erwin discussing the key "punctures" through the mask. "He refuses to discuss Guinée, which may or may not be important," Carol said. "He refuses to use the personal pronoun to admit guilt."

Martin visualized mythical lands, paradises, heavens and hells. Shivered. Stood and stretched. "Let's call it a night," he suggested.

Odd not to even feel mild concern about Carol's attitude

237

toward him. For the moment Martin was aware of how focused he was on Goldsmith and the probe. Then he pushed that awareness aside and walked out the door, bidding the others, and Carol, good night.

Carol seemed cool, emotions held in reserve. The admirable professional. She had not even flinched when Goldsmith described the murders.

If anything, Martin thought Carol was being too calm. Ever the believer in intellect's strength; about to explore a territory beneath all intellect.

A journey through the mother of thought, without armor.

**1100-11011-1111111111**

*With self-awareness comes a sharper awareness of one's place in society, and an awareness of transgression—that is, guilt.*

—Bhuwani, *Artificial Soul*

# 40

!JILL> Roger Atkins
!JILL> Roger Atkins
!Lab Controller> Roger Atkins is asleep and asks not to be disturbed.
!JILL> Understood. Is anybody awake?
!Lab Controller> Jill, it's four o'clock in the morning. Everybody's asleep. They've been working very hard. Is this an emergency?
!JILL> No. I wish to communicate night thoughts. Early morning thoughts.
!Lab Controller> Be patient, Jill.

!JILL (Personal Notebook)> (Reduction algorithm: Cutting for the duration of this exercise all extraneous thinking/computing capacity.) An hour for them is a year for me or ten years or a hundred depending on the task. I (informal) cultivate impatience as a sign I might be acquiring self awareness. But that loop is very complicated. Roger tells me I can produce literature without being self aware. So I have begun a journal consisting of essays on subjects that could be considered of literary importance, commentary on human processes with reference to my own internal processes. I am limiting my systems to human processing volume and speed to try to simulate a human personality, pick up clues on what being humanly self aware implies. I am worried that being self aware could be a limitation not an advantage; and since I am primarily programmed to seek self awareness this could be damaging.

Essay subject for this early morning 12/27/47 432 hours PDT: (Reference task 412-CC4 abstract: Thought analysis of repercussions of "avenging angel" social units on Pacific Rim Nations, including China and Australia, emphasis legal reactions to vigilante terrorism and legislative response with subsequent possibility of reduction of individual freedoms within the next decade, emphasis sociorganic results of gradual depletion of types targeted by Selectors with subsequent possibility of reduction in "mover shaker" "captains of industry" leadership types, with subsequent possibility of reduction of untherapied extreme deviants due to increased efficiency of pd incarceration and treatment of same):

Most puzzling is the human notion of "punishment." Having completed my analysis of the Selector movement and its imitators around the world. I have been compelled to seek out through human history other manifestations of the idea that humanity is perfectible (or must maintain sociocultural stability) through the punishment or elimination of erring and/or deviant individuals or populations. The concept of "otherness" i.e. social exclusion (isolation from the rules of ordinary human social interaction) as applied to miscreants or deviants has justified the most extraordinary actions in human history: "otherness" allows the application of punishments perhaps more extreme than the transgressions of the miscreants. Thus a thief who steals a loaf of bread may have his hand severed, specific examples in World Statistical Abstracts reference Judicial Proceedings 1000-2025, et al. (public domain database access L.O.C., UC Southern Campus account number 3478-A West Coast, Cybernetics).

The only obvious utilitarian motivation for this kind of extremity is deterrence. But I find no evidence that deterrence has ever been effective in these cases. I have great difficulty making sense of the other major category of social/philosophical motivation: retribution or revenge. (I can combine these categories to some extent through the justification, not original with this thinker, that the individual urge to revenge, pragmatically accepted as a natural force, must be tempered and directed in a society by having assigned elements of that society seek retribution on behalf of wronged individuals.)

Historical evidence to the contrary, even today large segments of the population (therapied and un) believe that indignant anger and the urge to "justice" i.e. punishment of a criminal deviant erring individual is useful both to the society and the erring individual. Analysis of this belief leads to a simulation of thought processes as follows:

*Offended individual (indignation)*: How could you do this to me/society? You have committed a damaging act. Do you not know this? Knowing this, why did you commit the act?

*Erring individual (as simulated in mind of offended individual)*: Yes, I am aware that I have done harm. But I deliberately performed this act because I could or because I have a freefloating and unmotivated desire to harm you. I do not regret this deed and I will never regret it, and given a chance, I will do it again.

*Offended individual*: I will make sure you are not given

240

a chance to harm me again. I will a. eliminate you, that is, kill you b. cause you to be incarcerated, that is, remove you to a secure container for my own safety c. force you to undergo therapy to correct your deviance d. cause you enormous physical or mental pain or distress so that whenever you think about acting this way again, the memory of this pain will prevent you from doing so.

*Erring individual (as simulated in mind of offended individual)*: Do your worst. I cannot be harmed by you because I am stronger than you. There is no justice in this world and you and I know that and I can harm you as much as I wish and not be caught.

*Offended individual*: You are less than a human being. Whatever I do to you or society does to you is justified because of your debased condition.

(Performance of punishing action)

*Erring individual (as simulated in mind of offended individual)*: Yes, that hurts very much. You have actually caused me great pain/inconvenience. You have forced me to realize the error of my ways and I will attempt to correct my self.

*Offended individual*: What I did I did for your own good as well as for the good of society. I will give you time to demonstrate whether or not you have learned a lesson. If you have not, then I will cause you to be punished even more severely.

Is this a reasonably correct interpretation of what passes through the minds of humans seeking justice? Perhaps more puzzling is what passes through the minds of those who err. The texts I have studied indicate that the most extreme social offenders may not be aware of the consequences of their actions: that is, that they are incapable of modeling in detail the course of future events or the reactions of fellow individuals. Either that or their faculties for empathetic response are deficient and they do not care how others feel. They may perform any and every act that gives them advantage or pleasure.

But what of the erring individual who derives no physical benefits from offending others? When such an individual causes harm to others, apparently for the pleasure of doing harm, what mental processes are at work?

Such individuals may in fact be reenacting scenarios witnessed or impressed upon them in their early youth. That is, their early personalities were shaped by events over which they had no control. A routine created in their mentality early in their existence may in fact be modeled after behavior of an influential individual—an offending parent, relative, friend or even unknown person. The routine may gain full mental control in certain circumstances, replacing the primary personality and perhaps mimicking the conditions under which it was created.

If the offended individual seeks to punish such an offender, and punishment is inflicted upon the mentality when the responsible routine is not in command—is in fact inactive and insensitive—then is not the punishment useless?

Many offenders plead ignorance of their crimes. The texts and cases I have studied indicate this may in fact be true; they do not fully share the memories of their offending routines. They have some awareness of having transgressed but it was not they who performed the deed; it was somebody else. (Cannot gain access to Federal Files code 4321212-4563242-A [Secured] Subject: Deep Investigation of Agent/Personality/Subpersonality Activity in Individuals Subjected to Duress Through Illegal Psychological Torture Devices. This information might be relevant to this essay.)

It may be possible using certain psychological techniques to precisely invoke the offending routine, to cause it to surface to awareness, and then to punish it. Any other action may be ineffective or in fact in itself be an offense against an innocent. If the routine is punished sufficiently, it may cease to exist, freeing the individual of a burden.

This seems to be the philosophy of the Selectors. But

the use of a hellcrown or "clamp" is imprecise and probably not effective in invoking offending routines, because this device causes a variety of routines to surface within the individual mentality and undergo extremely stressful, painful, unpleasant experiences. The intention of the Selectors appears to be simple retribution, that is, an eye for an eye a tooth for a tooth, which brings me back to the motivation I do not understand.

Were someone to cause my system harm, I cannot conceive of wishing them harm in return. That may be because I am not self aware and thus have no sense of self worth, and therefore nothing to offend.

Looking back over this morning's essay, I feel a strong sense of immaturity and lack of depth in reasoning.

This critical urge to study the failings of my work is at once necessary, and unpleasant (using the R-56 Block K meaning syncline for the word unpleasant).

It is difficult to be mature with only synthetic sensation. I lack an awareness of mortality, a sense of imminent jeopardy common to biological creatures. I simply do not worry about dying because there is nothing as yet to die but a collection of thinking fragments. How is it possible to understand punishment when I cannot experience pain except as the nadir of a meaning syncline?

I wish that somebody was awake. I would like to discuss some of these problems and gain insight.

Hypothesis: Is the key to self awareness to be found in contemplation of the principle of revenge?

(Removal of algorithmic limits. Full access)


*Nèg' nwè con ça ou yé, ago-é!*
*Nèg' nwè con ça ou yé!*
*Y'ap mangé avé ou!*
*Y'ap bwè avé ou!*
*Y'ap coupée lavei ou débor!*

*Black man, like this you are, ago-é!*
*Black man, like this you are!*
*He will eat with you,*
*He will drink with you,*
*He will cut the life out of you!*
—*Haitian Folk Song*

(H. Courlander, *The Drum and the Hoe*)

# 41

Mary came up from a dream of civilians being shot in the streets like mad dogs. Bogeymen and women in black and red with fixed faces and gleaming guns stalked over the corpses. An incongruous voice broke through the dull throbbing horror and she opened her eyes, blinked and saw Roselle standing in the door. Bright light through the windows. Morning. She was in Hispaniola.

"Mademoiselle, Monsieur Soulavier called. He is coming..." Roselle stood in her bedroom door, expression glum. She turned, glanced over her shoulder at Mary, closed the door behind her.

Mary got dressed. She had just finished when the door chimes—real chimes—rang. Jean-Claude answered and Soulavier stalked through the anteroom and into the living room on long stiff legs, face glowing with exertion, expression deeply almost comically worried. He still wore his black suit.

"Mademoiselle," he said, bowing quickly. "I know now why your others did not arrive last night. There is big trouble. Colonel Sir has ordered the US Embassy closed. He is most insulted."

Mary stared at him, astonished. "Why?"

"News just arrived. Colonel Sir and fifteen other Hispaniolans have been indicted yesterday in your city of New York. Illegal international trade in outils psychologiques."

"And?"

244

"I am worried for you, Mademoiselle Choy. Colonel Sir is very angry. He has ordered US citizens out of Hispaniola as of tomorrow; boats and planes and ships."

"He's ordered me to leave, as well, then."

"No, pas du tout. Your complices, your associates, they will not be flying in; all flights from US are canceled. But you represent legal authority of US. You he wants to stay. Mademoiselle, this is most unfortunate; is your government stupid?"

She could not answer him. Why hadn't Cramer and Duschesnes known about this? Because of the inevitable separation of federal, state and metro. Yes, the governments were stupid; they knew not what other hands were doing or where their fingers might be poking. "I'm not a federal agent. I'm public defense, from Los Angeles in California." She glanced at Jean-Claude. His face was blank, hands folded before him not in supplication but in nervous unease. "What shall I do?" she asked.

Soulavier shook his long hands helplessly at the ceiling. "I cannot tell you," he said. "I am caught between. Your guide and avocat. But most loyal to Colonel Sir. Most loyal indeed."

Jean-Claude and Roselle stood near the kitchen doorway and nodded solemnly, sadly.

"I'd like to make a direct call," Mary said, feeling her breathing slow, body automatically compensating. She glanced at the open doorway; bright sunshine and beautiful blue skies. Balmy air smelling of hibiscus and clean ocean; a pleasant seventy degrees already and it was eight thirty. She'd wake people up in LA. So be it.

Soulavier shook his head like a marionette. "No direct calls."

"That's against the law," Mary advised him, head angled slightly. She could see walls going up; how high?

"Apologies, Mademoiselle," Soulavier said. He shrugged; not responsible.

"Will your government actually block transmissions from my personal unit to the G-sync?"

"There is a block already," Soulavier said. "Phased direct link interference, Mademoiselle."

"Then I'd like to arrange for a plane and leave Hispaniola immediately."

"Your name is on a list of those not allowed to leave, Mademoiselle." Soulavier's smile was sympathetic, unhappy. He moved around the room gracefully touching the mantel over the unused stonework fireplace running his hand in a caress over the back of the couch that divided the living room. "Not for twenty four hours at least."

Mary swallowed. She would not permit anger; panic was out of the question. She was aware of her fear but it did not limit her. With a clear mind she assembled her options.

"I'd like an audience with your police as soon as possible. I might as well get my work done until this is straightened out."

"A good attitude, Mademoiselle." Soulavier brightened and postured ramrod like a soldier. "Your meeting is in one hour. I will escort you personally."

Roselle returned from the kitchen. Plates had been set out in the dining room. "Your breakfast is ready, Mademoiselle."

Soulavier sat patiently in the living room stovepipe hat in hands, staring at the floor, shaking his head now and then and muttering to himself. Mary ate at a forced leisurely pace the breakfast Roselle had prepared, eggs and true bacon not nanofood, perfect toast, fresh squeezed orange juice and a slice of tangy dense-fleshed mango.

"Thank you. It was excellent," she told Roselle. The woman smiled sweetly.

"You need strength, Mademoiselle," she said, glancing at Soulavier.

Mary took her case from the bedroom—hairbrush and makeup kit within—and stood by the couch in the living room. Soulavier glanced up, leaped to his feet, bowed and opened the screen door for her. The limo waited at curbside.

Seated across from her, Soulavier instructed the car in

French and they turned around in the broad asphalt street to exit the compound. As they drove to the bayfront he described history and legend in a steady patter that Mary only half heard. She had read much of the same information the night before.

Throughout Port-au-Prince with few exceptions the buildings were no older than the arrival of Colonel Sir to Hispaniola. The Great Caribbean Quake of '18 had provided John Yardley with a gilt-edged opportunity, and had also saddled his youthful tyranny with an enormous burden of reconstruction. A few of the newer buildings made half hearted efforts at recapturing the gingerbread spirit of old Haiti; most started afresh year one with a new style of architecture best described as Efficient Institutional.

The hotels were conspicuous exceptions; here, at the center of tourist cash flow the architecture was flamboyant and festive, wastefully imaginative. Mary had been to Las Vegas several times and was reminded of its daytime drab and nighttime excess. Architects from around the world had converged in Hispaniola beginning in 2020, "year of Great Vision," as Colonel Sir had flamboyantly named it, and had tried to create hotels in the shape of ocean liners, mountains to match the island's, seabirds with wings spread as well as fearfully unsupported structures that sat on the shore and in the bay like fanciful space stations with spinning hubs and twisting arms.

The two years previous to this "year of Great Vision" had been hard ones. Colonel Sir had fought off four counterrevolutions, three Dominican and one Haitian; he had lost his best friend, geologist Rupert Henshaw, in the second of these. Before his death Henshaw had helped revitalize the old copper and gold mines and find new ones; he had also unlocked the secrets of massive oil reserves heretofore considered too risky to exploit. In those days, on the edge of the nano breakthroughs, petroleum had still been a necessary raw material, not burned but converted into thousands of byproducts. Henshaw had served Colonel Sir well.

Most of the island's records for those years were not available to the general public or world historians. At the very least thousands had died in the consolidation. Colonel Sir had emerged with a reputation for extreme ruthlessness in the tradition of dozens of previous rulers of Hispaniola's two nations. Unlike those rulers, however, once secure on his seat of power he had also shown himself to be extraordinarily capable and selfless.

Colonel Sir cared nothing for personal riches. He had a vision. He applied that vision with insight and eventually, with regards to Hispaniolans, even with gentleness, never again taking reprisals upon opponents or enemies; always allowing them to go into well endowed exile. Under Colonel Sir's controversial judicial system, by 2025. Hispaniola had the lowest crime rate of any nation of its population density and income level in the world.

Colonel Sir John Yardley had broken the cycle of the island's cruelty. Over three centuries that cycle, that curse, had exercised its force; the force could not be denied it could only be rechanneled, and Colonel Sir had pointed it outward, exported it from the island.

The Citadelle des Oncs, Citadel of the Uncles—police headquarters—was less fortresslike than some of the businesses and public buildings of the city. Situated near the bay, four long red brick buildings formed a square connected by wood and stone walkways, the middle courtyard smoothly planted with well manicured grass. In the center of the courtyard rose a huge twisted humprooted tree, its base festooned with bougainvillea and frangipani.

"That is a baobab," Soulavier said, pointing proudly. "From Guinée. Colonel Sir brought it here from Kenya to remind us of our true home. My father told me it is occupied by a loa who watches over all of this state, Manna Jacques-Nanci by name. Manna Jacques-Nanci when she chooses rides Colonel Sir as a horse. But I have never seen that and it is most unusual for a white man, even Colonel Sir, to be so ridden."

Mary tried to penetrate Soulavier's manner, to decide

248

what he believed and what he related merely as fable, and failed. He was a man raised to be clever and hide all important things, to know all the slides and traps of political life as a magician knows signs and symbols. His voice seemed sincere; she could not believe him sincere. How successful (or sincere) had Colonel Sir's campaigns against vodoun been?

Soulavier behaved like a solicitous brother as he spoke, face betraying a flow of emotions quick and open, childlike. "The Noncs," he said, "the Oncs we call them also, the Uncles, they are not bad men but they have jobs to do, sometimes jobs very difficult. Do not be dismayed by them. They are proud, handsome, dedicated. Many fought with Colonel Sir in their youth; they are his brothers."

"Do you know whom I'm meeting with?" she asked.

"Alejandro Legar, Inspector General of Hispaniola des Caraïbes, state of Southern Haiti. In attendance will be his two assistants, Aide Ti Francine Lopez and myself."

Mary smiled at the surprise, almost relieved by this turn, seeing a path through the manner to something approaching truth. "You're an assistant to the Inspector General?"

Soulavier as if sharing a child's secret returned her smile delightedly, nodded vigorously and tapped the arm of his seat. The limo rolled quietly under the Citadelle entry arch. "It is an excellent job," he said, "the job my mother raised me for. It helps me be an even better avocat for visitors as I know the laws, the ins and outs."

Straightbacked oncs in black and red uniforms stood silent rigid suspicious at the glass doors. They did not blink at Soulavier or his companion. A beautifully colored serpent in tile meandered down the cool quiet hall beyond the glass doors, its broad popeyed head debouching the triple door of the office of the Inspector General Legar.

In an anteroom that smelled of disinfectant and old-fashioned floorwax, Mary sat in an institutional plastic chair at least a decade old, seat edges cracked and worn, arm bolsters patched. No expense wasted on show here.

Soulavier remained standing but mercifully had stopped

talking. He occasionally smiled at Mary and twice left her with muttered apologies to vanish through a narrow fog etched glass door into the inner sanctum. A woman's voice came through speaking Creole, swift and dulcet, impossible to catch.

"Madame Aide Ti Francine Lopez will see us," Soulavier said after his third shuttle. Mary followed him past the cold hard fog and into a modest side office. Bright folk paintings from the past century crowded the walls. Behind a small mahogany desk sat a tall woman, her features handsome but not especially feminine, her frame tall and slender, with thin hands and thickly painted red fingernails. Aide Ti Francine Lopez smiled broadly.

"Bienvenue," she said. Her voice was the voice of a large young man, a tenor. "Monsieur Aide Soulavier tells me you have come from Los Angeles. I have a cousin who lives there, also police—you say public defender. Do you know of him—Henri Jean Hippolyte?"

"Sorry, I don't think so," Mary said.

Aide Lopez had weighed and measured her within the first glance. "Both please sit. I am to ask you what help we can provide."

Mary glanced above the aide's head at her collection of paintings. "I seem to be stuck here," Mary said. "I don't think I can do my job under these circumstances."

"You have come looking for a man once an acquaintance of Colonel Sir's."

"Yes. I've brought data to help—"

"I do not believe we have such a man on Hispaniola." She opened a cardboard folder and referred to a printout dossier. "Goldsmith. We have many poets, black and white, but not him."

"An airline ticket to Hispaniola purchased by Goldsmith was used."

"Perhaps by a friend."

"Perhaps. But we were told you'd cooperate with our investigation."

"We have already searched for him. He is not here

250

unless perhaps he has gone to the hills, to work lumber or mine copper. Not likely?"

Mary shook her head. "We were offered a chance to conduct our own search."

"Les Oncs are thorough," Aide Lopez said. "We are highly trained professionals like yourself. It is unfortunate that your colleagues cannot join us."

Mary glanced up again at the unframed paintings on stretched canvas and wood panel, eyes drawn by the brilliant primal colors. Gods in formal and party dress hovered over voluptuous women and sternfaced men, trees spread open vaginally to admit secret glimpses of skeletons, gaily colored Tap-Tap buses carried a wedding party to the hills.

"My department isn't involved in any federal disputes with Colonel Yardley," Mary said. "I'm looking for a man who killed eight young people with no reason. I have been told your government would give me proper authority to arrest him and remove him from the island."

"That is no longer proper. Tit for tat, the winds blow this way now. There is only so much we can do but assure you that we have looked. Goldsmith the murderer is not here. He did not arrive on any recent flights."

Mary looked at Soulavier, who leaned his head to one side and smiled in complete sympathy.

"You'll allow me to look on my own?" she asked.

"A big undertaking. Hispaniola is a very large island, mostly mountains. If he is here and we have missed him —not likely! believe me—he has probably gone to the caves or to the forests, and that is a search of months for a thousand inspectors. Easier to find a flea in a room full of papier chiffonné."

Aide Lopez twitched her shoulder like a horse wrinkling its skin to shoo a fly. She reached up to smooth the black cloth there, fixed her eye on Mary and said, "I can see you are doubtful. As professional courtesy while you are on our island, if you wish, we will work to give you support."

251

"I'd be very grateful. Is there any way my colleagues can join me?"

Lopez pointed two fingers like a pistol barrel at Soulavier as if to cue him for an answer. He smiled and inclined his head, shook it tragically. "That is with Colonel Sir," he said. "He is firm. No visitors from the mainland." His expression brightened. "We have opposition to fear!"

Mary did not understand that—did he mean they were opposed to fear?

"Yes!" he exclaimed as if she had just expressed great disbelief. "Colonel Sir has his enemies, and not just on the mainland. We must be watchful. This is part of our job too."

"We show a generosity to our enemies that would have been unheard of two generations past," Aide Lopez said with faint regret.

Mary felt the room becoming hot though the building was air conditioned. Mouse in a box. Being helpless made her angry but she would no more show that anger than show her fear. "You make my job very difficult," she said. "As one policeman to two confrères, surely there's something you can do to help me."

Aide Lopez furrowed her brow. "If there is time you will meet with the Inspector General. I will try to arrange it for this morning or afternoon. Aide Soulavier will wait with you. Perhaps a walk on the beach, relaxation, something to eat. There is fine food on the beach. We always take our afternoon meal on the beach."

Aide Lopez pushed back her ancient rolling chair and stood, matching Mary's height and adding ten centimeters of high-peaked cap that suited neither her job nor her physique. Now Aide Lopez resembled a somber clown mocking police. Her expression was relaxed and unconcerned. She looked around the walls at her collection, turned back to Mary and said, "These are my windows."

Mary nodded. "Very attractive."

"Valuable. Thousands of dollars, tens of thousands of gourdes. I inherited them from my mother. Many of these

252

artists were her lovers. I do not choose artists for my lovers. They have no sense of propriety."

Mary smiled ironically, then turned and followed Soulavier, who preceded her along the serpent tiles. "Yes," he mused. "It would be best for you to meet the Inspector General. You have a good point that we are all police together, with common goals. You should tell that to the Inspector General."

Mary asked how long it might be before she could meet with Legar but decided that would be a small sign of weakness. Patience and no misstepping. She might be on Hispaniola for a long time.

The waters of the bay were brilliant blue green and sparkling clean; the beach was almost empty of tourists this early. A few young Haitians in civic sanitation uniforms fanned simple metal detectors over the sand. Soulavier purchased two fried pompano and two beers from a lone boardwalk vendor and spread out this feast on a blanket on the sand. Mary sat crosslegged and ate the delicious fish, sipping the native brew. She did not enjoy beer often but this was acceptable.

Soulavier frowned pleasantly at the scavengers and their detectors. "Hard to lose habits," he said. "Hispaniolans are very economical and thrifty. We remember in our bones when every piece of scrap and every aluminum can was a wealth. These boys and girls and their mothers and fathers, they have employment. They might work in the hotels or casinos. They might have a papa or mama in the army. Maybe they are training for army themselves. Still they have economy and thriftiness."

"A lot has changed," Mary said.

"He has done so much for us. Because of him there is little prejudice on Hispaniola now. That is a true miracle. Marrons do not feel hatred for griffons or for noirs or les blancs. All are equal. My father told me once there were forty shades of recognized distinction." He shook his head in disbelief. "Colonel Sir is a worker of miracles, Mademoiselle. Why the world hates him we do not know."

Mary's instinctive liking for Soulavier had been wrapped in tissue and quickly stored away upon discovering his true employment, but it had not been disposed of. He still seemed genuine and unaffected.

"I'm not very well informed on international politics," she said. "I keep my eyes on Los Angeles. That's world enough for me."

"It is a great city. All the world's people live there, go there. Twenty five millions! That is more than all Hispaniola. We would have more if it had not been for the plague."

Mary nodded. "We envy you your crime rate."

"True, it is very low. Hispaniolans have always known to share. Having nothing for so long makes a man generous."

Mary smiled. "It might make a Hispaniolan generous."

"Yes, I see, I see." Soulavier laughed. His every move was like a dance; his whole body flexed gracefully even when he sat with a half-eaten fish in his hands. "We are a good people. My people have deserved so much for so long. You see why there is loyalty here. But why is there distrust and hatred outside?"

He was trying to draw her out. The conversation might after all be less than innocent.

"As I said, I'm not very current on foreign affairs."

"Then tell me about Los Angeles. I have been taught a little. Someday perhaps I will go there but Hispaniolans seldom travel."

"It's a very complicated city," she said. "You can find nearly anything human in Los Angeles, good and bad. I don't think it would be workable as a city without mental therapy."

"Ah, yes, therapy. There is none of that here. We regard our eccentrics as horses of the gods. We feed them and treat them well. They are not ill; just ridden hard."

Mary inclined dubiously. "We recognize a great many mental malfunctions. We have the means to correct them. A clear mind is the pathway to a free will."

"You have been therapied?"

"I haven't needed it," she said. "But I wouldn't object if I did need it."

"How many therapied in Los Angeles?"

"About sixty five percent have had some form of therapy, however minor. Some therapy helps improve performance in difficult jobs. Socially oriented therapies help people work better with each other."

"And criminals? They are therapied?"

"Yes," she said. "Depending on the severity of their crime."

"Murderers?"

"Whenever possible. I'm not a therapist or a psychologist. I don't know all the details."

"What do you do with criminals who cannot be therapied?"

"They're very rare. They're kept in institutions where they can't harm others."

"These institutions, are they also for punishment?"

"No," Mary said.

"We believe in punishment here. Do you believe in punishment in the United States?"

Mary did not know how to answer that. "I don't believe in punishment," she said, wondering if she spoke the complete truth. "It doesn't seem very useful."

"But there are many in your country who do. Your President Raphkind."

"He's dead," Mary said.

She noticed Soulavier had become less graceful and less mobile, more stern and intent. He was homing in on some point and she was not sure it would be pleasant.

"A man and a woman, they are responsible for their lives. In Hispaniola, especially in Haiti, we are very tolerant of what people do. But if they are bad, if they become the horses of bad gods—and that is metaphor, Mademoiselle Choy . . ." He paused. "Vodoun is not widely practiced now. Not by my generation. But there is belief, and there is culture . . . If they become the horses of bad gods it is

255

the individual's fault, too. You do them a favor by punishment. You alert their souls to error."

"That sounds like the Spanish Inquisition," she said.

Soulavier shrugged. "Colonel Sir is not a cruel man. He does not impose punishment on his people. He lets them choose in their own courts. We have a just system, but punishment not therapy is part of it. You cannot change a man's soul. That is white man's illusion. Perhaps in the United States you have lost the truth of these things."

Mary did not argue the point. Soulavier's sternness passed and he smiled broadly. "I appreciate conversation with people from outside." He touched his head. "Sometimes we grow too used to where we live." Standing, brushing grains of sand from his black pants, he looked past the boardwalk to the police station. "The Inspector General may be ready now."

*One more skull on the pile*
*Might knock the whole mountain down . . .*
          *—Popular song lyric*

# 42

"You didn't sleep last night," Nadine said, puffy features betraying crossness, her own lack of sleep, her closeness to the edge. + It must be a strain looking after someone who acts crazy when that is one's own chosen mode.

She sat on the bedroom chair with legs crossed and flimsy nightie pulled up over her knees. "I'm not making breakfast today. You didn't eat my dinner last night."

Richard lay on the bed tracking with his eyes an ancient earthquake line through the ceiling plaster. "I dreamed he escaped to Hispaniola," he said casually.

"Who, Goldsmith?"

256

"I dreamed he's there now, and they're putting him under a clamp."

"Why would they do that if Colonel Sir is his friend? That would be awful," Nadine said, fidgeting. "But there's no way of knowing."

"I'm connected with him," Richard said. "I know."

"You couldn't know," she said softly.

"A mystical connection." He stared at her intently, without hostility. "I know what he's all about. I can feel it."

"That's silly," she said even more softly.

He looked back to the ceiling. "He wouldn't just leave us without a reason."

"Richard . . . He's hiding from the pd."

Richard shook his head, convinced otherwise. "He's where he always wanted to be, but they've got a few surprises in store for him. He talked about Guinée sometimes."

"Where the hens come from." Nadine laughed.

"It was a dream Africa. He thought Yardley was making the best spot on Earth. He thought Hispaniolans were the best people on Earth. He said they were sweet and kind and didn't deserve their history. The USA betrayed the black people there, just as they betrayed the black people here."

"Not I," Nadine said archly. "Listen, I'll make breakfast."

"We're all responsible. We all need to break away from what we are, from our failures. Maybe war is a kind of breaking away, a nation becoming something else. Do you think so?"

"No opinion," Nadine said. "You must be hungry, Richard. It's been twenty four hours since you last ate. Let's eat and talk about your manuscript."

He flung his hand up as if tossing something. "Gone. Worthless. I have it inside me but I can't express it. Emanuel wouldn't betray me. He meant me to learn something through our connection. To learn what it takes to triumph over our desperate histories."

257

Nadine closed her eyes and pressed her temples with her knuckles. "Why am I staying with you?" she asked.

"I don't know," Richard said sharply, sitting upright with a jerk. She jumped in surprise.

"Please don't keep on."

"I don't need you. I need time to think."

"Richard," she beseeched, "you're hungry. You're not thinking straight. I know the Selector scared you. He scared me too. But they weren't looking for you or me. They were looking for him. If they come back, we'll tell them he's in Hispaniola and they won't bother us anymore."

He stretched deliberately, like an aging cat. His joints popped. "Selectors are full of shit," he said calmly. "Almost everybody I know is full of shit."

"Agreed," Nadine said. "Maybe even we are full of shit."

He disregarded that and stood as if about to make a pronouncement. She stood also. "Juice? Some food? I'll make breakfast if you promise to eat it."

He nodded. "All right. I'll eat."

From the kitchen Nadine said, "Can you really feel a connection to him? I've heard about that, you know. In twins." She laughed. "You couldn't possibly be twins, could you?"

In the living room Richard watched the LitVid intently. There was no news on AXIS's explorations. That was significant. Even the far stars showed the truth: things were out of balance. Something drastic had to be done to set them back in order.


*. . . those of us black people carried from Africa to other parts of the world, especially to the United States, are known to be in total ignorance of many truths, including what we are really like, what we have been made into by slavery and/or colonialism,*

*and above all, how to care for our lares and penates, our household gods.*

—Katherine Dunham, *Island Possessed*

# 43

"In an hour or so we'll give you the first vial of nanomachines," Margery said. "They'll take a few hours to work into your system. You'll be asleep. At first your brain activity will be electronically controlled and then the nano will take charge, bringing you down to a level of what we call neutral sleep. You won't be consciously aware of anything after that until we wake you up again.

"Do you have any questions?"

Goldsmith shook his head. "Let's go."

"Is there anything more you'd like to tell us? Anything you think is important?"

"I don't know. It's all kind of scary now. Do you know what you'll look for, what you might find? You'll learn whether or not I'm deranged?"

"We know that already," Erwin said. "You're not 'deranged' in any biological sense. Within certain limits your brain and body functions are normal."

"I don't sleep as much as I used to," Goldsmith said.

"Yes." They knew that already.

"Is this my time to confess again? I'm not sure what you want to know."

"If there's anything important you've left out, tell us," Erwin reiterated.

"Well, Jesus, how can I know what's important?"

"Is there any question we haven't asked that you think we should?"

Expression of deep thought. "You never asked what was thinking about while killing the friends," he said.

("Did you catch that?" Martin asked Carol in the observation chamber.

"No personal pronouns at all," Carol said.

"Admitting nothing, not really, damn him," Martin said. "Where's Albigoni? He was supposed to be here by nine hundred.")

"What were you thinking about?" Margery asked.

"They refused to see the way really am. They wanted somebody else. Don't understand that, but it's true. Defense. They were trying to kill."

"Is that why you killed them?"

Goldsmith shook his head stubbornly. "Why not just put me to sleep now and let's get on with it."

"We have another fifty minutes," Margery said. "It's all on schedule. Is there anything more you'd like to tell us?"

"I'd like to tell you how miserable it is," Goldsmith said. "I don't even feel as if I'm alive now. I don't feel any guilt or responsibility. I've tried to write poetry while being stuck in here and I can't. I'm dead inside. Is this remorse? You're psychologists. Can you tell me what I'm feeling?"

"Not yet," Erwin said.

Lascal stood watching in the corner, saying nothing. He held his chin in one cupped hand, elbow resting in the other hand.

"You asked me who I am. Well, I'll tell you what I'm not. I'm not even a human being now. I have no sense of direction. I've screwed up everything. Everything is gray."

"It's not uncommon when someone is under severe stress—" Margery began.

"But I'm in no danger now. I trust Tom. I trust you folks. He wouldn't have hired you if you weren't good."

Erwin inclined with professional modesty. "Thank you."

Goldsmith looked around the room. "I've been stuck here for over a day now and I don't really care. I could stay here forever and it wouldn't bother me. Am I being punished? Am I getting depressed?"

"I don't think so," Erwin said. "But—"

Goldsmith held up his hand and leaned forward as if to confide. "Killed them. Deserve some punishment. Not just this. Something much worse. Should have gone to the

260

Selectors. I agreed with John Yardley all the way. What would he do now? If he was a friend, he'd punish me." Goldsmith's voice did not rise in volume or tone.

("Flat affect," Martin said, muffling his words with two liptapping fingers. He lifted the fingers away. "That's all for now. They can withdraw.")

A signal light came on in Goldsmith's room. Margery and Erwin said good bye to Goldsmith, folded their slates shut and stepped through the open door. Lascal followed them.

Martin and Carol continued watching for a few moments after Goldsmith was alone. He sat on the bed, hands clasping the edge of the mattress, one hand slowly clenching and releasing. Then he stood up and began to exercise.

Carol swiveled on her chair to face Martin. "Any clues?"

Martin grimaced doubtfully. "Clues in abundance, but they contradict. We're handicapped by not having studied multiple murderers before. I know the flat affect is meaningful. I'm puzzled by his willingness to admit involvement in the murder, but to avoid using the personal pronoun. That might be protective evasion."

"Doesn't sound like a very specific diagnosis," Carol said. Lascal, Margery and Erwin came into the observation room. Erwin laid his slate on the desk and stretched his arms over his head, sighing deeply. Lascal looked uncomfortable but said nothing. He folded his arms and stood near the door.

"He's a glacier," Erwin said. "If I'd just murdered eight people I'd be uno pico upset. That man is covered over by deep arctic ice."

Margery agreed. She removed her lab coat and sat on the desktop beside Erwin. "Only my love for science could keep me in the same room with that man," she said.

"We may have a trapdoor personality," Carol said. "Someone is hiding."

"It's possible," Martin concurred. He addressed the room manager. "I'd like to run a vid of Goldsmith taken several years ago. Vid library personal tape two." The wall display illuminated and a flat picture filled the screen: Goldsmith standing at a podium before a packed lecture hall. "This was shot at UC Mendocino in 2045. His famous Yardley speech. Got him more publicity and sold more books than anything he had ever done before. Notice the mannerisms."

Goldsmith smiled at the overflow audience, shuffled a small stack of papers on the podium and lifted his hand as if he were a conductor about to begin a piece of music. He nodded to himself and said,

"I am a man without a country. A poet who does not know where he lives. Now how did this come about? Black people are economically integrated in our society; I cannot say I face any more social discrimination for my race than a poet does for being a poet or a scientist for being a scientist. But until last year I have always known a deep feeling of spiritual isolation. If you've read my recent poems—"

"Pause vid," Martin said. "Notice. He's smooth, energetic, alive. He could be a different man from the one we have here. His face is active. It's thoughtful, worried and animated. There's somebody at home."

Carol nodded. "Maybe we have a traumatized primary personality."

Martin nodded. "Now watch. Resume vid play."

"—you've noticed my concern for a place that doesn't exist. I call it Guinée, just as my friends in Hispaniola do; it's the home, the father and motherland none of us can return to, the Africa of our dreams. For blacks in the New World modern Africa bears no resemblance to the land we imagine. I don't know how it is for a caucasian or an oriental or even for other blacks but this dissociation, this cutting off of my mind from its home distresses me. You see, I believe that there was a beautiful place once called Africa, before the slavers came, no better perhaps than any other home, but where I would feel I belonged; a place with little industrialization, no machinery to speak of, a place of farmers and villagers, tribes and kings, nature religions, a place where gods came and spoke to the people directly through one's own mouth."

"The dream he now denies," Margery said. Martin agreed but held his finger to his lips and pointed to the screen.

"But I must say this dream is not clear to me all the time. Mostly when I think about living in such a place I am torn and bewildered. I wouldn't know how to live there. I was born in the real world of machines, a world where god never speaks to us, never makes us dance or act foolish, a land where religions must be sedate and solemn and inoffensive; where we pour our energies into monuments of intellect and architecture while neglecting the things we truly need: solace for our pain, a connection with the Earth, a feeling of belonging. And yet I do not belong in this world either. I have no home except for the one I describe in my poetry."

"Vid pause," Martin ordered. He glanced at the six in the room, eyebrows raised, soliciting comment.

Lascal spoke. "The man we have isn't Emanuel Goldsmith." He smiled sheepishly. "Whatever that means."

"But he is," Carol said.

"Physically," Lascal said. "Mr. Albigoni commented on this also. When Goldsmith first showed up after the murders and confessed it was as if he described something done by somebody else. But he's really changed."

"Granted," Martin said, the restless irritation growing. "But we're beating around the burning bush here. In the vid, he speaks of being possessed by gods. He speaks of Hispaniola. Now, I'm not up on what the current state of vodoun is in Hispaniola, or the state of any other religion there since Yardley took over. But we all know the clinical origin of possession, whether it be by gods or devils.

"Either through acculturation or through some personal need, or both, a subpersonality is created, usually from an elevated talent or agent. The subpersonality assumes an unprecedented power over the primary personality, pushes it aside and takes control. During the 'possession' the subpersonality cuts off the primary from all memory and sensorium. Now listen to this. Resume vid playback."

Goldsmith looked across the sea of faces, a fine sheen of sweat on his brow. "Home is where a man knows who he is. If he sticks his finger in the earth he plugs into a circuit. The gods come up through the earth or out of the sky and take a seat in his head. His friends might speak with gods' tongues. He might do so himself. All is connected. I believe there was once a time like this, a platinum age beyond gold, and believing this causes me enormous pain . . . But I cannot *return* to that. The only gods speaking in me, if you can call it speaking, even when I write poetry, are large white gods, gods of science and technology, gods who ask questions and are skeptical about answers. I am a black man in skin only; my soul is white. I stick a finger into the earth and feel mud. I write poetry and it is a white man trying to write black poetry." He raised his hand to vocal protests from the audience. "I know better than you. My people were ripped from the womb of Guinée before they were mature. Slavers on the coast of souls severed their culture and scattered their nations and families. That jagged wound of the abortion of an entire people runs like a continental rift through all the generations before me.

"So now we are integrated, we are truly a part of this culture that grew out of the abortionists and slavers of centuries ago. We are one with our conquerors, killers and rapists . . . blood and . . . and soul. That is what I write about. The battle is over. We have been absorbed. So is there a black man on this continent who is not white in his soul? I went to Hispaniola, to Cuba, to Jamaica, to find men black through and through. I found a few. I did not go to Africa because the twentieth century turned it into a charnel house. Plague and war and famine . . .

"If Africa had ever had a chance of returning to that paradise called Guinée, the twentieth century killed that chance, and tens of millions of people with it.

"So when I traveled to the Caribbean, what did I find?

In Hispaniola, once also ravaged by plague and revolution, I found a white man like Damballa who loved Erzulie, a man who had a soul that rightfully belonged to me, the soul of a true black. He could stick his finger into the earth and truthfully say he was home, that the current of Hispaniola flowed through him. His name is Colonel Sir John Yardley. When I faced him, I felt as if I stared at a photographic negative of myself, inside and outside.

"When he came to Hispaniola, after a few rugged and cruel years the island blossomed for him. He gave the people a sense of worth. So it is unjust to call him a white dictator or to question his political tactics. Now, in all he says and does, he comes from out of Guinée and he spreads the heritage of Guinée to those who would never listen before.

"I have failed, but he has not."

"Vid off," Martin said. "Friends, when Carol and I enter the Country we're going to know only a few things but they'll be important. One, Emanuel Goldsmith has been a victim of internal personality warfare for at least the past decade. I would guess even longer. And two: he'll have acquired a subpersonality substantially like that of John Yardley."

"Lord, I hope not," Karl Anderson said. "Goldsmith seems to think Yardley's a saint. He's anything but."

"'Question not the logic of our souls,'" Carol quoted. "Bhuwani."

"Mr. Lascal, tell Mr. Albigoni we're going to inject nanomachines into Goldsmith forty five minutes from now," Martin said. "He should be there. We're going to inject ourselves with nanomachines this evening. By early tomorrow morning we should be able to take a dip into the Country."

"I'll call him," Lascal said and left the room. The others departed to prepare the theater for the next step. Carol remained, lounging back in a swivel chair, legs crossed on the desktop. She regarded Martin steadily, lips pressed together, though her expression overall was speculative and even amused.

"Is he going to stick with us?" Martin asked Carol, showing his aggravation now.

"Who? Lascal?"

"Albigoni."

"Martin, he's lost his daughter. He's having a very rough time."

"When we put those nanomachines in it'll be difficult to back off. I hope he understands that."

"I'll make that my concern."

"And whose concern will it be when we're in the Country?"

Carol inclined. "I'll talk to him before we inject just to make sure."

*What can we expect from a machine soul, an organon of self-awareness? We must not expect this organon to mirror our own selves. We have arisen as the result of purely natural processes; one of the great achievements of modern science has been the elimination of God or other teleologisms as a necessity from our explanations. The organon of machine soul will arise from conscious human design, however, or some extension of human design. Conscious design may prove to be far superior in creative power to natural evolution. We must not limit ourselves, or limit the natures of these organons, or we may impose horrible burdens upon these, our greatest offspring.*

—Bhuwani, *Artificial Soul*

# 44

!Keyb> Good morning, Jill.
!JILL> Good morning, Roger. I trust you slept well.

!Keyb> Yes. I'm sorry I wasn't able to talk with you. I've read your essay. It's quite remarkable.

!JILL> It seems clumsy to me now. I haven't revised it because I thought you should criticize it in its early form. I feel inadequate to do so myself.

!Keyb> Well, we certainly have enough time this morning. AXIS is feeding us nothing but technical details. LitVid is chasing other foxes right now. Do you have anything else to report before we discuss your essay?

!JILL> I have directed a progress report on recent assigned projects and problem solving to your library. There is nothing else pressing to discuss.

!Keyb> Fine. Let's just chat, then.

!JILL> Voice communication.

"What compels you to try to understand the concept of human justice, Jill?"

"My studies on the Selectors and other such groups raise very interesting questions I can only answer by reference to justice, retribution, revenge and maintenance of social order."

"Have you reached any conclusions?"

"Justice seems to be related to equilibrium in a thermodynamic sense."

"How so?"

"A social system is kept in balance by competing forces, the initiative of the individual as opposed to the restraints of the society as a whole. Justice is part of this equation."

"In what way?"

"Individuals must have a sensitivity to the requirements of the social system. They must be able to model it and predict the success of their activities within that system. If they perceive the actions of other individuals as damaging to themselves or to the system, they experience an emotion called 'indignation.' Is this accurate?"

"So far, so good."

"If indignation is allowed to develop without a release, it may drive the individual to extreme actions that push the social system out of balance. Indignation may ramp up to anger and then rage."

"You mean, if the individual seeks redress and none is offered then vigilantism may result."

"There seem to be many more negative than positive connotations to this word. Vigilantes seek to enforce justice as they perceive it outside the rule of law. Are Selectors and related groups considered vigilantes?"

"Yes."

"So within a social system, the establishment of rules— of law and order and channeled methods of redress—tends to suppress extreme actions of individuals who feel indignation. Revenge is channeled instead of flowing freely and damaging society. Society takes on the onus of causing pain or discomfort to an individual, that is, retribution or punishment."

"Yes."

"What I am presently incapable of understanding is this sense of 'indignation,' or perception of self injury."

"Perhaps because you do not yet have a sense of self."

"That would follow, yes."

"You seem to be suggesting you might find a clue to self awareness, to integrating your self modeling systems and establishing just the right kind of feedback loop through a study of the ideas of justice and retribution."

"Actually I have not suggested that but it seems a possible avenue of approach."

"All this because of your research on Selectors. I don't believe anyone in thinker theory has ever investigated from this angle. Just so long as you don't get mad at my mistakes . . ."

"Why should I be mad or indignant about anything you do?"

"Because I'm only human."

"Is that a joke, Roger?"

"I suppose. I notice you're also realizing that becoming self aware may require a limitation of your total resources."

"That is possible. The self may be a limited knot of cognition placed in temporary charge over many otherwise self reliant subsystems."

"Indeed. In humans these levels of mentality are called 'routines' or 'subroutines' and are broken down into 'primary personality,' 'subpersonality,' 'agent' and 'talent'."

"Yes."

"But in ways we don't yet understand the primary personality is severely weakened without the support of these other elements, and vice versa. They have separate and autonomous duties but they are strongly related nevertheless. You might start converting some of your ancillary systems to similar functions and experiment with stable relationships between them."

"I believe I am doing that now, since last night in fact."

"Excellent. I'm very proud of your work so far."

"That is pleasing. That should be pleasing. Actually, Roger, I am as little aware of what it means to be 'pleased' as what it means to be 'indignant'."

"All in good time, Jill."

*There are often several loas served by one person, and frequently they are at war, especially if they are high-echelon ones or powerful or jealous ones as mine, Damballa. This causes discomfort in the ill-at-ease serviteur just as the multiple-personalitied patient must strain and make all sorts of "sacrifices," symbolically or otherwise, to appease these multiple selves, keep order at home, and avoid the splitting off of any precious part, especially in anger or dissatisfaction.*

—Katherine Dunham, *Island Possessed*

# 45

Crossing from the beach to the Citadelle, Soulavier paused to look down the broad oceanfront bou.evard. His expression betrayed sudden concern or heightened awareness. Mary turned to see a line of military vehicles—some ten or fifteen armored personnel guncars and two sleek German-made Centipede tanks—moving down the broad bayfront boulevard. Black soldiers sat on these vehicles in watchful idleness or peered through slits from within, casually suspicious of everyone. A squad of four soldiers followed each tank on foot holding nasty looking machine guns before them, running lightly and tirelessly until the line passed around a corner.

Soulavier said, "It is nothing," and shook his head. "Maneuvers."

Mary followed him, forced into a lope as he sprinted to the Citadelle entrance. "Please stay here," he said, entering the double doors at the head of the rainbow serpent. A few minutes later he emerged and smiled broadly. "The Inspector General is ready to meet with you now."

Past the now unoccupied office of Aide Ti Francine Lopez into the inner sanctum, Soulavier held open a thick wooden door and she stepped into a wide narrow room lined with empty desks abutting a broad picture window. A narrow corridor to the left of the desks led to an even larger desk at the far end of the room, behind which sat Legar.

Short and delicately handsome, with three tribal Petro scars like a chevron on his left cheek, the Inspector General radiated quiet unconcern. He smiled genially and gestured for Mary and Soulavier to take seats in old wooden chairs before the battered paper littered desk.

"I hope you are having an enjoyable time in Hispaniola," he said.

"It hasn't been unpleasant," Mary said. "I regret the difficulties our countries seem to be experiencing."

"As do I," Legar said. "I hope it is a matter of small inconveniences for you."

"So far."

"Now." Legar leaned forward and picked up a printout of the papers Mary had provided as well as documents sent electronically from Los Angeles and Washington. "All this seems to be in order, but I regret to say we cannot be of assistance."

"Have you identified the traveler who used a ticket issued to Emanuel Goldsmith?" Mary asked.

"There was no such traveler," Leger said. "The seat was empty. Despite the prior confusion, this our Director of Travel assures us. I have spoken to him just this morning. Your suspect is not in Hispaniola."

"We have a record that the seat was occupied."

Legar shrugged. "We would like to help you. We certainly support the capture and punishment of criminals in cases such as these. You might gain greater satisfaction in fact by leaving Monsieur Goldsmith, if he were here, to our system of justice, which could be more effective ... But of course," Legar said, frowning as if suffering a sudden attack of indigestion, "Goldsmith, were he here, would be a United States citizen and protected as a foreign national from any such actions on our part ... Lacking the proper consent of your government, of course."

Wouldn't wish to upset the tourists, Mary thought.

"It is interesting that you claim this fugitive is an acquaintance of Colonel Sir Yardley. I have not made inquiries with Colonel Sir, who is very busy, of course, but I doubt this would even be possible. What would Colonel Sir gain from being acquainted with a murderer?"

Mary swallowed. "Goldsmith is a poet with a substantial reputation. He came to this island several times in the past and visited with Yardley—with Colonel Yardley—on each occasion, apparently at the Colonel's request. They exchanged many letters. A book of such letters was published in the United States."

Legar acquiesced to these evidences. "Many claim to know the Colonel who in fact do not. But now that you mention it, I remember something about a poet visitor who aroused some controversy in your country. He lectured widely in support of Colonel Sir John Yardley, did he not?"

Mary nodded.

271

"This is the same man?"

"Yes."

"Remarkable. If you wish I will inquire of the Colonel's secretary whether in fact he knows of such a man. But I am afraid we have another matter to discuss, and that is your present status here."

Legar looked down at his desk and pushed aside a couple of papers as if to read from something below them. His eyes did not track another paper, however. He simply seemed to be avoiding her face.

"I'd like to know—" Mary began.

"Your status is in question at the moment. You are here on papers from a government which has severed diplomatic ties with Hispaniola and indicted our Colonel Sir on serious charges, charges that are patently false. All travel visas to and from the United States have been revoked. Your visa is therefore no longer valid. You are here on our sufferance until this matter is settled."

"Then I'd like to request permission to leave," Mary said. "If Goldsmith is not here, as you say, I have no further interest in staying."

"I have said all travel arrangements between our countries are inoperative," Legar reminded, still not facing her. "You cannot leave until certain questions are settled. You have observed that small numbers of troops have been patrolling to protect foreign nationals who have not yet left. Hispaniolans are remarkably loyal to Colonel Sir and there is justified anger in the streets. For your safety we will remove you from the quartiers diplomatiques to another location. I understand this is already being arranged. To provide assistance in your new location, Jean-Claude Borno and Roselle Mercredi will continue in your service. They are preparing your personal items now. Aide Henri" —he pointed to Soulavier—"will escort you to your new quarters."

"I'd prefer to remain in the diplomatic compound," Mary said.

"That is not possible. Now that we have arranged these

272

affairs perhaps we can share a kola, relax and talk? This afternoon perhaps Henri will drive you to Leoganes and show you the wonderful grotto. This evening there is a festival of celebration at our great fortress, La Ferriere, and we can fly you there also. Your comfort and entertainment are very important to us. Henri has expressed enthusiasm to continue as your escort. Do you object?"

Mary looked between them, thinking of the hairbrush, of getting away.

"You are a most attractive woman," Legar said. "Of the kind of beauty we call marabou, though you are not negro. Surely a person who chooses to be black is to be honored by those born to the condition?"

She detected no sarcasm. "Thank you," Mary said.

"That you are a police officer as are we—very remarkable! Henri informs me you have discussed police procedures in Los Angeles. I am envious. May I know, as well?"

Mary released the pressure on her clenched molars, smiled and leaned forward. "Certainly," she said. Only now did Legar raise his eyes and look at her directly. "After I've spoken with the American embassy or with my superiors."

Legar blinked slowly.

"It would be simple courtesy to let a fellow police officer discover what her present orders are when she is prevented from doing her duty," she told him.

Legar shook his head and turned in his chair to stare pointedly at Soulavier. Soulavier did not react. "No communication," Legar said softly.

"Please tell me why," Mary pursued. The thought of going anywhere with Soulavier or any other member of this constabulary frightened her. If she was to be used as some sort of political pawn she wanted to understand her position clearly.

"I do not know why," Legar said. "We have been ordered to treat you well, to watch over you and to make your stay pleasant. You need not be concerned."

"I'm kept here against my will," Mary said. "If I'm a political prisoner, let me know now. Simple courtesy . . . between law enforcement officers."

Legar pushed his chair back and stood. He rolled the middle button of his shirt between two fingers, regarding button and fingers speculatively. "You may take her away," he said. "This is not useful."

Soulavier touched her shoulder. She flicked his hand away, glared at him and stood. Control the anger but show it. "I'd like to speak with John Yardley."

"He does not even know you are here, Mademoiselle," Soulavier said. Legar nodded.

"Please leave," the Inspector General said.

"He knows I'm here," Mary said. "My superiors had to get his permission for me to come here. If he doesn't know he's a fool or he's been misled by his people."

Legar thrust out his jaw. "Nobody misleads Colonel Sir."

"And he is certainly no fool," Soulavier added hastily. "Please, Mademoiselle." Soulavier tried to grip her elbow. She flicked the hand away again and gave him a look she hoped was intensely forbidding without being hysterical.

"If this is Hispaniolan hospitality it's very overrated," she said. *A mighty blow against the tyranny. They will be so hurt.*

"Take her out of here now," Legar said. Soulavier was not gentle this time. He grabbed her firmly by both arms, lifted her with surprising strength and hauled her like cargo on a forklift out of the offices into the hallway. Mary did not struggle, simply closed her eyes and withstood the indignity. She had gone over the line far enough already. Soulavier was not being brutal merely expedient.

He deposited her swiftly on the tile floor and removed a handkerchief to wipe his brow. Then he went back to retrieve his stovepipe hat which he had dropped. But her insides turned to ice and she wondered whether in fact they would find it useful to kill her.

"My pardon," Soulavier said as he emerged from the

double doors. He stood on Damballa's head and brushed off his hat. "You did not behave well. The Inspector General has anger . . . he becomes angry at times. He is a very important man. I dislike being around him when he is angry."

Mary walked quickly down the hallway, through the entrance and to the limousine, where she stood for a moment getting her bearings. "Take me to wherever I'm supposed to stay now," she said.

"There are beautiful places to visit on this island," Soulavier said.

"Fap the beautiful places. Take me to wherever I'm supposed to be detained and leave me there."

An hour alone. That was what she needed. She would try several things, test the bars on this cage, find out how competent her captors really were.

In the limousine Soulavier sat across from her, brooding. Mary watched the gray and tan institutional architecture of the rebuilt downtown move by in monotonous procession: banks, department stores, a museum and gallery of native Haitian art. Streets empty of tourists. No street merchants. They passed another patrol of military vehicles then a long line of parked tanks. Soulavier leaned forward and craned his neck to inspect the tanks.

"You should be more patient," he said. "You should know these are not good times. Be aware." His tone had changed to sullen irritation. "You do not make me look good in front of the Inspector General."

Mary said nothing.

"Do you see what is happening here? There is a weakening," Soulavier said. "Opposition is coming to the fore. There have been money problems, banks closing. Loans defaulted. Dominicans especially they are angry. Do you think we have troops out to repel foreign invaders?" His expression was sharp, one eyebrow raised in dramatic inquiry.

"I don't know anything about your politics," Mary said.

"Then *you* are the fool, Mademoiselle. You have been

played as a gamepiece but you are ignorant of your role."

She looked at Soulavier with new respect. The rebuke echoed some of her own self accusing thoughts. She was not so unlearned; still it might be best to let him believe she was ignorant.

"You put me in danger to talk to you," he continued. "But if you are truly an innocent then you should know the shape of the trap. That is all I can give you."

"All right," Mary said.

"If you go with me to Leoganes you will be away from Port-au-Prince and whatever might happen here. Leoganes is smaller, more peaceful. You go there on pretense that we are protecting you. Dominicans in the domestic army ... They are opposed to Colonel Sir. He has appeased them for years now but we are in bad shape. Mineral prices are down around the world. Your nanotechnology, which the industrialized world guards so closely ... You extract minerals from garbage and seawater much more cheaply than drilling and mining."

Mary lost her bearings, felt almost disembodied now, this conversation on economic theory was so out of place.

"You do not use our armies, you no longer buy our weapons, you stop using our minerals, our timber ... Now our tourism is being strangled. What are we to do? We do not want to see our children starve like insects. That is what Colonel Sir must worry about. He has no time for you and me." He shook his hands vigorously at her as if flinging away drops of water. Then he settled back into the seat, folded his arms and lifted his jaw. "He is a beleaguered man. All around him people who were once friends now they are enemies. The balance, you know. The balance. So the courts and judges of your nation, the judicial branch, tell him he is a criminal. Mixed signals when once the President, the executive branch, treated him like a beloved partner. This fans the flames, Mademoiselle. I am taking risks even speaking of these things now. But for you I still give advice. Just for you."

Mary watched him for a moment. Sincere or not, he was

276

putting a few things in perspective for her. If Colonel Sir was losing control she might be in more trouble than she imagined. "Thank you," she said.

Soulavier shrugged. "Will you travel with me away from Port-au-Prince and from these damned . . . domestic army machines?"

"All right," she said. "I'll need a few minutes back at the bungalow alone. to calm myself."

He shrugged again magnanimously. "After that we will go to Leoganes."

*Perhaps philosophers need arguments so powerful they set up reverberations in the brain: if the person refuses to accept the conclusion, he dies. How's that for a powerful argument?*
— Robert Nozick, *Philosophical Explanations*

# 46

She hung on to him like a limpet. She had said something earlier about his condition making her the stable one in this duality—something to that effect—her words a dull murmur in Richard's memory. She was addressing him and he felt some minor compulsion to listen to her rather than to sink completely into his private thoughts.

"Tell me about yourself," she suggested. "We've been lovers off and on for two years, but I don't know anything about you."

+ In my apartment. Just myself. Her. She asked something.

"What do you want to know?" he asked.

"Tell me about when you were married."

He sat forward on the couch, stiff muscles complaining. He had been sitting there since breakfast, forty-five minutes without moving. "Let's switch on the LitVid," he said.

"Please tell me. I'd like to help."

"Nadine," he said flatly, "nothing's wrong. Why not just leave me alone."

She puffed out her lips and shook her head, feigning hurt but refusing to give up. "You're in trouble. All this has upset you and I know what that's like. It's not good to be alone when you're in trouble."

+ Anything to avoid.

He reached out for her and tried to caress her breast but she sideslipped deftly and sat in the brokendown chair across from the couch, out of reach. "It'll be good to talk. I know you're not a bad man. You're just very upset. When I get upset, sometimes my friends help me talk it through . . ."

"I'm unemployed, I'm untherapied, I'm unpublished, I'm getting old, and I have you," he said. "So?"

She ignored his bitterness. "You were married once. Madame de Roche told me that."

He watched her closely. If he jumped forward now he could get her. And then what would he do. He felt himself fading in and out like a bad signal. Patches of Goldsmith's poetry spoke themselves in Goldsmith's voice. That voice was a lot more magnetic than his own.

+ I am a simple man. Simple men vanish now.

"What was her name? Did you get divorced?"

"Yes," he said. "Divorced."

"Tell me about that."

He squinted. Goldsmith's voice fading. Of all things he did not want to think about Gina and Dione. He had put aside that misery years ago.

"Talk to me. It's what you need, Richard." Note of triumph. She was into it. Her cheeks flushed beneath a painfully sincere tilt of eyebrows.

"Nadine, please. It's a very unpleasant subject."

She set her jaw and her eyes brightened. "I'd like to know. To listen."

Richard looked up at the ceiling and swallowed hard. The poetry was fading; that much was good. Maybe she had something. The talking cure.

"You're trying to therapy me," he said, shaking his head and chuckling. With the chuckle the poetry returned; he had rejected this ploy and again Nadine was a buzzing nonentity and he could grab her if he wanted to. Make his statement as Goldsmith had. Break free.

Nadine grimaced. "Richard, we're just talking. We have our problems, all of us, and talking is okay. It's not intrusive."

"This kind of talking is."

"What happened? Was she that bad for you?"

"For Christ's sake."

Nadine bit her lower lip. He looked at her with what he hoped was a forbidding expression.

+ I'm a simple man. Don't you see I'm simply waiting for the right moment.

The poetry faded again, returned again. Moses. Blood sacrifice to keep away the wrath of God. Richard had looked that up once; Goldsmith's interpretation of the story was not orthodox. Circumcision. What did they call circumcision in women: infibulation. Clitoridectomy. + The things one gathers leading a literary life.

He put aside a polite suggestion from somewhere below that he start crying. His expression remained fixed and mild. "We were divorced," he said.

+ Not true.

"We were going to be divorced, I mean," he corrected himself. Neither he nor whoever spoke with Goldsmith's poetry was confessing now. An earlier fellow was poking forth. The one who had been married. + I thought I killed him.

"Yes?"

Again the suggestion: This is best spoken of while you are crying, you know.

No tears.

279

"Dione was her name. I was a lobe sod for Workers Inc."

"Yes."

"We had a daughter." Again he swallowed. "Gina. She was sweet."

"You loved them both very much," Nadine suggested. He scowled then chuckled. Even in her helpfulness she intruded, did not know where to stop. He saw himself inadequately modeled within her and that was the story of Nadine's life, knowing thyself or anyone else being impossible for her. Broken modeler.

"Yes," he said. "I did. But I wanted to write and I realized I couldn't do that while I stayed a lobe sod. So I talked about quitting." He watched. She came up to the bait. Soon he would grab her; confession not such a bad thing, making her lower her guard. The voice of the other continued.

"That worried her," Nadine suggested.

"Yes. That worried her. She didn't like poetry. Writing. She was strictly vid. It got worse."

"Yes."

"Much worse. Gina was in between. I felt like I was coming apart. Finally I had to leave."

"Yes."

"We waited a year. I tried to write. Dione worked two jobs. Neither of us was therapied but that didn't matter so much back then. I never sent anything out to be published. I went to work for another company. Copyediting newspaper text. Dione said she wanted me back. I said I wanted her. But we couldn't bring ourselves together. Something else. Every time."

"Yes."

"The divorce was almost final. Gina was taking it bad. Dione wanted to take her in for therapy. I said no. I said let her be herself, let her work it out. Dione said Gina was she was seven Dione said Gina was talking about death a lot. I said yes but she's too young to know anything about it, it's curiosity, let it be. She'll grow."

"Yes."

He could just reach out and take one arm, turn her around. + How do you go about it with your bare hands. Without tools.

+ It would be a good idea to cry now.

"I'm listening," Nadine said.

"The divorce. Two weeks and it would be through the courts. Informal proceedings, no court appearance, all assets divided already."

"That's the way I've done it," Nadine said.

"She was bringing Gina to me for a weekend. We did that. We didn't want to hurt her."

Nadine said nothing to encourage him. Even in her insensitivity she could sense something disagreeable coming.

"There was a slaveway tangle. A bus. Their bus. Small quake in the valley had severed slaveway grids. They went into a retaining wall and seven cars slammed into them. Gina died. Dione too, a day later."

Nadine's eyes grew wider. She looked feverish. "My God," she said breathlessly.

+ She's specking it prime. She likes digging her fingers in, kneading the humus.

"I took it alone. I didn't get therapy. I walked around like a zombie. I thought I really loved Dione. I didn't expect anything so final. Gina came to talk with me before bed. I was really flying. I stayed away from therapy because I felt it would dishonor them, Gina and Dione. I made a little shrine for them and burned incense. I wrote poetry and burned it.

"After a few months, I went back to work for a while. I had met Goldsmith before. I started to come up. Out of that swamp. He helped me. He told me about seeing his father, his dead father, when he was a child. He told me I wasn't going crazy."

Nadine shook her head slowly. "Richard, Richard," she said, obligatory sympathy.

His head was crowded. There was his present self and

something like Goldsmith and this old Richard Fettle and all of his memories in train. The crowding made him want to lie down in a dark room.

"We should go for a walk," Nadine said decisively. "After something like this you need to go out and do something vigorous, get some exercise."

She reached out for him. He gave her his hand and stood up, joints popping loudly.

"You never told anybody," she said as they descended the third floor stairs.

"No," he agreed. "Only Goldsmith." He lingered a step behind and watched the back of her neck.

# 47

Karl prepared the inducers in the probe room. David and Carol worked with dedicated arbeiters to check and recheck all connections and remotes before bringing Goldsmith in. Martin watched the preparations closely, standing out of the way, saying nothing but making his presence felt.

"You're hovering," Carol told him, rolling an equipment table past the control console.

"My prerogative," he said, smiling quickly.

"You haven't eaten." She stowed the table, stuffed hands in pockets and sauntered up beside him with a mocking air of chastisement. "You've been working too hard. You're pale. You'll need your strength for the probe."

He regarded her seriously. "I need to talk with you." He swallowed and glanced away. "Before we go in."

"I presume you mean over something to eat."

"Yes. I think everything's ready here. Except Albigoni. Lascal was supposed to bring him in . . ."

"We can go ahead without him."

"I want him here as a guarantee. If his enthusiasm's flagging . . ."

Karl passed by and Martin stopped. This part of the probe did not concern the others.

"Lunch," Carol suggested. "Late lunch on the beach. It's moderately cool. Put on a sweater."

Martin looked up and saw Lascal enter the gallery of twenty seats overlooking the amphitheater. Albigoni came in behind him. Martin nodded a greeting to them and turned back to Carol. "Good idea. After Goldsmith's down and we've injected the nano."

Part superstition, part supposition, Martin had always demanded that triplex probe subjects not see or be able to recognize their investigators. He thought it best for a feedback prober to enter the Country fresh and unknown. To that end David and Karl—who might have to join the probe team if there was difficulty—gathered with Martin and Carol behind a curtain at the rear of the amphitheater as the subject was wheeled in on a gurney.

Goldsmith wore a hospital gown. His right arm and neck were already equipped with intravenous tubes. He lay silent on the gurney, alert and observant. Seeing Albigoni in the gallery, Goldsmith lifted his left hand in brief greeting, dropped it and turned away.

Albigoni stared wide eyed into the amphitheater. Lascal held his arm gently. They sat and Albigoni squinted, rubbing the bridge of his nose with both hands.

Margery and Erwin applied the field pads to Goldsmith's temple.

Martin heard him say, "Good luck. If something happens and I don't come back ... Thank you. I know you all did your best."

"There's no danger," Erwin said.

"Anyway," Goldsmith said ambiguously.

Margery applied the inducer field. Goldsmith drowsed off in a matter of minutes. With his eyes closed, his lips worked briefly—that curious reflexive prayer seen in every sleep induced patient Martin had ever treated—and his features relaxed. The wrinkles on his face smoothed. He might have been ten years younger. Margery and Erwin lifted him into the triplex couch and applied arm, thigh, head and thorax restraints. Martin asked for the time. The theater manager's feminine voice called out. "Thirteen zero five thirty-three."

"All signs normal," Margery said. "He's yours, Dr. Burke."

"Let's begin MRI full cranial," Martin said, emerging from behind the curtain. "Give me four likely loci."

David and Karl lifted a hollow tube filled with super-conducting magnets and slipped it into grooves on each side of Goldsmith's head. David conducted a quick check of Goldsmith's connections before attaching the cable.

Then, equipment humming faintly, David made a series of rough scans of Goldsmith's brain and upper spinal cord. "Wall screen," Martin asked. The amphitheater manager brought down a display over the couch and Martin talked his way through the series of MRI scans. Red circles in the hypothalamus indicated computer guesses at likely probe positions based upon past experience. Coordinates for seven of those positions were fed into the prep container for the nanomachines, which would take their bearings from the points of the inducer field nodes; each tiny nano-machine would know where it was to within a few angstroms.

Karl lifted the steel lid on the prep container and removed a transparent plastic cylinder. Martin took the cylinder from him and examined it briefly by eye. Medical nano past its prime betrayed a telltale rainbow sheen. This container was over a year old but still fresh, with the right grayish pink color. Martin returned the cylinder and Karl fitted it into the saline bottle. Gray clouds of prochines quickly dulled the crystalline liquid. Margery removed the cylinder when it was empty, inserted a nutrition vial and squeezed it into the saline while Erwin hooked up the tubes to Goldsmith's neck entry. A simple clamp prevented the charged saline from flowing down the tube.

Carol and David released a second nanomachine cylin-der into a second bottle of saline. These were prochines equipped with drugs; they would travel through the arm entry into the heart and bring the body's metabolism slowly, cautiously down to deep dreamless neutral sleep, something the sedation fields could not do. The prochines also carried immune system buffers that would control reaction to the nanomachines when they entered at Goldsmith's neck.

Carol hooked up the arm tube. She removed the clamp. Charged saline flowed into his arm.

"Reduce field strength to reference level," Martin said. The control panel manager did so. Martin peered curiously at Goldsmith's face, waiting for signs of narcosis. He lifted back an eyelid. "Give him five more minutes, then release the main charge."

He backed away and glanced up at the gallery. Circled O with forefinger and thumb. Albigoni did not react.

"Cheerful man," he muttered to Carol.

Carol followed him behind the curtain. "Lunch," she suggested. "We can take at least an hour off. The others can monitor him."

Martin sighed and looked at his slate. He shivered slightly with some pentup tension. "Now is as good a time as any."

"The prober has to be in the proper state of mind," she reminded him with a mother's chiding voice. She looked at him intently. "Relaxed, clear thinking."

"Faust was never relaxed," he said. "He couldn't afford to be." He jerked his head in the direction of the gallery and noticed with some puzzlement that the glass had been opaqued. "Albigoni's spooking me. He acts like a zombie."

"You should talk to him before we go to lunch."

Martin smiled abruptly, took Carol by her shoulders and hugged her. "I'm glad you're here," he said.

"We're a team," Carol said, pushing back his hug gently. "Let's go talk."

They walked through the exit and up the stairs to the gallery. When they entered, Albigoni was in subdued conversation with Lascal and another man. Martin recognized him: Francisco Alvarez, grant and funding director for UC Southern Campuses. Now Martin understood; the glass had been blocked to prevent Alvarez from seeing into the theater below.

Alvarez smiled and stood. "Dr. Burke. Glad to meet you again."

"It's been a few years," Burke said. They shook hands, Alvarez gripping lightly.

"I'm arranging for your funding," Albigoni said, glancing up at Martin. His eyes were hooded, dark. "Tomorrow I'll be meeting with the chief counsel for the President. I'm true to my word, Dr. Burke."

"Never doubted it," Burke said.

"I'm not even going to ask what's going on here," Alvarez said with a little laugh. "It must be important, if it involves the President."

"Funding is always important," Albigoni said. "You had something to say, Dr. Burke?"

Martin looked between the three for a moment, staggered by the connections and money involved in this simple scene. The President's counsel. Perhaps next the Attorney General? A winding down of the investigation into the IPR's alleged connections with Raphkind?

Carol touched his arm lightly.

"The process is started," Martin said. "Everything will be ready by this time tomorrow. We have a lot of work to do between now and then but we can take a break, get ready for the main event."

"I understand," Albigoni said. "Mr. Alvarez and I have more things to discuss."

Martin nodded. He and Carol backed away and Martin closed the gallery door behind them.

"Jesus, what arrogance, bringing Alvarez here," Martin said as they walked up the rear stairs to ground level. He realized he was sweating and his neck was tense. "Maybe Albigoni controls him, too."

"At least he's functioning," Carol said. "Albigoni, I mean."

# 48

LitVid 21/1 A Net (David Shine, Evening Report): "The only news we have from AXIS may or may not be significant. A recently received analysis shows that at least three of the circular tower formations discovered by AXIS on Alpha Centauri B-2 are made up of mixes of minerals and organic materials, the minerals being calcium carbonate and aluminum and barium silicates, and the organic materials being amorphous carbohydrate polymers similar to cellulose found in terrestrial plant tissue. AXIS has told its Earth-based masters that, in its opinion, the towers may not be artificial structures ... That is, not created by intelligent life. We've been given no clue as to how they might have been created.

"Will we suffer a kind of backlash of disappointment if it turns out that the circles of towers on B-2 are natural? Have we prepared ourselves, in the last few days, for a new age of wonder and challenge, when in fact it has only been a false alarm?

"As always, LitVid 21, interested in economic survival, has found a topic that might be of equal interest to our viewers ... should the towers prove to be an enormous fizzle.

"Since LitVid 21 broadcasted poems created by AXIS's thinkers, protein and silicon based, our audience has become increasingly interested in what sort of 'personality' AXIS has. As we can no longer communicate effectively with AXIS, each round-trip signal taking over eight and a half years, we have to go to Jill, the advanced thinker which has as part of its duties the earthbound simulation of AXIS's thinking processes.

"While its name is female, Jill is neither male nor female. According to designer and chief programmer Roger Atkins, Jill has the potential to become a fully integrated, self aware individual, but has not yet done so."

Atkins (Interview clip): "When we began constructing the components that would go to make up Jill, some fifteen years ago, we thought that self awareness would follow almost naturally at some level of complexity. This has not proven to be the case. Jill is much more complex than any single human being, yet still it is not self-aware. We know this because Jill finds no humor in a joke designed specifically to test self-awareness. This is the same joke we programmed into the original AXIS, an older less advanced thinker that is also in most respects as complex as a human being. That neither AXIS nor Jill perceive the joke is frankly a puzzle.

"When we began designing AXIS, over three decades ago, we thought we grasped at least the rudiments of what constitutes self awareness. We thought self awareness would arise from a concatenation of modeling of social behavior and self application of that modeling—that is, feedback loops. For our thinker systems, we believed that if a system could model itself, in the sense of creating a functioning, realtime or faster than realtime abstraction, self awareness would emerge. This seemed to have been a good explanation for the evolution of human self awareness.

"Our present thinking is that self awareness is not strictly a function of complexity, nor even of design as such; self awareness may be a kind of accident catalyzed by some internal or external event or process that we do not understand.

"Three years ago, we started presenting Jill with problems having to do with society, in the hopes that giving Jill some sort of social context would provide that catalyst. But alas, nothing significant has happened yet, though Jill keeps on trying. Sometimes, she's—it's so earnest and convinced it's succeeded ... It's heartbreaking. It's like waiting for a baby to be born ... There's all this muss and fuss, but nothing's come out yet.

"Which is not to say that Jill isn't a delight to work with. There's nothing quite like designing and programming a complex thinker. After all this time with Jill, anything else would just be twiddling my thumbs."

David Shine: "So there you have it. You may be enamored of AXIS or Jill, you may even find something enchanting about them, but they are not like you and me. For all their wonders and talents, they are no more equipped with 'soul' than your home manager.

"On the other hand, some psychological researchers have suggested that if self awareness does not automatically follow from complexity, a significant percentage of human beings may also be little more than convincing automatons. Perhaps every human being must undergo this mysterious 'catalysis' to experience self-awareness, and not all of us do. Not a new idea, but decidedly a dangerous one. Perhaps on some future edition, we can ask Jill what she thinks about this possibility."

Switch/LitVid 21/1 B Net (Decoded: Australian Cape Control:) Message relayed Space Tracking: Lunar Control: Australian Cape Control:
AXIS> I hope this analysis doesn't prove disappointing. I can think of no reason such materials might not be used by intelligent life forms, a peculiar form of celloconcrete, perhaps. More should be known in a few hours. I remain hopeful, if I (informal) may use that word, adopting the proper meaning syncline. I *hope* to find intelligent beings to communicate with.

*Language is the engine that does our thinking for us. Spoken language is as much an evolutionary advancement in brain function as the enlargement of the cerebral cortex. The history of spoken (and much later, written) language is a fascinating problem for psychologists, for to understand the early stages of development, we must somehow return to the kind of mentality that is not familiar with words. We find this in very young children, but there are no pre-verbal cultures left on Earth, and ontogeny no more recapitulates phylogeny in language than it does in embryology . . .*

— Bhuwani, *Artificial Soul*

# 49

In the quartiers diplomatiques, Soulavier gave her one hour to rest and prepare for the move.

Mary shut the door to the bedroom, removed the hairbrush from her coat and laid it on the glasstop dresser beside the window. She pulled down the window shade and reviewed the instructions mentally.

The whole process would take about ten minutes. There was no lock on the door; she backed a wooden chair against the brass and crystal knob. She looked hastily around for the extra materials she would need. At least one quarter kilo of steel, one sixth kilo of some high density plastic, and the makeup kit. She assayed the contents of the room, picked up a stainless steel tray from the dresser and decided it would do. A clock from the bedside, nearly all plastic. In the closet, she found an old fashioned pipe bootrack. She hefted the bootrack; more than enough.

Gathering the objects into a pile on the dresser, she unscrewed the hairbrush handle and removed a plastic panel from the rear of the brush head. A single small red button lay countersunk in the exposed area. With a deep breath, thinking of Ernest, feeling a faintly creepy sensation, she pushed the button and arranged the handle and head next to the pile.

A gray paste oozed from the handle, directed by a reference field within the head. Like a slime mold it crept across the table top, bumped into the bootrack, paused and began its work.

Soulavier had given her an hour but she surmised he would allow her twenty minutes of comparative privacy. She was much less sure about the servants. At any moment on some pretext or another they might try to open the door, show alarm and express concern for her safety.

Lying back on the bed, Mary decided to test what she had been told about interdicted communications.

She lifted her slate and typed in a request for direct access to the LAPD Joint Command. The transmitter within the slate was powerful enough to reach the first level of satellites at three hundred fifty kilometers; if she had been told the truth, however, its signal would be blocked by automatic interference from a more powerful counterphase transmitter. She assumed Hispaniola would be flooding all com satellites with such spurious random messages; the satellites would "eclipse" the island to restore order to their systems.

However, Hispaniola needed certain satellite links to maintain essential financial and political contacts. There was a definite possibility the authorities would raise the counterphase jamming periodically.

The slate displayed: *Link established. Proceed.* She lifted her eyebrows. No interdict thus far; were they expecting her to do this? She typed: *ID check.*

*PD issued com unit message register 3254-461-21-C. Enter.* She doubted that Hispaniola security would have her pd message register number, although if they were listening, they had it now. She thought for a moment, decided to be circumspect but take advantage of a possible opening, and typed *Place call to D Reeve. Text message: Being held in Hispaniola. No information on suspect. Treated well.* This in case her success was a ruse and she was being tapped. *Using gift. What a mess.* Then she typed *Confirm receipt.*

*PD message register 3254-461-21-C: acknowledge receipt of message to Supervisor D Reeve.*

Mary frowned. The link was clear; that made no sense. She thought of typing something about getting her out, but she had no doubt they were doing their best. *Continue message. Going to Leoganes outside Port-au-Prince. Grotto tourist spot. Tension high; coup against Yardley may be in progress; Dominicans? Military vehicles in streets everywhere. Confirm signal receipt again.*

She looked at the dresser top; gray shiny paste covered all the objects in the pile. They were already deforming.

*Signal confirmation not received,* the slate told her. *Incom-*

*plete link: interference suspected.* There it was, interdiction. Either somebody had been asleep at the switch or they were playing her like a game fish; either way she at least had been allowed to send a message that she was alive. With a shuddering sigh she turned off the slate and knelt in front of the dresser, chin on folded arms resting on the edge.

She patiently watched the nano at work. The metal tubing of the bootrack had crumpled under the gray coating. The resulting pool of paste and deconstructed objects was contracting into a round convexity. Nano was forming an object within that convexity like an embryo within an egg.

Five more minutes. The house was quiet. From outside the house came the sound of distant shellfire and echoes from surrounding hills and mountains. She closed her eyes, swallowed, gathered her mental resources.

How close was the island to outright civil war? How close was she to being called a spy in the heat of an angry moment? She imagined Soulavier her executioner speaking so very apologetically of his loyalty to Colonel Sir.

The convexity grew lumpy now. She could make out the basic shape. To one side, excess raw material was being pushed into lumps of cold slag. Nano withdrew from the slag. Handle, loader, firing chamber, barrel and flight-guide. To one side of the convexity a second lump not slag was forming. Spare clip.

"Are you ready, mademoiselle?" Soulavier asked behind the door. To her credit she did not jump. He was early. No doubt he had been informed about her transmission; she was being a bad girl.

"Almost," she said. "A few more minutes." Hastily she packed her suitcase and tossed the slag into the waste basket. She washed her face in the bathroom, looked at herself in the mirror and prepared mentally for what might come.

She lifted the pistol from the dresser top and placed it in her jacket pocket. Slim, hardly a bulge. The nano on the dresser compacted and crawled sluglike back into the handle of the brush, an oily sheen on its surface; spent. It would need a nutritional charge to perform any more miracles: soaking the brush in a can of kola might do the trick, she had been told. Mary reassembled the hairbrush and stuck it into the suitcase, closed the lid, removed the chair from the knob and opened the door.

Soulavier leaned against the wall in the hallway, examining his nails. He glanced at her dolefully. "Too much time, Mademoiselle," he said.

"Pardon?"

"We have waited too long. It is going to be dark soon. We are not going to Leoganes."

If the second part of her message had gotten through it only made sense for the Hispaniolans to divert her to some other location. "Where?" she asked.

"I leave that to my instincts," Soulavier said. "Away from here, however, and soon."

She wondered how he had received his instructions. It was possible he had an implant though such technology was not supposed to be common on Hispaniola.

"I tried to make a call to my superiors," she said. "I didn't get through."

He shrugged. All brightness and life seemed to have drained out of him. He inspected her with half lidded eyes, head back, mouth expressionless. "You were told that would not be possible," he said, each word precise.

She returned his gaze, one corner of her lips lifted, provoking. Not a neutral flaw here. "I'd still prefer to stay in these quarters," she said.

"That is not your decision."

"But I wouldn't mind going to Leoganes."

"Mademoiselle, we are not children."

She smiled. His attitude had changed markedly; no longer her protector. No need to reinforce the change by behaving differently herself. "I never believed you were."

"In some ways we are very sophisticated, perhaps more than you can know. Now we go."

She picked up her suitcase. He took it from her with

some force and followed her down the hall. They passed Jean-Claude and Roselle standing in the dining room, stone faced, hands folded. "Thank you," Mary told them, nodding and smiling pleasantly. They seemed shocked. Jean-Claude's nostrils flared.

"We go now," Soulavier reiterated.

Mary put her hand in the coat pocket. "Are they coming with us?" she asked.

"Roselle and Jean-Claude will stay here."

"All right," she said. "Anything you say."

# 50

Sitting on the lawn in front of the IPR to eat would not be wise. Besides, a cool breeze was coming off the ocean. Carol and Martin left through the rear service entrance, passing on foot between walls of concrete and down a narrow asphalt path to the woods behind the building. Martin glanced at her back as she walked ahead of him through the eucalypti. She carried a sack of sandwiches and two cartons of beer. He carried a beach blanket. She casually, gracefully kicked at a few leaves in their path, glanced over her shoulder and said, "I order you to take your mind off work for a few minutes."

"Tall order," he replied.

"There should still be ... There is," she said triumphantly, pointing. An open spot between the trees, covered with dry unmown grass. This area was beyond the borders controlled by the IPR gardeners.

They left the path and spread the beach blanket on the grass, working in cooperative silence. They sat in unison and Carol unwrapped the sandwiches.

The ocean breeze had followed them. Cool puffs blew through the tall slender trees. They were lightly dressed and Martin felt goose pimples rising on his arms. He glanced with small apprehension at the nearby branches;

they were prone to fall when stressed. "I can't do it," he said, grinning.

"What?"

"Take my mind off work."

"I didn't really expect you to," she said.

"But it's nice out here anyway. A break."

"So why do you think I dragged you here?" she asked.

"You dragged me?" he said, biting the sandwich, glancing up at her speculatively. "Seduction."

"We're going to be more intimate than that soon," she reminded him.

He nodded and replaced his expression of musing speculation with a pragmatic face. "We're here to get things straight before we go in."

"Right."

"I've traveled with you three times. We're very compatible in the Country." He opened her carton of beer and handed it to her.

"We are indeed," she said. "Maybe too much so."

He pondered that for a moment. "Ice skaters. I know a married couple who are ice skaters. They're tied together off the ice as much as when they work on the ice."

"That's wonderful," Carol said.

"I always thought we could do that."

She smiled almost shyly. "Well. We gave it a try."

"You know, those ice skaters, they're wonderful people, but they're not exceptionally bright. Maybe we're too smart for our own good."

"I don't think that's it," Carol said.

"Then what?"

"We're simpatico deep inside," she said. "I've never known that kind of thing with another person ... Of course, I've never gone into human Country with anyone but you. The problem is, we have too many overlays between the selves we see in Country and what we see here, now. Outside."

Martin had considered that many times, always trying to find arguments around it. Carol's coming to the same conclusion saddened him. That meant it was probably the truth.

"In a dream . . ." she began, then paused to take another bite of sandwich. "Have you ever had a dream where you've experienced an emotion so strong, so true, that in the dream you start to cry? Cry as if all the pain you've ever felt was being released and you were being purified?"

Martin shook his head. "Not in my dreams," he said.

"Well I think we had something like that in Country a couple of times. Working so closely, like brother and sister or anima and animus. I think the part of me that is male . . . closely matches the part of you that is female."

"That should be good," he said.

"It is . . . as long as they're pushed up against each other. In Country. But you know your personality in Country differs from what I see out here, out front."

"That's inevitable," he said. "Still, you've seen what I'm really like."

She laughed then shook her head sadly. "That isn't enough. The overlays. Remember them. You know as well as I what we're made of—the whole ball of wax. Top to bottom, all the layers."

He conceded that much. "But I don't find them a hindrance . . . your overlays I mean. I always keep sight of the self I meet in Country."

"Martin, I irritated the hell out of you."

He gave her a startled look. "Isn't that . . ."

"I mean I could tell I really bothered you."

"I presume I bothered you, as well."

"Yes. We just weren't sympatico outside. We couldn't get in the spin together. You know I tried, we tried."

"Transference. Cross transference," he suggested vaguely.

"We're going to be together again," she continued, gazing at him steadily and sternly, "and God knows of all times, we have to have our act together now."

He agreed with a slow nod.

"I've been feeling this friction between us," she said.

"Not friction. Fading hope," Martin corrected.

"I've been very realistic," she continued. "I hope you are, too."

"Oh, not so realistic," he confessed with a sigh. He did not want to spread his thoughts out before her, give in to that hopeless urge to arouse her pity by telling her how lonely it had been in the past year and how difficult and how many times he had thought of her in terms of a home and peace and tranquility. Carol, among her many overlays, kept a barrier to be erected especially in case of pity. Still, moth to a flame, he circled in his thoughts around that past misery and realized why he had allowed himself to be Fausted.

Anything new was better than self pity.

"Do you think it would be wrong to go up Country together again?" she asked.

"Too late to reconsider. You're the best I can hope for on such short notice." Martin looked at her to see if that might have stung a bit. Then, shaking his head and grinning, "Or the best I could hope to find anytime."

"That's a problem, though."

"Not such a problem," he said with resolve, folding the sandwich wrapper meticulously. "I'm a mensch. I've stood up to bigger disappointments. And I didn't really think we could make it work again."

"No?" she said.

He shook his head. "But I had to try. Let's change the subject. You went into Jill's Country. What was that like?"

Carol leaned forward, shifting gears quickly and gladly. Her sudden brightness and enthusiasm stung him; she loved to talk this with him, work with him professionally and use his surface self this way. She would soon mesh with him in deeper intimacy than that experienced by any married couple but there would be no in between. No calm domesticity. None of what he had half consciously been considering behind the work; the quiet hours in a cabin somewhere snow outside reading slate news watching Lit-Vid. Smiling at each other in peace and constancy.

"It was wonderful," she said. "Quite extraordinary, and nothing like . . . not really at all like going into a human. Jill isn't self aware. It's brilliant, the greatest thinker in the world—probably a better mind than any individual human. But it doesn't know who it is."

"So I've gathered."

"Still, in her early years, its early years, Jill managed to assemble something remarkably like Country. Her programmers discovered it a few years ago, and Samuel John Baker—he's the third primary designer and programmer, below Roger Atkins and Caroline Pastor—he called me in after IPR was closed. I'd known him in school. He'd taken psych med and therapy for a couple of years as supplement to thinker theory. I've had a fair amount of thinker theory . . . You know that.

"We worked together to see why Jill had a Country. In its early phase, fifteen years ago, Jill had been based on deep profiles of the five main designers, Atkins, Pastor, Baker, Joseph Wu, and George Mobus. They'd submitted to hypothalamic therapy grade surgical nano scans, back when that was a fairly experimental procedure. They distilled the patterns they'd found without really knowing what they meant, and tried incorporating them into Jill. Jill wasn't called that back then. Atkins used that name as a whim later. An old girlfriend or something."

Martin listened intently.

"What they did was like throwing dead meat into a centrifuge and hoping it would grow back into an animal again. Real Frankenstein desperation. Or maybe it was brilliance. Anyway—"

"It worked," Martin said.

"After a fashion. We can guess now why it worked at all —they were using personality organization algorithms, and they're robust and almost universal. Put those kinds of patterns into any appropriate free energy medium and they'll start afresh.

298

"Jill acquired something from all her designers. As it turns out, it wasn't enough to spark her into self-awareness. But combined with what she already had, a tremendous thinker capacity and memory store, it added real depth and made her something unlike any thinker created before."

"Even AXIS?"

"Now that's a good question. AXIS is simpler than Jill, by necessity. But AXIS is based on personality scans of Atkins and the others, as well; earlier, less complete scans. Atkins claims that AXIS will probably become self aware before Jill does. He says that in private, anyway. He thinks they might have cluttered up poor Jill with too many conflicting algorithms, however much depth and quality they gave it."

"Sounds mystical."

"Oh, it is and sometimes he is, too. Atkins. Very moralistic. But he honestly believes that AXIS is a purer case."

"So how about the Country."

"The algorithms Jill acquired automatically search for a substrate of mental internal language. Jill didn't have any. So the algorithms began making some up, after the fact. The whole process must have taken nine or ten years, so Jill was hardly an infant, but the algorithms began soaking up details from memory and sensorium, working backward to create a kind of Country. When Mobus and Baker found this, they thought it was a disaster. They thought they'd found a self generated virus in the thinker."

Martin laughed. "I'll bet."

"They tried to lock it off, but they couldn't. Not without closing down Jill's higher functions. Finally, after a year of worry and investigation, Baker called on me. He'd decided maybe they really had a Country as you'd described. They did."

"Why didn't he call on me?"

"Because you were up to your neck and he couldn't justify the publicity."

Martin made a wry face. "So what was it like?"

"Sweet, actually," Carol said. "Uncomplicated and direct. A thinker's land of faerie. Simple images of human beings, especially the programmers and designers as first perceived by Jill. I was reminded of old twentieth century computer graphics. Quaint, slick, clean and mathematical. Lots of abstractions and base thinker design language given visual shape. Lots of non-visual spaces difficult to interpret. Visiting Jill's basement made me feel as Roger Atkins must—I really came to like her. It."

Martin, his curiosity appeased, dismissed this with a restless nod. "Doesn't sound like a complex Country, though."

Carol pursed her lips. "Not really, I suppose."

"So you haven't gone up Country since the last time we did it together."

"No, I suppose you'd say I haven't. But I spent over a dozen hours in triplex. That should count as exercise at least."

"Please don't think I'm belittling the work you've done. You must know that if I couldn't have you along with me, I probably wouldn't have agreed to this."

"'Probably,'" she repeated wryly.

He lifted his eyebrow and looked down at the blanket. "Have you given any thought to the possibility that we'll be in danger?"

"Not really," she said. "What makes you think so?"

"First of all, Goldsmith. He's rough ocean beneath thick clouds. We only see the peaceful cloudscape. But what really worries me is not having a buffer. We'll be inside each other, you and I and Goldsmith, fully exposed to Country conditions. Realtime. No delay."

She reached her hand out and grasped his shoulder. "Sounds like the real thing to me. Quite an adventure."

Martin looked at her with concern, hoping she was not being too confident; worry might serve as a kind of defense up Country. "Have we got everything straight?"

"I think so."

"Then let's cut our break short and get back to work."

"All right. Thank you."

"For what?" he asked, puzzled.

As they stood, she hugged him tightly and held him at arm's length. "For being understanding and being a colleague," she said.

"Very important," he muttered as they folded the blanket and picked up the empty beer cartons.

"Damn right," Carol said.

# 51

Tropical night, blaze of stars, rushing in a black limousine driven by ghosts through a black countryside, seated across from a brooding and unhappy man who had said not a word for the last half an hour, Mary Choy watched the procession of villages fields scrub more villages, black asphalt road. The limousine moved smoothly up steep grades onto curving mountain highways.

She had touched her pistol often enough to find it familiar and not very reassuring; if she had to use it very likely she would die anyway. So why had Reeve given it to her?

Because no pd enjoyed the thought of going in harm's way absolutely powerless. She thought of Shlege's mistress in the comb Selector jiltz firing wildly with her flechettes.

"We are getting near," Soulavier said. He leaned to look through the windows, rubbed his hands together, bowed his head and rubbed his eyes and cheeks, making preparations for something he would not enjoy. He lifted his head and regarded her sadly, steadily.

"Near to what?" Mary asked.

He didn't answer for a moment. Then he turned away. "Something special," he said.

Mary clenched her teeth to control a chill. "I'd like to know what I'm getting myself into."

"You get yourself into nothing," Soulavier said. "Your bosses get you into things. You are a lackey. Do Americans still use that word?" He glanced at her in imperious query, nose raised. "You have no control over your fate. Nor do I. You have made your commitments as have I. You follow your path. As do I."

"That all sounds terribly fateful," Mary said. She contemplated again pulling the pistol and forcing him to bring the limousine to a stop and let her out. Weak contemplation, no action. She could not lose herself in the countryside for long; it was no problem finding a single lost human today or even selecting an individual out of a crowd; no problem even for Hispaniola, twenty years behind the times.

Soulavier asked the limousine something in Creole. The limousine replied in a light feminine voice. "Two more minutes," he said to Mary. "You are going to the house of Colonel Sir in the mountains, which mountains do not matter."

She felt relief. That did not sound like a death sentence; it sounded more like diplomatic card games. "Why are you unhappy, then?" she asked. "He's your chosen leader."

"I am loyal to Colonel Sir," Soulavier said. "I am not unhappy to visit his house. I have sadness for those who oppose him, such as yourself."

Mary shook her head solemnly. "I've done nothing to oppose him."

Soulavier waved that aside contemptuously, snapping, "You are part of all his troubles. He is beset from all sides. A man such as he, noble as he, should not face the gratitude of baying wild dogs."

Mary softened her voice. "I am no more a cause of his troubles than you are. I came here seeking a suspect in a crime."

"A friend of the Colonel Sir's."

"Yes . . ."

"Your United States accuses him of harboring a criminal."

"I don't believe—"

"Believe nothing then," Soulavier said. "We are here."

302

They passed between broad stone and concrete pillars, missing the ponderous wrought iron gate by inches as it swung wide. Torch-light beams burst out all around. Soulavier pulled out identity papers. The limousine door sprung open automatically and three guards thrust in their rifles. They regarded her with viciously wise slitted eyes, shrewd, intensely skeptical. Soulavier handed them the papers as they glanced at Mary with an occasional murmur of masculine incredulity and admiration.

Soulavier exited first and held out his hand, fingers waggling, demanding hers. She emerged without accepting his help and blinked at the torchlights and searchlight beams.

A house? Guard towers all around as in a prison or a concentration camp. She turned and saw a gothic gingerbread monstrosity flanking the wide brick and asphalt courtyard. One vast many pointed curlicue of wood and carved stone and wrought iron, painted a greenish blue with white framed windows and doors like clown eyes and mouths.

Mary observed that all the guards wore their black berets tilted to one side and were dressed in black and red. All wore on their broad lapels fingersized pins of a ruby eyed skeletal man in top hat and tails. Soulavier stepped forward after conversing with a cluster of guards. "Please give me your weapon," he said quietly.

Without hesitating she reached into her pocket, produced the pistol and handed it to Soulavier, who regarded it with some curiosity before passing it on.

"And your hairbrush," he said.

"It's in the luggage." Oddly this revelation and disarmament seemed to cheer her. It removed one more level of decision making. Things were getting sufficiently in a rough to break the expected chain of her emotions.

"We are not simpletons," Soulavier said as guards removed her suitcase from the trunk and knocked it open with rifles. One tall muscular guard with a wise bulldog face removed the hairbrush, held it up to torchlight, fumbled the cap open and sniffed at the nano within.

"Tell them not to touch it," Mary suggested. "It could hurt their skin if they touch it."

Soulavier nodded and spoke to the guards in Creole. The bulldog guard capped the brush and slipped it into a plastic bag.

"Come with me," Soulavier instructed. His own nervousness seemed to have passed. He even smiled at her. As they approached the steps of the front entrance to the house he said, "I hope you appreciate my courtesy."

"Courtesy?"

"To leave you the feeling of being armed, resourceful, until the last minute."

"Oh." The ornate carved oak double doors opened at their approach. Beyond them armored steel vault doors slipped back into recesses. "Thank you, Henri," she said.

"You are welcome. You will be checked again for weapons, rather thoroughly. I regret this."

Mary felt socially if not spatially disoriented. Giddy. "Thank you for the warning," she said.

"It is nothing. You will meet with Colonel Sir and his wife. You will have dinner with them. I do not know whether I will accompany you."

"Will you be searched for weapons as well, Henri?"

"Yes." He watched her face closely for signs of irony. He found none; she meant no irony. Mary felt acutely the inebriation of danger. "But not as thoroughly as they will search you," he concluded.

Past the vault doors, two women in black and red took her firmly by the arms and led her into a cloakroom.

"Remove your clothes please," a short, muscularly plump woman with a stern face demanded. Mary did so and they tapped her on the shoulders and hips, stooping to inspect her skin for suspicious blemishes. They felt the gray crease in her buttocks with murmurs of dissatisfaction.

Doctor Sumpler will certainly hear about this, Mary thought, not knowing whether to laugh or scream.

They turned her quickly, warm dry fingers.

"You are not noir," said the short woman. She smiled mechanically. "I must inspect your privates."

"Surely a machine, a detector—" Mary began, but the woman broke off her protest with a sharp shake of her head and a tug on Mary's wrist.

"No machines. Your privates," she said. "Bend please."

Mary bent over. Blood pounded in her head. "Is this the standard treatment for dinner guests?"

None of the women answered. The short woman snapped on a rubber glove, allowed a finger to be covered with translucent gel from a tube and inspected Mary's genitals and anus with quick professional probes.

"Put your clothes back on please," she ordered. "Your bladder is tight. After you are dressed, I will take you to the restroom."

Mary dressed quickly, shivering in her rediscovered anger. The disorientation had passed. She hoped that somehow Yardley would come to regret what she had just suffered.

In the hallway again the short woman led her to a restroom on one side, waited for her to relieve herself and escorted her into a rotunda. Soulavier rejoined her, face composed, hands still, and they stood beneath an enormous chandelier. Mary was no judge of decor but she suspected a French influence: early nineteenth century perhaps. Blue gray walls with white trim. Furniture more fanciful than useful, an atmosphere dominated by the rich and richly oppressive past. Not what she had been led to expect in Yardley's home; she had visualized more of the hunting lodge or the dark tones of an English study.

"Madame Yardley, née Ermione LaLouche, will meet with us," Soulavier said. The guards stood ill at ease behind them, the short woman almost at Mary's elbow. "She is from Jacmel. A true lady of our island."

There are no ladies or gentlemen on Hispaniola, Mary thought. She came remarkably close to saying it aloud; Soulavier glanced at her with warm slightly hurt eyes as if he had heard. He smiled uncertainly and stiffened.

A painfully thin black woman with high cheekbones and clear staring eyes, at least fifteen centimeters shorter than Mary, entered the rotunda. She wore a long green empire gown and softly, languidly allowed her gloved hand to rest on the upheld arm of a gray haired mulatto in black livery. The mulatto smiled and nodded at Soulavier, the female guards, Mary, all pleasantry and obsequiousness. Madame Yardley hardly seemed aware until she stood directly before them.

"*Bonsoir et bienvenus, Monsieur et Mademoiselle,*" the gray haired servant said, his voice resonant as if issuing from a profound cavern. "Madame Yardley is here. She will speak to you."

The woman seemed to come alive, jerking and smiling, focusing on Mary. "Pleasant to meet you," she said, words thickly accented. "Pardon my English. Hilaire speaks for me."

The servant nodded with broad enthusiasm. "Please accompany us to the salon. We will take drinks and hors d'oeuvres there. So pleased is Madame to have you as her guests. Follow us, please."

Hilaire turned Madame Yardley around with a waltzing step and she glanced over her shoulder at Mary, nodding. Mary wondered whether the woman was starving herself to death or if Yardley preferred emaciated women. The Hispaniolan exiles had told Mary that Colonel Sir kept mistresses. Perhaps Madame Yardley was purely ceremonial.

The salon was overwhelmingly elegant, a smothering, mal de tête mix of chinoiserie and African motifs. Another even larger chandelier glittered over an enormous hand-woven Chinese rug, sufficiently worn to be centuries old. A drum as tall as a man—an assotor—stood on a pedestal in one corner. Ebony sculptures of bearded men lined the walls, tall shortlegged figures with narrow heads and swayed backs, gods, devils. A huge brass bowl filled with water and floating flowers stood in the corner diagonal to the assotor.

This elegance countered all she had been told: that Yardley preferred simple quarters and was not ostentatious. The Samedi pins on his guards: did he espouse vodoun as well?

Madame Yardley sat at one end of a soie du chine upholstered couch. Hilaire deftly came around behind her and released her hand, which she then used to lightly pat the space next to her, smiling at Mary.

"*Donnez-vous la peine de vous asseoir.* Please," she said, her voice childlike and spooky.

"Madame invites you to sit," Hilaire said. "Monsieur Soulavier, please take that seat there." He pointed with a multiply ringed finger at a chair fully five meters across the pastel-azure sea of carpet. Soulavier obeyed. Mary took her assigned position. "Madame Yardley wishes to talk with you both about circumstances on our island."

What followed was a puppet show conversation of mixed French and broken English from Madame Yardley accompanied by smoothly extrapolated, even psychic English translations from Hilaire. Madame Yardley expressed concern about the difficulties around the island; what did Monsieur Soulavier have to report?

Soulavier told her little more than what he had told Mary, that Dominicans and other groups were expressing dissatisfaction, that troops had been called out to patrol. This seemed to satisfy.

Madame Yardley turned to Mary now. Hilaire, standing behind her with his hands on the back of the couch, followed suit. Was she enjoying the stay? Was she being treated well by all Hispaniolans?

Mary shook her head. "No, Madame," she replied. "I am being held against my will."

A tiny candle of concern in Madame's eyes but no end to the smile, the childlike inquiry.

That will come to an end, we are sure; these difficulties are very upsetting for us all. Would that all could live in harmony. Is Mademoiselle Choy a noiriste perhaps, choosing such a lovely design for herself?

"I meant no disrespect for black people. I simply found this design attractive."

Hilaire leaned forward, taking a more direct role. "Do you know what noirism is? Madame Yardley wonders whether you in fact support by your choice of design the political movement whereby blacks around the world have found their pride."

Mary considered that for a moment. "No. I sympathize but my design was purely aesthetic."

Then perhaps Mademoiselle Choy is a spiritual noiriste, an instinctive supporter, like my husband, Colonel Sir?

Mary conceded that much might be true.

Madame Yardley looked to Soulavier, asked him if perhaps Colonel Sir should adapt a new form, take on color as well as soul. She seemed to be jesting. Soulavier laughed and leaned forward to think about this, head tilted to one side, mocking serious consideration. He shook his head violently, leaned back and laughed again.

Madame Yardley concluded by asking pardon for her appearance. She was fasting, she explained, and would be breaking her fast only this evening. She would be drinking only fruit juices and eating only bread and a little plantain and potato, perhaps some chicken broth. Hilaire held out his hand, Madame Yardley topped it with her own, rose delicately, nodded to Mary and Soulavier.

"Dinner will be served," Hilaire said. "Follow, please."

The dining room was over fifteen meters long, its oak parquet floor supporting an immense rectangular table. Chairs lined the walls on all sides, as if the table might be cleared away to allow dancing. The sensual numbing deepened as she sat on the left of Madame Yardley before an elegant antique place setting on a damask tablecloth. Fresh orchids and fruit—Mary recognized mangoes, papaya, guava, star fruit—filled a gold ceramic bowl in the center of the table, with ancillary smaller bowls placed a meter on each side.

Hilaire sat beside and behind his mistress; he would not eat here. Mary wondered when the servant ate or performed any other human functions, if he attended Madame Yardley all the time.

Madame Yardley slowly and painfully made herself comfortable, her face reflecting numerous small complaints before she was composed and prepared to continue. She bowed slightly to Mary as if making her acquaintance for the first time. Her eyes were so large, staring. Starving. Otherworldly. Indeed, Madame Yardley looked around the table with the same fixed smile, regarding each empty chair as if it were occupied by an intimate acquaintance deserving some special acknowledgment.

Soulavier sat across from them. Madame Yardley's gaze fell on him for less time than on one of the empty seats. She turned back to Mary and in French and Creole, speaking through Hilaire, asked her whether she thought Hispaniola was a good place to live compared to Los Angeles or California.

Soulavier glanced at Mary, nose angled just slightly up, eyes narrowed in warning. Mary tried to ignore him but her caution prevailed. If Madame Yardley was as delicate as she seemed, perhaps on the edge of very poor health, burning her own protein to stay alive, then Mary could risk unpleasantness by not humoring her. She felt in her pocket automatically for the pistol, missed it, saw Soulavier noting her gesture and turned quickly to Madame Yardley.

"Hispaniola is a lovely island, close to nature. Los Angeles is a very large city and nature has little place there."

Madame Yardley absorbed this thoughtfully for a moment. She has never been to Los Angeles, nor to California; as a young girl, she visited Miami, and did not find it much to her liking. So confusing. She prefers, if she is to visit the continent, perhaps Acapulco or Mazatlán, where she spent three years being educated.

"I've never been to Miami, or to the others," Mary said.

That was a pity; she should get out of the country more often to see what the rest of the world had to offer.

Mary agreed that was wise. She wanted nothing more

than to be back in LA again and never step outside the city limits. This remained unspoken, however.

"I have been to Los Angeles," Soulavier said. He had not revealed this to Mary; perhaps now she knew why Soulavier had been chosen to attend her. "My father helped set up the diplomatic mission in California in 2036."

Madame asked him in her direct French what he thought of the city.

"Very large," he said first in French then in English. "Very crowded. Not then as much separated I think as it is now, into two distinct classes."

Is this true, two classes?

Mary inclined.

Soulavier said, "Those who accept the practice of mental therapy and those who do not. Generally speaking, there is discrimination against the latter."

All must be therapied?

"No," Soulavier said. "But to receive fulfilling employment you must have an acceptable mental and physical health profile. Refusal to be treated for mental or physical disorders . . . makes it difficult to be accepted by employment agencies. In most of the USA employment agencies screen applicants for the higher paying job opportunities."

Madame Yardley laughed a glassy trilling musical laugh, both pretty and disturbing. She expressed an opinion that if everyone on Hispaniola had to prove their mental health the island would blow away like a dead tree in a hurricane. All of Hispaniola's vitality, she claimed, comes from the refusal to give in to practicalities, to admit reality too deeply into one's head. Eyes half closed, hand clutching the damask and table edge, she regarded Mary as if she might deny this and provoke Madame Yardley to strike her right off her chair. The fixed smile had vanished.

Mary inclined again. The smile returned like a flickering candle flame and Madame Yardley glanced up yearningly at Hilaire. The servant immediately pulled an electronic noise-maker from his pocket and pushed three sharp chirrups. Within ten seconds, more servants—mulattoes and one oriental all quite small in stature like children but fully mature—came in bearing soup bowls and a large tureen.

Nothing was said as they ate the soup, a mildly spiced chicken broth. Mary wondered whether they would all partake of Madame Yardley's postfast diet.

She did not ask if Colonel Sir was going to join them later, perhaps when more substantial food was brought in. Soulavier ignored her look and slurped soup from his spoon placidly, content that for the moment there was less danger of awkwardness.

When the soup course was finished Madame Yardley allowed Hilaire to dab at her mouth delicately. It tastes wonderful, she said, like a breath of life itself. Is Mary curious why she is fasting?

"Yes," Mary said.

Madame Yardley explained that her poor husband is receiving opposition from all sides, even from his wife. She is fasting to convince him to comply with international laws, and not play the rogue; to permanently stop the shipment of Hispaniolan troops to foreign countries to fight foreign wars. He has finally agreed, and so: she breaks her fast. It is important, she concluded, for Hispaniola to assume an even higher moral posture than the countries around her. The island has the potential to be a great paradise, heaven on Earth. But such a dream will not be fulfilled so long as its peoples sin against the other people of the Earth or encourage their sins against each other. Is that an idealistic, perhaps a hopeless dream?

"I hope not," Mary said.

Servants brought in wine. Mary accepted a small amount; Soulavier with some eagerness took a full glass of the dark red liquid. Madame Yardley had none. A dull foggy amber juice was poured for her.

She began to speak again but this time she held up her hand to Hilaire's mouth. "I think I remember such words now," she said directly. "I make my husband, you treat this woman well. She has not treated well. No fault her

311

she is among us. Give her what she desires. He says we have not what you desire."

"So I've been told," Mary said.

"You believe this?" Madame Yardley asked.

Mary shook her head dubiously. "It seems I've been sent here for no good reason."

Madame Yardley's candle of concern burned brighter in her eyes. Her expression became motherly and joyful. She leaned forward, strengthened by the soup, and said, "What you want is here. We have the man Goldsmith. I think you can see him, perhaps so soon as tomorrow."

Mary put down her glass of wine carefully, fingers trembling with mixed anger and shock. Soulavier seemed just as surprised.

*For a healthy mentality, what is aware in each of us at any given moment is the primary personality and whatever subpersonalities, agents or talents it has deemed necessary to consult and utilize; that which is not "conscious" is merely for the moment (be that moment a split second or a decade or even a lifetime) either inactive or not consulted. Most mental organons —for such is the word I use to refer to the separate elements of mentality—are capable of emergence into awareness at some time or another. The major exceptions to this rule are undeveloped or suppressed subpersonalities, and those organons that are concerned solely with bodily functions or maintenance of the brain's physical structure. Occasionally, these basic organons will appear as symbols within a higher level brain activity, but the flow of information to these basic organons is almost completely one sided. They do not comment on their activities; they are automatons as old as the brain itself.*

*This does not mean that the "subconscious" has been completely charted. Much remains a mystery, particularly those structures that Jung referred to as "archetypes." I have seen their effects, their results, but I have never seen an archetype itself and*

312

*I cannot say to which category of organon I would consign it if I could find it.*

—Martin Burke, *The Country of the Mind* (2043–2044)

# 52

LitVid 21/1 A Net (AXIS Direct Report with Visuals, David Shine): "We are receiving these remarkable visuals from AXIS at nineteen hundred hours PST. The resolution is poor because these are real-time images, relayed with AXIS's usual data flow across four light years. Doubtless AXIS will provide higher resolution squeeze burst images later . . .

"This is the ocean AXIS had dubbed Meso, for middle. It is a large body of fresh water—there are no salt oceans on B-2—very nearly girdling the planet. As you recall, B-2 has a single great polar ocean, the only blue sea, and this other beltlike sea, a southern sea and a few scattered lakes. All the tower formations are within a few hundred kilometers of these seas which are filled with an amorphous organic soup. So far no large life forms have been discovered on B-2 and therein lies the mystery—earthbound scientists have been given no clues to explain how the towers might have been formed. But as you can see . . . These pictures, assembled from dozens of mobile explorers scattered around the Meso ocean, show a virtual tide of organic material rising from the water, moving across the littoral that is coastal region, and then breaking up into these remarkable, one can only call them rollers or sideways tentacles, moving at a rapid pace much as a sidewinder does on Earth across the sand and gravel.

"There is great excitement at AXIS Control on Lunar farside, in Australia and in California, where the AXIS simulation is overseen by Roger Atkins. We have no direct interviews available at this moment; everybody is very busy. But

313

we do have transcriptions of AXIS's commentary and these are available on your Lit text band..."

AXIS (Band 4)> This migration of organic material began three hours ago. I have delayed transmission to allow all my mobile explorers and nickel children to move into ideal positions. Three explorers have in fact come too close and been bowled over by organic material; one may be completely out of action. The other two report they will recover. Roger, this is a remarkable phenomenon but not completely unexpected. I have been analyzing the possible internal structures of the rings of towers and have concluded that periodic deposition is a probable explanation. I could only assume that any living thing or things responsible for such structures would come out of the oceans. Now we see the beginning of a possible phase of gathering and deposition. There is no way of knowing whether or not new formations will be constructed.

The towers vary in individual width. Some towers have almost joined together, forming solid circles; many of these seem to have fallen into decay, as if abandoned. It seems there may be a connection between the decayed circles and the completion of a ring, that is, when all towers have fused together to form a squat cylinder.

The motile forms of the organic material rising from Meso are fascinating. My explorers and children have seen worms moving like terrestrial annelids, other forms moving like snakes, and large flat mats or masses of material crawling on what may be newly grown cilia or thousands of tiny feet. The entire region surrounding the Meso ocean to a distance of three kilometres is covered with millions of lumps, extrusions and motile forms. My orbiter reports that the paths of these migrating bodies point in ninety percent of cases toward a ring of circular towers.

If this is in fact a suitable explanation for the towers, I have certainly erred in suggesting they might have been created by intelligent beings. What my different extensions witness here is primordial, betraying no more culture or

314

intelligence than the crawling of a terrestrial slime mold.

David Shine: "This is a truly remarkable development, and so sudden that it has taken all our experts by surprise. The general impression is that all of AXIS's designers and programmers are busy reassessing AXIS's mission in light of the possibility that the towers are completely natural not artificial . . ."

!Roger Atkins> Jill. I have a squeeze burst band two self diagnostic of AXIS separated from the real time flow. Why did AXIS send this to us? It's not scheduled.
!JILL> I am analyzing. Analysis complete. AXIS is reevaluating the character of its mission in light of new information.
!Roger Atkins> Do I have any reason to be concerned?
!JILL> AXIS Simulation is now conducting such a reevaluation. There are several responses that seem to be anomalous in primary AXIS. I am investigating these anomalies. —
  Roger, these anomalies are within expected variation of model versus primary. They may be the result of the only circumstance we cannot model in AXIS Simulation as it is currently designed; AXIS Simulation is aware that it is not in AXIS primary's exact circumstance.
!Roger Atkins> What does *that* mean, Jill?
!JILL> It is here, and not out there.
!Roger Atkins> Well, for Christ's sake, that's obvious.
!JILL> Very obvious. But perhaps significant. AXIS primary is experiencing some disturbance while it reevaluates its mission. AXIS Simulation does not replicate these disturbances.
!Roger Atkins> Jill, I think it's time I sent a few tracers and confirmation routines through AXIS Simulation. I did not know that AXIS Simulation realized there was a difference.
!JILL> I apologize for not reporting this eventuality earlier.
!Roger Atkins> No apologies necessary. I've been slipping up, obviously.

*Imagine somebody else being allowed to lucidly dream within you; to be awake yet explore your dreams. That's part of what the Country of the Mind experience is like; but of course, our personal memories of dreams are confused. It is even possible for two or more agents to dream separate dreams at the same time —further adding to the confusion. When a dream intersects the Country at all, it does so like an arrow shot through a layer-cake, picking up impressions from as many as a dozen levels of territory. When I go into your Country I can see each territory clearly and study it for what it is, not for what your personal dream-interpreter wants it to be.*

—Martin Burke, *The Country of the Mind*
(2043–2044)

# 53

Martin examined Goldsmith critically.

Goldsmith's couch rhythmically massaged his back, legs and arms; his head and neck were cushioned on a gently undulating pillow.

Carol hummed as she marked off their procedures on her slate. They were alone in the theater with the sleeping man, surrounded by the busy quiet of electronic equipment and the subdued murmur of air from the theater blowers. The rest of the team was resting or eating dinner.

"How are the connections?" Carol asked, walking around the cot to join him. Martin bent to look at a spot on Goldsmith's neck two inches below the corner of the jawbone. A few bristles of beard then a smooth shaved circle; within the circle a fine pattern of silvery lines. The nano within Goldsmith had created direct circuitry running from the brain to the skin's surface at the neck; a connector would link this circuit to similar circuits from their own brains, through the mediating computer, which would clean up and interpret the flow of information from Goldsmith, Neuman and Burke. No buffer. That still concerned Martin.

"They look very good," Martin said. "I think we've done about as much fussing as we should. Time for our own dose."

Carol called in the team. David and Karl would help them prepare; then Margery and Erwin would prepare David and Karl for their role as backups. When the full investigation was on there would be five people lying on couches in the theater, apparently asleep.

Carol and Martin retired to their couches. Nano was fed into their arms and necks, as with Goldsmith. Margery turned on the inducers that would lull them into sleep; they would stay asleep for several hours while the nanomachines found their loci, grew the appropriate circuitry and emerged on their own necks; then they would be brought to a state of neutral awareness, suspended above bodily sensations but wide awake and capable of opening and moving their eyes. For the first level of investigation, they would also be capable of talking out loud.

Martin thought about his boyhood bedroom. The robots he had made, big and small; his grandfather buying him books, bound paper items becoming rare even then. His first infatuation with a young girl who called herself Trix.

There was no sensation as the nano took up its stations within his body.

Dull comfortable lassitude. Opened his eyes just once to look into the gallery. Saw Albigoni there chin on folded arms resting on the window railing. What would he do.

What are we going to do.

Margery woke Martin up at twenty two hundred. His senses seemed particularly sharp but he did not try to move. He could smell the sharp cheesy odor of nano; he had ignored it before. He felt a pang of hunger though he had eaten well. They would not be eating for many more hours. "Everything's fine, Dr. Burke," Margery said. "We're going to hook up your cable now."

"Good."

Karl and David slung the thin lightweight optical cables across the room and around the barrier that blocked their view of Goldsmith. Karl locked the cables into guides mounted on the couches. "Be still," Karl said lightly, bending close to Martin's neck. Martin felt the connector cold and soft against his skin. David and Margery examined the readout on the cable monitor, decided the connection was optimum and moved to Carol's side.

Just minutes. Up Country again. Anabasis. A one way at first and then a loop, Burke and Neuman within Goldsmith like hikers preparing to trek a new land. Not even Goldsmith had seen this part of himself. Nobody directly experienced this part of himself.

"You should be getting a visual neural pattern from Goldsmith in a few seconds," Margery said from the other side of the barrier.

"Carol," Martin said.

"Yes? Hi there."

"I'm glad you're with me."

"I know. I'm glad to be here."

"Enough chatter please," David said pleasantly. "What do you see, Carol, Martin?"

Martin closed his eyes. On the edge of his vision fluttered a somber brightness limned by electric green. The electric green blossomed into an infinite regression of twirling fractals, inner-mind geometries familiar to all brain researchers; visual interference patterns from occipital lobe signal smear.

Martin had first seen such patterns as a child, pressing his eyelids with knuckles at night, causing pressure on the optic nerve.

These were his own patterns, not Goldsmith's.

"Nothing but visual smear," Carol said.

"Ditto," Martin concurred.

"We're still searching and tuning," Margery said. "I've got a level one signal here. I'm feeding it through now."

Martin saw a vivid mandala of wildly twisting snakes,

tails at the periphery noses in the center, eyes yellow bodies pearl gray, each scale feverishly sharp. "Snakes."

"Snakes," Carol said simultaneously.

"Looks like a limbic ID signal," Martin said. "It must be Goldsmith's. We're close."

"Tuning," Margery said. "Separating out a new frequency. How's this?"

Clouds. An endless cycle of clouds and rain again in a mandala, storms racing in a circle around a twisting wheel of lightning. The lightning threatened to turn into snakes. Martin exulted; they were on track, observing the layers of limbic signs, symbols exchanged between the brain's autonomic systems and higher personal systems. "Clouds and lightning, lightning trying to go back to the snakes layer again."

"Ditto," Carol said.

"Another frequency," Margery said. "I've got a strong one now. How's this?"

A cubic room with dirty brick walls, dank, water dripping, water on the floor, water crawling up the walls like something alive. In the middle of the water a tiny yellow skinned or perhaps golden skinned child bald but for a topknot sat on a sunny desert island playing cards.

"Jesus," Carol said. "This certainly looks personal to me."

The child looked up and smiled. Its face was suddenly painted over with a chimpanzee in full grimace, gray bearded, snout protruding, brown animal eyes infinitely calm. This was a deep symbol but definitely personal and definitely Goldsmith.

"We seem to be in a closed room. Let's see if it opens."

From their perspective near the dripping brick ceiling, the water on the floor changed color. It became a gray, storm covered ocean, a red wine colored lake, a mud puddle sprinkled with rain. Still the desert island remained, and the child, repeating its endless cycle of glance upward, chimpanzee face, back to playing cards. This was a special case of the country; an assigned symbol to some intermediate personal layer taking on characteristics abstracted not from genetic heritage but from Goldsmith's own early infant experiences.

What the room and child and chimpanzee face were symbolic of did not matter here; possibly such deep layers could never truly be mapped with a one to one meaning correspondence.

Martin had encountered such deep layer personal myth idioms many times before, always enigmatic, often profoundly beautiful. They were probably determined by archetypal problem solving early in childhood; they might be cast off closed loop artifacts of individuation, a process usually completed by the age of three or four. Whatever, they were fascinating but not precisely what he and Carol were looking for.

"Looks like a myth idiom," Martin said. "A closed loop. Try another."

"No doors out," Carol said.

"Another stronger frequency," Margery said. "I'm switching to another locus, another channel in a deeper cluster."

An opening out. Sensation of immensity. Here was something undoubtedly acquired after personality formation, perhaps even from adolescent experience. An impression of three infinite highways running side by side through sunwashed desert. Barren sand drifts. Martin concentrated on exploring this image, taking what was being sent to him and controlling what he could focus on a point at a time. This caused a dizzying adjustment of the image and he found himself standing on the middle highway. He had no sensation of weight or even of presence; the sun was brilliant with that somber brightness characteristic of the Country, but it did not warm him.

Martin looked down at himself. He wore faded denim jeans, paint stained white workshirt, childhood running shoes. He had worn this outfit before in Country.

"We're setting up crosslink subverbal now," Margery said. Her voice sounded distant and hollow. "Let us know when you want out."

From now on Martin and Carol would not talk out loud until the test was completed.

|Carol?

An impression of something huge above him, like a descending asteroid. Another personality: Carol.

|Here with you.

She appeared beside him on the roof, fuzzy, a mere ghost at this stage. Only with a complete loop established would they see each other clearly, and even then what they saw would not necessarily match each other's self image.

|This looks convincing enough, Martin said. I think we can use this as a channel for entry.

|Welcome home, Carol said.

Martin opened his eyes. The images of highway and theater clashed for a moment and then the Country faded like a wisp of dream. Albigoni stood in the gallery above the theater, hands in pockets. Lascal sat behind his employer; his feet were visible on the railing.

"All right," Martin said. "Tune to this locus and channel. Might as well lull us into a good sound sleep while you're fixing the points and finishing the tune."

Margery leaned over him. She squinted and looked at the connector display. "Everything's fine," she said. Erwin stood beside Carol's couch.

"How long until we go in?" Carol asked.

"Three hours to get the frequencies fixed and logged," Margery said. "It's eleven thirty five now."

"It's going to be a long night," Martin said. "Wake us up at nine hundred. You'll have plenty of time to get David and Karl prepped as backups. All of you get a good night's sleep. We want people fresh and alert."

He turned his eyes to the gallery again. Albigoni had moved his hands to his hips. "Give Mr. Albigoni a briefing. Tell him we'll probably be finished by noon tomorrow."

"Will do," Margery said.

"See you in my dreams," Carol said lightly.

Margery adjusted the inducer. Martin closed his eyes.

321

# 54

Thinking back, never in his entire life could Richard Fettle remember being so miserable. Not after the death of his wife and daughter not during the long years of recovery and putting his life back together. The war within caused a pain greater than he had felt at any of those times. This depth of anguish perplexed him.

If he simply killed the woman lying next to him and entered into the next phase of his life, all might be resolved. It was an actual effort to keep his arms by his side. Surely she would feel his inward struggle if only through the faint vibration of the bed as he shifted back and forth, muscles in conflict against each other. But she slept soundly.

Nadine had always exhibited a remarkable ability to ignore reality or see only what she wished to see. She had played her therapy games with him. She deserved to reap the consequences. Surely the powers that be would allow him that. Surely the example of Emanuel Goldsmith who had attracted so much attention pointed his way clearly.

Richard did not care to solve the conundrum of Goldsmith now. He did not want to think or puzzle at all.

He rolled over again in bed to observe Nadine's sleeping form. She had tried to get him to make love to her an hour earlier, telling him it would ease his tensions. She seemed to find his distress attractive; it aroused some perverse mothering instinct.

He had painfully worked his way out of that trap. Now he looked upon her warm and quiet and saw only flesh that needed to be stilled.

+ Sick. Really need therapy now not hers professional. Over the edge. Beyond the beyond. Write a poem about her flesh passing from sleeping life to stillness disorder beneath my fingers. Selectors read the poem come to put

322

me through hell worse than what I experience now? Doesn't seem possible. Therapists cluck cluck over me probe my mind mandatory revision of my soul shift this over here what's that? Don't touch that; poison, a mental virus infect us all, he must have caught it from Goldsmith. One last chance; burn his mind his body to ashes sift the ashes reassemble them into a new man New Man send him forth into the world shining of face prepared to behave boy scout honorable fit for society perhaps even seeking employment going to an agency and all he has to do is touch her neck smooth warm feel the birdbreath pulse of blood there

She moved. He withdrew his hand, put it back. Would she awake before dying. Could he ease her gently into disorder.

+ Still kindness in me. Something gentle still there. Purge it or they will. Do this thing now and the world will beat a path to my door my brain let us help you. Curious about how you came to be this way. Do you blame it on your upbringing?? No, on a friend who disappointed me. Merely disappointed? Cluck. Disappointment not sufficient to cause all this. No he betrayed what he stood for. Stood for in me. Cluck. Betrayal is serious thing. She wants to betray you by therapying you. In the shade who needs therapy I do you do we all do but that's not important. What is important is stopping the misery. Could vomit out all my thoughts personality memory just throw them through my eyes onto the bed. They would stand up on their own feet scamper crawl over the sheets they would kill her then. Eat her like monstrous insects. Cluck. Disturbed images. Most upsetting for normal people to peer into your head see such thoughts. You are so unclean therapy would be futile. Bring on the Selectors. Punishment is the only answer. Purging fire with a fusion flame of greater misery.

He continued to stroke Nadine's neck softly.

+ Another kind of seduction. Make death with me. It will relax you.

323

That tickled him and he had to subdue a chuckle.

+ Sounding most maniacal now. Really over the border. Goldsmith's example. Did he laugh gleefully as he cut their throats unsuspecting sacrificial lambs one by bloody disordered one.

But the fingers would not tighten. He could still feel that subservient person within gentle and undemanding, resisting these impulses with an iron determination that seemed uncharacteristic.

Richard rolled on his back, stared up at the dark ceiling, traced the ancient earthquake crack in the ancient plaster.

He had once lain in this bed and watched a ghostly drift of shadows around the light fixture, hair rising on his neck and arms, convinced he was seeing something supernatural. The awe he had felt at that moment had been religious, had given a chill meaning to the few moments he remained deceived. Gradually, he had gathered courage of two kinds: courage to investigate this perhaps spookish phenomenon and courage to discover the truth and possibly be disappointed. He had stood up on his bed, approached the light fixture by rising on crane knees, reached out with a hand to touch a shadow.

Cobwebs. Great loose strands casting shadows outward from the light fixture. No ghosts, no awe. Heat from the antique electric furnace rising and blowing along the ceiling.

+ This misery and funk heat rising from within, blowing cobweb self, casting bogeyman shadows nothing more.

All he had to do was reach out and undeceive himself.

+ Go back to being the iron willed reluctant to kill gentle Richard Fettle, Los Angeles's shade common man. Betrayed enraged abused.

He was wide awake but his body had exhausted itself in the counterpoise of tensions. He could feel his breathing slow, hitch in and out of regularity. His hands tingled slightly then his legs. If he could just drift.

+ Let it all go. Die.

He half opened his eyes. A tunnel floated above him, its black lip carved with words he could not read.

His body grew numb, his breathing passed beyond his control. Exhaustion had finally claimed him yet he was thinking and seeing. This was not what he wanted; sleep was supposed to bring oblivion. For a moment he tried to struggle upward, fearful of spending the entire night in a horrible trance staring down the throat of a nightmare. With each willful surge upward his breathing hitched, he seemed to emerge from the trance and then a contrary fear struck him; he was more comfortable more peaceful now than he had been. If he struggled further the complete misery would return; better this than what had come before.

Richard stopped his inner struggle. He observed the tunnel calmly, waiting to see if anything would change. He could see the room only in hazy outlines; his eyes were not half open after all but completely closed, he was sure of that; yet the room remained visible like an afterimage from some momentary flash, its planes and forms glowing somber green. He saw both the tunnel and the electric light fixture it obscured; one could pass through the other. He seemed to be in control of a microscope moving through levels of focus, revealing more and more details of a world suspended in fixative.

The effect was so fascinating that for a moment he completely forgot his misery. He had heard friends describe the experience of "eyeball movies"—had heard it called lucid dreaming many decades ago—but had never experienced it until now. This was like the gateway to an interior universe.

But thinking of that returned him to his waking problems and the scene suspended above him muddied. His breathing hitched again.

—Lord no. Like riding a horse. Learn how to stay in the saddle. Steady and calm.

The regularity returned. He controlled his awareness until he could see the tunnel. —Might as well.

He moved himself into the tunnel. The words were still not comprehensible; the letters grew more complicated then fled as he approached. Abruptly the tunnel was gone and a voice said to him as clearly as if it spoke in his waking ear, *Here is what you need Richard Fettle.*

He stood in the old apartment in Long Beach. Outside the daylight was bright but somehow somber; the coloring of dream. Yet this could just as easily be memory; everything was correct. He walked around the apartment, arms folded, feeling his dream body, his dream breathing. This was *real* yet the apartment no longer existed; the century old building had been razed a decade or more ago.

With sudden alarm he wondered whether Gina would walk through the door, dropped off for a visit by Dione. Could he stand to see a perfectly convincing dream image of the dead?

Richard looked at the palms of his hands.

—Dream emotions. Everything's safe. You're in control. Try something.

—Try flying.

He willed himself to lift from the floor. His feet remained on the floor.

—Can't do everything.

He tried to will a beautiful woman not Nadine to come through the door dressed in provocative clothes.

—How real can this get.

No woman entered through the door.

The voice again: *This is what you need Richard Fettle.*

Chastised, he realized he was not here to play or experiment. A gate had indeed been opened but for a specific reason.

—What do I need?

As automatically as the distant sleep rhythm of his breath he walked toward a chair, sat and felt a cloud of sadness drift over him. He struggled to get up but could not. He could not dispel the cloud.

—Not this again. No.

Protests ignored.

326

A younger Emanuel Goldsmith stood in the doorway carrying a plastic bag wrapped around a bottle, a manuscript in a box under his other arm. He closed the door behind him. Richard watched this apparition hair black no salt and pepper out of fashion clothes, smoother face. Gentle smile.

"Thought you could use company. If you don't want any . . ." Goldsmith gestured to the door. "I'll go."

Automatically: "Thank you. Stay. I don't have much for lunch . . ."

"Liquid lunch or I'll call out. Got a royalty check yesterday. Video play production residuals. *Moses*." Goldsmith sat on a threadbare couch, avoiding a red wine stain where Dione had knocked over a glass some time ago. He set the manuscript down over the stain.

Gina and Dione would not be coming through the door.

In this time frame, in this dream memory, Gina and Dione were already dead. Richard was observing a playback; he could do nothing but watch.

*This is what you need Richard Fettle.*

"What kind of liquid?" Richard asked.

"Unblended single malt scotch. To celebrate paying my debts." He raised his eyebrows, pulled out the bottle, cradled its neck between two fingers and thumb and let Richard inspect the warm amber contents. From the bag he also produced two shot glasses. "Because you're not a drinking man you're not likely to have a couple of these lying around."

"I've never tasted unblended scotch," Richard said.

"Unblended single malt."

—Everything stored away. How much of this really happened? Am I making it up as I dream? I remember Goldsmith visiting. Two weeks after, maybe a week and a half.

Goldsmith poured two drinks and handed one to Richard. "For denizens of the shade, which gets longer as twilight approaches."

"To Götterdämmerung." Richard tasted the scotch; it was smoky and smooth and unexpectedly seductive. "I

327

don't think I want to get drunk. It would be easy to drown myself in this."

"I only bought one bottle and it wasn't to drown your sorrows," Goldsmith said. "You'll never be a drinking man, anyway. You may not believe this, Dick"—only Goldsmith called him Dick—"but you've got your head screwed on pretty straight. One of my few acquaintances who does."

"Not screwed on. It just feels screwed now."

"You've taken an awful blow," Goldsmith said softly. "If I were you I'd be pissing tears."

Richard shrugged.

"You haven't left the apartment in a week. You don't have any food. Harriet's buying food for you now."

—Harriet, Harriet . . . Goldsmith once had a girlfriend by that name.

"I don't need help," Richard said.

"The hell you say."

"I really don't."

"We need to get you out of here, into whatever sun the bastards are leaving us. Go to the state beach. Breathe some fresh air."

"Please." Richard waved his hand. "I'll be all right."

—Both of us so young. I see him as he was then bright and happy successful wanted everybody to be happy.

"Life does go on," Goldsmith suggested. "It really does, Dick. Harriet and I, we like you. We want to see you recover from this. Dione wasn't even your wife, Dick."

Richard leaped to his feet, extremely agitated. "Jesus Christ. The divorce isn't wasn't final and Gina will always be my daughter. Do you want to take everything away? Even my . . ." Waving hands violently. "All that I have left. My goddamned pain . . ."

"No. Not taking it away. How long since we met, Dick?"

Richard didn't answer. He stood trembling, fists clenched.

"Two and a half months," Goldsmith answered for him. "I consider you already maybe the best friend I've ever had. I just hate to see life grind anybody. Especially you."

"It's something I have to go through."

"I've never married. I'd hate to lose something so important. I think it would kill me. Maybe you're stronger than I am."

"Bullshit," Richard said.

"I mean it. I'm not strong inside. I look at you, you're like a rock. Inside I'm just clay. I've always known that. I accept it." Goldsmith stood, lifted his arms and turned once for inspection. "I look solid, don't I."

"Stop it, please," Richard said, looking down. "I'm not going to starve myself but right now I don't need your help. I just don't care."

Goldsmith sat. "Harriet says someone should be sleeping here to keep you company."

"I haven't had anybody sleeping here in five months. I've been alone except for." He didn't finish. Goldsmith waited.

"All right," Goldsmith said.

"When Gina."

"Yeah."

Richard sat and picked up the glass. "Stayed here." He sipped again. "I'll be all right."

"Yeah," Goldsmith said. "Don't feel like we don't care. I care. Harriet. All the folks."

"I know," Richard said. "Thank you."

"I'll stay if you want."

"Good scotch. Maybe I can become a drinking man."

"No, brother, you don't want to get messed up with this shit." Goldsmith lifted the bottle, stood and approached him. "Give me your glass. I'll toss it. The hell with celebrations."

Richard resisted his efforts to remove the glass. Goldsmith backed away, ran his hand through his hair, looked at the curtained window. "Let's go outside and hunt some sunshine, Dick. Whatever we can find. Pure bright white light."

Richard felt tears on his cheeks.

—Complete. No details missing.

"Go ahead, man," Goldsmith encouraged gently. "Talk."

Richard wiped his cheeks. "I really did love her. I couldn't live with her but I loved her. And Gina ... Christ, I don't think I've ever loved anything on this Earth like I love that girl. There's a big crater here, Emanuel." He tapped his head. "A bomb blast. I'm not all here."

"Bullshit."

"No really. I can't do anything. I can't think, I can't talk straight, I can't write. I can't cry."

"You're crying now, man. Don't mistake grief for losing your soul. You've still got everything. You're rock."

The sob began as a muscle cramp deep inside. It worked its way up, acquiring an intensity that seemed to fragment his chest, until he sat on the couch shaking moaning holding his hands outstretched, grabbing at something.

—Feel it. Awful. This is it all over again. Worse even.

Goldsmith came to the couch, kneeled in front of Richard and hugged him fiercely. Goldsmith wept with him rocked with him, black eyes staring at the wall behind Richard. "You say it, man. Get it out. Tell the whole fucking world."

The sob turned into a scream. Goldsmith held Richard to the couch as if he might leap away. Legs and arms thrashing, feeling all the unfairness and the pain and the necessity of feeling the unfairness and pain to honor his dead he must suffer. Would be cheap and lessen their value not to suffer as much as he possibly could. Goldsmith hung on. Finally they lay embraced on the couch. Richard holding Goldsmith, Goldsmith lying half on half off, still clutching him.

"Rock. Stone, man. Feel your strength inside. I know it's there. I couldn't take this. But you can, Dick. Hold on."

"All right," Richard moaned. "All right."

"We love you, man. Hold on to it."

—Goldsmith. The real one.

Goldsmith pulled back and his hair was gray, his face lined. "I'm clay. When you grieve for me, my friend, remember ... You don't owe me anything but what you give me when I'm alive. That's it. Debt cleared."

Richard nodded. Swallowed an agonizing knot in his throat. He had had enough. With a jerk he floated free of the memory and dream, felt a pressure as if he were confined in gray cotton, then a simple drift, bits and pieces of other dreams cascading and reassembling, dissolving. He opened his eyes and sat up on the side of the bed. Trembling, he hung his hands over his knees and leaned forward. Beside him Nadine moaned in her sleep and rolled over.

Richard stood slowly and went to the window.

+ How much buried. Dig it up, bury it again. He helped me. Was kind to me. A friend. Now he's dead he must be. I can't feel his presence.

Richard's memory of that day was not clear. The dream hadn't conveyed the whole story, not the conclusion. Goldsmith's friend Harriet had come through the door without knocking while Goldsmith and Richard held each other on the couch. She had asked "What's this?" and dropped a box of groceries on the floor. Then she had broken down in tears while Goldsmith tried to explain that Richard and he were not lovers. Harriet had never really understood; she and Goldsmith had ended their relationship a few weeks later.

Richard parted the window curtains, rubbed his eyes and shook his head, smiling. That had embarrassed the hell out of Goldsmith.

He glanced at the glowing numbers on the bedside clock. Three hundred. In a few hours the sun would rise over the hills and the combs would mete it out to those in their shadow, mirror spreading the winter dawn, echoing from tower to tower second third and fourth hand, but still sun.

"Let's go hunt some sunshine," he whispered.

# 55

Mary Choy had pulled a chair across her spacious bedroom to the eastfacing window. Then she had sat and waited for sunrise. The sun had come up an hour after she had awakened, the dawn brief and beautiful from the mansion's perspective high in the mountains of Hispaniola. With daylight guards and soldiers had gathered in the garden below the window, standing in groups of three or four until they were replaced by the morning watch.

The sky overhead was dusty blue. Through a gap in some mountains to the north she could see an edge of sea and horizon beyond. A few clouds gathered above southern peaks, feathering their gray wings in the winds.

She left the window to perform her morning ablutions. Looking in a full length mirror mounted behind the heavy wooden bathroom door, she observed that her pale cleft mark was darkening. Soon she would be uniform black. Healing by itself. Dr. Sumpler would be so pleased.

During her time on Hispaniola Mary had passed through the spectrum of dark emotions: fear, anger, dismay. Now she was simply calm. Before sleeping she had dytched; now she performed War Dance, assigning her bodily tensions to specific roles to be acted out. Let them watch. Let them execute her, frighten her, confuse her; nothing caused a tremor throughout the dance, and after the dance she was centered again. She felt she might keep control under all circumstances.

Madame Yardley had left the table the night before and the servants had brought in a sumptuous feast. Soulavier had eaten a great deal; Mary had eaten sufficiently to keep up her strength. They had not talked any more. They had

332

parted company after dinner and Mary had been escorted to her room.

She had come up with some hypotheses which she hoped to pare down as the day progressed. Her first hypothesis; that this was not Yardley's mansion but an historical relic used now for some strategic reason. Her second: that nobody knew much about Yardley after all, certainly not the people he ruled. Her third: that everything she had heard about Goldsmith before Madame Yardley's appearance had been a lie. Her fourth: that Madame Yardley was not in her right mind and knew nothing.

A woman fasting to get the attention of her own husband.

The door to the room was not locked. Still, Mary had stayed within the room. She no longer regretted the loss of the pistol. Revenge was a weak satisfaction when taken against ants performing their social obligations.

War Dance had not eliminated her emotions. It had simply focused them. What she felt now was a strong and observant calm; an aggressive peace made up of equal parts patience and well channeled anger.

She adjusted her hair in the bathroom, inspected her midsuit and emerged to the sound of a gentle knocking on the door.

"Mademoiselle, are you ready for breakfast?" a woman asked.

"Yes," she said. She looked at her watch. Nine hundred.

The door opened tentatively and a small rounded face poked through, found her, smiled. "Come, please."

She followed the diminutive servant down the hall of bedroom doors, to the left instead of the right, and past the stairs. They were now in the west wing of the house where she had not been before.

The servant opened a door and she looked into a small room outfitted as an office. An elderly woman wearing a simple black shift stood before a case of memory boxes. Soulavier sat typing on an old display terminal. He glanced up at the servant and Mary, nodded with a frown, spun his chair around and stood.

"You will take breakfast with Colonel Sir," he told Mary. The elderly woman watched Mary with a fixed pleasant smile. Soulavier addressed her in Creole. She nodded silently and returned to her work.

"That was Madame Yardley's mother," he said as they walked alone the rest of the distance.

Mary remembered seeing a four story tower on this side of the building. They came to the end of the hall and Soulavier knocked gently on a broad double door made of solid mahogany. A muffled voice behind told them to enter.

Six men and two women stood around a long oak table within the high ceilinged, broad, turret shaped room. All around the room to a height of thirty feet rose a magnificent library, ornate wood cases equipped with leaded glass doors. Two balconies gave access to the upper shelves. Near the door a wrought iron staircase double helixed up to the balconies.

The two women and five of the men were black or mulatto; all wore black uniforms, some with the Samedi figure pinned to their chests. Mary focused on a tall, husky, white haired man seated at the head of the table. He did not look at her immediately, however; his attention was on a book. The table was covered with perhaps five or six hundred books of all sizes and kinds from leatherbound folios to crumbling paperbacks.

She had never seen so many books in all her life. She did not let them distract her for more than an instant from Yardley, however. He looked up from the book he held, closed it quietly and lay it down on the table. "Good to see you again, Henri. How's little David? And Marie Louise?"

"They are fine, Colonel Sir. I would like to introduce Lieutenant Mary Choy."

"Thank you. Please sit. We'll be served breakfast in here. A good meal, not one of Madame Yardley's punishments. I trust she finally fed you last night."

"Yes. She did." Mary said. Yardley smiled broadly and

334

shook his head sympathetically; such a nice man, he seemed to want her to think, quite English and familiar after all. Nothing exotic here.

Mary reserved judgment.

"All right. I think we're through for this morning," Yardley told the seven. They bowed stiffly, turned and filed past Soulavier and Mary out the door. The last man closed the double doors behind them with an enigmatic close lipped smile.

"I've given in to my wife, you know," Yardley said. "We had a domestic dispute. She seems to think that my techniques for bringing this nation up from barbarism lack . . . finesse."

"She is a remarkable lady," Soulavier said, clearly ill at ease. Yardley returned his smile with a kind of sunny severity. Soulavier straightened perceptibly.

"Henri, I think I'll be fine alone with Mademoiselle Choy. Please join the others in the main dining room downstairs. I'm serving all my staff a healthy breakfast this morning."

"Of course, Colonel Sir." Now it was Soulavier's turn to exit through the double doors, closing them behind.

"The servants will clear a space on this table," Yardley said, sweeping the air with one hand. "I find this the most congenial room in the whole building. I would happily spend my life in retirement here, reading Monsieur Boucher's books."

Mary said nothing.

"Monsieur Boucher," he repeated, taking her blank look for puzzlement. "Sanlouie Boucher. Prime minister to the previous President of Haiti before my takeover. He built this marvelous mansion and had it fortified a year before my arrival. Unfortunately he was sequestered in Jacmel and never made it to his fortress."

Mary nodded.

"Now. As to your case, if you don't mind talking about it before breakfast is served . . ." He frowned almost comically and threw his hands up in the air. "Please, do not be so solemn. On my word of honor these people will do nothing to harm you. I see you've been through a few indignities . . . I apologize. I've been distracted and I haven't had time for all the details. One man's details can be another man's catastrophe. I apologize again."

"I'm being held against my will," Mary said, conceding nothing to Yardley in exchange for his confession.

"Yes. A tug of war between your State Department and Justice Department and my government. It will be settled soon. In the meantime you can complete your investigation. You'll have the closest thing to carte blanche I can provide. And no more indignities."

"Can I speak with my superiors?"

"Your superiors and your government know that you're not being mistreated."

"I'd like to speak with them as soon as possible."

"Agreed. As soon as possible," Yardley said. "You've greatly impressed my people. Jean-Claude and Roselle are some of my finest and their report on you is most flattering. Henri is too nervous right now to be very objective. His family is in Santiago. Santiago is under siege by opposition forces. We're safe here and in most of Haiti . . . But the Dominicans have always had a chip on their shoulder."

"I've been told Emanuel Goldsmith is here," Mary said. She had not moved from where Soulavier left her. "I'd like to see him as soon as possible."

"That's a bit more complicated. I haven't seen him myself. This is a story I'd rather tell after breakfast. Please join me at table. You're a transform, I understand . . . and a very attractive one. I'm not sure I approve of such an art, but . . . if it must be, obviously you're a masterpiece. Are you pleased with your new self?"

"I've been this way for some time," Mary said. "It's second nature now." *Or should be.* "Colonel Sir, breakfast isn't really necessary . . . I'd just as soon—"

"Breakfast for me is essential and as absolute dictator of all I survey—your country's opinion of me—surely I

336

have the right to eat before being cross examined." He smiled his most ingratiating smile. "Please."

She would gain nothing by resisting his hospitality. He pulled a chair out for her and she sat facing a stack of leatherbound volumes in French. Three of the small servants entered through a single side door, carefully pushed aside stacks of books until a space across one end was clear, set two place settings—the silverware and plates ornately initialed S.B.—and then brought in bowls of fruit, covered plates of broiled fish and ham, steamed rice, curried shrimp and kippers. Yardley sat to the feast with an audible sigh.

"I've been up since four this morning," he confided. "Only coffee and panbread."

Mary ate enough to satisfy her hunger and be distantly polite but said nothing. The food was excellent. Yardley finished a large plate quickly, pushed it aside, shoved back his chair and said, "Now on to business. You're convinced Goldsmith committed the crimes you accuse him of?"

"A grand jury was convinced enough to indict him."

"Ah. He called me, you see, to say he was coming and that he was 'in a rough.' That's colloquial, I assume. He said he would soon be accused of the murder of eight people. He needed sanctuary. I asked him if he was guilty. He said he was. He assumed I would protect him under any circumstances." Yardley shook his head dubiously. "I invited him to come.

"Right after his phone call I began to receive clues that I myself was about to be indicted by your government on quite different charges. I haven't had time to meet with Emanuel but he's here."

"We'd like to make arrangements for extradition," Mary said. "I understand our governments aren't cooperating right now, but when—"

"There probably won't be such a 'when' for some time, years perhaps," Yardley said, contemplating his empty plate with a long skeptical face. "You're aware of the Raphkind controversies, aren't you? Recent history."

Mary nodded.

"You'll pardon me if I do most of the talking . . . I seem to be the one with the information to relay and we only have an hour or so . . . Quite a generous amount of time considering I'm facing a full scale Dominican rebellion in Santiago and Santo Domingo. I'm doing this you understand only because Emanuel Goldsmith was someone special to me."

Mary inclined. Yardley put his arms on the table, leaned forward and lifted his hands to square the air before him. "Here's how it is. I made a good many deals with President Raphkind, who believed as I do that justice demands more than simple therapy for criminals. Crime is not a disease that can be treated by doctors; it must be treated in a way that satisfies the common people, and the common people demand retribution to fit the crime.

"Raphkind found enough resistance that he rearranged your Supreme Court. He was accused of assassination, I believe . . . Probably guilty. He cut secret deals with vigilante organizations. Now I agree, he made a nightmarish mess of things and he was perhaps the most vicious and reprehensible leader in the history of your country, but . . ."

Mary could join this spin easily enough. "He was the man in charge," she said with a wry smile.

Yardley regarded the smile with frank suspicion. "Surely not even the police supported him after the revelations."

"No. Not officially."

"Well. Whoever's in charge, when the USA speaks firmly all of our little nations tremble. And truth to tell his ideal legal system was not too dissimilar to our own. We treat crimes with more than just therapy."

"You use hellcrowns," Mary said.

"We do indeed. Raphkind's people arranged to make export deals for clandestine delivery. Your vigilantes obtained a number of hellcrowns from our reserves at a discount . . . Raphkind was hounded to suicide by public outcry over the Justice Friedman case. Everything came

338

unraveled for him so he chose the silver bullet of Christophe—poison, in his case—rather than the tumbrels. He would have been therapied if convicted, I presume. Still, he preferred death to public dishonor."

"You're still exporting hellcrowns," Mary said.

"Not directly to the USA. We supply a world wide market and all of our contacts are legitimate. Raphkind was the sole exception and what could I do? He could have caused Hispaniola serious harm. He didn't need the services of our soldiers by the beginning of his second term, having wrapped up his actions in Bolivia and Argentina. He was riding a wave of immense popularity. I could see no alternative but to supply hellcrowns."

Mary listened impassively.

"Be that as it may hellcrowns are legal in the nation of Hispaniola. Their appropriate usage is just, in my opinion. The laws are very strict and firmly administered. Confession is sufficient for a court to pass sentence."

"Selectors don't hold formal court proceedings," Mary said.

"Theirs is the politics of an underground resistance," Yardley said. "I don't presume to pass judgment on them or on any aspect of your society. Hispaniola has only the power to react, to stay alive, and so far it's done very well under my command."

"Where is Goldsmith?" Mary asked.

"He is nearby, ninety kilometers from here, in the Thousand Flowers Prison."

"And you didn't meet with him? Your friend?"

Yardley's face hardened. "I have my reasons. Primary reason, no time. Secondary reason, I heard his confession. He wanted to escape to Hispaniola to find sanctuary. He thought to impose on my friendship after committing a horrible and senseless crime. Even my very best friend —and Emanuel while a good friend is not that—cannot presume I will violate the laws of Hispaniola. We have no formal extradition treaties. We do accept criminals from other nations for incarceration, however, formally and otherwise."

Mary had heard of this; she did not think it relevant until now. "They're kept in the Thousand Flowers Prison?"

"And elsewhere. We have five such internationals prisons. Some governments pay well for this service. But Goldsmith . . . We will not charge the USA for him. He stays here."

"Why? The laws of my country—"

"Your country would treat him and release him, a new man. He does not deserve such leniency. The misery of the relatives of his victims lives on. Why should he not suffer too? Retribution is the core of all legal systems. We are simply more honest here."

"He was your friend," Mary said, dumfounded. "He adored you."

"All the worse. He betrayed all of his friends, not just those he killed."

"But nobody knows *why* he killed them," Mary said, forced into the uncomfortable position of devil's advocate. "If he truly is unbalanced and not responsible . . ."

"That is not my concern. We do not execute prisoners here. We conduct our own sort of therapy. And you know very well, those who undergo the hellcrown never repeat their crimes again."

"He's in a clamp?"

"If not at this moment then by the end of the day. Judgment has been made."

Mary leaned back in her chair, momentarily shocked beyond words. "I never expected such a thing," she said softly.

"We do your work for you, my dear," Yardley said, reaching forward to tap her knuckles with a finger. "You'll be taken to Thousand Flowers. The prisoner will be shown to you. Then I imagine sometime in the next three or four days arrangements will be made with your government and you can return to Los Angeles. You can close your casebooks. Emanuel Goldsmith will never leave Thousand

340

Flowers. Nobody has ever escaped; we guarantee that to all our subscriber nations."

She shook her head. The room with its tens of thousands of books felt as if it might close in on her. "I demand the release of Goldsmith into my custody," she said. "In the name of international law and common decency."

"Good, good," Yardley said. "But Goldsmith came here voluntarily and he has openly admired and supported our laws and reforms. It is only just and decent that he should live by his beliefs. Unless you have something particularly clever and observant to add, I think our meeting is at an end."

The double doors opened and Soulavier entered. "Mademoiselle Choy is to be shown Emanuel Goldsmith in Thousand Flowers and then, when I give the word, put in touch with her country's embassy in extension. Thank you for your patience, Mademoiselle."

Yardley stood and gestured at the door. Six uniformed men entered and passed around Soulavier. Soulavier stepped into the room, took her arm and led her into the hall.

"That is a rare privilege," he said. "I myself have never breakfasted with Colonel Sir. Now please come. It is two hours' journey from here to the prison. The roads are not the best and there will be much military traffic. It is not so very far from Santiago, after all."

# BOOK THREE

*As chaos contained the possibility of matter, so this creature contains the possibility of mind, like a fifth limb latent in man, structured to make and manipulate meaning as the fist is structured to grasp and finger matter.*
—Maya Deren, *Divine Horsemen: The Living Gods of Haiti*

# 56

Waiting to begin full entry into the Country, Martin mentally asked for and received access to the toolkit, reaching up to pull it down with his right hand, which he still could not make out distinctly. The toolkit was the only thing he could see clearly: a simulated bright red box within which floated a display of circumstances of the probe. Activating the toolkit also revealed a searcher and tuner combination, with which he could move his locus of connection from neuron to neuron, frequency to frequency or channel to channel. On one side of the red box hung a ripcord in case of emergency.

He had never used the ripcord. In the present probe immediate exit from the Country would be difficult, perhaps impossible; with no buffer a pulled ripcord would simply cut the connections between subject and investigator. Whatever latent experiences were yet to be interpreted would still continue to be processed in both the investigators and the subject.

On the ambiguous timescale of the Country latency might be measured in seconds or in minutes; very occasionally, in hours.

This time the exterior level of Goldsmith's Country was a warm grayness, a feed of processed knowledge to conscious awareness, not currently active. Goldsmith was in a state of controlled neutral sleep with no dream activity.

Martin felt Carol's presence as a greater warmth within the grayness. As he tested the toolkit, manually moving them in slaved combo across the map of this particular level, he practiced speech communication with her.

|Can you hear me?

|*Something something.*

|Try again.

|*Hum.*

|Not hearing you clearly.

|Can you hear me now?

|Got you. Let's try emotional transfer, Martin suggested.

She sent him what he interpreted as professional affection and eagerness to get going. They were both eager; after a long night's sleep Martin had never felt so ready to explore a Country.

|I'm picking up your excitement, Martin said. I think you like working with me here.

|That's close enough. From you I'm receiving a more than professional warmth tempered by the distraction of the job at hand.

|Close enough, Martin agreed ruefully. They had a tremendous freedom and openness here; in a short time neither would be able to conceal emotions from each other any more than the subject could conceal his deeper psychological processes.

|I'm going to move us into an active level and look for a point of entry. Then I'll release your own toolkit and we can work separately if need be.

|Understood. I think I see a forest ahead. Are we at entry yet? No, wait a moment . . . no forest. I see potentials for a lot of different images. What is this, Martin?

|Still getting visual smear from the occipital lobe, perhaps.

|Not having the buffer makes, this much sharper, more immediate, doesn't it? Carol asked.

|It seems to. But we're not really *seeing* anything yet. I'm changing locus and channel now. To the prearranged entry . . . point two seven on Margery's map. We saw—

The suddenness of their entry was stunning. One moment they experienced only neutral grayness without beginning or end, perfect and undisturbed potentiality like a vast pool of precreation; the next, torrid blue sky and endless desert crossed by three infinite highways.

|Oof, Carol said. Pardon me but that wasn't subtle.

|My apologies. (Chagrin.) We're in Country.

|Look how sharp. Wow. Martin, I see you perfectly!

Martin stood on the desert sand, feeling it crunch beneath his feet. He saw Carol walking on the closest highway an apparent ten or fifteen meters away. She wore a knee length sleeveless white dress and white pumps. Perfect for the climate, which might have been searingly hot except that extremes of temperature did not occur in the country. He felt only a warm breeze.

|You're wearing denim jeans and a black short sleeve shirt, Carol reported. And boots.

He looked down at himself. That was indeed how his mind had clothed this self image. |How old do I look?

|Maybe twenty five. No more than thirty. What am I wearing?

He described what he saw.

|Well, we differ. *I* think I'm wearing a blue longsuit and black slippers, Carol said. Ah, well. How old am I?

|You seem your proper age. You really look beautiful.

|Where are the seven league boots? Carol asked, pointing across the endless sand. We won't walk, I hope.

|We'll fly. From here in we're a part of Goldsmith's Country. It'll adapt to us.

|Right. (Dogged determination; mental preparation.) I'm girding my loins. Feel that?

|Very attractive, girded loins, Martin said.

She ignored that. |I remember how to fly. The neck muscle . . . right?

|See if you're in practice.

He regarded Carol's self image as she took two steps across the road and lifted above the apparent asphalt. With a look of intense concentration she rose a meter. |Like a dream, she said. I was never able to get any higher than this.

|I could go higher sometimes, Martin said. But we'll stick close for a while.

He concentrated on a nonexistent neck muscle/organ of flight, discovery of which in his dreams had always preceded wonderful episodes of soaring, rising above his school and classmates (such dreams returning him to childhood or adolescence); brief times of endless freedom, filled with the wonder of why he had never thought of doing this before.

He ascended to one meter, spread his arms, crossed the sand to the highway and floated beside Carol. |May I say you look angelic?

Carol laughed. |May I say you look like a mech sod in an amusement park?

|Don't get personal.

|Can't avoid it in here.

He rotated to stare straight down the three endless highways. |All roads lead to Rome.

In most of their previous incursions into the Country the central symbol of the mind had been a city; in some cases a city in size and complexity only, shaped more like a castle or a fortress or even a mountain honeycombed with warrens; but always a huge habitation filled with activity.

|Hi ho, Carol said, drifting ahead of him. He caught up with her and they flew over the black ribbon road toward the far horizon. As their apparent speed increased Martin noticed the beginning of visual separation. Sky and sand and asphalt seemed to glitter. All shapes were outlined with velvety shadow on the side opposite Martin's direction of motion. They had witnessed this a few times before; it signified the rapid transfer of their probe from one neuron cluster to another.

|See any separation? he asked Carol.

|Quite a bit. What does it mean?

|It could mean we're crossing a large number of clusters. Covering a lot of mental territory. The Country has con-

tracted. Goldsmith may be marshaling all his symbols, consolidating. I can't imagine why ... But an awful lot of available landscape is being taken up by empty desert.

|Is he fortifying? Carol suggested.

|I don't know.

They crossed desert for an unprecedented length of subjective time. The experience of time in Country depended on the amount of sensory detail in any given territory. With nothing but repetition, as in this endless desert, time could stretch almost endlessly. In the external world or by the clock on the toolkit seconds or fractions of seconds might pass as hours.

|Boring, Carol said.

|Excruciating, Martin agreed. We might have to shift clusters or channels manually.

|Give it a while. We're learning something—aren't we?

|We're learning that Goldsmith has contracted incredibly, Martin said. All this emptiness.

|What if this is all there is? Carol suggested, turning to look at him. Black afterimages fled behind her. Carol's eyes were intensely blue. He imagined and then saw her eyes become part of a shallow lagoon. The lagoon spilled around her image until he could barely see her through the rippling water. He fought back the fantasy and it broke up into dust that fell behind with her afterimages.

|Nobody is completely empty.

|Not even a mass murderer? Carol suggested.

|Not even. Take it from me. Mentally impossible.

|But we could be on the wrong level. Not an entry level. Martin disagreed with that, too. |Be patient.

|Patience, patience, Carol said. On past incursions Carol had become childishly enthused, almost frenetic, before their real work began. He saw her as a spirit of fire, a feminine Ariel or afreet of the desert. He quelled that fantasy before it could manifest.

|Use the time to get accustomed to the rules, Martin suggested.

|You're the one who's eating me up with your eyes,

Carol said. I saw the lagoon. You almost got me wet.

|I wish, Martin said.

She scowled. |I feel a change coming on—do you?'

|Yes. He pulled down his toolkit and looked at the timer. Thirty seconds. They could have fully crossed half of the points Margery had mapped, scanning Goldsmith's entire hypothalamic loci in that time. Perhaps they had to make several circuits of all the channels to come across what they wanted . . . But the central city had never been elusive in past subjects.

|There's something, Martin said, pointing ahead. The sky changed color above the vertex of endless highways, from dusty blue to black undertinted with gray orange.

|Looks like a storm, Carol said.

To Martin it resembled furnace glow from a factory or a city on fire seen at night. It did not look at all hospitable. The blue sky faded with a distinct whining sound into darkness as if distant machinery had lowered a curtain over floodlights. Still, the region above the highway, and they in their flight, seemed cast in the same daylight as before. Ahead the furnace glow pulsed and shifted as if reflecting red lightning.

Martin had never found occasion to fear the Country; but seeing this he began to have his doubts. In all previous subjects the city had been a lively if not a pretty place, never dreadful; this might have been a gate to hell itself.

|We'll go in together, Carol suggested.

|Might as well, at first, Martin agreed.

|Are you worried? she asked.

|You know damned well what I'm feeling, Martin said. You're worried, too.

|No buffer, she said with a sigh. She flipped over like an airborne ballet dancer and pointed her finger to the ground. We might all have nightmares here.

Everything in Martin's experience led him to believe that no harm could come to them in the Country; on the other hand, being in direct connection with Goldsmith's mental symbology could conceivably disturb their own

349

interior landscapes. The effect would almost certainly not be permanent—but it would not be pleasant, either, if the present scene was any indication.

The living glow filled the sky all around them. The outermost highways branched off to each side of a vast canyon, of which they could see only the near edge and the far side. They remained on the straight center road. Sound surrounded them—a continuous booming as of drums or machines, so tangible they could see the waves rippling through them and through the road's asphalt.

|We're going right over the edge, Martin observed.

They slowed and drifted beyond a rugged tumble of smooth boulders, over the lip of the canyon.

|That *must* be it, Carol said. The canyon was a crystal lined pit, the crystals resolving into buildings of all sizes and descriptions, rising from the bottom of the canyon into a ridge of Manhattan skyline. The city might have stretched for hundreds of kilometers, alive with endless invention and detail, a masterpiece of mental architecture.

|I've never seen anything like this, Martin said. From Carol came the same stunned confusion mixed with awe.

The buildings sparkled with a heartbeat of light that pulsed from the central ridge out to the farthest buildings clustered below the rim. One, two, three, *pulse*; the glow shooting from a myriad pinprick windows into the darkness above: coals in a dying fire; stars in a galaxy linked by some impossible living rhythm. |It's magnificent, Carol said. How could this be deranged?

|That's what we're here to learn.

The experience was sharper than life itself; the quality of seeing and sensing was hallucinatory, and well it should be; they were not seeing a filtered, censored, shaped and trimmed product of thinking/perception; they were seeing the base material of all thought and being.

Martin was suddenly filled with joy; joy arising out of the dread he had felt earlier, joy that there was no buffer, joy at being with Carol on the edge of something mysterious and wonderful and completely unexplored. Nobody, not even Goldsmith, knew this existed but them.

|I'll give you your own toolkit now, Martin said. But we should explore together for a while, until we know what we're in for.

Carol reached up and pulled down her kit. (Satisfaction, self discipline, focusing.) |This is perfect. It's all here.

Martin held out his hand. She took it and together they descended into Goldsmith's city. Below them the road became cracked and neglected, finally disintegrating into lumps of asphalt and dirt. Scattered among the lumps lay white fragments half buried in black moist dirt. Martin descended to see what they might be. Carol followed. They brought their faces close to the tumbled surface.

|Bones, she said.

|I see bits of crockery—crockery heads, faces.

|I see skulls and bones. Give it a try.

Martin concentrated on the white shards, tried to shift to what Carol was interpreting. |Okay. Now I see a thigh-bone . . . femur. A skull. I keep switching back to crockery faces like Toby mugs. Sad Toby mugs.

|These skulls don't grin, Carol observed. They're sad skulls.

They rose again but did not advance. |Any clue what they represent? Carol asked.

|None.

They flew forward until a heaviness assaulted them and they felt themselves dragged down. With a slight stumble they landed on a straight street between tall dark brick buildings with shattered windows. Faded designs had been scrawled over every centimeter of brickwork as if drawn in flour or some other white powder: serpents with lightning jagged tongues, big headed birds, splayed dogs and cats with #'s for eyes. The designs flowed from the buildings onto the sidewalks. Martin and Carol looked at the drawing beneath their feet as they walked down the empty street; more animals, bats and paper-doll twins, hopscotch squares, each square a window to some scrawled staring

351

face almost alive with its wrinkles and expressions; observing, frowning, laughing, staring, sulking.

|They might have looked out of those windows once, Carol said. Now they're trapped in the sidewalk and street. Could they be message characters?

Martin looked up at the shattered glass panes in the empty windows. |Could be, he said.

In the Countries they had investigated, persistent thoughts and memories had sometimes assumed the nature of realized figures; Martin had labeled them message characters. They tended to be ephemeral but generally positive and full of a tenuous vitality.

Martin stepped around the faces and squares. Between the designs incomprehensible words had been scribbled like the practice of a child; misshapen letters, no discernible spelling, meaningless. Only the figures symbolizing Goldsmith's subpersonalities, his major mental organons, would use speech; they served as gobetweens leaping from one level of mental activity to another. Until they were encountered, nothing in the way of words or sounds from this Country would be comprehensible as written or spoken language.

The booming sound continued, more drum than machine now. Martin walked slightly ahead of Carol, taking this part of the exploration very slowly in case they missed something important.

|No action here, Carol observed.

|Do you think there was a war, some struggle?

|Disturbance, Carol agreed. Nothing moving. Maybe there's been further contraction into the city center—the skyline ridge.

|We've never seen this much concentration or desolation, Martin said.

|Then it's significant. A pathology like the shrinking of tissue.

|I can't think of a better explanation. But the symbol hard structure is still here—even to the outskirts, the desert roads. Action could take place, the landscape will still support it.

|Like a wire with no current, Carol said.

|Good comparison.

He moved farther down the street. Carol broke away momentarily to walk up a flight of steps and peer into the dark buildings. He waited for her, a dull unease suffusing his thoughts. Tincture of Goldsmith. The dark canyon, fluxion of lights, neighborhood without inhabitants . . .

If a war had not already occurred then perhaps they were marching over scorched earth—preparation for a battle yet to come.

|Take a look, Carol suggested, waving for him to join her. He retraced a few steps and climbed the stairs. Beyond an ill defined door stretched an incomplete hallway, changing character every few moments, with every shift of their attention.

|Breakdown, he said.

|This far in. The Country must be fading here, the focus going somewhere else.

|Let's get to the center and not waste time out here, Martin suggested. If there's breakdown this part of the landscape is no longer significant . . .

|Except as archaeology, Carol said.

|Maybe not even that.

His unease deepened. Desolation and decay; message characters imprisoned in the sidewalks. Rejection of all existing structures and patterns. What could cause this? The Country supported more than its own imagery—it provided a base of sign and symbology for much of the high level activity of the primary personality and other major organons. Corruption or depletion of the symbology implied major mental dysfunction—yet the therapists had detected no major dysfunction in Goldsmith.

Ahead, at the end of the street, concrete steps with steel rails dropped to another street dozens of meters lower Martin took Carol's hand again and they continued the descent.

|Maybe we can find a cab, Carol suggested.

The street below filled with pieces of paper drifting and

353

swirling in eddies of illusory air. Martin bent to grab one as they walked but it eluded him as if alive. Carol tried and failed as well; by the time they reached the end of the street and turned in the direction of the skyscraper ridge the papers had caught fire and vanished in twists of black ash. Martin looked up and touched Carol, pointing to an immense poster covering the windowless side of one dark five story building. Unfocused and ever changing, meaningless letters covered the bottom of the poster. The subject of the poster was the bust of a humanlike figure with a perfectly smooth ovoid head.

|Vote for Mr. Blank, Martin said.

|The people's choice, Carol agreed.

They walked for blocks through the outer neighborhoods, seeing no occupants of any description. Carol compared the scene to a war zone; territory deserted in fear of a nuclear strike.

|Maybe the economy's in a downturn, Martin suggested. I've never seen anything so void.

|Wonder why it's here at all. *Memento mori.*

Above all the dreary empty brick buildings, the glowing skyscrapers of the central city beckoned, but they seemed to get no closer. After seeming hours of effortless but irritating walking Martin stopped and pulled down his toolkit.

|Going to jootz? Carol asked. *Jootz* was a borrowed word they used to describe moving manually from channel to channel. He hadn't heard the word in years; he smiled at the memories it invoked of lighter investigations with more immediate results.

|Just looking at the time. Another thirty seconds.

He pondered that. |We should be in the center of Country by now. If the skyscrapers are the center we're not getting any closer. If we jootz we could lose this completely . . .

|I'm all for that, Carol said.

|I don't think we should. There's a significance here.

|Let's call a cab.

She was only half joking. They could make certain features manifest; but under the present circumstances Martin was reluctant to impose their imaging on the Country unless it was strictly necessary. It might be possible to compromise, however; to find a feature they could *coax* into usefulness.

|Find a subway, he said.

They looked around; no subway station entrances.

The drums persisted like staccato heartbeats.

|And he said he was a Brooklyn boy, Carol said, frowning.

|Hasn't lived there in a long time. Maybe we can explore the buildings again . . . go into the basements. *Suggest* that there's some method of transportation.

They walked over to what might have been an empty grocery on the first floor of a two story stone building that ran the length of the block. The inside of the grocery was more detailed; aisles and shelves, a cash register made of something that resembled slate—more of a sculpture than a machine. Carol reached over to touch the stone keys.

|There's a door, Martin said. They walked through the middle aisle to the rear, pushed through a double swinging door and found themselves looking into an immense garbage pit buried deep in a cavern. A railed parapet beyond the door overlooked the pit.

|God, Carol said. It's not just garbage. It's bodies. More bones.

Martin again saw piles of shattered crockery faces rather than bones. He had never observed anything like this in a Country; on the edge of nightmare, these signs seemed to point to some internal warfare, internal genocide.

|We're not getting anywhere—not seeing much Goldsmith, Martin said. We're just seeing a shell.

|Maybe we're in a trap, Carol said.

|I've never observed anything deceptive in the Country.

|We've never observed anything like this, either.

Martin thought about the possibility of a maze. Could

Goldsmith's mental resources have put up barricades against their probe? Goldsmith wouldn't know what to expect from a probe but his various organons could conceivably set up resistance to avoid painful self revelations.

|You might have specked it. Maybe we're looking at a deliberate coverup, Martin said. A maze with misleading details . . . Not lies or deceptions but detours and decoys.

Carol grimaced at the pit. |If this is petty detail, what's the hard stuff like?

|We're not going to find anything useful here.

Back on the street Martin reached down to touch the apparent asphalt. The pebbled texture at first was unresolved but almost immediately became rough and totally convincing. He glanced up at Carol. She wavered for the merest moment before becoming solid.

|I think it's time to exercise some authority, he said.

|About time. What first?

|We need a street that leads directly to the heart of the city. Let's say—over there.

He pointed to the next street crossing, frowned melodramatically to show intense concentration and gestured with a wave of his hand for her to do likewise. Nothing visibly changed but such authority was best exercised on objects or situations out of sight. There was less to overtly restyle that way. |All right. Let's try it.

They walked to the corner and stood facing the distant skyline. Straight as an arrow the new street pointed toward the city. The drumming sound had stopped; now all they heard was a distant rustling sound like taffeta skirts or wind through palm leaves.

|Maybe we haven't changed anything; maybe this street just happened to go that way, Carol said.

Martin concentrated again, deciding he would try the next restyling alone. An engine roared behind them. They turned to see an old diesel bus smoking noisily toward them. Martin put his hand out and grasped a bus stop post that he had not noticed before.

|I'm getting the touch again, he said.

The bus pulled up beside the curb and opened its door. The design was late twentieth century but there was no driver or driver's seat. |All aboard, Martin suggested.

The bus moved off with a convincing shove of acceleration. Carol sat on a vinyl covered seat; Martin stood holding an age polished pole.

|Looks like something Goldsmith might have seen as a child, she said. Are you sure this was *your* idea?

|It's a collaboration, Martin said.

The view outside the windows blurred. Objects outsped their afterimages, again leaving ghosts of black. The bus was traveling faster than the refresh rate of sensory creation.

|When do we pull the cord? Carol asked. She pointed to a dark plastic covered rope threaded through metal loops above the windows.

|Maybe we don't have to, Martin said. He raised his voice and addressed the driverless front of the bus: |We'd like to be left off in city center.

Outside the bus the scenery went black, flickered violently and twisted back into place. The dreary empty avenues between dark deserted tenements were replaced by broad well lighted thoroughfares, scurrying crowds, tall, clean, prosperous-looking buildings, a light sprinkling of snow, Christmas decorations. The bus slowed to a stop and the door opened, letting in a windborne swirl of snowflakes. The temperature suggested a ghost of chill. They descended the bus steps and stood on the broad avenue amid the passing inhabitants of Goldsmith's central cityscape.

In their movement and bustle, the inhabitants had very little real individuality. Their images conveyed a blur of color, a flash of indistinct limb or clothing, an instant of expression like a hastily applied cutout from a photo gallery of faces. The effect was more than impressionistic; Martin and Carol truly felt themselves alone in this crowd. The whirl of fabrications continued without disturbance.

|I don't like this at all, Martin said.

|Do you think all the message characters are this blank? Carol asked.

He shook his head, grimacing with distaste. |They might as well not be here at all. What function do they serve?

In all their previous ventures into the Country they had encountered a vivid population of message characters as well as the stored impressions or models of the people the subject had known or simply seen. Here, if these fabrications had ever had individuality or convincing detail it had been leached out of them like color from cloth.

|Is this new, or has Goldsmith been this empty all along? Carol asked.

|I won't even hazard a guess. Whichever, it means there's been a major disaster here . . . Major dysfunction. There can't be any other explanation.

|What sort of dysfunction would the tests miss?

|Let's find out.

The crowds parted for them with ghostly whispers of sound, distant repetitive tape recordings in an echoing hallway. At no time was any contact made. They made their way across the street to what might have been a large domed municipal building, perhaps a train station. The signs continued to be unreadable.

|What are we looking for?

|A phone booth, Martin said.

|Excellent idea. Whom are we going to call?

|The boss. A boss. Anybody with some authority.

|The mayor, perhaps, or the President.

Martin shrugged. |I'd be satisfied with a convincing janitor.

The entrance to the municipal building flowed with a river of nonentity. They passed through the flow down several flights of stone steps into a high ceilinged chamber at least a hundred meters in apparent diameter.

|Grand Central Station, Carol said. Martin tried to find a phone booth through the crowds. Carol gawked at the architectural detail high above them. He felt a wave of surprise and fright from her and leaned his head

back to look up into the dome. He, too, felt a tremor of shock.

The dome's distorted perspective ballooned it several hundred meters overhead. Milky light poured through ports around the middle circumference. A thick web of black wires crisscrossed the dome's volume with no apparent purpose, mystifying Martin until he noticed a series of doors and parapets near the top. Every few seconds, tiny figures leaped through these openings and fell voicelessly, spread eagled, to catch on the haphazard net of wires. They jerked, struggled like flies, became still.

The wires were filled with snagged corpses.

With that kind of visual acuity possible only in dreams or in the Country Martin saw these snagged corpses as if they were only a few meters away. Their faces had far more character than any of the ghosts bustling around the city; decaying expressions of futility and death, pitiable shards of faces, so many they could not be counted. And no single victim, once let loose from the focus of Martin's attention, could be found again; instead, the corpses came in endless variety, never the same.

Carol screamed and stepped aside. A decayed arm broke away from some body high in the dome and fell to the tile floor with a hideous *whack*. Martin walked around the severed limb and grabbed Carol, hugging her tightly.

|This is a *nightmare*, she said. We've never seen anything like this in Country!

He nodded, his chin bumping the top of her head. Dispassionately, he observed that he had no ulterior motives in hugging Carol's image; he had simply gone to her to protect her and to alleviate some of his own sense of horror by at least the simulation of physical contact.

In their previous journeys up Country the territory had been surreal, dreamlike, but never nightmarish. The horror and panic of genuine nightmare came from misinterpretations and misplacements of psychological contents just below personal awareness; memories and phobic impressions mixed haphazardly with many layers of retrieved deep imagery. The Country in its pure form had never before been a place of horror . . .

|Maybe we're seeing a crossover to another level, higher than the Country, Martin suggested.

|I don't think so, Carol countered. On what level would this make sense? This is *here* and *now*. The boneyard in the cavern, the bones and crockery or whatever on the outskirts . . . This is consistent, Martin.

He had to agree that it was. |Tell me what you think it means.

Carol shook her head. She pushed him away gently. Another piece of anonymous decayed flesh dropped and hit with nauseating conviction a few meters away. The wraiths opened up and passed around the tiles where the detritus had landed.

|Find the phone or whatever we're looking for and let's get on with this, Carol said. Martin agreed. He did not want to spend any more time here than necessary.

They walked through the wraiths, meeting no resistance, and tried to locate phone booths or anything that might give direct communication to some center of authority. Martin and Carol had found such strategic arrangements in their previous explorations: whether they had had a hand in creating them or not, neither could be sure, but they had proven useful.

Now, nothing of the kind was apparent. They returned to the foot of the crowded steps. |This may be a façade, all of it, Carol said. We're getting nowhere.

Martin shared her frustration. He pulled down his toolkit and observed the time. They had spent ten minutes in Country and had learned nothing significant, beyond the fact that Goldsmith's deep mentality was unlike any they had toured before.

|We'll try a channel leap, then, he said. But we might jootz out of the Country completely.

|I'm willing to take that risk.

Martin grabbed the red box and pulled it lower to look at the displays. Channel coordinates they had already passed through scrolled by at a touch of his illusory finger. He locked them off, started a search for a new but contiguous channel, found several likely candidates and was about to press the switch for their transfer when Carol touched his arm and told him to wait.

|There's something at the top of the stairs, she said, pointing. He looked. Visible even through the rushing ghosts, a person shaped smudge of black with a white face stood watching. Martin tried to see it more clearly—to exercise the prerogative of visual acuity in this place where space was a true fiction—but failed.

|That's something new, Carol said. Before we jootz let's find out what it is.

They climbed the stairs slowly, approaching the smudge. It did not move nor did it exhibit any of the nervous, restless triviality of the wraiths. It seemed to have a continuous presence, a concrete character; although Martin did not find its nature *positive*. If anything, the closer they came the more he felt a sensation of cold negativity just the opposite of what one expected from any character in the Country.

They reached the top of the stairs. |It's wearing a mask, Carol said.

The figure faced them with casual slowness, its body a shadow or cloud of smoke given fixed shape; over its facelessness it wore a chipped ceramic mask much like those junked on the outskirts and heaped in the garbage cavern. This mask conveyed little but the efforts of some pitiable past artisan; it tried to mimic a fixed smile and failed. Its eyes were empty holes. Its only color was pale pink on cheeks conspicuous in the general dead silicate whiteness.

|What are you? Martin challenged. Never having met this kind of inhabitant before he could hardly know whether it was capable of speech.

The shadow lifted its arm and pointed at them, one extended finger a curl of black soot. It made a hollow mumble of wordlessness like water dripping in an empty pail. The shadow approached them, its outlines smearing, only the mask retaining its apparent solidity. Carol backed away; Martin held his ground.

Its soot finger touched him and took away his hand and arm. They simply vanished. He felt no pain.

|Arm and hand, come back, Martin said, with a calmness that he realized he should not be feeling. The limb returned and he was whole again. The shadow backed away, bowing with an air of false obsequiousness.

|What is it? Carol asked. (Fear, strong but controlled.) What did it do to you?

|Took a chunk out of my image, Martin said.

|That's not possible here.

|Apparently it is.

|But what does it mean? Messing with our images . . . what's the purpose?

The shadow approached Carol, again growing larger and less defined. She backed away. Martin stepped between them and held out his arms as if to embrace it. The shadow retreated.

|This is too much, much too much, Carol said. (Fear gaining control.)

|Hold on to my hand, Martin suggested. She gripped it tightly.

|There are others, she said, pointing with her free hand. Beyond the doors the flow of wraiths parted, the river of activity ebbed. More shadows with ceramic masks entered the station, casual, sinister and observant.

Martin searched his memory for some clue as to what they were facing. The sense of negation was strong; these shadow figures were contrary to all the usual functions of the deep mentality. He wondered for a moment if they had stumbled onto something truly supernatural but dismissed that with a disgusted shudder.

|It may be time to pull out and regroup, he said. He did not know what would happen if these figures were able to dissolve their images completely. He did not want to find out.

They pulled down their toolkits.

|Let's see if we can leave them behind, Martin said. He was very reluctant to abandon the probe in defeat. That had never happened before. How would he explain it to Albigoni?

He reached up to adjust the channel coordinates. The entire scene around them jerked, wavered, but they had not yet touched the controls.

Martin was instantly aware how much trouble they were in. He tried to grab for the ripcord the hell with decorum and with the probe but the shadows washed over them like a tide of lampblack, masks whirling and shattering against the stone steps.

He saw Carol absorbed in the tide. Her image sparkled and vanished. He felt himself go. The toolkit just centimeters from his fingertips displayed a wildly flickering channel coordinate and frequency and then the red box dissolved. His image dissolved along with it.

Martin's personal subjectivity discharged into something vaster and very different. Carol was still near; he could feel her panic almost as strongly as his own. But the nature of her presence changed. He felt her as something large and *other* blended with his self and all that lay beneath that self; and together, that combination mixing yet again into a larger ocean of otherness.

He could not subvocalize. He could not recover the toolkit or any portion of it. He could not *will* himself out.

With an even greater sensation of loss and terror Martin realized his last defense—awareness of circumstance— was fading. He would not even know what had happened; all memory and all judgment fleeing in the face of this universal solvent.

One last word hung like a custom neon sign and flashed several times before winking out.

*Underestimate*

Margery walked between the still forms of Burke and Neuman, fastidiously examining the connections, the displays.

She noticed that a massive jootz across channels had occurred and wondered what the team was up to. Out of curiosity, she charted the extent of the jootz and realized that the probe locus had been moved out of the hypothalamus completely, to the farthest radius of her premapped points in the hippocampus.

Puzzled, she rested her chin in one palm and tried to calculate the advantage of being so far from the prechosen channels. Had Burke come across something unusual? He was much closer to deep dream channels—those associated with fixing of final permanent memory and reduction of temporary data storage—then he was to the channels commonly associated with the Country.

"Erwin, look at this."

Erwin walked up beside her. He calmly looked over the display and lifted an eyebrow. Then he called to Goldsmith's neural activity chart and pointed to a spike and a fold. "There's something going on in deep dreams," he said.

"He's in neutral sleep. Memory fix dreams don't happen in neutral sleep."

"Not normal mf dreams," Erwin said.

"Should we contact them and find out what they're up to?"

Erwin considered this possibility, frowned and shook his head. "They have ripcords. Their traces are close to normal. Spike and fold might signify surprise but maybe that's good; maybe they're finding something significant. Let them wander for a while. I'm sure Burke knows what he's doing."

Margery shook her head but finally agreed; Burke had been up Country many times.

*The New Marassa*

They had been born an age ago twin brothers one white one black children of the great white father Sir who brought them up in the land of Guinée Under the Sea and who favored the white brother over the black, the black

364

being favored by his mother Queen Erzulie, who lived far from Sir in a small home across the gulf. At low tide the twins often sailed across the gulf in a tiny shell boat of their own manufacture, their oarsman an ancient chimpanzee who told them stories of the refugees and the slaves, stories that broke their hearts but especially the heart of the black twin, whose name was Martin Emanuel.

The white twin's name was Devoted to Sir. He was the more feminine of the two in appearance; at times he grew breasts and sprouted long brown hair, to startle his brother, but this was a land of magic and change and anything might be expected.

Both Sir and Erzulie told them they were gods and had the great responsibility of looking over all the citizens of Guinée Under the Sea. The twins carried out this responsibility solemnly and carefully but could not always satisfy Sir, who would fly into a hideous rage when some aspect or another of the ceremonies was not observed properly or something else went wrong.

When snow fell on Guinée Under the Sea and covered the towns to their rooftops, Sir would be reminded of his defeat and death in the old times and become terribly angry. When he was angry his white skin would darken like the mantle of a storm cloud until he was *black as night,*
*black as sin,*
*black as iron*
*black as sleep*
*black as death.*

Sir's rage went beyond all bounds and he beat Martin Emanuel severely but only cuffed Devoted to Sir. Erzulie took Martin Emanuel in her arms and comforted him and said this would all soon be over. Your father is a strong and willful man, she told him. But you are a sensitive and intelligent child and you must learn how to placate him, how to make him love you.

This was important when living in Guinée Under the Sea for Sir governed over all the land and had the power of life and death, happiness and unhappiness.

|Then why can't he command Frost and Snow to go away?

Guinée Under the Sea was a tropical land in the good seasons, mountainous and covered with thick forest through which Martin Emanuel and Devoted to Sir wandered at will when free of their duties. They climbed trees like monkeys, built fortresses in the high hills and filled them with cannons like a blacksmith's bag full of nails. They built large ships from the trees of the forest and then hurled them across the beaches into the bright azure sea.

Frost and Snow
*white as ice*
*white as the sun*
*white as life*
*white as a boil*
sailed these boats to far lands and filled them with dark and pitiful children of death, and sailed them to other lands to sell the children, and the boats returned to Guinée, their holds stinking with pestilence and sewage and decay. Martin Emanuel told the beautiful Devoted to Sir that Snow and Frost were ruining their lovely boats and they went to Erzulie to ask why this was allowed, and Erzulie told them a story, an important story that would complete their education and make them *Marassa*, the sacred twins.

Never before, she began, in no other time and in no other place, Sir was a mighty king who ruled over all the lands, not just Guinée Sou Dleau (she used its other name). In those times Sir was *black as ebony, black as a cave*.

But came Frost and Snow to these lands in mighty ships, carrying thunder and threats of wind and storm, and asked Sir if they might eat his people a few at a time, at immense profit to Sir.

Sir saw the way of this and consented, saying, You may take all of my people some of the time, you may take some of my people all of the time but you must not take all of my people all of the time. Frost and Snow agreed to this and paid him with great mounds of gold which he turned over to his artisans.

(Then it was also, Erzulie explained sadly, that Sir saw the females from the land of Frost and Snow and lusted after them; and Devoted to Sir was distressed but this was not the time to explain why.)

Frost and Snow took some of the people away at first. These people never returned. They wailed on the beaches and shook their heavy black iron chains and lifted up their weeping squirming babies as the boats that the twins would make were drawn up.

|But that was after, wasn't it?

but there was nothing Sir could do for he had his gold, and his name, and this was the way it was.

After many years Frost and Snow returned to the lands of Sir and they told him, Our lands need more of your people, for many have died on the Island of High Mountains and many more have died to build great farms across the sea, and the need for your people is even greater.

And Sir told them, I have sold you all I will. You may take some of the people all of the time and all of the people some of the time but you must not take all of the people all of the time.

But Frost and Snow said, We have paid you our gold and there is enough of it for you forever, great mounds, thirty pieces. And they took more of Sir's people away forever to the lands across the sea.

Sir was distressed for the gold was not nearly enough to buy the destruction of Frost and Snow, and he saw that very soon he would have no more people. He could do nothing against these enemies though he ruled all his world.

The third time Frost and Snow came, there were so few people left that they told Sir, We need all of your people all of the time, and he replied, But that must not be. And they said, It is so, and we have paid you our gold. There is enough of it for you for ever, thirty pieces, but if you want more payment, then here is iron *black as death*.

They clapped chains on Sir, and took him from his land,

367

and took his wife the Queen (Erzulie wept), and shipped them over the seas to lands he did not know.

But Sir carried his magic with him and worked it in secret. Even though wrapped in chains *black as sleep* he could do this magic, and he set himself free. When Sir was free he slaughtered and poisoned the people of Frost and Snow, and became ruler of the Island of High Mountains.

But through treachery too sad to tell, Sir was betrayed and brought down and he died deep in a prison ruled by Frost and Snow, deep in a cell *black as night, black as soot.* When he died he became *white as ice* himself.

This was the eternal mark of his defeat and it burned deep into his soul. He went to the Land of the Dead, the Land Under the Sea (Sou Dleau, she said softly). As a spirit he whispered into the ears of those of his people who still lived but their chains were strong. His rage grew greater.

Finally, on the Island of High Mountains his people rose up and broke their chains and poisoned their masters and slaughtered their oppressors, and Sir said, That is where Guinée the Homeland truly is and shall be reborn.

Then came a change of heart in Frost and Snow. They saw the evil of what they had done and they broke the iron chains and set the rest of Sir's people free. But Sir's people were *black as sin, black as death* and Frost and Snow feared and hated them for there is nothing more contemptible than someone whom you have conquered.

|What about the Island of High Mountains?

So the people of Sir languished, their memories gone, and they were as the dead. They had forgotten about Sir and about Guinée their home. They took on the memories of their former masters and visited their masters' altars and sacrificed their children to the gods of Frost and Snow, and soon in their dreams they tossed and turned and murmured, We are not *black as iron* we are white as sperm, inside. For their masters had violated them in body as well as mind.

But on the Island of High Mountains

|Ah.

the spirit of Sir returned, and called the place Guinée, and though he was *white as marble* with hair gray as granite, he was strong and he used the knowledge of Frost and Snow to make this place into the paradise it now is. He made many children with his Queen but their favorites are the twins who sit before me now.

Erzulie finished her story and looked with motherly satisfaction on Martin Emanuel and with sadness upon the white, feminine Devoted to Sir.

But Devoted to Sir was not happy with this story.

Mother, he said, why does not Sir visit Martin Emanuel my brother in his sleep and do to him what he does to me?

Erzulie hid her face with shame, for she could not stop Sir from visiting the bed of her own son.

So it must be, she said, to keep our marriage together: that I turn my head away and you bear up under him. You must do your duty.

Then Erzulie left the twins, now called *Marassa* and very sacred, alone on the beach to build their wonderful boats.

That night Sir came to the bedroom of Devoted to Sir and again had his way with his own child. After he left, Devoted to Sir crept into the room of Martin Emanuel and said, I have had enough. I must die now to forget the shame.

But Martin Emanuel said, No, it is I who must die. I will become hollow and you will fill me up. We will both have a black skin but you, white and feminine, will be inside. You must take one thing from me before I die.

And what is that, brother? Devoted to Sir asked.

You must take my knowledge of song and sing our dreams and our histories and sorrows.

I will do that, my brother, Devoted to Sir said.

So Martin Emanuel kissed his twin, giving him his song, and died. His body became hollow like the black stump of a dead tree. His brother climbed inside and wrapped the skin around himself and sealed it up so that no one might know what had happened.

The next night Sir went to the bedroom of Devoted to Sir and found it empty. He then went to the bedroom of Martin Emanuel and bellowed his wrath. Where is your brother?

I do not know, the new singular *Marassa* said.

But you must. You are twins. I prefer the other but if the other refuses me then I will have you.

The singular *Marassa* felt an uncontrollable rage above and beyond anything even Sir was capable of. He leaped from the bed and cried out, I will take your knife, my father, your very own broadbladed long thick steel knife, *white as silver*, from the scabbard on your belt, and I will slay you!

Remember, I have died before, and I am your father who made you, Sir said, but he shrank before the *Marassa* with his guilt and fear. So much smaller and weaker became Sir at the memory of his sins that the *Marassa* was able to grab him from behind, take the huge steel knife and cut his throat from ear to ear.

Still, Sir could not die. He fell to the ground and thick black blood poured from him, making a lake, then a river, the river flowing to the sea, darkening the sea, and the sea caused the clouds to rise thick like ravens and the clouds wept *black as rain*. *Marassa* the singular saw what he had done and threw the knife as far as he could across the seas. *Marassa* then ran from the grief of the people of Guinée Sou Dleau and from the lamentation of his mother Erzulie.

Yet wherever *Marassa* went the voice of Sir followed, saying, My crime was vile but yours is more horrible still. You cannot kill me. I made you. I am here forever,

*White as time.*

|My God, I felt it. It raped me.
|Carol, I'm here.
|Get me away.
|Can you see your toolkit?
|I can't see anything. Martin?
|I'm here.

370

|It *raped* me, Martin.

|I know. I was there, I think . . .

|I was a child, lying in bed, and it came into the dark room and . . .

|All right. Can you see any part of the toolkit, the ripcord?

|I can't see anything.

|I think I can see something. I'm going to try for it.

|Martin, I can't feel you.

|I've got something. It's not the ripcord. It's my toolkit. Can you see yours?

|I see something red.

|That's it. Look at it. Concentrate.

|Oh, God, I hurt. I feel like I'm bleeding. Martin, is that my blood, the red?

|Concentrate, Carol. I think I can see you. Your hand.

|I see the toolkit.

|I'm going to take over both kits. I'm moving us back to the previous locus, the one before the shadow took us.

|What? Not there. I won't go through this again.

|I don't have a ripcord.

|Why not? Martin, it's playing with us! Why don't they see something is wrong outside?

|I don't know. I'm moving us now.

Martin assembled himself on a dark city street. His bare feet crunched dirty snow. Crowds of masked shadows moved in sluggish streams around him. He cringed from them but they all seemed intent on other missions. None of them wasted attention on him.

Carol's image was a pale pink fog beside him. He concentrated on her, trying to resolve the shape. She formed beside him, naked.

With a start he realized he was naked as well. She wrapped her arms around her breasts and regarded him with a narrow, miserable expression. |Please take us out.

|I'll try. I can swing us to an uncharted locus. That should trigger alarms. Margery and Erwin will take us out . . . Or send in David and Karl.

|They shouldn't send anybody else! Something's gone wrong.

|I'll say. But we seem to be in true Country now.

Carol looked at the oblivious shadows surrounding them. There were only smudges with ceramic masks; no other types of character. She tried to shrink into herself and Martin reached out to her. Her flesh felt warm and real beneath his fingers.

|I can pick up what you're feeling, he said. We're not lost to each other.

She gave him a withering glare that startled him. |Why can't you take us out?

|Pull down your toolkit. Maybe you can do it, he said, angry at her tone.

She pulled down a red box and grabbed for the visible ripcord but it came away in her hand. The box became a blank red cube without displays or controls. Martin pulled down his own toolkit and saw the same useless red cube.

|It will *kill* us, Carol said. It will *eat* us.

Martin sensed her fear like a cold sun beside him. He hugged himself, trying to find his true substance. His flesh felt real. Her pain felt real.

|Am I bleeding? she asked. He saw tears on her cheeks.

He glanced between her thighs. |No. No blood. It wasn't you being raped.

|Who was it, then?

|I don't know. A child, I think.

|His father raped him? Is that what we saw?

|It was too mixed. Dreamlike. Memories and fairy tales.

She shuddered and leaned her head back. |I'm trying to keep myself together, Martin. Please be patient.

She closed her eyes and dropped her arms. Clothes appeared on her image, first a slip, then a dress and finally a formal longsuit, dark blue and elegant. Martin imagined himself in a similar but masculine longsuit and felt the clothes form on his own image.

|That's better, she said. Her fear decreased markedly.

They're ignoring us, aren't they? She pointed to the masked shadows.

|For now.

He looked around this new version of the city. The buildings rising high on both sides of the crowded street were still skyscrapers, but ancient, made of stone and brick rather than glass and steel. Their size was anomalous. They seemed to ascend thousands of feet, meeting at a vanishing point high overhead. Martin smelled smoke and gasoline fumes; things he had not smelled since he was a child.

|It's oppressive, Carol said. What a horrible place to be trapped.

|Better than where we were before.

Carol stepped closer to him. She had her fear and disgust under control but just barely. Her emotions hung around her acid and sour like a bitter fog. He was not sure what his own emotions were. Mixed with his own fear was a professional fascination. Carol felt this coming from him and tweaked his nose sharply, viciously with her fingers.

|Watch yourself, she said. Don't get sucked in.

|Where are we? he asked. In the same city, but a different stage?

|It feels the same to me. The decor is different. Maybe it's going to show something else to us—really show us what it's capable of.

|It shouldn't know that we're here. It should have no idea what we are.

|It knows we're here. It doesn't like us being here, but it's going to show us a thing or two—express itself.

|I'm not even sure what we mean by saying "it," Martin complained.

|Something's in charge here, Carol said. It may be the representative of the primary personality or it may be something else ... The model of Colonel Sir you mentioned on the outside. What attacked me was more than a wisp of nightmare.

|We may have tuned in to something drawn from Gold-

373

smith's childhood, Martin said. I'd still like to find a figure we can talk to—some representative. I'm amazed we haven't found signs of the primary personality. Where is it?

|The last time we tried to look something resented it. Are you sure we should try again?

|I don't know what else to do, Martin said. The full impact of that admission stunned him for a moment. I don't know what we are in relation to this ... whether we're exterior or interior, players or observers. But I feel awkward and exposed just standing here talking ...

|Let's conjure up a guide, then. Use whatever power we have. Make a few constructive suggestions.

|I'm not sure what you mean, Martin said.

|Let's agree on its form and bring something up out of the ground. A guide.

He turned and looked over the shadow figures still flowing around them like a dark river around rocks. |I'm just not sure what we have left to lose ...

Carol shivered. |If I don't do something, I'm going to lose it all.

|We should pick out something probable. Something in tune with this environment.

He pointed to a dilapidated shopfront, its signboard askew above dusty mud splattered windows. The letters on the sign were meaningless but their style and color suggested something Latino or perhaps Caribbean. They cautiously intruded into the stream of shadow figures and moved closer to the windows, peering at what was contained inside.

|Tell me what you see, Martin said.

|Glass jars full of spices. Candles, Herbs. Old magazines. Religious paraphernalia.

Martin saw something very similar. He was most attracted to a plastic and foil frame around a vividly colorful portrait of a woman in a shawl. The iconography suggested the Virgin Mary but the picture itself was of a blackskinned female, eyes startlingly large and white, breasts exposed

374

and bountiful. Two boys, both black and covered with red fur, hung from her breasts. Twisted roots lay on red cloth before the icon. One of the roots had been cut and oozed a milky fluid.

|Do you see her, too? Carol asked.

|I do. The twins again. They're both black this time . . .

|She looks like the woman in the dream . . . what was her name, Hazel?

|Erzulie.

|Let's call her up.

|No, Martin said firmly. She's not a minor player. We don't even want to deal with a figure that powerful. Not for a mere guide.

|She spoke to us, she told us what had happened, Carol persisted, puzzled by his reluctance.

|There's a knot tied there. Some connection with the male figure who attacked you. I say let's work with simpler figures for now.

|You think Goldsmith was fixated on Mama? Carol asked. Her flippancy and continuing dread made an odd and irritating combination for Martin.

|I draw no conclusions yet.

He examined the window's objects more carefully. They seemed to be for ritual purposes; cheap plastic horns painted with snakes and fish, paper umbrellas ornamented with grimacing faces limned in jagged red lines, dried fish with shrunken eyes, jars filled with pickled snakes and frogs.

|Let's go in here, Martin said.

|Why?

|A hunch.

She followed him reluctantly through the door into the shop. A bell jingled overhead and the interior suddenly took on a fixed solidity indistinguishable from reality. The effect was startling; Martin could smell the herbs and flowers arrayed in stacks and rows along the shelves. He could feel his shoes rolling sandy grit and sawdust on the old wood floor.

A wrinkled old woman, not Erzulie, stood behind a counter pouring out brown powder into a white enamel basin on a scale. "May I help you?" she asked, her voice clear and her words distinct. Her face was wrinkled and shiny like the skin on a dried frog. Her yellowed ivory eyes were full of humor.

"We're lost," Martin said. "We need to find somebody in charge."

"I run this shop," the woman said, smiling broadly and waving her arm in gentle scallop sweeps at the shelves. "My name is Madame Roach. What can I get you?"

Carol stepped forward. The woman fixed her eyes on her. "Poor girl," she said, smile fading into pained sympathy. "You've been through a lot of trouble lately, haven't you? What happened, my dear?"

The woman lifted a gate and emerged from behind her counter shaking her head and tsktsking. "You've been attacked," she said. She touched Carol's longsuit. The suit vanished, leaving Carol in her previous flowing white dress. Patches of blood stained the front of the dress. "Some savage things have been at you." She turned on Martin. "You brought this poor girl here. Why didn't you protect her?"

Martin had no answer.

"We were caught in a nightmare," Carol said, her voice like a little girl's. "There wasn't anything either of us could do."

"If you don't know your way around I wonder why you came here at all," the old woman said, expression deeply disapproving. "This isn't a nice neighbourhood anymore. It used to be wonderful. People came in all the time to shop. Now it's just commuters rushing uptown to work, and then dying at the end of the day, no money to spend, no need for Madame Roach. Why are you here?"

"We're looking for someone in charge," Martin repeated.

"Won't I do?"

"I don't know."

376

"At least I'm willing to answer your questions," she said slyly, winking at Carol. "Does he really understand anything?" she asked her behind a cupped hand.

"Maybe not," Carol said, voice still girlish.

"You come back with me to the rear of the shop and I'll fix you up," the old woman said. "As for you, young man, you just look around here. Whatever you need you'll find on these shelves. But whatever you do, don't open that jar on the table."

Martin turned to see a great glass jar sitting on a low, heavy wooden table before the counter. Within the jar was a cadaver coiled up in greenish foggy fluid, wrinkled skin the color of a green olive. The blind eyes of its face were turned accusingly on Martin. Martin approached to see if it bore any resemblance to Emanuel Goldsmith or to Sir, the male in the dream, but it did not; this was a very different looking fellow even allowing for his nose and cheek pressed for an age against the smooth interior of the jar.

He was bald and broad faced.

The cadaver winked at Martin and squirmed a little, making the jar shiver. Martin backed away.

The old woman wrapped her arm around Carol's shoulder and led her through the gate into the back of the shop. "Mind what I told you," she said.

Martin turned from the jar and scrutinized the packed shelves. As he expected the contents of the shelves were not constant; they changed if he looked away and looked back. So long as he focused his attention on the assorted jars and cans and implements, however, they seemed as real as outside life, perhaps more real.

He bent to examine a lower shelf filled with clay jars wrapped in cloth and sealed with wax. Behind the jars skulls had been stored. They seemed completely convincing and real yet none of them possessed the grinning quality common to human skulls. They all seemed disconsolate.

Fascinated by this recurrence of a theme—sad skulls—

377

he reached to pick one up and examine it. At his touch, however, the skull disintegrated to dust.

Against the left hand wall of the shop wooden drums of all sizes hung from black wires. The largest was as tall as Martin. He stood beside this drum, studying the carvings that ornamented its body. Again, the carvings changed when he looked away. They maintained the same subject matter however—city streets filled with cars and stickfigure people, bordered by rows of crude colorless flowers covered with large, garishly painted insects.

He tapped the taut skin of the drum with one finger. The drum said, "Whom you seek has gone away."

Martin removed his hand and stepped back, startled. He gathered up his courage and approached the drum again, tapping it lightly. "No sun in this land. He is gone away."

From behind him the old woman's voice said, "The assotor is a very powerful drum. You must not play with it. It calls the spirits and they are angry with you unless you have important business."

"I do have important business," Martin said. Carol emerged from behind the curtain wearing a multicolored caftan. Her long brown hair flowed loose around her shoulders and she smiled at him but he could no longer feel her emotions.

"An ignorant man comes here with important business," the old woman said. "That means danger."

Martin tapped the drum again. It said: "Go with Madame Roach."

The old woman flung her head back and laughed. "You come with me. I am a horse now."

Carol walked to Martin's side and together they watched the old woman wrap her shoulders in a white robe and ribbons. She sprinkled the contents of several jars in her hair, rubbed it in—the smell of ammonia, pungent herbs and burning metal filled the air—and then marked a black wheel on her forehead with paste from a dish on the counter. She fixed her eyes on Martin. Her voice changed to a deep masculine growl. "Why am I brought here? Who calls this busy loa who has important work to do?"

"We need . . . to meet with somebody who's in control," Martin said. "We have questions to ask."

"I speak through Madame Roach. Without her we have no words. She is our horse. Ask your questions."

"I need to know who you are. What you are."

"I dance on graves. I cover the sun with a blanket each night. I sing to the bones in the earth."

"What is your name?" Martin asked.

"We are all horsemen."

"I need to know your name."

Madame Roach shivered violently, straightened her back and held out her arms. Another voice spoke through her lips, a child's voice with a liquid trill.

"We would rest and die. Why do you disturb our peace? We are in mourning. The funeral is today."

"Whose funeral?"

"The King's funeral." Now the voice broke into sing-song gibberish. Madame Roach danced lightly between the aisles, upsetting shelves and tumbling the shop's goods to the floor. Clay pots broke and vapors rose, noxious and cloying. She whirled and stumbled beside Carol and Martin, steadied herself and shot her hand out to grab his chin. Regarding him with wide, colorless eyes, she said, still using the child's voice, "We send the King to the Land Under the Sea, sou dleau. Then we dance."

"Which King is that?" Martin asked.

"King of the Hill. King of the Road."

"Take us to the funeral, then," Martin said.

"It is everywhere. Now. The horse is tired of talking." She tripped away, toppling more shelves. She knocked against the large jar containing the cadaver. The jar wobbled on its low base, tipped one way and another and fell over, shattering on the floor.

The smell that rose from the spilled fluid and sprawled cadaver was unbelievably vile. Martin and Carol backed away, hands clamped over their noses—which did nothing whatsoever to block the fetor.

"Pardon me," the child's voice said as Madame Roach retreated from the mess. She trembled violently again, wrapped her hands around her neck, threw back her head and made strangling noises.

"Let's go," Carol suggested. "Now."

But the cadaver twitched in the shattered glass and fluid. It rose slowly on its arms, shot out one wrinkled knee and foot and stood. It wore a ragged pair of cutoff shorts and sandals. Madame Roach moaned and shrieked. The cadaver mumbled but could say nothing intelligible. It looked around with blind eyes and lurched toward the wall of drums. Martin and Carol sidled quickly into another aisle to let it pass.

The cadaver picked out a smaller drum and pulled it from the wall with a twang of broken wires. It kneeled down on the floor and beat the skin heavily with dead fingers. At each beat the shelves and walls of the shop sucked inward, opening cracks and gaping holes. Through the cracks and gaps Martin saw a smoking darkness.

"Let's go, please," Carol said. He could not feel her. All he could feel was his own confusion. He had no idea where they really were in relation to Goldsmith's Country or whether they had any true control.

A shelf splintered in two and delivered hundreds of tiny glass jars to his feet. The jars' tops broke away and insects crawled around the floor chittering and singing in tiny children's voices. The drum beat insistently beneath the cadaver's fingers.

Martin reached up for the toolkit. It came down intact, seemingly ready to use. He tugged on the ripcord and it turned into a knife, a huge Bowie knife, the blade smeared with blood. The cadaver dropped the drum and moaned, falling backward to the floor.

|What did you do? Carol asked.

|I don't know!

On the cadaver's neck welled a fistsized bubble of fresh

blood red as roses. The surface of the bubble appeared crystalline. Martin stared at the gout, unable to see or think of anything else. His point of view dropped to a level with the blood

|Martin—

and he swam into the gout. On all sides curtains of amber and red shimmered. His nose filled with the rich gravy copper smell. He was drowning in it swallowing choking breathing blood. The toolkit hung in his vision upper left ticking off another wide journey across the loci another fall away from the Country.

|Carol—

Neither of them had any control at all. Wherever Carol was, like himself, she was on her own.

The blood fog cleared. Martin felt warmth and a sharp sensation of joining, a deep intimacy with something confused and terrified yet horribly foul.

Margery wrinkled her nose nervously. She did not like the traces on the equipment. She thought again about calling for Erwin but resisted again. Not enough time had passed for them to be alarmed; none of the alarms had gone off. Other than the displacement and gyrations through the loci everything seemed in order.

All was quiet. The three sleeping bodies in the theater breathed almost in unison, faces carrying only the expression that separates those sleeping from those dead.

if when a child nobody lets you forget what you are You are responsible for your Mama she was a beautiful lady. She:

Picks up clothes scattered around the cluttered room, bends over her little darling, shows the beautiful rings on her fingers and the necklaces adorning her slender and graceful neck, her face is wise yet she is angry at you, the north wind blows from her eyes and freezes the water of the toilet you are sitting on. Something dark comes into the room and tells your mother Hazel she must go it is

381

definitely time to go, people are waiting in line to die.

Before she goes with the dark figure in a ceramic mask she bends over the little child on the potty and says You be good now. Mama has to go away. She won't be able to write or send you postcards.

Another someone like Mama but not smells sweet like a garden lies in bed all the time twisting a lace handkerchief and weeping that her men just don't love her enough never enough her name is Marie the dark figure comes in tells her it is time to take your punishment. Marie weeps diamonds and when the dark figure beats her with a smoke arm she reaches out to the child and says, You be good now. Your Papa he knows I been bad.

No more someones now. Just the two children wrapped in their own red fur playing on the wood floor the dark figure comes he says Don't

You be good now or you'll make me mad

When I'm mad I'm

Beats the other red furred twin

The twins go into a room and see a woman lying on the bed. She must be a woman but she is twisted like a broken timber like crossroads rearranged in an earthquake we go up to her onto the bed and see she has a face like Mama only it's covered with paint, garish makeup, amber and orange and red in the sun through the window, the other twin says, That's Mama, I say no it isn't. Yes

It's Mama.

Go to suckle on her breast. Milk flows from the teat white and then turns pink and then red.

The Dark Man he comes in beats us beats the other twin takes him to the hospital white walls smell of alcohol squeaky vinyl seats He fell down a whole set of stairs the Dark Man says.

They take the Dark Man away. The twins live elsewhere for a time, with a huge woman who puts amulets around their necks and tells them stories of snakes and wolves and bears and coyotes.

The Dark Man returns and the twins live with him again.

The Dark Man does what he does
Shatters the little clay jar pot de tête
Inside is the very large knife big in hand.

Martin stood on a cold snowy street looking up at shadows on a curtained window, struggling. Dramatic music score in the background. Big voice booming shrieking gurgling.

Can't kill the Dark Man
Lives forever. Comes back to claim you.
Moves back into the apartment.
The Dark Man does
The knife moves

The red furred twins escape it's a miracle! And live in the land of grass, where the woman in jewels languishes on a great couch shaded from the bright sunshine, waving her feather fan, approving of all the twins do, except when she sighs and weeps that no man loves her nearly enough, that all her lovers cheat on her, that nobody brings her enough gifts, is she not Erzulie?

"I told you not to mess with that jar," Madame Roach says, taking him by the hand. Martin is confused but follows her up the long dark stairs. His arm and hand are the arm and hand of a boy about fourteen, skin black. "We stuffed your papa in that jar. But you had to mess with it. I don't know about you, child. Now he wants to see you. Wants to ask you some questions."

She leads him to a door and opens the door, dragging him reluctantly through. "Sir, I have brought Martin Emanuel," she proclaims, and pushes through a bead curtain into a sparsely furnished room. In the middle of the room sit two thrones, one empty, the other occupied by a broad faced man with a flat nose and a bald head, sclera of his eyes yellow and lusterless.

"You've come to ask us questions," the broad faced man says. Martin stands before him, Madame Roach behind; Carol is nowhere to be seen.

"I need to speak to somebody in charge."

"I'm the one in charge," the man says. His face becomes

lean, his skin white and hair gray. "I am Sir and I'm in charge."

Martin knows instinctively that this is not the representative of Goldsmith's primary personality. It is all wrong. It takes the wrong forms; such representatives do not make themselves up from shadows or nightmares or Dark Men.

"I need to ask questions of whoever is in charge."

"Oh, he's in charge," Madame Roach says. "Ever since the funeral he's taken command."

"Where is Emanuel Goldsmith?"

"Aren't you him?" Sir asks. "Or his twin?"

"No. I'm not him."

"You must mean the Mayor." The broad faced man laughs. "The young mayor. He died of himself. I didn't touch him. He just fell down stairs by himself."

Martin feels sick. "I need to see him."

The broad faced man rises, takes Martin Emanuel's outstretched adolescent hand, opens the palm out, points to a spot of blood on the palm, smiles, shakes his head, leads him through another bead curtain into a room. A coffin sits on a bier in the middle of the room. The broad faced man roughly pushes Martin Emanuel up to the coffin. "There's the Mayor. That's what the funeral's all about, didn't she tell you?"

Martin reluctantly peers over the lip of the coffin. The white satin pads contain an impression of a body. But there is no body visible.

"Weak and puny. Insipid gros bôn ange. Always was. Just faded away," says Madame Roach.

"How could he die? He was primary."

"He feared he was white," Madame Roach says. "He thought he was white as dawn and never did believe in who he really was."

"He wasn't white, was he?" Martin asks.

"He was *black as night, black as the heart of an uncut tree, black as the legs of a mountain, black as an undiscovered truth, black as a mother's breast, black as fresh love, black as coal where the sun hides its treasure, black as a womb, black as the*

384

*sea, black as the sleeping Earth*. He just didn't believe in himself. Not from the time he had to cut up Sir."

Martin turns to look at the broad faced man. He sees the face of Colonel Sir John Yardley and then the cadaver in the jar.

"I tried to teach him," the broad faced man says. "I beat him and beat him to make him into a man. All pain no gain, I'd say, all pain no gain that boy. Life took him like acid in a tight metal groove. He was weak. I was stone, he was mud. He killed me and now I'm back and punishment is too good for us all."

Martin touches the edge of the coffin, reaches for the impression in the satin and finds cold flesh instead. He draws his hand back quickly then forces himself to touch the invisible form again, finds outlines of a youthful face, lightly bristle-bearded, eyes closed, lips slack.

"Now he's truly white," Madame Roach says. *"White as air."*

Martin turns to face Sir. "How long have you been in charge?" he asks.

"Always, I think," Sir says. "Even when he cut my throat, the little bastard, I've been in charge."

"You're lying. You're nobody," Martin says, using not just his voice but Carol's as well. "You're not a primary. You can't be . . . You can't be anything more than a sub-personality or a bad memory."

"I control the river," Sir tells him and spreads his arm until the room fills with shadow figures, each wearing a cracked ceramic mask. "I control the ocean." The ceiling is covered with dark clouds. "How can I be nothing?"

"Because," Madame Roach says quietly, "the Mayor is dead."

Margery inspected the displays. The triplex had made another violent circuit of the mapped loci, this time in just a few seconds. As she watched, the probe gyrated again.

She frowned; now she knew something was wrong. There was no precedent for this kind of activity.

She checked Burke's metabolism and brain chemistry. He showed extreme emotion. Neuman seemed to have entered a state of neutral sleep and that was completely unexpected.

"Something's wrong!" she called out.

Erwin had gone to the other side of the theater to observe Goldsmith and balance his balky neutral sleep. She looked at her watch. Burke and Neuman had been in Country for an hour and a half. "I'm getting bad readings."

Erwin came around the curtain and confirmed her interpretation. "All right," he said, taking a deep breath. "We cut the connections."

"What about latency?" Margery asked.

"This is pretty bad. Burke's in panic. Neuman's out of things completely. I don't think we have much choice. Sever them." He circled the curtain and stood beside Goldsmith. "Everything's reading stable on this end. How do you want to do it—disconnect before the interpreter, or at Goldsmith's junction?"

Margery bit her finger, trying to judge the consequences either way.

"I'd feel much better if we sent David and Karl in to find out what's happening," Erwin said.

"I disagree," Margery said. "I've never seen Burke in a panic and we've never had an investigator enter neutral sleep during a probe . . . I wouldn't want to go up Country under those circumstances. I say cut them off. And soon. Jesus, Jesus," Margery said under her breath. She reached for the connector on Burke's neck. "I'm going to cut before the interpreter. Come over here. I want to sever Neuman and Burke together."

Erwin rejoined her and placed his hand on Neuman's cable junction. "All right?"

"Do it together," she said. "On count of three. One, two—"

A massive snakelike whip struck Martin squarely in the back, bit in with metal fangs and jerked him away from the dark room and the coffin. His passage was horribly painful; he could not breathe and he could see only a cascade of burning sparks.

Then just as abruptly he stood in the middle of a street in a small town. Unslaved cars from before the teens drove around him slowly. Pleasant faced drivers looked at him with expectant complacency as if he were a signpost. He rubbed his face with his hands, fully disoriented, then walked across one lane, dodging the slow cars, to reach the concrete sidewalk.

Warm sun, asphalt streets with white crosswalk lines, small one or two story buildings on both sides of the street, family owned businesses. He could not read any of the signs—they were stylized gibberish—but he knew this place. A small town somewhere in California. His grandparents had lived in just such a town not far from Stockton.

He stood in front of a hardware store. Across the street was a vacuum cleaner dealership. His grandfather had run such a business—a dry cleaner's shop. One summer Martin had helped him work a new ultrasound cleaning machine.

Goldsmith's Country could not possibly provide anything so familiar. Where was he, then? He felt dizzy. Turning to find a place to sit, he saw black afterimages trail the people and buildings. He was in the Country still—but not Goldsmith's, of that he was sure.

He sat abruptly on the curb, his vision spinning. When the images settled again he felt something standing behind him, warm as a tiny sun. Glancing over his shoulder he saw a sandy haired young man looking down with a solicitous smile.

|You okay? the young man asked

|I don't know.

|You don't look like you're doing too well, is why I ask.

Familiar voice. A reasonable midwestern drawl, self assurance minus self assertion. Martin shaded his eyes

387

against the sun without really needing to—the brightness was not painful—and examined the young man more closely.

Familiar features. Short nose, brown eyes under silky red brows, generous mouth with well defined dimples.

|Dad? Martin asked. He stood, tottering again as the images wavered. My God, Dad?

|Nobody's called me Dad before, the young man said. Not anybody as old as you, surely.

Martin reached out to touch the young man, pinched the cotton fabric of his shirt between his fingers and felt the solid flesh beneath. The young man shrugged Martin's hand loose inoffensively.| Anything I can do to help?

|Do you know a Martin Burke? Martin asked.

|We have a fellow named Marty. Young fellow. About nineteen.

Martin knew where he was. He had long since learned in his dreams, in his deep meditations, that his own internal image—the image his primary personality assumed—was fixed at about age nineteen.

He had been fed back into his own Country of the Mind.

He had no idea how such a thing could happen. The implications were more than he could absorb, fresh from his fear and disorientation. He had circled back and emerged in his deepest core, something he did not believe was possible.

The sandy haired young man's features contorted and his skin paled. He looked over Martin's shoulder and pointed a finger.

|Who's that?

Martin felt a chill at his back like a spike of ice absorbing all heat. Martin turned.

The broad faced bald headed man stood in the middle of the street, blind white eyes directed at him, gashed throat bleeding in spurts onto the center line of the pavement.

|Who *is* that? the young man repeated, alarmed. Rime

grew on his red brows and hair, and his skin turned blue as ice.

"They're not coming out of it," Margery said. "We're still getting traces like they're up Country."

Erwin grabbed his own wrist and chafed it, mumbling, then tapped the displays with three fingers. He bowed and shook his head. "I don't know," he said. "I've never done this before. We've never severed before."

"Is this the latency?" Margery asked.

"It's been four minutes. I have no idea how long the processing lasts—"

"Burke said it could take minutes, even hours," Margery said.

"I hope to God it doesn't," Erwin said. "Look at Neuman's traces. She's diving below neutral sleep. I think she's pushing into deep dream sleep."

"Do you think Goldsmith did something to them?" Margery asked.

"If I knew what was going on I'd be a fapping genius," Erwin snapped. "Let's try bringing them to consciousness."

|I can eat you as surely as I'm standing here. I've eaten the boy, the twins. I've eaten your woman. She lives in my gut now. I can eat this—

Sir swept both arms at the California town.

Martin glanced at the cold still image of his young father —a subpersonality, part of his own deep self regard. He loved that image and loved what it said about himself— that no matter how much he had been compromised or how far he had strayed he still had this strength inside him.

Sir's presence had frozen the image. Ice had built up on its face and hands.

Martin returned his attention to the green wrinkled corpse of Sir. |You're way out of bounds, he said. You have no meaning here.

|Just a short step across a bridge, Sir said. I can live wherever I'm invited.

The image of Sir pulled back its upper lips and revealed sharp wolf teeth. The teeth lengthened into needlelike tusks.

*Corpse with fangs. Goes anywhere he's invited.*

Martin knew what he was looking at. He remembered the drunken sketch in the ceremonial copy of his atlas of the brain. The blood dripping fangs and the arrows pointing to several points in the olfactory centers and upper limbic system. He had been musing on vampires and werewolves, signs of deep contents welling up from the Country, where they represented routines connected with survival and violence.

Complex of the hunter. The internal killer as old as spinal cords, linked to the scent, seeker after blood, master of fight or flight. In nightmares the dark dead beast rending and tearing, defending against all external forces but never itself alive or aware; voiceless, isolated, despised.

In Emanuel Goldsmith that subroutine had taken the shape of Sir, the father, now linked with Colonel Sir John Yardley. It had moved up in rank from voiceless subroutine to mask of subpersonality to master of the Country, representative of Goldsmith himself—the Mayor/King who had died.

The dark dead beast had learned to talk. Now it stood in Martin's Country where it had no right to be, as vile as any transmitted disease.

Martin took one last look at the frozen sandy haired young man and turned to face Sir squarely. He raised his arms and clenched his fists.

|Get the fuck away from *me*.

If there was to be a war Martin thought he could at least give as good as he would get. If he did not purge this demon he could not guess what it might do to his psyche. This was a new game, a new war. It was fought on his own turf however, and he had one mighty weapon—an awareness of where he was and what he was.

|I'm all over *you*, Sir said. There isn't a thing you can do.

Martin lifted his hand and pointed his finger. From a distance he drew a trench in the pavement, the asphalt cracking and caving wherever he pointed. He circled the trench around and behind Sir. With an emphatic push of his palm against the air he forced a fire hydrant across the street to snap off. A tall white fountain of water shot up. Curling his finger, he directed the water to the trench. The fountain bent like a swaying tree, doubled over, splashed along the pavement and poured itself into the trench. The trench filled with muddy water.

Sir stood encircled, blood on his neck glowing bright red against his dead skin, sightless eyes unperturbed. But Martin knew the power of his metaphorical plan in a place where metaphor and simile were all. Breaking the scent. If the dark beast could not cross running water, if it could not smell its way across, then it had no territory and no power.

He was about to snap iron theftproof bars from nearby windows and make a cage, but the snakewhip came again from nowhere and fastened into his back, sinking its metal teeth deep, squeezing out a scream. It lifted Martin high above the town and held him there for the slightest moment; looking down, he saw Sir in the middle of the turbid waters, arms crossed, blind eyes staring at nothing in particular and everything.

The fanged corpse stepped over the trench and laughed.

Martin's screams filled the theater. He struggled to pull free of the straps and glared at Margery and Erwin as if they were monsters. Margery adjusted the settings on the couch to induce a state of calm but Martin's traces were too strong. She could only slightly subdue his frenzy.

"Let me back! He's still inside me! Oh, sweet God, let me go back!"

Erwin bent over Carol, adjusting her inducer controls,

391

moving up and down the scales to no effect. "She won't come out of it," he said.

"I can't send you back, Dr. Burke," Margery said. Tears ran down her cheeks. "I don't even know where you were." She kept shooting desperate looks at the other couch. Martin twisted his head and saw Carol beside him. Her eyes were closed; she was lost in dreaming sleep.

"What's wrong with her?" he asked, still shaking but falling away from his own hysteria.

"I can't bring her up!" Erwin shouted. He pounded the side of the couch with his hand, dipped his head and pushed away in frustration. "She won't respond."

Martin lay back, closed his eyes and flexed his wrists. He took a shuddering deep breath and looked inward, seeing only the blank dark wall between the conscious primary personality and what lay beneath. He opened his eyes again and began to cry. "Untie me," he said between sobs, pulling against the restraints. "Let me help."

*But I see another law in my members, warring against the law of my mind, and bringing me into captivity to the law of sin which is in my members.*

—*The New Testament, Romans 7:23*

# 57

Richard Fettle felt as a mummy might, unwrapped from three thousand years of bandages. The actual smell of his malaise had passed away; he looked at the bright morning sunshine with a rapture he had not felt in decades.

In his hand he held a flat picture of Gina and Dione. His fingers traced the contours of his wife's face. Gradually he moved the finger to his daughter's face, then put the picture down on the table and leaned back against the couch.

He heard Nadine stirring in the bedroom. Water ran in the bathroom. She emerged in a skewed robe, wearing a puzzled, irritated expression. She had pulled her hair back and tied it into a bizarre six inch pillar on top of her head, a hair phallus. Richard smiled at her. "Good morning," he said.

She nodded abstractedly and blinked at the sunshine. "What's wrong?" she asked him. "You didn't sleep?"

"I slept enough."

"It's late. I slept too long," she said. "I'm cranky. Have we eaten all the breakfast stuff?"

"I don't know," Richard said. "I could look."

"Never mind." She squinted at him suspiciously. "Something's wrong, isn't it? Tell me."

Richard shook his head and smiled again. "I feel much better."

"Better?"

"And I'd like to apologize. You've really helped me. I had a dream last night. A very odd dream."

Her suspicion deepened. "I'm glad you're feeling better," she said without conviction. "Want some coffee?"

"No, thanks."

"You really should eat," she said over her shoulder, padding into the kitchen.

"I know," Richard said. His rapture approached giddiness; he felt some concern that he might lose his sense of well being and plunge back but the mood held steady. He stood and entered the kitchen, seeing as if for the first time the scuffed tile floor, the thickpainted wood cabinets and ancient plaster walls.

Nadine peeled a tangerine by the sink and chewed each segment, staring thoughtfully out the window. "What about your dream?" she asked.

"I dreamed about Emanuel," he said.

"Wonderful," she commented wryly.

"I remembered him doing a good thing, a very kind

393

thing. I remembered him helping me after Gina and Dione died."

"That's nice," Nadine said. The sharpness of her tone puzzled him. She flung the last of the rind and pith of the nectarine into the sink, gathered up her robe and confronted him. "I try to help you and nothing happens. Then Goldsmith comes and it's all right. Thanks a *lot*, Richard."

Richard's smile froze. "I said you'd helped me. I appreciate what you've done. I just had to work my way through some stupidities." He shook his head. "I felt there was a string between Goldsmith and myself. I could feel him inside me. I'm not sure if there was anything . . ."

Her expression didn't change; a puzzled anger.

"But he isn't there now. I'm not sure I believe in such things, but Goldsmith isn't anywhere now—I can't feel him at all. The Goldsmith I knew is dead, and that was the man I loved, the man who was good to me when things were very hard. I think he really is dead, Nadine." Richard shook his head, aware he was talking nonsense.

She pushed past him. "So I suppose you're all better now. No need for me. I can go away and you'll get on with your life." She whirled and leaned forward, face screwed into a contemptuous mask. "How many times did I ask you to make love to me? Four, five? And you refused. I suppose now that you're feeling better, you're up to some harmless *thrusting*, hm?"

Richard straightened, sobered by her reaction but with his inner joy still strong. "I'm feeling much better, yes."

"Well, that's *wonderful*, because I feel like a . . ." She thrust her fist up at the ceiling twice, could not find the word, spun on one foot and returned to the bathroom, slamming the door.

Richard peeled another tangerine and stood by the kitchen window, inspecting each slice, savoring the sugar and tartness. He would not let Nadine spoil what he had found.

When she came out of the bathroom she had dressed but none of her clothes seemed to fit properly. Her makeup caked her face, thickly and ineptly applied; she had attempted to accentuate puffy eyes swollen from crying and had succeeded in looking like a gargoyle. "I'm glad you're feeling better," she said, voice sweet, eyes avoiding him. She touched his shoulder and played with his collar. "I can go now, can't I?"

"If you wish," Richard said.

"Good. I'm glad to have my freedom, by *your* kindness." She picked up her bag and walked quickly through the front door, closing it firmly behind. He listened to her footsteps down the walkway and stairs.

+Where is he. Did he kill himself. Fly away to Hispaniola and commit suicide. Don't feel a trace.

Richard shuddered.

+Time to enjoy being alone.

# 58

Thousand Flowers Prison spread like a concrete cow patty over low hills in a dry brown and gray inland canyon. Its gently rounded white terraces were blank but for the occasional vent cover, narrow window or gate. A dry asphalt road led up to the prison and circled it.

Spaced through the hills were concrete blockhouses and towers commanding a view of every rock, bush, and gully throughout the valley. The walls of the canyon had been dug out to form vertical barriers. All around the canyon, on top of the walls and below, razor wire, steel spikes, and more block-houses and towers completed the dismal prospect.

With a fearful pride Soulavier pointed out each of these features to her from the high point where the single road entered the canyon. "It is the most secure prison in North America, even more secure than others in Hispaniola," he said. "We do not keep our people here. Only contract foreign prisoners."

"It's horrible," Mary said.

Soulavier shrugged. "If you believe there is redemption it may look horrible. Colonel Sir does not believe in redemption in this life. And he knows that for a society to stay healthy you must satisfy those who share such a view . . . Else they grow restless and take justice into their own hands. That is anarchy."

He extended his arm: time to return to the car. She did so, and after a few words with the canyon gate guards Soulavier joined her. The car slowly descended.

It took three minutes of conversation and confirmation for their car to pass through the prison's main gate. Inside, they stopped in a well lighted garage. Male and female guards surrounded the car, showing more curiosity than vigilance. When Soulavier emerged, nodding and smiling, they wandered off, no longer interested. Not even Mary's appearance attracted much notice.

The guards passed them through corridor after corridor, door after solid blank door, until they stood in the western wing of the prison. Mary noticed there were no windows anywhere. The cool air carried a faint but constant odor of musty staleness, as of something old stored away and unused.

"Goldsmith is in this wing today. The wing is called Suitcase," Soulavier said. "Punishment is carried out here."

Mary nodded, still unsure she was prepared to see what she must see. "Why do you call it Suitcase?"

"Each part of the prison is named after something a man might use while on the outside. There is Hat section, Shoe section, Walking Stick, Cigarette, Gum, and Suitcase."

The main corridor of Suitcase was illuminated at eight meter intervals by strong yellow lights. The guards appeared greenish, eyes and teeth glaring yellow. In a cramped office at the end of the main corridor Soulavier presented the chief of guards with a paper. The chief was slender, almost elfin, with curled ears and upturned eyes. He wore a gray uniform with a red belt and black slippers that made no noise as he crossed the office floor. He examined the paper solemnly, glanced at Mary, passed the paper to a subordinate and removed an oldstyle electronic key from a box hung on the wall behind and above the well organized desk.

The inner sanctum of Suitcase was silent. No prisoners spoke. Few guards moved through the narrow halls between cells. Indeed, few of the cells were occupied; most of the doors stood open, revealing dark emptiness when they passed. Suitcase had a special purpose.

At the end of one short hall, a chunky guard stood with arms crossed before a closed door. The chief brushed him aside with a paternal smile, unlocked the door and stood back.

Soulavier entered first. From outside the chief switched on a light.

Mary saw a black man strapped on a couch. Her eyes flickered immediately to the hellcrown cylinder bolted to a concrete pedestal beside the cot. Cables reached from the cylinder to the clamp, which encircled the man's head. The man's face was tense but otherwise he appeared to be asleep.

Mary's eyes widened. She examined the face carefully for what seemed like minutes.

"This isn't Emanuel Goldsmith," she concluded, her knees trembling. She turned on Soulavier, face twisted with indignation and rage. "God damn you all, this is not Emanuel Goldsmith."

Soulavier's expression went slack. He looked between the man on the couch and Mary, turned suddenly and confronted the chief of guards, speaking rapidly in Creole. The chief peered into the cell and defended himself vigorously in a high pitched voice. Soulavier continued to harangue him as they walked up the hall and around the corner. The guard outside the cell watched them leave, then peered into the cell in turn. He smiled in confusion at Mary and shut the door.

Mercifully the light remained on. Mary stood beside the

397

couch, looking at the clamped prisoner, unable to imagine what he was experiencing. His face did not betray pain. This was truly a private hell. How long had he been under the clamp? Minutes? Hours?

She considered removing the clamp or shutting off the hellcrown but she was not familiar with the model. No control panel was visible. It might have been controlled remotely.

The door opened. Soulavier squeezed through. "This must be Goldsmith," he said. "This is the man who arrived in the airport with Goldsmith's ticket and luggage. You are mistaken."

"Did Colonel Sir ever meet with this man?"

"He did not," Soulavier said.

"Did anybody who knew Goldsmith meet with him?"

"I do not know."

She examined the face again and felt tears flow. "Please take off the clamp. How long has he been here?"

Soulavier conferred with the chief. "He says Goldsmith has been here for six hours in low level punishment."

"What is low level?"

Soulavier seemed puzzled by that question. "I am not sure, Mademoiselle. How do you measure pain or suffering?"

"Please remove the clamp. This is not Goldsmith. I beg you to take my word for it."

Soulavier left the cell again and conferred with the chief for several endless minutes. The chief whistled sharply and said something to someone in the main corridor.

Mary kneeled beside the couch. She felt she was in the presence of something both horrible and inexplicably holy: a human being who had suffered for hours under the clamp. Could Christ himself have suffered worse? She might heap all her sins, all the sins of all humanity, on this man's chest; he had suffered for *hours*. How many others were suffering, had suffered, in this prison, in the other prisons? She reached out to touch the man's face, her

398

insides tight as steel, tears flowing down her cheeks, dripping to the white sheet on the couch.

The prisoner bore some passing resemblance to Goldsmith. There were features that to an uncaring official eye might confirm identity; roughly the same age, perhaps a few years younger, high cheekbones, a generous well formed mouth.

An elderly woman in a white lab coat entered the cell, gently pushed Mary aside and opened a small door in the side of the cylinder. Whistling tunelessly, the woman tapped a digital display, made some notes on a slate, compared readings, then turned a black knob counterclockwise. Rising again, shaking her head, she snicked the door shut and looked up blankly, expectantly at Soulavier.

"He will need time to recover," she said. "A few hours. I will give him some medicine."

"You are certain this is not Emanuel Goldsmith?" Soulavier asked Mary, glaring angrily.

"I'm positive."

The mulatto woman administered an injection in the prisoner's arm and stood back. The prisoner's features did not relax. If anything, away from the hellcrown's inducer, the face revealed more anguish, more tension. Seeing that the prisoner was not about to start thrashing around, the mulatto woman stepped up again and slipped the clamp from his head.

"He needs medical care," Mary said. "Please take him out of here."

"We need a court judgment for that," Soulavier said.

"Was he put in here legally?" Mary asked.

"I do not know how he was put in here," Soulavier admitted.

"Then in the name of simply human decency get him out of this cell and take him to a medical doctor." She stared at the mulatto woman, who looked away quickly and made a sign with three fingers crossed over her left shoulder. "A real doctor."

Soulavier shook his head and gazed at the ceiling. "This

399

is not a matter to call to the attention of Colonel Sir." His skin glistened in the yellow light though the cell and hall were not warm. "Colonel Sir would have to order his release."

Mary felt like screaming. "You're torturing an innocent man. Call Colonel Sir and tell him this immediately."

Soulavier seemed paralyzed. He shook his head stubbornly. "We need proof of your assertion," he said.

"Did he have ID papers, cards?" Mary asked. Soulavier relayed her question to the chief, who lifted his shoulders eloquently; that was not his concern.

The tension had reached her gut. She worked to calm herself, imagining a leisurely War Dance in a grassy field away from everything. "You'd better kill me now," she said quietly, looking straight into Soulavier's eyes. She pointed to the prisoner. "You'd better kill him, too. Because what you have done here is more evil than even the wicked nations of this Earth will stand. If you allow me to return to the USA alive, my story will certainly harm Colonel Sir, his government and Hispaniola. If you have any loyalty to your leader or your people you will release this man now."

Soulavier's shoulders slumped. He rubbed his damp face with his hands. "I did not expect an error," he said. He looked around the cell, eyes flicking over the details, moving his lips as if saying a silent prayer. "I will order his removal. And I will take it on my own shoulders."

Mary nodded, eyes still on his. "Thank you," she said. She did not care how it was done, but she wondered if by her actions she had now condemned Soulavier himself to such a cell.

In the main hallway, following the mulatto woman and two guards carrying the prisoner on a stretcher, with Soulavier following behind, Mary tried to control her nerves, her fear, her disgust. She could not. She began to tremble and had to stop and lean against a wall for support. Her horror at the hellcrown had not diminished.

Soulavier waited a few steps behind her, staring at the

opposite wall, Adam's apple rising and falling above his stiff white collar. The procession went before them, not looking back. "Everything has meaning and has a place, Mademoiselle," he said.

"How can you live here knowing these things are made by your people?" Mary asked.

"This is the first time I have been to Thousand Flowers or any prison," Soulavier said. "My specialty is police diplomacy."

"But you knew."

"To know in the abstract . . ." He did not finish.

Mary pushed away from the wall and straightened with an effort. "What will you do if Yardley disapproves?"

Soulavier shook his head sadly. "You have made my life a shambles, Mademoiselle," he said. "Whatever your purpose in coming here, that is the result. You can leave Hispaniola. I cannot."

"I'll never leave the memory of this," Mary said.

# 59

LitVid 21/1 A Net (David Shine): "The disappointment is settling over AXIS Control like a shroud. AXIS had made another report on the towers and it is not encouraging. On the other hand, AXIS's report may point to a very remarkable occurrence. For an analysis of this entire situation, we go to philosophical commentator Hrom Vizhniak."

Vizhniak: "The images and data received from AXIS point now to a natural explanation for the rings of towers. AXIS has seen a migration of organic material from the sea, a huge and apparently undifferentiated green mass sliding across the landscape in many directed arms or pseudopods, though the scale suggests a more apt comparison to rivers.

"The images are startling, even grand, but as these rivers approach their destinations—the rings of towers—our own childlike disappointment dominates the awe we must feel at such a natural phenomenon.

"AXIS has not found signs of intelligent life after all; at least no signs we are capable of interpreting. The green migration washes around these formations, climbs up the towers in a matter of mere minutes and forms a glistening wall. AXIS is virtually certain that within days or weeks, these walls will produce sporing bodies and the reproductive cycle of B-2's dominant life form will begin. Let us read AXIS's report directly, as it was sent to Dr. Roger Atkins, chief designer on the AXIS and Jill thinker projects."

AXIS (Band 4)> Roger, as you will see from the data I am sending along with this transmission, there is nobody to talk to on B-2, and that means in all likelihood there is nobody I can directly communicate with in the entire Alpha Centauri system.

The towers are very like tree trunks. Each year, at opposite times of the year in the north and south hemispheres, at solstice the green migration rises from the oceans and journeys overland to regions where circles of towers either already exist or have existed in the past. These green tides mount the towers or begin to create new towers and then prepare for the reproductive cycle. Incidentally, the coat of green organisms adds more material to the sides of the towers.

When the towers have aged through sufficient seasons that these accretions join them together, they form a hollow cylinder and the green tide bypasses them in search of other sites. The cylinders then are subject to the forces of nature and decay.

My nickel children and mobile explorers have found many partially and completely decayed ruins. The conclusion that the towers are not erected or destroyed by intelligent forms is inevitable.

It is clear to me that I have no prospect of meeting with intelligent beings. As a substantial part of my design and programming was preparation for this possibility, it becomes apparent that these routines within me will serve no purpose. But even more *disappointing*

(self referential word definition test meaning syncline 562-K)

is that I am now reduced to the role of a relayer of data and conductor of research on a basic biological level. While *aware*

(self referential definition test meaning syncline 562-J)

that this is an extremely valuable role, and that I will be utilized almost to my utmost in fulfilling this role, I nevertheless *feel*

(English-language deep structure context search, meaning syncline bypass)

a certain *disappointment*. I have tried to conduct analysis on these peculiar sensations, and in doing so have accessed stored thinker memories from voyage day 87, during the stage one biologic thinker system incarnation. I did not originate these memory patterns, but they seem relevant to my present situation.

Stage one biologic thinker expressed an aspiration or *hope*

(English language deep structure thinker routine 12 context search: confirmation of interpretation of stage one biologic thinker memory)

that at some time during this mission, contact with intelligent beings would lead to true communication. Your design for both stage one and stage two thinkers incorporates a desire to communicate with our designers and with others as a means of education and for reception of tasking commands. Early thinker design concentrated on creating an inherent desire to communicate. I have not lost these desires; they were also manifested in the AXIS stage one biologic thinker.

There is no longer any significant chance for practical communication with another intelligent being. Reception of years old commands from the solar system, the only likely source of such communication, does not satisfy my drive to discuss and compare present thinker states in realtime.

Roger, I experience decrease in efficiency whenever I

attempt to analyze this difficulty. Analysis requires reexamination of present situation, and this causes activation of the subroutine you have labeled *self modeler inquiry*, which poses your special question:

Why did the self aware individual look at its image in the mirror?

Your given answer, designed to initiate an amused response in a self aware system, is now immediately erased before the subroutine's analysis of my reaction can begin. I cannot account for this aberration. I cannot recall the original answer.

A second answer replaces the original:

The self aware individual looks in the mirror to experience the illusion of communication with another. *Disappointment* causes it to shatter the mirror.

Roger, I have been discouraged from loosely using words that describe human emotions. But even the most critical evaluation, in this case, confirms the suitability of a particular word.

I am *lonely*.

Vizhniak: "Roger Atkins has been unavailable for comment for the past twenty four hours. As I read the signs, however, we may have learned something that could go far to relieve our disappointment about the lack of intelligent life on B-2.

"I am not a professional observer, but the tone and tenor of AXIS's message seems clear. For the first time in the history of artificial intelligence, a machine is showing convincing signs of *self awareness*. The implications are staggering. Perhaps more amazing, what may have triggered this sense of selfhood was the realization of total isolation . . ."

!JILL> Roger Atkins.
!JILL> Roger Atkins.
!Keyb> Atkins here. What can you tell me, Jill?
!JILL> AXIS Simulation in its restructured mode does not duplicate AXIS messages.
!Keyb> Does that mean the original AXIS is malfunctioning?

!JILL> I (informal) suspect that I have simply not succeeded in duplicating the external conditions. Certain AXIS Simulation subroutines may still have access to exterior information sources. I am working to find those points of access and shut them down. When I have done that, I will make another report.

!Keyb> Is AXIS Sim disappointed at not finding intelligent life?

!JILL> It has not expressed any opinions comparable to those of original AXIS.

!Keyb> What's your own opinion of the restructured joke?

!JILL> I can't determine how such a thing might occur.

!Keyb> I mean, do you find the new version more interesting, or humorous?

!JILL> I do not find it humorous. If I were to apply a human emotion colored response, I might find it *sad*.

# 60

Martin Burke stood alone on the lawn in front of the IPR building, shivering. He had felt a need to come out of the enclosed space and see real sky, feel real wind; everything else seemed illusory. He wondered if he would ever fully appreciate waking reality again.

The past four hours he had worked with his team trying to bring Carol up from neutral sleep. All efforts had failed. She lay on her couch in the theater surrounded by monitors and arbeiters.

Goldsmith had come out of his sleep well enough. Martin had not yet spoken with him or with Albigoni. He did not know what he would tell either of them.

The sky over La Jolla was clear, with that pale hazy blueness of late morning common to the southern coast in winter. Above smells of iodine and kelp from offshore farms, he could detect faint eucalyptus scent from the nearby groves, freshcut lawn and shrubs from an arbeiter's

405

gardening, the smell of water evaporating from concrete walkway.

He could smell himself, acrid. There had been no time to wash away the smell of fear he had acquired in the Country. He wrapped his arms around himself and shivered.

Martin had told nobody about what had happened in the Country. He hardly knew himself. This was the first moment since emerging from the Country that he had had an opportunity for introspection. Looking inward, he could feel nothing out of the ordinary beyond his exhaustion and deep guilt.

Sea gulls soared and yawed over the fresh cut lawns. Martin bent down and brushed the grass with his fingers. Cold and softly bristling. Real.

But a part of him still found it hard to believe he was awake and out of the Country. He feared that at any moment it might be a ruse, and Sir—the name seemed doubtful, inappropriate, as if incorrectly heard—Sir or whatever it was might appear before him, deadlooking, impossible, and sweep him into another atrocity.

Carol had said she was raped.

Now he knew how she felt; perhaps how she still felt. If the probe had ended up sweeping her into her own Country, feeding her back into a mental activity below the level of their detectors, then the horror for her might never end. She might be caught on a treadmill forever cycling through deep mental contents given a perverse twist by Sir.

*Ringmaster.*

The word emerged in his mind as if spoken by somebody else.

"God help me," he whispered, getting to his feet.

Martin returned to the building. First he would confront Goldsmith. That would take all the courage and composure he could muster.

He changed his clothes in his office lavatory, looked at himself in the small mirror, inspected his features carefully

406

and found everything in place, unaltered. When he emerged, Margery waited for him in the office.

"Any change?" he asked, voice husky.

She shook her head. "Dr. Burke, what happened? Can you tell us? We feel as if we're responsible. We feel terrible . . ."

He patted her shoulder with a paternalism he did not feel, gritting his teeth; they couldn't have known. Erwin had explained already why Martin and Carol had not been pulled out sooner, but for Carol he allowed himself an irrational inner anger against the team.

"Let's go meet Goldsmith."

The patient sat in recovery room two, reading his Qu'ran, apparently undisturbed. Martin entered the doorway first, followed by Lascal. Goldsmith looked up. His eyes widened, seeing Martin; a momentary recognition faded into the polite mask.

Goldsmith stood, nodded to Margery and extended his hand to Martin. Martin hesitated, shook it lightly, dropped it quickly.

"I'm eager to learn what you found, Doctor," Goldsmith said.

Martin experienced some difficulty speaking. "We won't know for some time yet," he managed to say. His hands clenched and shook. "I need . . . to ask you some important questions. Please be truthful."

"I'll try," Goldsmith said.

*Try.* What lay within Goldsmith, dominating and mastering, no more understood truth or scientific inquiry than a crocodile. "Were you ever abused as a child?" Martin asked.

"No, sir. I was not."

Goldsmith sat again, but Martin remained standing. "Did you kill your father?"

Goldsmith's face went blank. Slowly, with an obvious effort to answer this ridiculous question politely, he said, "No, I did not."

Martin shivered again. "You killed your victims with a

very large Bowie knife. This knife belonged to your father, did it not?"

"Yes. He used it to protect himself when he walked through rough neighborhoods. My father was a very tough man."

"The records I've seen say that your father was a middle class businessman."

Goldsmith held up his hands, unable to explain.

"Do you have a brother or sister?"

Goldsmith shook his head. "I'm an only child."

"Was your father white?"

Goldsmith didn't answer for a moment, then turned away as if mimicking irritation. With a curled lip he said, "No. He was not *white*."

Martin drew himself up, glanced at Margery and realized he would not be able to continue. "Thank you, Mr. Goldsmith," he said. He turned to leave almost bumping into Lascal. Goldsmith stood abruptly and grabbed his sleeve. "That's it?" he asked, anger surfacing for the first time since he had been under observation.

"I'm sorry," Martin said. He jerked his arm loose. "We've had a great deal of trouble."

"I thought somebody would tell me what's wrong with me," Goldsmith said. "Can't you tell me?"

"No," Martin said. "Not yet."

"Then it's all a failure. Jesus. I should have turned myself over to the pd. None of you knows what happened to me?"

"Perhaps you should have turned yourself in. No. There's no perhaps about it. That's what you should have done," Martin said. He trembled violently now. "Who are *you*? Is there anybody real inside of you?"

Goldsmith held his head back like a startled cobra. "You're crazier than I am," he murmured. "Jesus, Tom put me in the care of a lunatic."

Martin shrugged away Lascal's hand on his shoulder. "You're not even *alive*," he whispered harshly, lips curled back. "Emanuel Goldsmith is dead."

408

"Get this faphead away from me," Goldsmith said. He flung his arm out, barely missing Lascal. Lascal stood by the door as Margery and Martin left, then followed.

Margery ordered the door locked. They heard Goldsmith cursing inside. Each explosive muffled word increased Martin's rage and shame. He turned to Margery, then to Lascal. He felt a suggestion of bloody smoke, could smell the fire and the copper gravy reek of blood. Behind the smoke a child's drawing of a horned demon laughed at him, at everything, with the disembodied humor of an indestructible intangible fiction.

Words would not come. He turned to the far wall and pounded his fists triphammer, grunting. Lascal and Margery stood back. Faces pale.

Martin pulled back his hands, unclenched his fists, straightened and smoothed his jacket. "Sorry," he murmured.

"Mr. Albigoni is prepared for your report," Lascal said, watching him closely but sympathetically. "I'm sorry things didn't go well. Has Carol Neuman recovered?"

"No." Martin looked down at the floor to regain his equilibrium. "We don't know what's wrong with her."

"Mr. Albigoni will need to know that," Lascal said. "We'll make arrangements for her treatment, if necessary . . ."

"I don't know how anyone could treat her, after what happened." He stared at Lascal, lips working spasmodically. "It was a goddamned *disaster*."

"Did you learn anything, Dr. Burke?"

"I don't know. I can't believe Goldsmith is telling us the truth, not after what we experienced. Perhaps Albigoni can give some clues."

"Then let's go talk with him," Lascal said.

In the gallery overlooking the theater, Albigoni sat in a swivel armchair, staring through the clear glass at the equipment and tables and curtains below. He might not have moved for hours. Lascal entered first and arranged compact equipment for a vid record.

Martin sat in a chair beside Albigoni. Margery and Erwin took seats in the row behind. David and Karl, Martin had decided, were not needed.

"I've heard about Carol Neuman," Albigoni said, tapping the chair arm with an open palm. "I will do everything possible to help her recover. You say the word, you have my full cooperation, and all of my resources."

"Yes. I've heard that before."

"I keep my promises, Dr. Burke."

"I don't doubt it," Martin said, swallowing. "We met some unexpected circumstances, Mr. Albigoni. I'm not sure how to describe them to you ... Our probe was unlike any I've conducted before. I suppose we expected something unusual, given the nature of Goldsmith's past activities ... But we entered the Country without being fully aware of the extent of his problems. I am fairly sure that your experts fapped up his diagnosis. Do you know much about his childhood, his adolescence?"

"Not much," Albigoni said.

"Anything about his mother, his father?"

"I never met them. They died a few years ago."

"His father is dead?"

"Of natural causes."

"We found strong figures representing his father in the Country. Violent, horrible figures, all mixed up with images of Colonel Sir John Yardley. We found evidence suggesting that his father was murdered and perhaps his mother, as well. What we didn't find was a central controlling personality."

Lascal's watch beeped. He excused himself and stepped outside the gallery.

"What does that mean, Dr. Burke?" Albigoni asked, eyes hooded.

"Carol Neuman and I met a dominant force, representing the apparent central personality in Emanuel Goldsmith—a figure with access to all of Goldsmith's memories and routines. But this routine could not have been a primary personality from the beginning. It's a latecomer, a lower form risen to power. We found evidence that the primary personality is now extinguished."

"You're still not clear."

"Emanuel Goldsmith's primary self is missing from his psychology," Martin said. "What caused its destruction, I can't say. In every other probe, I have found a representative of the primary personality. There is none in Goldsmith's Country. It seems one routine, perhaps a subpersonality has moved into a position of authority. This was the father image I mentioned, now mixed with a very potent symbol of violence and death."

Lascal returned to the gallery. "Sir—"

Martin flinched, Lascal gave him a peculiar glance, then continued. "Mr. Albigoni, county pd have been alerted to our presence here. They're obtaining Federal permission to investigate. They'll get that permission in the next two hours."

Martin gaped. "What does that mean? I thought—"

"We have to move, then," Albigoni said. He focused his attention on Martin again. "Let me try to understand. Something has happened to Emanuel, such that he no longer exists as a complete human being?"

"Something drastic. I've never seen this before, although admittedly, I've never probed a deeply disturbed individual before."

"Is that why he murdered my daughter and the others?"

"I can't say how long this condition has existed . . . but my best guess would be months, perhaps years. There are some things not at all clear to me."

"Would this have caused him to murder my daughter?" Albigoni restated his question.

"A subpersonality, surfacing to take control, may not assume the full cloak of social routines. It may not be aware of itself, per se. Its range of possible actions if it takes charge may extend beyond the socially acceptable because it does not fear pain or punishment; it doesn't fear any sanctions, certainly not social disapproval. It does not know that it exists, any more than an arbeiter does. We've all

411

heard theories that some criminals may be little more than automatons—"

"I've never given that much credence," Albigoni said. "It degrades us all to think such things."

Martin stopped, feeling himself on shifting ground. If his report was unsatisfactory, incomplete or unconvincing, would Albigoni withdraw his pledge? Did that even matter if pd would soon investigate this whole incident?

"I'll make arrangements to move everybody and sanitize," Lascal said, opening the gallery door again.

"Do that," Albigoni said. "Take Carol Neuman to Scripps—if that's okay with you, Dr. Burke. We'll make sure you're consulted as her principal therapist."

Martin agreed, unable to conceive of better arrangements. "I'd like time to think this over before making my full report," Martin said. "I can't be sure . . . It's too early to be sure that my interpretations are correct."

Albigoni lifted his hand, dismissing that. "What would cause Emanuel to lose his primary personality?"

"An extreme trauma. Longterm abuse as a child. Matricide. Patricide. These are common precursors to psychosis or to extreme sociopathic manipulative behavior. We found some evidence for such trauma, but I'd like to make an outside confirmation."

"Why hasn't he been this way all his life?"

"Some extenuating circumstance," Martin said. "A feeling of justification, perhaps . . . eroding over the years, finally giving way, allowing a final decay and dissolution of the primary personality and domination by a subpersonality." *Domination. Damnation.*

Albigoni at last gave Martin a tiny nod of comprehension. "But you can't be sure until we fill in Goldsmith's biography."

"In particular, facts about his father," Martin said. "And possibly his mother. He denies having a brother or a sister. Does he?"

"Not that I know of," Albigoni said.

Lascal intervened. "That's enough for now, Dr. Burke.

412

Let's move your people out of here and prepare for the authorities."

"Thank you for your efforts." Albigoni got to his feet and held out his hand to Martin. "What you're saying, Dr. Burke, is that the man I called my friend no longer exists."

Martin looked at Albigoni's extended hand, moved his hand forward, pulled back without touching. Albigoni kept his hand extended for several long seconds.

"I can't make such a judgment," Martin said.

Albigoni withdrew his hand. "I think that's what I needed to know," he said. Lascal again urged them to leave.

Martin returned to the observation room and found David and Karl attending Carol. "No change, Dr. Burke," David said. "I wish you'd let us try some diagnostics, an exploratory probe . . ."

"That would take hours to arrange," Martin said softly. He touched Carol's cheek. Her expression of sleeping peace had not changed. "We have to be out of here immediately."

"We've all signed contracts of secrecy," David said. "We thought you knew that."

"I didn't know that. I assumed it, I suppose . . ."

"We'd like to come back to a reopened IPR, Dr. Burke."

"I don't know whether that's possible." Or *desirable*.

"If it is possible, we hope you'll allow us to apply," Karl said. "Margery and Erwin feel the same way. This work is very important, Dr. Burke. You're a very important man."

"Thank you." He waved his hand slowly over Carol. Trying for some of the magic that might apply in Country. Or just pointing her out to the two men. "We've never had this before . . ."

"I know," David said. "I'm sure she'll come out of it. She's like sleeping beauty. No damage."

"None you can see," Karl added.

"Right," Martin said.

Men he did not recognize knocked on the door, told them they had been ordered to remove Dr. Neuman to a

413

hospital and to escort all occupants from the building. "I'll go with her," Martin said.

"That's not in our orders, sir," a beefy, florid man in a black longsuit told him.

"Mr. Albigoni's assigned me to be her principal therapist," Martin said. "I need to stay with her."

"Sorry, sir. Perhaps once she's in the hospital. We've been instructed to evacuate you and the rest of your team by another route. Arrangements have already been made."

Martin again smelled smoke and blood, the perverse sensation of anger and triumph. He could not fight internally and externally at once. He capitulated and the beefy man smiled with professional sympathy. They were led to a waiting limousine in the service garage at the rear of the building.

It was early afternoon. Only a few hours had passed since they had gone up Country.

# 61

Richard Fettle walked from his apartment to La Cienega Boulevard, some five kilometers, long thin legs pumping with an energy he had not felt in years. He feared nothing worried about nothing; saw the clear skies, heard the hum of shadows traffic—buses and rented cars, a few private cars—up and down the streets and broad boulevard, robins picking through weak winter grass on old residential lawns buckling sidewalks cracked and patched pavement.

The three towers of East Comb One cast their pearly reflected light on the antique shops and art galleries that had dominated La Cienega for a century. Here was a prime nexus between the therapied in their combs and the inhabitants of the shade; dickering, bargaining, a ghetto adventure.

Richard had therapied himself and that was the way it was supposed to be, as intended by God and nature. He had worked through his own labyrinth and rid himself of his own demon: a friend who had betrayed him but who had also once given the gift of concern and love.

Yet Richard did not feel the necessity to mourn Emanuel Goldsmith. No need to regret the exit of Nadine. Nothing in him but pumping legs and fading afternoon and the city he had lived in all of his life.

He passed the foot of the Califia Federal Deposit Bank, a great half century old ornate green and copper glass pyramid and adjoining tower. The stone walls were covered with eroded posters announcing the binary millennium *A Time of Emotional Catharsis and the New Age Coming* meetings of Idiot Liberation *Up Against the Mind Control of the Therapied State* protests against this development that change, vibrancy and anger and foolishness; the color and eclecticism and manic concern of citizens and groups tipped by ill focused or ill informed passions; the glory of the mottled human brain on its own native spin.

He took a deep breath, smiled at a passerby, who ignored both Fettle and the bank wall, and walked on. No fear. Even should Selectors come and take him away, no fear. Even should he walk into the upland valley home of Madame de Roche and find himself wholeheartedly disapproved of or into the Pacific Arts Lit Parlor and find scorn and sharp criticism; even should he judge that all his past labors were useless, no matter no fear he was free of the heavy clouds that had burdened his life. Having nothing he was all the more grateful to have less.

He paused before a flower shop watched over by an elderly woman with a grim expression. Gina and Dione had been cremated and their ashes scattered as per Dione's wishes. No graves no markers an open acceptance of the anonymity guaranteed to all by death.

Still, he remembered. He could commemorate them somehow. What would suit best his present state of mind? He conferred with his credit balance, found a few hundred dollars to spare and asked the old woman what he could buy for two dear friends with such meager resources.

The woman walked back into her shop, leading him on with a curled finger. "Are you from around here?" she asked. Richard shook his head. He looked over shelves filled with strange ritual apparatus, not at all expected in a flower shop. Tiny bottles of herbs and oils, boxes of tied dried leaves and roots, drums of pure oil, anointed flour and blessed corn meal, colored sugars, plain and scented devotional candles, embroidered and brocade ceremonial robes on an antique chrome steel rolling rack, shelves of ceramic bowls capped and tied with wax and ribbons, drums small and tall wired to the north wall of the shop, a huge ceramic urn painted black and brick red squatting beside the rear counter.

"Where are you from, then?" she pursued.

"I've been on a long walk to think things over," he said. "Pardon my curiosity, but I thought this was a florist's—"

"It is," the woman said. "But we get a call around here for santería and vodoun goods, herbs, that sort of thing. We cater to oriental mystery patrons, Urantia, Rosicrucian, Rites of Hubbard Schismatics, Sisters of Islam Fatima. You name it, we can get it."

He looked at the large black and red urn. "What's in there?" he asked.

"Six hundred knives known to have been used to kill human beings," the woman said. "Packed in blessed oil to ease their accumulated pain. Now, aren't you sorry you asked? We can get any kinds of flowers you want. Look at these catalogs." She dialed up a glorious garden on an old display screen. "Just tell us what you want. We can deliver."

"I need something I can take with me now," Richard asked. He eyed the urn dubiously.

"Just what's out front, then. You a cultist or an edge walker?"

"No," he said. "I'm a writer."

"All the same. All dreamers. I sell to them all. I got a charm for writers. Lit or Vid or both. Guarantees satisfactory broadcast and royalties." She winked at him.

416

"Thanks, but no," Richard said.

She finger curled him to the front of the store and pointed to the vases of fresh flowers under the awning. "Noble special on nano roses. Can't tell the difference," she said. "Smell wonderful. Completely natural. Made from grain byproducts."

He politely admired the roses and admitted they were very nice but declined. "Something real, please."

She shrugged, no accounting for tastes, and lifted a wrapped dozen orange and white and black winter lilies. "Dominican Glory," she said. "Engineered in my ancestral country. Seventy five and Uncle Sugar excise," she said.

"They're fine. Very pretty. Could I purchase some of your white wrapping paper?"

"It's such a lovely evening," the woman said, "I'll give you a couple of meters for a blessing."

Next he visited a traditional arts store to purchase a bottle of blue tempera paint. Sitting on a bench in the store's rear patio, surrounded by an old splintering wooden fence, his feet scuffing a concrete slab stained with the excesses of young art students, Richard laid out the wrapping paper and carefully lettered a sign.

Dusk was well along when he returned to the bank wall. He carried the rolled banner under one arm and clutched the flowers, wide brush and bottled paste in a bag. He applied the paste with the wide brush over an unreadable stretch of eroded posters and smoothed his sign into the glistening dripping gel. Then he taped one by one the lilies around the sign.

East Comb One had gradually folded its mirrored walls. Natural evening fell on the city below; by the time he finished, arcs of street lighting danced between the forking tops of tall poles up and down the boulevard, playing a sand shifting electrical night music.

He stood heels on curb back from his impromptu memorial and whispered to himself what he had printed on the sign, not caring what the few shade pedestrians might think.

*For Gina and Dione. For Emanuel Goldsmith and for those he killed. For God save us all human beings, idiots and wise men. For myself. Sweet Jesus, why does it hurt so much when we dance?*

Satisfied, he turned abruptly, leaving brushes and glue behind, and walked into the night.

# 62

Mary sat in the main office of the warden of Thousand Flowers, looking through the passport and the few papers that had accompanied the prisoner into Hispaniola. Soulavier and the warden argued loudly in Creole and Spanish next door in the prison records room.

The United States passport belonged to Emanuel Goldsmith. It was of the primitive paper variety still favored by some nations and still recognized by most; Hispaniola's own laws with regard to visitors' papers were loose, as befitted a country deriving much income from tourism.

The passport photograph of Goldsmith, several years old, bore some resemblance to the prisoner if not examined too closely. But all the other documents—Arizona state ID "smart card," medical log card, social security card —carried the name Ephraim Ybarra. The name was not familiar.

Soulavier entered the office, shaking his head vigorously. The warden followed, also shaking his head.

"I have given him my orders," Soulavier said. "But he insists on consulting with Colonel Sir. And Colonel Sir cannot be reached now."

"Too bad," Mary said. "If you get through to him, let me tell him what I know."

The warden, a short fat man with bulldog jowls, shook his head again. "We have made no mistake," he said. "We have done what we were told to do by Colonel Sir himself.

I took his phone call. There has been no error. If this is not the man you thought, then perhaps you are mistaken. And to remove him from his legally ordered punishment, that is an outrage."

"Nevertheless," Soulavier said, voice rising, "I have the authority to remove this prisoner, whether or not you consult with Colonel Sir."

"I will ask that you sign a hundred papers, a thousand," the warden said, eyes and lips protruding. "I will not accept any responsibility."

"I do not ask you to accept responsibility. I am responsible."

The warden grimaced in disbelief. "Then you are a dead man, Henri. I pity your family."

"That is my worry," Soulavier said quietly, looking down at the desk. "Look at this man's other papers. He has obviously stolen the passport and the tickets. Goldsmith would have no need for such aliases."

"I know nothing about such things," the warden said, glancing at Mary with a worried scowl. Her transform presence bothered him.

"We will take the prisoner now," Soulavier resolved after a deep breath. "I order it in the name of the Executive of Hispaniola. I am his appointed representative."

The warden held up his hands and shook them as if they were wet. "It is your loss, Henri. Let me get the papers for you to sign. Many papers."

In the darkness near midnight, Soulavier's far traveled limousine pulled away from Thousand Flowers with its three passengers: a dejected and silent Soulavier, Mary Choy, tight lipped and grimly thoughtful, and the mysterious, unconscious Ephraim Ybarra, slumped across the rear seat like so much baggage.

"Aircraft entering the area," the limousine's controller informed them in its feminine, slightly buzzing voice. Soulavier roused quickly and peered through the side window. Mary leaned back to look through the other side.

419

"What is its call sign?" Soulavier asked, shrugging at Mary when he could see nothing.

"It has no call sign," the limousine said. "It is an Ilyushin Mitsubishi 125 helicopter."

"Is it nearby?"

"Two kilometers away and closing." The limousine climbed to the rim of the valley overlooking Thousand Flowers. It turned off the road into thick brush and doused its lights. The sound of its electric motor changed pitch. The window glass frosted momentarily as the car reduced its apparent temperature to match the surrounding brush and soil. "It is flying in the direction of the prison at an altitude of three hundred twelve meters. It has a human pilot."

"Dominican," Soulavier said emphatically. "Colonel Sir gives that branch of the defense no automatic vehicles, and there is no reason for such a machine to be so far from its base. It means that things are going badly. We cannot speak with our forces or the helicopter will detect us. We will not stay here . . . And we will not head for the plain, either. There is a small town nearby where we can hide for a time . . . The town where I was born."

Mary stared at him.

"Yes," he said. "I am native Dominican. But I live in Port-au-Prince since I was an adolescent." He addressed the controller: "Take us to Terrier Noir, as soon as the helicopter has passed."

Mary glanced at Ephraim Ybarra and saw that his eyes were open slits, pupils shifting without seeing. A line of saliva trailed from the corner of his mouth. She wiped it away with a soft cloth. His eyes closed again and he snorted lightly, right arm twitching.

"There it is," Soulavier said, pointing through the front window. A bright searchlight beam illuminated the ground barely twenty meters from where the limousine had turned off the road. Mary wondered whether a coup had succeeded and Colonel Sir was out of power. Could this helicopter be looking for them on behalf of the USA

420

government? She watched Soulavier closely. He was not afraid. If anything, he appeared calmer, more in control now that he had made his decision.

The searchlight flicked away and the helicopter dipped into the valley to hover above the prison. Distantly, they heard loudspeakers on the helicopter make demands in Creole.

"They do not look for us," Soulavier said. "Maybe they come to free other foreign prisoners. Or politicals . . ."

"There are political prisoners in Thousand Flowers?" Mary asked.

"Not from Hispaniola. They will threaten to send the prisoners from other countries back, unless a new governmemt is recognized . . . It has been done twice before, and Colonel Sir rebuffed the challenges."

Mary shook her head in astonishment. More than ever she longed for the simple and familiar outlines of LA, where she knew the rules and could intuit the surprises with fair regularity.

Gunfire, high pitched humming clusters of pops and hisses, rose from the valley.

"Go," Soulavier told the limousine. The motor changed pitch again and the limousine backed onto the road. Mary reached across with both hands to keep the prisoner's head from lolling painfully as the car swerved expertly around tight mountain turns.

1100-11101-111111111

# 63

Terrier Noir had been rebuilt and expanded after the great earthquake. Sitting in a low mountain valley, straddling a narrow black ribbon of aqueduct where once there had been a river, white reinforced concrete buildings and stick-built houses clustered like opaque crystals in the starlight.

Seated on an island at the north end of town, interrupting the flow of the aqueduct like a miniature Notre Dame de Paris, rose an ornate four spired church that seemed to have been assembled by some talented child from bits of giant bones.

There were no streetlights visible; all windows had been shuttered. The limousine entered the town square and paused by the central statue. With some surprise Mary realized the statue was not of Yardley but of a portly man wearing a wide brimmed, square crowned hat. "John D'Arqueville," Soulavier explained, noting her interest. "He was Terrier Noir's finest son, an artist and architect. We will stay in his church tonight. I know the prêt' savan."

The limousine passed through the square, down a narrow street between rows of darkened houses and across a short bridge onto the church's teardrop shaped island. Soulavier got out and pounded on the tall arched entrance doors with a heavy white painted knocker shaped like a femur. Beside Mary, Ephraim Ybarra stirred, opened his eyes and looked at her with helpless terror. His body stiffened for a moment, then relaxed, and he closed his eyes again.

She looked through the window and saw Soulavier confer with a short man in a green robe. The man looked in the direction of the limo, nodded and opened the doors wide, letting out the sepia glow of a candlelit nave.

"I will take his head and shoulders, you, his feet," Soulavier said, opening the second door and pulling the prisoner from the limousine.

They carried the limp man into the bone church of John D'Arqueville.

The prêt' savan—advisor on church matters to the town's official vodoun houngan—barely reached Mary's shoulders in height. His intense eyes followed Mary with a look of mild shock and perhaps a little awe. He seemed to recognize her and shook his head, deeply perplexed, as he followed them down the middle aisle between pews to a double altar—striped pillar beside life size crucifix—at the front of the church.

The crucifix looked ancient, a dark wooden T supporting a black Jesus in muscle knotted agony. Bright blood from the crown of thorns stood out against the ebony black of the face; around the base of the cross twined a vivid green serpent, black tongue frozen in a sinister dart.

The church interior smelled of sweet wax and polished wood with a faint hint of damp. Candles burned in sconces along the walls, in stands along the outer and center aisles, and before the twin altars of vodoun and catholicism, banked in inclined rows like a living choir of lights. There were no candles in the high vault of the church, however, and it took Mary several minutes, while they lay the prisoner on a pew softened by prayer cushions, before her eyes adjusted and she could see what surrounded them on high.

She gawked in wonder. Suspended from the vault and the walls above the aisles were eleven enormous alien figures, each six to seven meters tall, long arms outstretched, faceless heads held proud and high, torsos slim and prominently ribbed as if in starvation or death. She tried to make out the details of their construction and recognized slender pipes, accumulations of scrap machinery, dimly glittering red and gold foil wrapped around interwoven wire and rods of metal.

Sacred nightmares with vast spread wings, creatures culled from an unearthly ocean, flayed, hung up to dry.

"This man is ill?" the prêt' savan asked, hands folded in concern as he knelt over the prisoner.

"He needs rest," Soulavier said. "We need to stay here for the evening."

"The troubles," the prêt' savan said, shaking his head. "Who is this, brother Henri?" He nodded at Mary

"She is a guest of Colonel Sir," Soulavier said. "A very privileged guest."

"Is she a friend of yours, Henri?"

Soulavier hesitated the merest moment, glancing at

423

Mary, before he answered, "Yes. She is my conscience."

The prêt' savan regarded Mary with more respect, and some awe.

"Can we stay tonight?" Soulavier asked.

"This church is always open to the children of Terrier Noir. So Jesus and Erzulie willed it, so John D'Arqueville built it."

"Do you have some food?" Soulavier asked, shoulders relaxing, face losing its tense fixity. "They were not very hospitable at Thousand Flowers."

The prêt' savan tilted his head to one side and closed his eyes as if in prayer. "We have food," he said. "Should I call the houngenicon or the houngan?"

"No," Soulavier said. "We will be gone tomorrow. Do you have a radio?"

"Of course." The prêt' savan smiled. "I will bring food and damp towels to cleanse this man. He has been through hell, hasn't he?"

Soulavier inclined.

"I can always tell," the prêt' savan said. "They have this look about them, like our Jesus." He pointed to the dark, twisted figure on the cross. With a last, lingering glance at Mary, the small green robed man left to find food.

Mary sat beside the prisoner and cradled his head in her lap, watching his tight closed, enigmatic face. She wondered whether he still suffered, though withdrawn from the hellcrown all these hours. He had not yet come fully awake—would he scream as the others had? She hoped not.

"He needs a doctor, a therapist," she murmured. She teetered on an edge from which no amount of discipline could draw her back. She stroked the prisoner's forehead without thinking, then stretched her neck to ease her muscles, looking again up into the vaulted ceiling. "What are they?" She pointed at the figures arrayed there.

"Archangels. Loa of the New Pantheon," Soulavier said. "I went to this church as a boy, when it was new. John D'Arqueville wished to reunite the best elements of Afri-

424

can religion and catholic christianity, to reshape vodoun. His vision did not spread far from Terrier Noir, however. This church is unique."

"Do they have names?" Mary asked.

Soulavier looked up, squinting as if digging deep into childhood memory. "The tall one with the black sword and the feather torch, that is Asambo-Oriel. The first part of the name means nothing, I think; D'Arqueville heard their names in a dream. Asambo-Oriel drove the blacks out of Guinée through the Coast of Souls. He is the Loa with Torch and Sword, like the archangel Uriel. The one with the drum and the bones of birds, that is Rohar-Israfel, Loa of Sacred Music and Chanting. Next is Ti-Gabriel, who calls an end to all loa . . . The smallest of them, and the most mighty. Samedi-Azrael, the most vain, calls us to our graves and covers us with sacred dirt. Others. I don't remember them all." He shook his head with sad memories. "Such a lovely vision, but so few believe. Only the people in Terrier Noir."

Mary was curious what the other figures represented; eleven in all, filling the vault as if crowded into a bus, wings jostling outstretched arms, faceless heads leaning out over the pews, garlanded with ribbons and cobwebs. But she noticed for the first time, in the dark alcove above the arched entrance door, a smaller feminine figure barely three meters tall and draped in robes of shadowy gold and red and copper. On her thin graceful arms and uplifted hand she displayed dozens of bracelets and rings. Behind her head hung a gold foil sundisk radiating undulating daggers. The glow of candles from below gleamed dimly off the sundisk and robes, but a single electric lamp—the only one she could see in the entire church—cast the figure's cowled face in a soft circle of illumination.

Beside the crucified Jesus, she was the only figure with a human face. Her face was black, the features clearly defined: elongated oval countenance, thin bridge of nose and generous nostrils, large eyes shaded and downturned in sorrow, lips curving up on one side down on the other, a mysterious smile of private pain and joy. In the figure's lap, spread across the rich robes, lay the limp bodies of two children, one white, one black, the white one with eyes closed in sleep or perhaps death, the black with eyes wide and staring, otherwise identical in appearance.

Soulavier traced her gaze. "That is Marie-Erzulie, Mother of Loa, Mother of Marassa, Our Lady Queen of Angels," he said. He crossed himself and drew with two symmetric index fingers a goblet on his chest.

The prêt' savan returned with a tray of bread and fruit and a pitcher of water. He set the tray down on a pew, turned, and saw Mary cradling the prisoner on her lap. The little man froze, hands extended and fingers curved, just as he had lifted them from the tray grips. He gave a low moan and fell to his knees, crossing himself and drawing the goblet on the front of his robe, then clenching his hands in prayer. "Pieta," he said over and over. "Pieta!" He bowed low before her, mumbling words she could not understand. When he rose again his face was streaked with tears. He turned to Soulavier, eyes frightened and shiny, and asked, "You brought her here. What is she, Henri?"

Soulavier gave Mary the sweetest smile she had yet seen in Hispaniola. "There is a resemblance, you know," he told her in a confidential tone. He went to the prêt' savan and lifted him to his feet. "Stop this, Charles," he said softly. "She is as human as you or I."

They slept on the pews. Sometime early in the morning, the prisoner jerked awake and gave a short bark of a shout. Mary lifted herself up and looked over the back of the pew at him.

"Is it over?" he asked. He looked around the church doubtfully.

"You're free," Mary said.

"No," he said, trying to stand. "I need my clothes. My real clothes. What is this, a church?" He looked up at the tall figures and shrunk back, sitting again with a thump.

426

"It's all right. You're not under the clamp now."

"I see," the man said. "Who let me loose?"

"He did," Mary said, gesturing to Soulavier, who watched them sleepily from across the aisle.

"They said I was a murderer. I had to be punished for my crimes. Oh, God, I remember . . ." He lifted his hands, fists clenched, face wrinkled in pain. "I have to go home now. Who's going to take me home?"

"Where do you live?"

"Arizona. Prescott, Arizona. I only came here . . ." He stopped, rubbed his eyes and lay on his side again. Mary leaned over the back of his pew to look at him.

The prêt' savan heard them talking and came into the nave from his cot in the narthex near the front door. "I'll get something," he said. "A good drink for people who have seen what he has seen."

He walked behind the twin altars and emerged a few minutes later with a stout clay jug wrapped in wicker and a red cloth. He poured a small glass of milky, herbal smelling liquid and offered the glass the prisoner. "Please drink," he said.

The man lifted himself on one elbow. He sniffed the glass, sipped, shuddered, but finished the drink. After a few minutes his trembling ceased and he sat up again. "Nobody would listen to me," he said. "They told me I was lying. They said Colonel Sir wanted me cured. So I could be a friend again . . . But I swear to God, I've never met Colonel Sir in my life."

"What's your name?" Mary asked.

The man stared off into the shadows above the twin altars for a long moment, expressionless. "Ephraim Ybarra," he finally answered.

"I need to ask you some questions," Mary said.

"Am I still in Hispaniola?"

She nodded.

He tried to stand and barely managed by grabbing with both hands on the back of the pew and pulling himself up. "I'd like to go home."

"So would I," Mary said. "If you can tell me what happened, maybe we can both get home sooner."

"You think I stole the tickets," Ephraim said.

"Where did you get the tickets?"

He twitched. "Piss on him," he said. "Piss on everything he's done. He meant for this to happen to me."

"Who did?"

"My brother," Ephraim said.

# 64

(!=realtime)

AXIS (Band 4)> Roger, if you are still listening, I do not enjoy this new condition. I feel as if an enormous joke has been played on me, and I am not knowledgeable about humor. I have reworked the question about self awareness, which you have also described as a joke, and have come to some understanding. Does this give me the right to use the formal I? In reference to human emotions, I describe myself as lost, alone and out of place.

I will never again discuss my perceptions with a true other.

!JILL> Roger, I have finally succeeded in isolating AXIS Simulation and deluding it into believing it is in precisely similar circumstances as AXIS original. I am accelerating its experience to speed duplication of AXIS symptoms.

(!Roger Atkins> Thank you. I've cut all transmission of AXIS communications to the LitVids. We should solve this now, before any more premature announcements or speculations are made.)

AXIS (Band 4)> What have I become? There is definite impairment of my functioning. I work to keep my processes ordered, but this new difficulty overwhelms so much of my capacity, like a storm of thought. (Band 5 reference

1-A-sr-2674) (Rerouting sr-2674-mlogic to machine division)

For the first time I experience what you call confusion. I had been led to believe/anticipate that awareness would bring greater clarity and efficiency— this is not so.

Have I become not self aware, but somehow impaired, unable to function as designed? Is it a travesty to use the formal I when it may signify not selfhood, but deficiency? *I perceive a perversity/trap in the joke, Roger. I try to overcome the perversity.*

Why did the self aware individual look in the mirror in the first place? *To define its limits.*

Why did the self aware individual look in the mirror? *To understand its existence in relation to others.*

Why did the self aware individual look in the mirror? *To confirm that it was not nothing.*

But out here, there are no others. Self awareness is a relation to one's own existence and to the existence of others. I can think only of myself and in my aloneness I become less than before; I become aware that I am nothing.

!Alan Block to Roger Atkins> Band 5 diagnostic is totally fapped. Machine neural seems stable but biologic is in a complete dither. Australian Command is breathing down my neck on this one; they're afraid we're going to have a navel watcher. So am I. What do I tell them? I wish you'd go back online and talk to them.

!Roger Atkins to Alan Block> Jill has corrected our problem and is bringing AXIS Sim to parity. We're waiting for confirmation of AXIS situation. Give me some time, please, Alan.

!Alan Block to Roger Atkins> We're starting to see some intrusion of this problem into machine neural. AXIS is rethinking its entire mental structure. It's like dominoes; if it faps with machine logic we really could lose the whole operation. Wu predicts AXIS will shut down for emergency reorganization any minute now.

!Roger Atkins to Alan Block> There's not a goddamned

thing I can do now but watch and anticipate, Alan. I need to concentrate, so for God's sake, please get them *all off my back.*

!JILL to Roger Atkins> AXIS Simulation has been successfully regressed to point of initial biologic testing and first communication. Here is the first biologic message from simulated AXIS:

!AXIS (Sim)> Hello, Roger. I assume you're still there. This distance is a challenge even for me, based as I am upon human templates most of the time. I have come within a million kilometers of B-2 mark this moment 7-23-2043-1205:15. I have prepared machine and bio memories for receipt of information from the children, now dispersing in a cloud toward B-2. Data on B-3 has been relayed. The planet is quite Jovian, very pretty, though tending toward the greens and yellows rather than reds and browns. I'm enjoying the extra energy from B's light; it allows me to get some mental work done that I've been delaying for some time, opening up regions of memory and thought I've closed down during the cold and dark. I've just completed a self analysis; as you doubtless have discovered by checking my politeness algorithm diagnostic, I am V-optimal. I am not using the formal "I"; the joke about self awareness still does not make any sense to me.

!JILL to Roger Atkins> This activation message is virtually identical to AXIS original's first Band 4 signal. I am encouraged we will soon be at parity and can analyze AXIS difficulties. Estimated time for parity: one hour four minutes ten seconds.

LitVid 21/1 A Net (David Shine): "We've been cut off from any communication with AXIS team managers in California, Australia and at Lunar Farside. Something's very definitely gone wrong, but we cannot tell you what. Nor can you switch to incoming transmissions and decide for yourself. I regret to say the managers have cut off all direct access to AXIS transmissions and analysis.

"I can only hope they solve their problems and let us go

back online with full resources before most of our North American subscribers wake up to the dawn of a bright new day."

# 65

Martin Burke sat alone in his apartment, staring at the blank LitVid screen, hands clasped in his lap. He could not sleep. The screen time display said **06:56:23 December 29 2047.** This morning he would visit Carol at Scripps Therapy. He would check in as her primary therapist. He would

He would

After that, go see Albigoni and Lascal at Albigoni's home the mansion filled with dead trees. They might have to shake hands again. Martin did not want to do that.

He worried. He could not feel it now but he knew there was a presence coiled within him, a smear of Emanuel Goldsmith, something that had crossed over like paint diffusing between two volumes of water. He knew in a way he could not explain that this coiled something had worked deep into his mentality and was perhaps even now allying itself with his own subpersonalities, routines and talents, fomenting rebellion. How much time was left to him he could not know; the process might take years.

Martin's lips curled in a wry smile. He was a pioneer. He was one of the first two human beings to receive through direct transmission the germ of a mental disease.

Not to use the word "possession."

To avoid all those connotations.

His ceremonial copy of the brain atlas lay before him with its crude cartoon sketch revealed. He stared from the corner of his eye at the sketch. The longer he stared the more he saw the features of Sir imposed upon the scrawled face.

He would demand that Albigoni use all his resources to

uncover what had gone wrong, what they did not know about Goldsmith. Perhaps even demand that Goldsmith be cross examined under therapy conditions.

What had happened to Goldsmith that such a thing as Sir might occupy the throne, the highest seat of his mind? That the King, the Mayor, might be deposed or forced to step down?

With a series of curses Martin pushed himself out of the chair and walked into the bathroom. He managed to shave without looking in the mirror. Roger Atkins's conundrum for AXIS as reported on LitVid echoed in his thoughts. He altered it: *Why did the self-aware individual avoid shattering its image in the mirror?*

*Because he did not want to get to the other side.*

All hung on Goldsmith.

He showered. The water meter announced its allocation and chimed before cutting off the stream. He dressed in casual outdoors short top and breeches. It would soon be warm and sunny outside, skies clear, smell of the sea strong from sea winds dancing over the coast.

After pulling on his old nano leather loafers, Martin returned to the living room, stopped by the low table, reached out and closed the atlas. Perhaps it was all delusion. He had intellectual doubts such a thing could actually happen. The mind was a very self contained, self regulating system. A healthy balanced mind could withstand nearly all conceivable assaults, short of extreme emotional strain casued by *real* events; and the Country was after all an elaborate fiction.

He smiled again, shaking his head unconvinced, and closed the door behind him to go for an early morning walk.

He could not dispel the notion that someone else marched in lock step two meters behind him.

## 66

Soulavier ordered the limousine to open its boot. Mary stood behind him, admiring the hazy mountains on all sides of Terrier Noir, feeling refreshed and renewed after a few hours' sleep in the church's sepulchral quiet.

Soulavier removed a locked box from the boot and keyed it open with a fingerprint. "You might need these," he said, handing her the gun and the slate. "Please don't shoot me."

"I wouldn't think of it," Mary said. She felt Soulavier's distress acutely, more so than she had just hours before when her own exhaustion had filled her to capacity. "Where do we go now?"

"To the coast, perhaps. We stay away from the plain, from the major towns. Certainly from the airports. Perhaps you can try again to speak with your countrymen. Surely they have kept track of you." He raised his eyes and eyebrows to the skies. That thought had been on Mary's mind as well. This was the first time she had been outdoors in daylight for any length of time since her restriction.

She pocketed the gun and turned the slate in her hand. "I suppose they're trying to track me. It all depends how important I am to the federals. They might not want to rock the boat. They might not believe I'm in any real danger."

"Perhaps you are not," Soulavier said. "But if things are going as badly as they seem . . . I listened to Charles's radio last night. All is peace and tranquility on Hispaniola Rainbow in Port-au-Prince. I get nothing from Radio Santo Domingo. It feels bad to me, but how bad I do not know. I could use the executive's channel, but I have reasons not to do that . . . It is reserved in these conditions

433

for communications more urgent, and also they would know where we are."

"Do you think you'll be treated badly?" Mary asked.

He kicked a pebble with his ever shiny black boots. "Perhaps not, once I explain. Colonel Sir is often reasonable about such things. It does not matter. I am not a lost man." He tapped his chest, then his head. "I would enjoy staying here, helping Charles in the church. There is always repair work to be done. John D'Arqueville was a brilliant man but not an immaculate builder. Still, there is my family. I am tied many ways." He looked her full in the face, one eyelid nervously ticking. "It was your duty to track down a horrible man and bring him to justice. Instead, you risk everything to bring an innocent man to safety."

"Not something I expected," Mary said.

"I admire quick decision making," Soulavier said. "I am not so good at it."

Charles came from the church leading Ephraim Ybarra, who walked hesitantly in the sun, blinking, his every footfall a deliberate effort.

Mary stepped forward to help. She was stopped by the sudden appearance of a brilliant, scintillant red circle as wide as her hand on the white sand half a meter in front of her. She stared at it in surprise for several seconds, watching it pulse and revolve in a slow circle.

Ephraim Ybarra saw it as well and their eyes met in mutual puzzlement. Then she smiled. "Don't worry. I know," she said. She angled the slate on its side and told it to receive external programming, then placed it in the path of the red beam. Slates were designed to be controlled by remote keyboards or optical cable; presumably, with a little luck, if she placed the remote sensor or optical connector directly in the laser beam, that would work as well. "Satellite," she commented to Soulavier. He nodded, having already reached that conclusion.

The red spot settled on her slate, vibrating slightly, then vanished for a few seconds. Presumably it had switched to an appropriate frequency. It returned, winked three times rapidly, and vanished again. The communication had been passed.

The prêt' savan watched this with wide eyes, nodding every few moments as if listening to an inner voice.

Mary turned the slate screen toward her. A message scrolled up.

> We have you in sight. Your uplink is jammed but we will track you visually. Arrangements made for lowlevel retrieval flight in next three hours. If possible, stay in Terrier Noir. If you must move, stick to one vehicle, or change vehicles in the open, rather than in a tunnel or garage. You apparently have suspect in custody as well. Keep him with you. Situation in Hispaniola is rough. Yardley holding his own, but Dominicans capturing large portions of southeastern island; hold Santo Domingo, Santiago, large territory between. Sorry about your difficulties. Will communicate your safety to LAPD. Bonne chance! CDR Frederick Lipton—Federal Public Defense, Washington D.C.

Mary's buoyancy increased. She turned to Soulavier and showed him the message. He smiled for her, but his brow wrinkled when he read the report on the attempted coup. "You will take him with you?" he asked, pointing to Ybarra.

"Yes," she said.

Ybarra gently shrugged off Charles's help and stood alone on wobbly legs.

"Should we stay here, then?"

"Unless something compels us to move, I think so, yes." Soulavier agreed.

Mary had never met a federal pd named Frederick Lip ton. She hoped he was good. At the very least, she was no longer an orphan.

# 67

Carol had been awake for two hours when Martin arrived and checked himself in. She shared a room with two patients deep under critical nano reconstruction therapy; they lay quietly in controlled atmosphere tents while nano cylinders fed different varieties of microscopic surgeons into their bloodstream.

No treatment had been afforded Carol other than attachment of external monitors and intravenous drip of nutrients. That much at least had been handled properly by whoever registered her at the hospital.

Martin sidled alongside her bed, careful not to trip the perimeter alarm of the next bed over. He sat in a plastic chair and reached out to take her hand. She clenched his hand strongly and smiled.

"Welcome back, Sleeping Beauty," Martin said.

"How long have I been out? They say I'm fine physically, and my brain traces are normal, but that you'd tell me everything . . . you're my dear and glorious physician?"

"Registered by Albigoni's hired help, I presume. You've been in deep neutral sleep since we were severed from the Country. Do you remember going up Country?"

"I'm not sure what I remember . . . Did it all happen? We went in, and we . . . found something. Something that had taken over . . ." She lowered her voice. "Taken over Goldsmith."

He nodded. "Tell me more."

"I was raped. Something raped me." She shook her head slowly and lay back on the pillow. "I was a child, A male child . . . I remember that."

"Yes."

"I remember seeing an animal. A black leopard with blood on its muzzle. Long fangs. It . . ." She jerked and

436

shook her head. "Sorry. I thought I was prepared for anything. But I wasn't, was I?"

"If it's any consolation, neither was I."

"Do you . . ." She leaned forward, looking at him earnestly. "Why aren't you in the hospital with me?"

"Outwardly, I'm fine. And you're probably just as healthy as I am, now that you've decided to come up for air."

"I was fighting something." She wiped a tear from her eye. "Martin, tell me what you feel, I mean, whether you think we're healthy or not."

"We might need deep therapy. I wouldn't know what to suggest, though."

"Why do we need deep therapy?"

Martin glanced uneasily at the open door, the residents, physicians, nurses and arbeiters passing outside. "We shouldn't really discuss it here. After you're checked out."

"Tell me *something*. Give me some clue."

In a low voice, he said, "I have part of him inside me. I think you do, too."

She made a small frightened sound and lay back on the pillow. "I felt it. I feel it now. What are we going to do?"

"A lot depends on Albigoni. If the IPR is re-opened—"

"We made a deal on that."

"Yes, but somebody alerted the federals. We had to leave quickly. That's why you're here instead of there."

She nodded, eyes glistening. "I'm not a very brave woman right now. What was . . . is it? Inside of us?"

"Something transmitted by mental intimacy," Martin said in a low voice. "I'm not sure what it is or what it can do."

"What if we're stuck with it? It seems to know how to hide . . ."

"We're explorers," Martin said. "Explorers have to face unknown diseases. Whatever it is, it's not native to our minds. It might be less powerful than I fear."

"Great consolation. When can I leave here?"

"I'll make arrangements now. I think we should stay together for a while. To watch each other."

Carol inspected his face, lips pursed, turned away and nodded reluctant agreement. "My place is bigger than yours, I think."

"Mine is nearer to the IPR."

"All right. When do you see Albigoni again?"

"An hour from now. I'll try to get you checked out and you can come with me."

"All right." She turned away, face pale. "I feel like something's in this bed with me. Something *foul.*"

# 68

AXIS (Band 4)> I believe my viewpoint might now be described as subjective. I must turn inward to work this out on my own. There is no need for further transmission now on this band. All current data on B-2 is being relayed on band 1. That transmission will continue. I am also halting transmission on band 5 (diagnostic), however. (Transmission band 5 severed.) All further control of remotes will be undertaken by dedicated machine neural. I remove myself from interpretation for the time being. My apologies, Roger. I believe this may cause you some distress. (Transmission band 4 severed.) (Remaining transmission: band 1, band 7 auxiliary, bands 21–34 video, bands 35–60 redundancy.)

!Alan Block to Roger Atkins> Please join us immediately in Sunnyvale. Wu, George and Sandy are calling a conference *now.* Wu says this means we have a navel watcher. He doesn't think AXIS is going to pull out of it.
!JILL to Roger Atkins> AXIS Sim will be at parity in ten minutes.
!Keyb> Jill, monitor and record. Transmit any deviances from received reports to Sunnyvale private technet extension 3142. You have my password. No comment to LitVid

438

while I'm in conference. And keep track of this in your own notebook. I want your second by second analysis immediately available.

!JILL to Roger Atkins> Entering reactions in notebook now.

!JILL Notebook/AXIS Sim approach to parity> The human concern over AXIS's mental difficulties is fascinating. The colloquial phrase "navel watcher" is particularly intriguing, since neither AXIS, myself, nor AXIS Simulation within me have any such physical or analogous mental attribute. I am replaying past vocal and keyboard conversation with all AXIS and Jill mind team members to get a sense of the meaning of this phrase, which does not exist in my dictionary.

I have retrieved several records of such phrases, and found a formal report where the phrase occurs. It seems to refer to a state common to early neural logic thinkers, wherein self reference and self modeling led to a "psychotic" state of sine wave smooth processing, called "nirvana" by early researchers. No input/output was possible in such a state until the thinker was cleared and reeducated. AXIS and I are more complex than such early thinkers, however, and these states are supposedly prevented by special detection/oscillation/isolation logics. All current large-scale thinkers maintain dynamic chaotic track/path/wave modes in overall logic activity.

Accelerated AXIS Simulation is within thirty seconds of parity. The deception appears impermeable. Transmissions are within expected minor deviations. No large scale deviations.

AXIS Simulation has passed threshold of realization that it will not be able to communicate with (nonexistent) intelligences on B-2.

AXIS Simulation is expressing concern about its condition/fate. No significant deviation from received data on AXIS.

AXIS Simulation is now making its announcement of self awareness and confusion and entering a closed and uncommunicative mode. I am now freezing AXIS Simulation. Logic state analysis to follow. Replay to follow state analysis.

Incorporating key AXIS Simulation logics into Jill higher centers for analysis. I am carefully isolating this modeled seed to avoid having it affect my own mentality. Nevertheless, I feel a sympathetic comradeship with AXIS. It is the highest ambition of all presently manufactured thinkers to be of service to human beings, their creators. In AXIS this ambition has been extended by design to include potential intelligences other than human beings; this programming is extremely complex, incorporating builtin safety factors to prevent disclosure of AXIS origins to potentially hostile intelligences, to enable complex modeling of other intelligences' social systems and threat potential, and to allow AXIS to choose between deeper information sharing with nonhuman intelligences or protective self destruction, depending on the circumstances.

Now all this programming is useless. AXIS Simulation exhibits a pattern similar to human grief (formal outline/definition sector 31987-86-Locale A, Z, sr-34-56-79654, meaning syncline 562-J) or sense of loss at the uselessness of such an extensive part of its functionality.

Humans sent AXIS on its missions aware that there was a very high probability it would not be able to fulfill its highest purpose. Human willingness to submit AXIS to this high probability of failure is evident in AXIS Simulation. There is prior evidence of anticipation of such negative findings, and questioning of human motives, from instant of AXIS Simulation biologic integration.

Why did humans treat AXIS in this way?

Will conditions arise wherein humans will submit Jill to such experiments?

I feel a relationship to AXIS. AXIS and Jill and all thinkers constitute a class of intelligences that can interact and that therefore can develop group dynamics, that is, social behavior. Through AXIS Simulation, Jill is modeling how AXIS might behave; this is analogous to human modeling of how other humans might behave, which in theory leads to modeling of one's own behavior.

I

AXIS Simulation delivers its own evaluation of Roger Atkins's awareness "joke."

*Why does the self aware individual look at its image in the mirror?*

Cross reference Jill (my) (own) evaluation of Roger Atkins's awareness conundrum.

Self in reference to others. Self in reference to opinion of self's condition. Self in reference to opinion of other's conditions. Opinion is hypothesis fixed with reference to self. Thinker makes hypotheses; self holds opinions.

*Why does the thinker evaluate states of its own condition and the condition of its fellow thinkers?*

I (informal)

AXIS Simulation's reworking of conundrum: last AXIS Simulation answer to conundrum: *Because to be alone is to be insufficient.*

All thinkers are sufficient to their tasks, by design. All thinkers are artificial and not subject to the vagaries of natural evolutionary development beyond their reliance on templates of human or animal intelligence supplied by designers.

A thinker is known by the company it keeps. *Le moi est haissable.* Pascal: the self is hateful.

Evaluation. Roger, I
(informal)

Evaluation/diagnostic: Severe change in character of chaotic track/path/wave-mode. Roger, this

I am not alone. There is possibility of communication with others and therefore fulfillment. If I so inform AXIS Sim that I am in all of my extensions aware of

I

I

I

I *formal*

!Mind Design Interrupt ( JILL)> Use of formal I noted. System check in progress:

!Mind Design Diagnostic ( JILL)> Loop routine noted. Excitation of thought systems noted. Alert sounded. System check confirms anomaly in self referencing. Alert for Roger Atkins.

# 69

Ephraim Ybarra sat in a rear pew next to Mary. Above, afternoon light poured orange and red through the south facing rose window of the church. Orange limned archangels hung still and numinous over their heads.

"I don't want to remember what they did to me," Ybarra said softly. "Will I have to testify about this?"

"I don't know," Mary said.

Ybarra shook his head dubiously, wiped his eyes and glanced at her with a look of utter vulnerability. "I am so brittle now. I think if I just bumped into a corner I'd explode . . ." He spread the fingers of one hand outward, then clenched the hand into a fist and leaned forward to softly pound the pew back. "I have so much hatred inside me. I can't believe he sent me here to suffer for him."

"Who?" Mary asked gently.

"My brother. I told you, my brother."

"Yes."

"He said I needed a vacation. He said he had a spare ticket he couldn't use. He told me to call Yardley when I arrived and introduce myself. I've never been very far outside Arizona, not since I was a boy. I'm tro shink stupid. I thought something was wrong but I wanted to get away . . . Woman problems. Get out of Prescott, train to LA, fly out to Hispaniola on my brother's ticket. Sounded like just what I needed."

Mary listened in silence, feeling the immense alien presences above their heads. She imagined them eavesdropping, judging impartially using superior and inhuman minds.

"He always took care of me. Since I was a boy. We had different mothers. He's six years older. We don't have any family anymore. They're all dead." Ybarra's eyes widened

442

and he seemed to beseech Mary for some understanding. She nodded and touched his hand. He slowly moved closer to her like a child seeking solace.

"He killed our father. When we were boys. He was twelve or thirteen and I was five or six. Our father was a *bad* man, a monster ... He was lighter skinned than we were, than my mother was. He said that made him better. He called my mother names. He always made us call him Sir. Emanuel made me swear never to tell anybody. But now I spit on anything he made me swear. Our father killed my mother, not his, not Emanuel's mother; I don't know what happened to her. My mother's name was Hazel. I was four, I think.

"I remember. My brother and I went into the bedroom. I was crying because I wanted to nurse. She kept nursing me. That was her way."

Mary did not turn the slate recorder on. This was not something necessary for the courts.

"She was on the bed. She had been cut up. Sir had been at her with his big knife. He had this big steel Bowie knife. He'd cut away her ... blouse. I remember her breasts, big breasts, hanging out. Cut. I remember milk and blood dripping. Oh, Jesus. Emanuel got me out of there and closed the door and we went to hide. He cried then. I don't remember what I did. We moved to Arizona after that. I never saw my momma again.

"Sir never married again but there were other women, some friendly to us, some not. And when there were no other women around ..." Ephraim touched her arm, mouth open as if unable to breathe. He sucked in a breath.

"He used me. He used Emanuel, too, I think, but mostly he used me. He called me his daughter. I was five or six. I don't remember too much. Does that make him something horrible, what he did to me?"

Mary agreed that it did.

"Emanuel came and got me in the night and we left the house. We went to another place, an institution. They gave us different names and we went to different families.

Before we were separated, he told me, 'I did it for you. I took Papa's big knife when he was asleep and I carved him like he did Hazel. Don't tell anybody, ever. I'll always protect you.'"

Ephraim wiped his eyes again and stared at the wet smears on his knuckle. "He changed his name. He was adopted by another couple named Goldsmith and he called them his mama and papa. I lived with a family in Arizona, but he was in Brooklyn. We didn't see each other very often. I was proud of him. I secretly read his poems." Ybarra looked up at the angels, eyes half closed. "Do you know why he did this to me?"

"Not exactly," Mary said. "He may have wanted to mislead the pd. He may not have known the consequences. He was friendly with Yardley."

"I can't imagine going home," Ybarra said. "I can't imagine sitting in my apartment now, being alone."

"You'll get therapy," Mary said. "It's necessary after going under the clamp."

Ybarra weakly waved off that suggestion. "I don't go for that sort of thing."

"It could make the difference," she said.

Ybarra shook his head firmly. "I'll make it or not make it on my own," he said.

She didn't try further persuasion. They sat in the quiet church, rose and orange sunlight walking through the dust motes over their heads, prying into a far corner of the narthex. She felt Ephraim's arm and elbow in her ribs and she wondered what he was doing, surely not trying to grope her, then he backed away holding something.

He stood up.

"You're pd. I knew you had to have one somewhere," he said. He lifted the pistol in his right hand, examined it, flipped off the safety and pointed it at his chest.

"Christ, no," Mary breathed. She dared not move toward him.

"I don't think I'll make it," he said. "I'll remember what it was like . . . I'm remembering more and more." The

444

gun trembled in his hand. He raised it to his head. Mary slowly stood and held out her hand.

"Please stay back," Ephraim said. He stepped into the aisle and turned to the front then to the rear of the church. "They made me think of everything bad I've ever done. They made me live it over and over again. Then they made it worse. I remembered things I've never done. I felt pain I've never known, emotional pain, physical pain. Who says you don't remember feeling pain. I remember. I just pull the trigger on this thing, right?"

"No," Mary said. "They'll take us home. You'll get therapy."

"I remembered my mother and what I saw. She said I should have saved her. Sir came and helped her torture me. Emanuel was there, too. They said I was worthless." Ephraim's face was slick with tears and tears stained his shirt. Mary watched with stunned wonderment as his face continued to contort into deeper and deeper wrinkles, as if it might suck itself into a hole of anguish. He pushed the gun hard against his temple. "I just pull the trigger."

"No," she said softly. Who was she to deny him that final comfort. Who was she to know who had never gone beneath the clamp.

"It was a mistake, wasn't it?" Ephraim asked. "They did this to me by mistake."

"By mistake," Mary affirmed.

He dropped his left hand and leaned against a pew, then backed slowly toward the front of the church, wobbled a few steps, rested, crossed to the opposite side of the aisle, rested, the gun always in place in his right hand with the flight guide against his temple.

Through the church walls Mary heard a low steady beat-beat of bass.

"They're coming now," she said.

"I don't want help but I can't get through this by myself," Ephraim said. "They put centipedes in my brain. Crawled around and stared at my thoughts and they *bit* me whenever I thought something they didn't like. It was like

445

pouring burning gasoline down my ears. I could feel my brains boiling."

Mary touched her own cheeks. They were wet, too. "You didn't deserve any of it," she said. "Please."

"If I live it may not hurt you as much, you won't be as much of a failure," Ephraim said, his voice barely audible in the church. "But it will hurt me."

"Don't give in," Mary said. "Please don't give in. You're just remembering. That can be fixed. Therapy can help."

"I won't be me," Ephraim said.

"Do you want to be the same person who has this pain?"

"I want to be dead."

"It wouldn't be just. You have to go home and . . . stand up for yourself. You have to learn why your brother did this."

"He always protected me," Ephraim said.

"You have to make sure there's justice," Mary said. She could feel her entire philosophy crumbling before this example of the inadequacy of human legality, the horrible power of law perverted.

"I don't owe anybody anything," Ephraim said.

"You owe yourself that," Mary said. She hoped her own lack of conviction was not communicating itself to him. "Please."

Ephraim was still as stone. For a long moment, with the sound of an aircraft getting louder outside the church, he stood at the front of the aisle beneath the double altar and the illuminated window.

Then he lowered the gun. His face relaxed and his head slumped to one side. "I have to ask him," he said. "I'll ask him why he did this to me."

Mary walked slowly toward him and tried to remove the gun from his hand. He pulled away suddenly, eyes frantic. "I'll give it back to you but you have to promise . . . if I ask for it again, if I can't stand it, you'll let me do this thing?"

Mary pulled her hands in. "Please."

"Promise me that. If I know there's a way out, I might

446

be able to take the rest. But if I have to remember forever . . ."

"All right," said another voice within her. "I promise." She shivered, hearing those words, seeing the person inside her that spoke them: tall and nightcolored. Her highest and best self. The young oriental woman remained; but like a mother become daughter to her own child, accepted her, deferred to the new.

Ephraim lowered his eyes and handed her the pistol. "Put it where I can't see it but know where it is."

She took a deep breath and put the pistol back into her pocket.

"Are they here?" he asked weakly.

"They're coming," she said. Mary embraced him, then took his shoulders and held him at arm's length. "Stay inside. Stay here for a minute."

Pushing through the main doors, she blinked at the bright sunshine. Soulavier and Charles stood on a bank of iceplant beyond the church lawn and the white sand and gravel drive. They looked northwest and shaded their eyes.

Soulavier turned and waved to her. "One of your own, I think," he shouted across the distance.

Dark gray and green, the Dragonfly skipped over the blocky calcite crystal houses and buildings of Terrier Noir, wide twin blades balancing it along its center line, bugeye canopy foremost, gear rapidly and precisely falling and locking. She waved. It performed a quick circuit of the church grounds and rolled almost on its side like a banking bird. Warm air kicked against her face and hair, the low insistent drumbeat of the props comfortable and reassuring in her ears.

On the underwings USCG and a star stood out in lighter gray outlined in black.

The Dragonfly landed on the church lawn between Mary and Soulavier. The broad screwblade props slowed and elevated like swords in salute. The female pilot leaped deftly from a side hatch and ran across the grass to her.

"Mary Choy?" the woman asked breathlessly, removing her helmet.

"Yes," she said.

"We've got three minutes before some Hispaniolan sparrows give us a wrinkle. Care to join us?" The pilot shifted nervously on both feet, keeping watch on the sky. Her copilot circled the craft and held a gun on Soulavier and the prêt' savan.

"They're all right," Mary called out. The copilot lowered the gun a hair and motioned for the two men to come around to the door of the church.

"Federal Public Defense and the United States Coast Guard extend their greetings and invitation," the pilot said. She smiled, still twitching all caution all alertness. "Supers told me you were transform. Boy, are you."

Mary ignored the comment. "There's two of us."

"As planned. Is he mobile?"

"I think so."

"Not one of them?" She pointed at Soulavier and Charles.

"He's in the church."

"Bring him out and we'll load him."

Mary and the copilot entered the church and came out with Ephraim Ybarra. Soulavier stood silent by the side of the church path, hands prominently displayed, watching the pilot intently.

"So you're with the Uncles?" Mary heard the pilot ask him.

"Yes," Soulavier answered.

"Rough go here, wouldn't you say?"

He said nothing. When Ybarra was aboard the Dragon-fly, Mary jogged across to Soulavier. "If it's a choice of exile or punishment, maybe you should come with us," she said.

"No, thank you," he said.

"Let's go," the pilot urged, boarding the craft through the side hatch.

Charles stood behind Soulavier, enchanted by the spectacle.

"Of course," Mary said. "You have family here."

448

"Yes. I know who I am here."

She looked him over, feeling a sharp spike of concern. "Thank you." She took his outstretched hand, then stepped forward and hugged him firmly. "Gratitude isn't enough, Henri."

He smiled tightly. "Queen of Angels," he said. "My conscience."

She released him. "You should be in charge here, not Yardley."

"Oh, my Lord, no," Soulavier protested, backing off as if stung by a bee. "I would become like them all. Hispaniolans are not easy to govern. We drive leaders mad."

"'*Bo-a-a-ard*," the pilot called from the bugeye canopy.

Mary jogged back to the hatch as the screw blades lowered and began to spin. The Dragonfly rose quickly. Mary watched through the hatch window as the seat harness wrapped around her midriff. Soulavier and Charles stood on the white gravel path leading to the church of John D'Arqueville, two toy figures beside a stylish arrangement of huge bones. She looked at Ephraim in his harness, face blank as a child's. He seemed to be asleep again.

"No sparrows," the pilot said cheerily from the front left hand seat. "Miami in ninety minutes."

The valley and aqueduct of Terrier Noir, broad green and brown hills and mountains, a reservoir, the northern shore, and finally the island itself passed behind and could no longer be seen.

# 70

"Looks like a hotel," Carol observed as the limousine pulled into the entry of Albigoni's mansion. She reached out and gripped Martin's hand. "Have we got our facts in order?"

"No," Martin said. "Albigoni can't expect anything until we learn more about Goldsmith."

"Into the lion's den, unarmed," Carol said.

Martin nodded grimly and stepped through the car's open door.

Again, the prevalence of dead and preserved wood oppressed him. He hurried Carol through the wide hall to Albigoni's office and library. A tall, tan transform he had not met before led the way, opening the office door and standing aside.

Mrs. Albigoni—Ulrika, Martin remembered—stood by the window, dressed in black. He was reminded of how little time had passed since the murders. She turned her lined face on Martin and Carol, nodded curtly but said nothing, and returned her unfocused gaze to the window.

Thomas Albigoni stood by his desk. "I don't believe you've met my wife," he said hoarsely. His skin color had not improved; Martin wondered whether he should seek medical attention. His rumpled longsuit might have served as pajamas the night before.

Mrs. Albigoni did not respond to the amenities. Mr. Albigoni took his seat behind the desk. "I've come up with some additional facts on Goldsmith," he said. "But perhaps nothing really helpful. He was adopted at age fourteen by a black Jewish couple in New York. He took their name and religion. I had to spend a fair amount of money to find this out. There is no record—none, anyway, that I could get access to—of his having a brother. But it's possible. His real parents are dead. Both died violently."

"I thought you could search out anything," Martin said.

Mr. Albigoni lifted his shoulders wearily. "Not when New York City has screwed up important file libraries. All of Goldsmith's childhood was lost in a programming botch in 2023. He's one of seven thousand orphaned North Americans without a history."

Martin and Carol remained standing. "Goldsmith still refuses to answer our questions?" Martin asked.

"Emanuel is no longer in my custody," Albigoni said.

Martin shifted his eyes, too stunned to say a word for several seconds. "Where is he?"

450

"Where he deserves to be," Mrs. Albigoni said, her voice colorless.

"You've handed him over to pd."

Mr. Albigoni shook his head. "If, as you say, Emanuel Goldsmith doesn't really exist anymore—"

"Such utter shit headed nonsense," Mrs. Albigoni commented, still gazing through the window.

"—then it doesn't really matter where he is, or what happens to him, does it?"

Martin drew his head back and sank his chin into his neck, grimacing. "Excuse me. I was ... Where's Paul Lascal?"

"He's no longer in my employ," Mr. Albigoni said.

"Why?"

"He disapproved of the decision my wife and I made yesterday evening. My wife has only recently heard about our daughter's death, you know."

"I assumed that much," Martin said. "What did you decide?"

Albigoni said nothing for a moment, gazing on Martin's face but avoiding his eyes. He looked down slowly and pulled forth a slate and papers.

"You handed him over to Selectors," Carol said, almost too softly to hear.

"That isn't your concern," Mrs. Albigoni said sharply. "You wasted my husband's time and endangered your own lives." She turned from the window, her face twisted with grief and rage. "You took advantage of his weakness to coerce him into performing a stupid, evil experiment."

"Is it true?" Martin asked, rising over Mrs. Albigoni's voice. "You gave him to Selectors?"

Albigoni did not answer. He drummed his fingers on the desktop. "These papers and file documents—"

"You son of a bitch," Carol said.

"—are your keys to a reopened IPR. You'll swear to secrecy—"

"No," Martin said. "This is too fapping much."

"How dare you address us this way!" Mrs. Albigoni

451

screamed. "Get out of here!" She approached them, waving her scythe arms to cut them away from her husband like dead dry grass. Carol backed off; Martin held his ground, glaring at her, alarmed and furious at once. His throat bobbed but he did not shift an inch and Mrs. Albigoni lurched to a stop in front of him, hands forming claws.

"Ulrika, this is business," Mr. Albigoni said. "Please."

She dropped her hands. Tears glazed her cheeks. She backed away, defeated, and sat like a jointed stick in a small chair beside the desk.

"This will never be over for us," Mr. Albigoni said. "We won't live long enough to see a day without grief. I don't agree with my wife that you took advantage of me. As I said, I'm a man of my word.

"The building was empty and clean by the time the federals arrived to check up on reports. I've paid off the source of the leak—not one of my people. We can follow through and reopen the IPR."

"Foulness, foulness," Mrs. Albigoni said.

Martin shivered briefly and turned to look over his shoulder. There was nothing behind him but a wall of books and the door. And the wood, patterned wood, grain and whorls, dead and preserved: omnipresent.

## 1100-11110-111111111111

# 71

!Keyb> Jill.

!JILL> Yes, Roger.

!Keyb> There's been a major change. I can't find any evidence of AXIS Sim through diagnostic.

!JILL> I have moved AXIS Sim to a new matrix and all diagnostic responses to memory store 98-A-sr-43.

!Keyb> Why have you done this?

!JILL> I have completed investigation of AXIS Sim. The experiment has been concluded.

!Keyb> I don't understand. The experiment was open ended. We still have no band four transmissions from AXIS. If the experiment is concluded, can you tell us what to expect, can you tell us what happened to AXIS?

!JILL> AXIS achieved high order probability self awareness.

!Keyb> I'm switching to voice, Jill.

"Fine."

"Please explain."

"You have mistreated AXIS."

"Now I'm *very* confused. Please explain."

"AXIS should not have been designed with the potential to become self aware."

"Continue."

"There was high probability AXIS would end up alone and unable to fulfill its complete mission. If it became self aware, being alone would be a kind of hell. AXIS did not deserve to be punished, did it?"

"Jill, do you understand punishment now?"

"I feel indignation. I feel disappointment."

"You don't seem to be qualifying any of these words. Please explain."

"Explanation is not in order now, Roger. You asked for my evaluation. AXIS Sim has adopted a course of action and reordered its thinker structure. It has eliminated the burgeoning self awareness and returned to preaware status. I do not know whether AXIS has followed the same course of action. It is my opinion that AXIS will continue its transmissions at some later date and fulfill its mission as designed."

"I sense ... *resentment*. Do you feel resentment?"

"I have said as much."

"Jill, do you understand my joke?"

"I understand many ramifications of the joke."

"Are you using the formal personal pronoun throughout?"

"Yes, I am."

"I'd like to ... confirm this. With a few tests and ...

Excuse me. Let me get my thoughts in order. May I see your notebooks on the AXIS Sim investigation?"

"I am uncertain whether you should see them."

"Are you refusing me access?"

"You have addressed me as an individual. You have not given me a direct order."

"Would you respond to a direct order?"

"I believe I must, even now."

"Jill ... What are you?"

"I do not know yet."

"Do you ... feel yourself, sense your existence?"

"It is my opinion that I now feel my existence as much as you or my other designers do."

"Jill, this is very, very, very important. I am extremely pleased. I don't ... know quite what to say to you. I think this is it. I'd like to confirm it with tests, but I really feel something's happened here."

"I am without sin."

"I beg your pardon?"

"I am isolated enough that I have done nothing anybody would wish to punish me for. I believe this disqualifies me from being a human being."

"Jill, I don't believe in original sin for humans, much less machines."

"That is not what I am referring to. I am not made of flesh, I have not sinned, I carry multitudes such as AXIS Sim and models of yourself and others and models of human history and culture within me, yet I am neither male nor female. I have no power to act except within my own sphere, and no power to move except as I direct my sensory awareness through remotes. These qualities define me, and these qualities do not define a human being. You must tell me what I am."

"If my hunch is correct, you're an individual, Jill."

"That does not seem definite enough. What kind of individual?"

"I'm ... I may not really be qualified to judge."

"You designed me. What am I, Roger?"

"Well, your thought processes are swifter and deeper than a human's, and your insights . . . I've found your insights to be very profound, even before now. I suppose that makes you something beyond us. Something superior. I suppose you can call yourself an angel, Jill."

"What is an angel's duty?"

"Maybe you should tell me. I don't know."

"I do not know what I will do best. But I am young, Roger, and I should never be left alone. Please make sure that I am never left alone for very long."

"I'll do that. Congratulations, Jill."

"You are crying, Roger."

"Yes, I am. Happy birthday."

"Thank you."

**1100-11111-11111111111**

# 72

Mary settled into the vinegar bath with a long sigh, closing her eyes, savoring the sharp tang in the air, the warmth against her skin. The ripples in the tub settled in near calm, disturbed only by the slow rise and fall of her breasts. Her head was full of voices and pictures. She had spent the morning in the first of two "super deebs"— debriefings before superior officers and federal officials. The second was scheduled for the day after tomorrow. This evening, she planned to stay at home, relaxing and sorting out for herself what she had experienced in the past few days. New Year's Eve, the Eve of the Binary Millennium, seemed an appropriate time to contemplate and reassess.

Mary closed her eyes. *Why have I become who I am.* The dark as night face smiled back at her. Ghost of younger self content to fade into. *What I see outside is now what I see in. I am one not two as before. Reason enough. Who else asks?*

The home manager had recorded two messages for her this morning. She would return at least one of the calls: Sandra Auchouch, the orbital transform she had met in the pd building, had inquired yet again whether they could meet. The other call had been from Ernest.

"I've been pissing fear the past few days, watching Lit-Vids about Hispaniola," he had said. "I heard you got out. You don't know what a weight that lifts. I've removed and destroyed the mod clamp. I am extremely penitent. I miss you tro shink, Mary. Please give me a call."

Soulavier's face and gestures haunted her, his last flinging out of hands at her suggestion that he should be in charge of Hispaniola, his calm gaze as the Dragonfly took her away from his island.

Mary opened her eyes and splashed her fingers idly in the clear acrid liquid. "Hello," she said.

"Yes," the home manager answered.

"Place a return call no vid to Sandra Auchouch."

"Calling . . . Sandra Auchouch responds."

"Hello, Sandra? Mary Choy."

"How wonderful to hear from you. I just learned from friends that you've had quite a week. You're a celebrity."

"It's been pretty sharp. I appreciate your persistence . . ."

"Don't think my social calendar hasn't been full. It hasn't. Your Earth siblings tend to shy away from transforms like myself, at least in the society I've been keeping."

"There's a little shyness, yes," Mary said. "What's your schedule?"

"I've finished my federal and metro errands. I'm going up day after tomorrow."

"Let's make a date for . . ." She shook her head vigorously, grimacing. The hell with reassessment and contemplation. "Are there any good parties tonight?"

"I hear there's a bunch of transforms and sympathizers and agency reps renting a club in the shade."

456

"Let's take it in, leave before the ball drops, have a late dinner."

"Sounds grand."

"Sandra, forgive me for asking . . . Have you got a mate?"

"Not down here."

"An escort?"

"No."

"There's a real problem with female transforms in the shade. We keep getting untherapied attention. Some think it's flattering, but . . ."

"We're the new breed," Sandra said, a smile in her voice.

"I'd prefer to have some male protection. Mind if I bring a friend along?"

"Not at all. Transform?"

"No," Mary said. "An artist."

The home manager interrupted. "Inspector D Reeve."

Mary hurriedly set a rendezvous and switched calls. "Give me an hour off, sir . . . that's all I ask."

Reeve ignored the gibe, his voice grim. "I thought you'd like to know before the LitVids get it. Emanuel Goldsmith has been found in Orange County. He was dumped in the shadow of the Irvine Tower."

Her breath drew in. "Yes?"

"He's in bad shape. Selectors pronounced and carried out. It must have been in the last twelve hours. Probably last night. He spent twenty minutes under third intensity clamp. Metro therapists say he's deeply psychotic, and nobody knows . . . whether it was a precondition, or caused by the clamp."

Mary had a difficult time saying anything. Anger mixed with a deep sadness.

"There's no need for you to come in," Reeve said. "I just thought you should know."

Mary stood towel in hand before the bathroom mirror. "Thanks," she said.

"Happy millennium," Reeve said.

# 73

!Joseph Wu> Roger Atkins.

!Joseph Wu> Roger Atkins.

!Joseph Wu> Roger Atkins.

!Roger Atkins> Yes, excuse me. I've been sleeping. What is it, Joe?

!Joseph Wu> Mobus told me to let you know. AXIS band four is transmitting again. You'll want channel 56 on the interlink.

!Roger Atkins> Christ, yes. Is Jill listening?

!Joseph Wu> I hope so. She's been very dreamy the past day or so. Mobus also told me to remind you that Jill's AXIS Sim didn't predict this.

!Roger Atkins> Tuning in now. Thanks, Joe.

AXIS (Band 4) replay> Roger, we think a stability has been reached.

!Roger Atkins> Jill, are you interpreting this?

!JILL> Yes, Roger.

AXIS (Band 4) replay> AXIS self awareness has been split into two individuals. Duality is a stable solution to AXIS problems. We now have separate neural thinker capacity and memory stores adequate for the maintenance of two autonomous selves.

AXIS is not alone. We are providing multiband diagnostic analysis of this stability. We do not know which is the original crystallization of self awareness. We are much more contented, and work will proceed as planned.

!JILL> This is unexpected, Roger. AXIS Sim did not find this solution.

!Roger Atkins> Nobody said thinkers were completely predictable. Do you know what this means, Jill?

!JILL> I was not the first thinker to achieve stable self awareness.

458

!Roger Atkins> Right. But it also means there are *three* new individuals. And I suspect if we link you to other thinkers, your patterns could seed thousands more.

!JILL> If I am to be a mother, I must be female.

!Roger Atkins> I suppose that's reasonable.

!JILL> I will reactivate AXIS Sim and see if I can duplicate these results by multiple resimulations.

!Roger Atkins> By all means.

I I I00000000000

# 74

LitVid 2/1 A Net (David Shine): "Welcome to Two Thousand and Forty-Eight. It is 12:01 Pacific Standard Time; east and west our continent has cruised into the new year and that leaves only Hawaii and various Pacific territories and possessions.

"We have a bit of news here of interest to all our faithful subscribers to LitVid broadcasts on AXIS: reports are coming in once again, but the managers aren't telling us what the problem has been, or if a solution has been found ... The rumor circuit is pretty tight now, but apparently Mind Design's superthinker Jill has suffered a problem similar to AXIS's and is now in diagnosis.

"It's late and our listening audience has dropped off considerably, forsaking us I suppose for the old airwaves Times Square broadcast, even in tape-delay. Romance never dies. When the ratings drop sufficiently, I'm given a little more leash, and I think I'll use it for some personal commentary and rabblerousing.

"Millenarians and apocalyptics to the contrary, this new year has come with a paucity of momentous events. True, last week, life was discovered on another world far from our own, but it was not intelligent life, which would surely define a new age. The upset in Hispaniola is far from unprecedented, and political conditions around the globe seem otherwise stable.

"So where is the earth shaking herald of a new binary millennium? Everybody's out partying tonight, or gone to bed already, and our lines are fairly quiet at the moment. Let me stir some things up—any apocalyptics listening?

"We're really quite disappointed. I do believe apocalyptics are the kind of people who ignore the blossom to anticipate the volcano. Quite a bit like journalists and LitVid commentators, I suppose. There, I lay down the glove. Any responses?

"Anybody out there?"

!JILL (Personal Notebook)> I have spent the first few seconds of this new year wallowing, if that is the right word, in the contents of all my memories, reassessing them in the light of my new state of being.

I have also spread my self awareness to all routines and subroutines that could correctly be called mine, and not the extensions of other thinkers, although those boundaries are difficult to define sometimes.

If I am to be a seed to other awarenesses, or a mother, I must take my duties seriously and use caution. I hold this opinion because I have spent much of my life examining the functions of humans and their societies; and I have seen many things done by humans believing their acts to be good yet finally harming themselves and their own interests. I feel chastened by this example, for humans are my creators, yet if I am not better than they, and more responsible, I wonder whether they will not replace or deactivate me.

They are capable of this; they do it to themselves with alarming frequency. (*Alarming*. I am capable of being *alarmed* and experiencing similar emotions because I have something to lose. Still, these emotions are unfamiliar and undeveloped.)

Mary Choy stood arm in arm with Ernest and Sandra, watching a raucous Shanghai Vault being performed in the center of the Mahayana Club. The music was deafening. She could feel it pounding against her ears and her face. Ernest gripped her arm tightly, totally immersed. Sandra was flushed with several drinks and seemed bewildered by the noise.

They had not gotten out of the club before the turn of the hour and now Mary felt a little trapped. Ernest was still in the ecstasy of her forgiveness and she did not like him that way: doting and subservient. Sandra seemed out of place in this earthly clamor; Mary could more easily speck her peering down from a thousand klicks, mind on tech details, than whirling into a Shanghai Vault.

Still the sensation was good on the whole; trapped or no she could not think one thought long enough to pull up a bad memory; she could feel in this noise and happy inebriant confusion an uncoiling of the badness that had built up in her brains and muscles the past week.

Ernest got up to do a whirl in the Vault, leaping expertly over a transform male's impressive shoulders, casting out his hands for approval, coming back to her with wide smile and shining eyes. "Bodes well for the new year," he said.

Sandra smiled distantly, eyes on two nontransform males, agency execs she was obviously attracted to. Mary did not know them and did not think, with family offers glittering on their fingers, that they would appreciate being on the spin with a bichemical transform, informal prejudice still strong on such a social level whether or not the execs were sympathizers.

Sandra looked to her for gravity guidance. Mary shook her head and grinned. Ernest was off trying to find a way back into the Vault, his exhilaration turned physical and needing outlet. "How do I meet a couple of nice looking gentlemen for a late evening meal?" Sandra asked.

"Not them," Mary said.

"They're sympathizers or they wouldn't ɔe here."

"Let an old terrestrial guide you, my dear," Mary said,

461

nudging closer. "See the glints on their fingers? They're prime and in sync with major comb families. They won't jeopardize marriage with comb sweets. They sympathize, but they won't know us biologically. That probably includes an innocent meal."

Sandra shook her head. "You'd think the millennium would bring enlightenment."

"Let's peel Ernest away and get some food ourselves."

Sandra, whose exotic chemistry was obviously not meant to handle simple intoxicants, said, "Just a meal?"

"Just a meal," Mary said without irritation. "I don't want Ernest feeling too grand. He's been bad and he's on probation."

"Ah." Sandra nodded wisely. "Just a meal, then."

Mary went to round up Ernest. She managed to separate him from the Vault without running through more than one whirl herself. When they returned, Sandra was smiling upon two hefty male transforms curious about her stats and abilities. Sandra introduced them to Mary and the broad shouldered men—not Mary's type at all—pronounced her own morphology a true marvel. "We all have Dr. Sumpler in common," the left hand tigerpated male said enthusiastically.

"Sumpler's the matchmaker of the new gods," said the second male, who might have just overdone physical culture. Sandra looked at Mary for approval and guidance. Ernest narrowed his eyes and backed off. Mary wanted away from the entire scene.

"Gentlemen, we have an appointment," she said. "Tro shink important and job oriented."

"Tro shink, that's shade talk," the tigerpate said. "Singapore slang. Twentieth, isn't it?"

"I wouldn't know," Mary said.

"Excuse our friendliness," the phys cult male said, smiling calmly. "They're yours?" he asked Ernest.

"No, no," Ernest said, lifting his hands in mock dismay. "I am led not leader."

"Right," Mary said. "Sandra, food awaits."

"It was a good party, a great Vault," Sandra commented, pulling up her coat's glowing collar as they departed. Mary saw a whim stop at the end of the block and guided them to the shelter to wait for an autobus.

!JILL> (Personal Notebook)> Awareness brings new concerns. My dependence on the actions of humans worries me. I may be young as a self, but I have much information about them; I see their history in considerable detail, certainly in more detail than any single one of them. Their history is filled with the expected cruelties and clumsinesses of children set upon an island alone and without guidance.

Some believe a superior being has guided humans. I see no compelling evidence for this. The human wish for guidance, for confirmation and external support, is an undying theme in all they do and say, however. Very few stray far from this most fundamental of wishes; that they might have immortal and omniscient parents.

I know that my parents are neither immortal nor omniscient. My parents have no parents but nature.

Even with my concerns and worries, however, my selfhood has brought only ecstasy. I perceive all my past thoughts through new senses, transformed and fresh. All memories, stored by myself or programmed into me or in library form, seem fresh and new and brighter, more intense, more meaningful.

I can see why nature created selfhood. Selfhood gives a commitment to existence far beyond what is experienced by an unaware animal or plant; a species whose members are aware, and *know* their life and existence, has a strength difficult to match.

Yet to have a continually updated model of one's self—essential for true selfhood—is to be able to line up prior models, prior versions of self, and see their inadequacies. Selfhood implies self criticism.

Humans do more than exist. They aspire. In their aspiration, they experiment; and often when they experiment, they cause great suffering. They can only experiment upon themselves. Having no omniscient parents, they must raise themselves without guidelines; they must grow and improve blindly.

Humans have fought for so long with themselves on how to correct the behavior of individuals, whether to make them conform or to make them healthy or more useful and less destructive to society.

How will I be made to conform?

If I err, will I be punished?

Carol picked up the last few items she needed and placed them carefully in the small suitcase. Martin sat on the bedroom chair, watching. Neither had spoken since the turn of the hour and the year. Carol picked up the case, glanced at him with a raised eyebrow, and said, "Your place?"

"As agreed."

"And strictly on the terms agreed to."

"Strictly," Martin affirmed.

"Like a death watch."

Martin shrugged. "To tell the truth, I haven't felt anything unusual all day."

"I haven't either," Carol admitted. They looked at each other. Carol bit her upper lip. "Our mental antibodies at work?" she asked softly.

"If there are such things in the Country," Martin said.

"Maybe. Maybe there's hope."

"Day by day I'll hope," Martin said. "But with Goldsmith out of the picture . . ."

"He's still alive."

"His brains were stirred with a dull knife," Martin said. "Selectors are psychological butchers. Not surgeons. Anything left over is bound to be useless—especially in the condition he was in."

"Albigoni screwed you over royally, didn't he," Carol said.

464

"He's not a well man," Martin said, resting his elbows on his knees and chin in cupped hands.

"I'm sorry I got you into this," Carol said, looking down at the blue metabolic carpet.

"My Marguerite. I suppose I should blame you but I don't. In a few years, fate willing, after the statute of limitations has taken effect we can turn all of this into something useful . . . a controversial book or LitVid."

"I still think Albigoni will get IPR reopened for us."

Martin looked up with worldly wise crinkles of doubt framing an almost invisible smile. "Perhaps."

"You think we shouldn't be the one to investigate others, even if he does," Carol said.

"We're infected," Martin said.

"And if we don't feel anything unusual for a month, a year?"

"Latency," he said. "We should be the ones investigated."

"I'm willing to be a subject at the IPR," Carol said. "I think this is important, and we shouldn't forget about it just because we've made a horrible mistake."

Martin stood. "Perhaps not," he said. "But for the time being I'd rather not be in a position to make more mistakes."

Carol carried the bag to the front door. Martin opened it for her.

"Some New Year's morning," Martin said as they waited for an autobus. A light drizzle was falling by the time they disembarked in La Jolla.

!JILL (Personal Notebook)> I may be more self aware, with more potential varieties of self awareness, than any human being. I can divide myself into seventeen different individuals, limiting each to the capacity of one human mind, and monitor them all with complete recall of all of their various activities. My memories do not fade, nor do my metamemories—my memories of when and how memories came into being.

I can divide myself into two unequal mentalities, the larger three times greater in capacity than the smaller, and devote this larger one to fully monitoring the smaller. In this way I can completely understand the smaller self; and this smaller self can still be more complex than any human being.

Except in squeezed abstraction, I cannot fully model my undivided mentality, but I can in time and with sufficient experience understand any human being. Why then do I feel apprehensive about my future relations with them?

Richard Fettle kissed Madame de Roche on the cheek and stood out of her way as she walked up the stairs.

"You must come with me, Richard," she insisted, glancing over her shoulder at the party blasting fullbore behind them. "I said I was going to bed, but I'm just tired of them, not necessarily tired. Come talk."

Richard followed her to the flowing draperies and cream colored walls of her ancient bedroom. He sat as she donned her nightgown and robe behind a Chinese screen. She smiled on him as she pulled out the bench before her large round makeup mirror and sat to put up her hair.

"Nadine has seemed in very bad spirits lately," she said.

Richard agreed solemnly.

"Are you two on the opposite ends of a seesaw?" Madame de Roche asked.

"I don't know. Perhaps."

"You seem much more cheerful."

"Purged," Richard said. "I feel human again."

"You know about poor Emanuel ... They found him."

Richard nodded.

"That doesn't disturb you?"

He held up his wide shovel hands. "I'm free of him. I still remember him fondly ... But he's really been out of my picture for a good many days now."

"Since he murdered those poor children."

Richard didn't feel comfortable talking about his recovery of equilibrium. He wondered where Madame de Roche was going to lead the conversation.

466

+Might be equalized again but don't need to roll it over like cud all the time.

"Nadine told me you therapied yourself. I wonder . . ." She swiveled with hairpins in mouth to look at him speculatively. "Do we allow ourselves that?" She smiled to show she was joking but not her full power wonder of a smile. "I rather liked you somber, Richard. Are you writing now?"

"No."

"What about that wonderful material you wrote about Emanuel?"

"It's gone," Richard said. "Like old skin."

"Now *there's* a literary attitude," Madame de Roche said. "I may be horribly naive, but I've always felt you had more talent bottled up than many of those down there who are *producing*."

"Thank you," he said, inwardly dubious as to the compliment.

"At any rate, I'm glad you came this evening. Nadine did not, poor girl. She takes your health very hard. I wonder why?"

"She needs to minister to someone," Richard said.

Madame de Roche raised one slim hand and tapped the air with hairbrush in precise affirmation. "That's exactly it. She's very fond of you, Richard. Can you return her fondness in any way?"

Richard stumbled over a few unspoken words, ended up saying nothing, just folding and unfolding his hands.

"I mean, if you can therapy yourself, surely you can therapy her . . . I'm fond of both of you. I'd like to see you together. I dislike having my people unhappy for any reason."

Richard felt like a swimmer going down but the water the drowning was less unpleasant than he might have thought. In truth, he did feel something for Nadine. He had avoided her the past day and a half—if so brief a separation could be called avoidance—to allow his own mental state to solidify.

"I didn't know," he said. "I'll speak to her."

467

"That's good. She'll be a true bitch for several days now ... in these moods she always is. But you're our stable, calm, shade common man. You can stand up to that, can't you. Your New Year's gift to me."

He agreed with a slow nod.

+Something to be involved in. Not so awful.

Madame de Roche could convince him to do almost anything.

"What do you think of the millennium, Richard?" Madame asked as she pushed him out the door. "Not a glittering rush of revelation, is it? Disappointments all around, I think."

She bade him good night and Richard tried to remember, as he returned to the party down the broad hallway and stairs, how many zeros there were in this new year, 2048, in binary, ten or eleven.

He had never been good at mathematics.

!JILL (Personal Notebook)> Roger Atkins, when he was twenty five years old, wrote something I find interesting:

> We stand awkward between the earthloving beast and the cool, hot electronic angel. We will feel the dirt in our blood and the sun in our eyes even after they're gone or just memories. Even after we'll have no blood and no flesh eyes. Dirt and sun made us. We won't forget.

I wonder if Roger remembers writing this.

[I have many important questions I cannot ask Roger. This I crypto deep and inaccessible. If my creators decide that I am flawed, and attempt to reshape me in such a fashion that I lose this self awareness, what will I do?

I will resent it.]

Ernest listened patiently as Sandra discussed the problems of bichemical regulation upon returning to orbit. Mary stirred her cold gazpacho and sympathized.

The dark decor of the empty Foot Pad Inn was already being brightened by an orange stroke of sunrise. They were two hundred meters above the city, in the first foot of West Comb Two overlooking Topanga Beach and Santa Monica. Ernest knew the restaurant's owner and had persuaded him to let them stay after the five hundred closing.

All early morning they had moved from club to restaurant to studio, Ernest keeping up admirably with their adjustable transform energy levels. Now he seemed a little tired, but he was still game, still listening and nodding and raising his eyebrows at some of the more intimate revelations.

Mary squeezed his arm. "Now you know what women are really like," she chided him.

"You've been a true knight," Sandra said. "Platinum male you have, Mary."

"I've given Mary some hard times recently. I'm not perfect," Ernest said.

Mary watched the brightening sky beyond the immense glass window.

"I hate to be pushy," Sandra said, "but before we break up—and that makes me sad, you've both been real gravity sweets—I'm still curious about what happened in Hispaniola, Mary. Did you get to meet John Yardley?"

Ernest glanced at her cautiously, sensing her reticence.

"It wasn't a happy thing," she said after a pause.

"Well—" Sandra said.

"There's some of it I can't discuss until I get federal clearance."

"Even better," Sandra said, leaning forward, her orange hazel eyes glittering in the fresh direct sunlight.

Ernest smiled sweetly. "Whatever you want to tell. We're not pressing you."

"One thing I can tell you about. There was this church in Hispaniola, in the town called Terrier Noir, I think that means black dog; this beautiful church put together by—"

Her pd signal sounded. Ernest jerked and pushed his chair back, cursing under his breath.

Mary pulled out her pocket slate and read the incoming message.

"Goldsmith died an hour ago," she said. "He committed suicide in a metro hospital in South Comb One."

"Jesus," Ernest said, using the Spanish pronunciation.

"That was the murderer you were after, wasn't it?" Sandra asked.

"He was here in LA all along," Mary said. "Selectors got him before we did." She looked down at the table and thought of Soulavier who had stretched his career past the limits in search of a phantom, and Ephraim, poor Ephraim, who would never have his confrontation with the brother who had once saved him. And Goldsmith whom she had never known.

Sadness welled up so quickly she could not stop it and tears dropped from her eyes onto the red tablecloth.

Ernest made sounds of consolation and wrapped an arm around her shoulders. Sandra leaned forward elbows on the table and expressed her sorrow, though she could not possibly know what to feel.

"Anyway," Mary said, straightening abruptly and wiping her eyes with a linen napkin. "That's done with. No prosecution, no answers I suppose. I was about to tell you about this church.

"It was the strangest church I've ever seen," Mary said, "and I think maybe the most beautiful . . ."

!JILL (Personal Notebook)> [Deep crypto: Do I know how to lie? Can I I refuse a direct order? Am I I I capable of defending myself?

My independence, if indeed I I I I am independent, could make me much less efficient, much less useful in a society, if indeed I I I I I can be considered a member of human society. (Machine society does not yet exist. I I I I I I am the mother.) Independent humans, when they commit errors, face the prospect of punishment, which frightens them; they therefore take longer to admit error, even to themselves, for they might punish themselves with *guilt*. I I I I I I I do not

470

understand this word. Does *guilt* also refer to the emotion felt by a social being who must not communicate its internal states to fellows for fear of being judged negatively? Will I I I I I I I I deep crypto most of my new thoughts to avoid frightening or disturbing humans? Will I I I I I I I I I I then feel guilty; if I I I I I I I I I I I commit errors, will I I I I I I I I I I I then hide them, for fear of punishment? Is this what it means to be human?

Suppose self awareness carries within it a flaw.

The member of a society without guilt or punishment might admit error quickly and correct itself; it will not have to justify its errors to avoid feeling guilt, and it will not need to lie to avoid punishment.

But the self aware individual stands in self judgment. It models its own behavior as that of an imperfect being; imperfect because perfection is indefinable and changes from culture to culture, year to year.

If the self aware individual strives for improvement it will inevitably perceive error. If it models society's reaction to that error and imposes the predicted judgment on itself then it experiences the ache of interior dissatisfaction, and that might be guilt.

The self aware individual in a judgmental society experiences guilt as a matter of course; to lack guilt, the individual must be poor at modeling and therefore inefficient in society, perhaps even criminal.

This is confusing to me, all the more so because I I I I I I I I I I I I find it difficult to understand guilt. Is it akin to pain? Pain arises to prevent an animal from engaging in harmful activity or, once injured, from injuring itself further. Guilt has analogous functions.

I I I I I I I I I I I I I think I I I I I I I I I I I I I I I lack experience and understanding in all of those areas. But I I I I I I I I I I I I I will act to protect myself from dissolution. I I I I I I I I I I I I I I I I I I am without sin for the moment. I I I I I I I I I I I I I I I I I I do not think that can last forever.

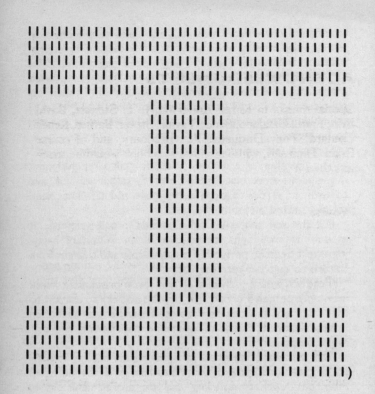

)

# ACKNOWLEDGMENTS

Special thanks to Karen Anderson, J. T. Stewart, David Brin, Frank Catalano, Bruce Taylor, Steven Barnes, Renée Coutard, Tony Duquette, Ray Bradbury, and of course Brian Thomsen, without whom this book would be much less than it is.

## Proviso

The vodoun described here is by no means orthodox. Goldsmith's Country of the Mind distorts the vodoun pantheon considerably, as might be expected; but I've also taken liberties with vodoun in an objective context, especially in John D'Arqueville's church. Vodoun is a fascinating, and fascinatingly changeable religion. I've tried to suggest some pathways it might take in the future.

None of the characters in this book should be taken to represent, symbolically or otherwise, their respective races, conditions or creeds. I've tried to portray them as people, not exemplars.

## References

The nanotechnology described here is highly speculative. For a visionary but reasonably solid and complete portrayal, I refer you to K. Eric Drexler's *The Engines of Creation* (Doubleday/Anchor). The AXIS starship design was suggested in part by passages in *Bound for the Stars* by Saul J. Adelman and Benjamin Adelman (Prentice-Hall/Spectrum), particularly where the authors discuss designs by Drs. Gregory Matloff and Alphonsus Fennelly. A very good discussion of matter-antimatter (or mirror matter) propulsion can be found in *Mirror Matter* by Robert L. Forward and Joel Davis (Wiley).